ACCLAIM FOR Allan Gurganus's

Plays Well with Others

"Captures the pulse and beat of an era and a world. Will remind the reader of F. Scott Fitzgerald on New York. . . . [The] narrator wants to write a book that will memorialize his friends' short lives . . . something Gurganus himself has achieved in this vexing and powerful novel."   —Michiko Kakutani, *The New York Times*

"A supremely affecting tale."   —*Chicago Tribune*

"With Southern aplomb that recalls literary forebears O'Connor and Faulkner, Gurganus makes his readers chuckle about the grimmest of circumstances."   —*Time Out*

"Gurganus succeeds in capturing a vanished place and time with poignancy . . . compassion and wit."   —*Boston Book Review*

"Gurganus is the worthy heir to Faulkner and Welty."   —*USA Today*

"A novel that laughs through the pain. Nothing about *Plays Well with Others* is coy, demure or otherwise closeted. [Gurganus] grounds catastrophe with humor."   —*Time*

"Gurganus writes without a safety net. . . . [He] can do anything he likes as a writer."   —Henry Louis Gates, Jr., *The Nation*

ALSO BY Allan Gurganus

Oldest Living Confederate Widow Tells All
White People

Allan Gurganus

Plays Well with Others

Allan Gurganus is the author of *Oldest Living Confederate Widow Tells All*, which was awarded the Sue Kaufmann Prize from the American Academy of Arts and Letters as best first work of fiction. Gurganus's collection of stories and novellas, *White People*, a finalist for the PEN/Faulkner Award, won the Los Angeles Times Book Prize. His short novel *The Practical Heart* was awarded the National Magazine Prize. Gurganus's work has been widely translated. He lives in a village of twenty-five hundred souls in his native North Carolina.

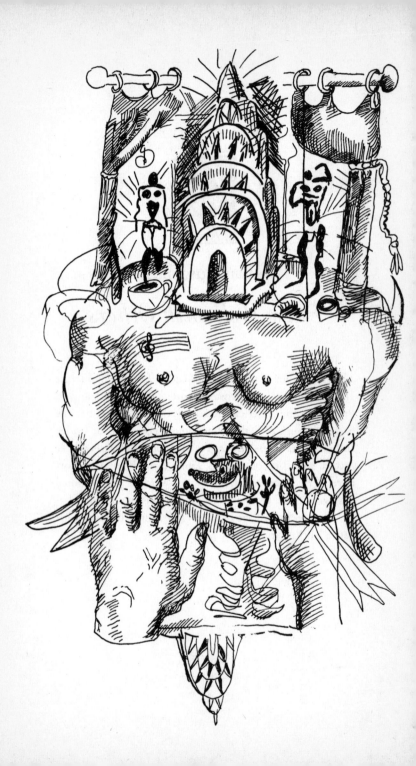

PLAYS WELL WITH OTHERS

Allan Gurganus

VINTAGE CONTEMPORARIES

Vintage Books

A Division of Random House, Inc.

New York

FIRST VINTAGE CONTEMPORARIES EDITION, FEBRUARY 1999

Portions of this work appeared, in slightly different form,
in *GQ* and *The New Yorker*.

The Library of Congress has cataloged the Knopf edition as follows:

Gurganus, Allan.
Plays well with others / Allan Gurganus.
p. cm.
ISBN 0-394-58914-9
I. Title.
PS3557.U814P57   1997
813'.54—dc21   97-36884
CIP

Vintage ISBN: 0-375-70203-2

Author photograph © Marion Ettlinger

Book design by Peter A. Andersen

www.randomhouse.com

Printed in the United States of America
10 9 8 7 6 5 4 3 2

For TOBIAS SCHNEEBAUM
and JOE CALDWELL,

friends, artists, and two beloved
heroes of our recent siege

It pleases me to thank my friends, this book's earliest readers. I am grateful to Mona Simpson, Helen Miranda Wilson, Joanne Meschery, Jane Holding, John Shoneman, Andrea Simon, Danny Kaiser, Tim Woodman, Chris Bram, Erica Eisdorfer, Charles Millard, Michael Pollan, Judith Belzer, George Eatman, David Vintinner, and Daisy Thorp. To my agent and compeer, Amanda Urban, warmest daily gratitude.

I am devoted to my editor, Dan Frank, for his intelligence, serenity, and character. For being there at the creation, for patience and imagination, a godfather's full rights.

Thank you, friends.

Contents

The Voyage As I Saw It

(1980-1995)

by

Hartley Mims jr.

During the terrible years of Yezhovshchina, I spent seventeen months in the prison queues of Leningrad. One day someone recognized me. Then a woman with lips blue from cold who was standing behind me, and of course had never heard my name, came out of the numbness which affected us all and whispered in my ear (we spoke in whispers there):

"Can you describe this?"

I said, "I can!"

Then something resembling a smile slipped over what had once been her face.

—ANNA AKHMATOVA, "Requiem"

PROLOGUE

The Comedy of Friends

Thirty Dildoes

I.

There are just two kinds of people in the world: those who will help you and those who won't.

In New York, New York, 1983, we—being this talented and so young—found but one roadblock to our careers.
It was called getting sick.

I myself seem able to help my friends. Know what?—I often hate it.

Nothing roused him from the sweet ice of his final coma. Nothing till we mentioned his parents' flying in today from Iowa. They'd arrive bearing baked goods and one greeting card signed by their entire Lutheran church—they would stay at our patient's very own apartment.

We'd tried everything to lift Robert, thirty-four, from his old-man stupor. We played him his favorite music: Mahler's Fourth and Ninth; Peter Pears doing English folk songs; lots of Bach; three shrill emotions from a Callas *Norma*; one whole summer's Donna Summer disco ecstasy. And I mean loud. Only after nurses complained did we clamp headphones directly onto him.

Above Robert's famous blue gaze, we held postcards—works by painters he loved best: "Here's some Balthus, a Francis Bacon, here's your top Vermeer . . . and, mmmm, Bonnard—look, a table in the garden, sunlight through trees, wine, fruit, nice lunch waiting. Like?"

* * *

Nothing.

We told Robert his own best jokes. Punch line hollered—"after all, what's time to a *pig*?"—we hovered above the face.

Still nothing.

Even whittled, the face had stayed so beautiful it was hard to look at, but for new reasons. Rote breaths, one at a time, decided provisionally to, maybe/yes/no, continue.

Robert must've overheard: "His parents' flight gets in from Cedar Rapids at, what? noon? And, since they say they 'don't feel comfortable paying New York hotel prices,' his folks asked to crash at Robert's place. And we just couldn't think fast enough to say why not . . . Of course, somebody'll have to wait over there and greet them, and explain about the six keys, and warn them against taking sugar cookies to that lunatic Serb Rasta man next door, and where not to wander after dark and . . ."

Robert had lain silent for three weeks. This boy so gently forward in life now hid far back in a cave he must've told himself he was learning to almost like. He lived beneath the manhole of a mask he left us on his pillow. Where his sexy raucous grin once worked, find only an "Occupant" sticker. By now, his body was crafted mainly of aerodynamic holes. "O! that this too solid flesh would melt, thaw, and resolve itself into a dew." Hamlet predicted a disease. Our friend's body, once lusted after citywide, had become all chiseled bone, Henry Moore's finest work. "Human form" rendered as hat rack.

"The prettiest boy in New York of his decade." You only get ten of those per century and here lay the incidentally living remains of the greatest beauty of the late 1970s Manhattan nights. Robert, his platinum hair once shaggy as some fashion-conscious Tom Sawyer's, Robert in a tailor-made bottle green velvet suit (created "on" him by his next-door neighbor, an ancient African-American seamstress who'd once Singered acreage ruffles for the Ziegfeld Follies); Robert pedestaled upon platform shoes as steep as cinder blocks; Robert sporting a tasteful rhinestone lapel pin shaped like, what else, a single star! It helped that he moved like a high school band major on Orange Bowl Day. His exceptional male stuff got so strutted, you laughed with the joy of watching him maneuver it, his.

Everybody wanted Robert, girls especially. Many got him, boys especially, once he finally declared. Back then, in ballrooms lit by mirror-mosaic spheres that were half joke, but mostly magic—it was Robert Robert Robert. A common name, but one he made glamorous and, even odder, fully only his.

Now, face up, eyes closed, doing what some witty visitor had recently called "Robert's exceptional Pharaoh imitation," our friend managed one final feat—superhuman.

The closed right eye trembled in sneezy little spasms all its own. Then both his eyes tore open with such sound, twin zippering rips, no louder than a mouse's scream, and exactly that terrifying.

We, lolling on windowsills, slumped in tacky plastic orange chairs, rushed to Robert's bed as if summoned by a thunderclap and forty French horns.

Radical as only being alive can make a guy, Robert strained upward to answer. I bent my head against his mouth. (We would press a compact mirror here in just four days.) Now, gusts of hard-earned air bore sound waves as Robert managed: "Kee po. Dee do. Gee ou. Fo com."

I had learned the language of his language ending. Not unproud of how my skill had evolved to coil inside the nautilus spiral of Robert's own exquisite devolving, I translated for marveling friends.

"Says, 'Kiddie porn. Dildoes. Get out, before The Folks come.' "

We watched him nod, our pal, Robert, the composer (already diatonic when only joyless twelve-tone cacophony still counted; already wooed and won by our best judge of male beauty and symphonic talent, Mr. Copland). Hearing his own last words replayed aloud, Robert nodded so.

"Don't tire yourself, Babes." Somebody touched his spindle shoulder. And one gigantic grateful tear—the size of something sold in your better gift shoppes—slid from the outer corner of a glazed crystal blue eye. It was one of two baby-blues that'd made Robert briefly yet intensely popular at steam baths and in the backs of parked trucks along West Street, where forthright boys passed fluids to and fro, passed jets of spit and spunk, a secret virus riding all that liquid living pleasure. Tax. Everything good is taxed so. On a 30 percent pleasure, a 1001 percent tax. Is that fair?

"Robert? Okay now, Robert ours." I drew closer. "I know you're listening and, buddy, look . . . no, here. —I'm guessing as how the kiddie porn is stuffed into that steamer trunk beside your bed, okay? 'kay . . . good. But where'd you tend to stash the majority of your dildoes, honey? —Robbie?"

There came the deepening dent between eyes. There came a setting of shoulders: A launchpad is readied for eventual rocket. You saw how much energy his speaking up from such a cave-in void would cost him. And, vertical achievement, here it came: "Boo ca."

That said, he fell so far back into pillows, it seemed he'd dropped down all nine floors, clear to Manhattan's cold stone platelets supporting this—our diseased, endearing St. Vincent's Hospital.

" 'Broom closet.' " I beamed.

And Robert, though hearing me, though gladdened that my translation proved correct, Robert was so asleep, we heard immediate snoring. Half comic. Half. We'd just received his final words. My friend, Robert Gustafson, composer of Symphony no. 1, his final words: "Broom closet."

II.

he parents would meet me at their only son's fourth-floor walkup. Rain seemed likely. After last month's hurricane, any sign of black sky brought merchants scurrying forth to roll up their awnings. The whole town still looked piratelike and scarred, plywood baffles left in place.

Just as the Gustafsons' plane was landing, I unlocked Robert's apartment, the red fire door. I figured I'd have time to haul incriminating loot to my place. Then I'd catch a subway back downtown and just wait on Robert's front stoop. His folks were strangers. But how hard could it be to spot a cab unloading the Lutheran minister and his wife, two silvering blond Iowans, tall—blinking around, toting Saran-wrapped datenut bars?

Beside Robert's four-posted bed, a steamer trunk that once contained his carpenter great-granddad's tools, all brought by boat from Sweden. The family name (also the name of their return-address village) was still spelled here in a Gothicy milk-based blue. Inside the heirloom trunk lined with 1840s chromolithos of fjords, I found Robbie's kiddie porn.

I'd feared something virulent. That had been disloyal. His proved mostly benign Swedish nudist pix, circa 1953—healthy male children, undraped al fresco, just before the onset of that mixed blessing called "the Pubic." Boys, colt-legged and scarily pretty, were shown sawing wood, getting into or out

6

of some lake, then toweling each other off, a lot. Boy-children of Sweden sure must swim often.

They must be all platinum and blush. Photographed in black and white, shown silver in an evergreen landscape, they made the most innocent meringue. I sat here on Robert's immense Federal bed, sat flipping pages—feigning a prim reproach of sorts. My erection shamed me. Then I remembered my mission. The preacher and his organist floral-print wife, bound here in minutes.

Robert's merciless if fond tales about his folks made them seem so real to me, made them seem already present in these rooms, present and watching me scout for cupid Bobby's little quiverful of dildo love projectiles. I felt (and fielded) their conventional toxic questions: "Why, son, in two rooms this postage stamp–tiny, would ya keep a four-posted bed the size of a cabin cruiser, Robbie? Not to criticize, mind you, just asking. Hmmm?"

They wouldn't know that Robert composed his music here (his Symphony no. 1, subtitled *The Titanic*, was already half afloat). Robert created while stretched out naked. It helped that his eyebrows and lashes were platinum. Leg hair by Harry Winston.

Given his looks, Robert's talent seemed redundant. He had the goods for immortality, according to "Mr. Copland" as Robbie called him, even after long sleepy weekends spent at Maestro's Peekskill retreat upriver. Robert's musical gift felt a spendthrift oversight by some God too briefly in too good a mood.

One snowy Manhattan night, we'd stood outside a famous club where everyone but Warhol got auditioned at the velvet cord. Robert, seeing that we two would not make the cut, called above crowd sounds, "Take off your shirt." Because he stripped of all finery, I undressed, my breath clouding blue. The bouncer, appraising Robert's flesh, considered. But I held us back. My chest was a solid A minus, not theatrical Manhattan's normative A plus.

"Pants," Robert barked. So we shucked off, despite its being four degrees. And got waved past an awed mob's tickling furs. I remember the sight of Robert's pink-gold back tapering before me. The respectful crowd divided, his head was crowned by platinum curls—snow had casually gathered there, forming natural Fabergé leaf shapes. Once into the sound, we checked everything but our jockey shorts. And, shoeless, stripped, we were soon offered hand mirrors spread with powder—white and snortable and, for us then, unaffordable. *So,* till dawn, we redefined fun. —Copying Robbie, I became immodest as a god.

The Gustafsons could not know how often and successfully their gorgeous charitable boy had entertained in this bed. They would not recognize the names of the many models and film stars of both sexes who had achieved out-of-body bodily experiences here with the help of their cheerful, guiltless Swedish-American boy.

This youngest Eagle Scout in Cedar Rapids history had, around 1980, right here, fucked a Rolling Stone, then his wife, and then once more the Stone, whose rocky butt was surely gathering no moss whatsoever. Here, Robert made history, and most everybody else. He enabled many stars to use these four posts, isometrically. Plaques of bronze have been attached to vessels far less culturally seminal.

The uprights were topped by carved pineapples, huge owl-sized things like phallic hand grenades. Robert had lovingly recalled how his mother, on seeing pineapples anywhere, could never refrain from saying, with the sealed sententiousness of someone thoroughly middle class, "Pineapples symbolize hospitality." Looking up at these four, I thought, Yes, alas.

12:03 p.m. Robert's innocent folks would now be waiting at the brushed-steel luggage carousel. Most domestic flights to Manhattan land at La Guardia. Theirs arrived at Kennedy—as if their trip were international. And, considering the distance they had come from Lutheran Youth Fellowship socials on the Iowa bluffs, to this world of skeleton gods and boy-children forcibly undressed, to 120 blocks of talented people selling their abstract ideas first, and then their bodily presentation of those ideas, and eventually, in several cases, their bodies—considering the Gustafsons' flying into the joy of careless rapture naked, with today's total stranger naked too, and the single night (the night he wore the 1970s inaugural bottle green velvet suit), the night a whole decade elected Robert "The Sexiest Boy Alive in Town Right Now," this poor couple's flight, it could've been inter-planetary.

If they didn't already know some of this, the poor things soon would. In his kitchen, I picked up an old Easter basket; I emptied it of vintage fountain pens, commenced harvesting raunchier images from under the fridge door's magnets. Now to open Robert's freezer, find an igloo with one central peep-hole and—in it—a single geological cannoli, one half-pint of sludgy Stoli circa 1979?, plus nine small brown glass screw-top bottles. I dropped these into my container, singing, to console myself, "Pickin' up poppers, puttin' 'em in de basket. Pickin' up . . ."

I felt glad, at least, that his folks wouldn't find their ancestral tool-trunk stuffed with peach-fuzz swimmers. And, God willing, I'd at least have purged the place of their son's few store-bought boners.

Basket over arm, I finally opened the broom closet. One broom tilted there, leaned on by a dingy mop. I had expected oh three dildoes, tops. I found about thirty.

Thirty dildoes are a lot of dildoes.

They were piled knee-high, like cordwood. Propped, bald, ridged, and spired. Set on end, they formed a little onion-domed Kremlin. Some used adjacent cleaning products as their splints. Clumped there, the dildo quorum appeared unionized yet disgruntled. —Like toys caught in the act of trying to become the Toy-maker. Here were Toys that'd crawled up off the floor, yeah, into an erect position, okay—but had not evolved much beyond.

Striving? yes.

Brainy? no.

They seemed to sniff up toward me, weak-eyed rats, startled by daylight. Their pointed ends—the business ends—considered my new scent. The dildoes resembled some half-familiar form of household tool (actually, I guess they were). But their reiterated shape fell somewhere between a vacuum cleaner's "wand" and the fuselage of an old-timey batter-beating Mixmaster. They seemed hybridized with that lanky, shameless, duck-faced go-between, The Plumber's Friend.

I counted thirty-two, then quit. One was red and white and blue. Most showed that sickly pink shade combining chewed bubble gum with old eyeglasses' nose rests and ear hooks meant to simulate caucasian skin tone. Others, browner, Latin or African, appeared tree-sized, ropey saplings. And all were lasciviously detailed: lariats of vein, cobra cowls that flared—fair warning.

They gaped up at me like an open-mouthed choir of retarded children, looking heavenward.

Some, I recognized, were actual casts from living porn stars; there was a Jeff Stryker, a monster, but somehow Roman in its genial fluted civic beauty. One such menace proved double-headed as the Russian imperial eagle.

III.

12:12 p.m. How, in twenty-four minutes, to get this rictus of disembodied yearning uptown? I couldn't afford the round-trip cab fare. Taking yet another day off work meant the usual: tending my dying buddies was not just exhausting; during these condensed, hypnotic years, it'd gotten extremely expensive. The Sickness followed a Health of almost its equal: our early frisky New York days.

Under Robert's kitchen sink, I found a huge blue Tiffany's shopping bag (the show off!), plus a Lord & Taylor one featuring an Old English plum-pudding Christmas. These bags would make fine protective coloration for my smuggler's chore. When uneasy in Manhattan, assume the city's protective camouflage: feign shopping.

Opening my backpack, I piled in Robert's porn. Then at the kitchen's corner, I knelt, commencing the loading of dildoes into toney, neutralizing shopping bags. You couldn't just throw these things in helter-skelter. Too many to fit. So I worked, tongue pressed between teeth, as if building some Scout-worthy, log-cabin doghouse. I crosshatched nearly three dozen dildoes, dovetailing, relying on my early expertise at boyhood Lincoln Logs. (No offense intended, Mr. Lincoln.)

First I wondered, "Robert, what did you *do* with all these things?" Then of course I knew, and switched to alternate imagery. ("If only you'd stuck with these," I said aloud. I'd lately found I was saying things aloud a lot in public, aloud to friends alive and dead and dying. Teasing them, mostly. It was rough on strangers but seemed to help me, so I kept doing it. Why not? Apart from hospitals, I'd had little social life since about '84 on. I mostly picked up people at memorial services; I'd briefly dated a male nurse. And now, this tired, when it came to muttering aloud on streets, at least I didn't need a prescription; at least the jokes to departed loved ones made them seem less shadowy. Made me feel half-opaque. And, hey, the price was right.)

My backpack weighed with thin Swedish boys outdoors, I hoisted two shopping bags containing maybe fourteen pounds apiece of premium-cut dildoes. "This here pecker pack mule's about to trot uptown. Head 'em up, move 'em out, Rawhiiiide!" Such quips helped give me strength. Don't ask why.

I locked everything, then rushed to the Christopher Street station. The rain caught me. Soaked, I jumped the local just as its rubber-edged door sucked shut behind me. How efficient I'd become. It was only 12:39.

Prologue

* * *

One forearm looped around the steel pole, I tried planning what to tell Robert's naïve, judgmental parents. His father mounted a weekly pulpit, preaching the need for Christian love. The pastor hadn't seen his son in five years. I knew it was my duty to lead these people, smiling their simulated smiles, bearing church homecoming keepsakes, into Robert's narrow room.

"Prepare yourselves," I'd warn these folks. They had somehow conceived, then spoiled, then offered organ lessons, then tooth-braced the former prettiest boy in New York. I loved them at least for that. I'd say, "It's still him." (Or is it "he," it's still "he?" I felt very tired. Syntax, an early casualty.) I was so tired, I could only compare today's tiredness with last month's, "At least I'm not that far gone." Pearl gray I contrasted to the brindled dove gray darkening most of last fall.

I gave my days away in handfuls, partly out of superstitious gratitude that I'd somehow been spared. I helped because I could, and just hoped this equation might continue. It made me feel less guilty if I kept myself nearly as exhausted as my beloved patients. Surely I had been undercharged. Therefore, I could brutally tax myself, passing along the savings to others. My own apartment, one block from Robert's, had recently flooded; just my luck the sublet was ninety blocks north. A beggar now hollered his spiel above the train's din. People groaned, sick to death of being cornered by such need. "Just got out of prison, folks, an' I don't want to have to hurt nobody for my six babies' food, but . . ."

Our hospital receptionist, Lourdes Amy Llamos, spoke mostly Spanish, but with such cheer you felt you understood it. Behind her desk—stocked with candy and *Reader's Digest*s—a stained-glass window burned. It showed Mary the Mother, receiving hurt children of all nations, kids wearing casts and head bandages. Three had wedged themselves under her either arm and, within robes too blue, even the Virgin stared up into yellow light as if for strength, further funding. Lourdes always greeted me like staff, never exhausting her own goodwill. Her melon-colored silk blouses became a fact I leaned toward. As I swept in daily, she'd wink and ask about the latest of my twenty-odd patient-friends: "He betterer or worserer?"

Squiring other parents into other rooms of other dying boys, I had done all this before. I could hardly remember ever doing anything else. I'd always coddled my New York men friends—like Wendy mothering the Lost Boys. (We'd all come to New York in search, natch, of Peter.)

Followed by my lost ones' spritely, terrified parents, I felt like one more West Village Virgil. I was starting to sound bored as that old gal who's done the Circle Line boat tour of New York for fifty years. "On your left, that green roof? The building where they filmed *The Apartment* . . ." My references had grown dated as hers. I'd nearly forgot an upstate paradise called "Before."

At times, truth is, I felt some fugitive urge to shock these remote-control parents who'd let their boys suffer alone. By telephone, they told us, "We *would* come to New York, but given our schedules till Christmas, we just can't. Besides, hospital rooms are small, we'd only be in your way." My way?

They were probably decent folks, perfectly willing to dare their son's city friends to abandon him. Within the safety of their walled suburbs, they absolved themselves: "Wouldn't other lepers know leprosy just a li'l better?"

They arrived for final tearful scenes. Then, in the hall, after the first sight of the blinky, grateful skeleton who'd replaced their plump Princeton son, they would ask us caretakers—in lowered tones, "I think his accounts are with Citibank, right, Ed? Perhaps the time has come to inquire as to the disposition of Hiram's things . . . ?" So the genteel ones phrased it.

And we, the nurses, waited, knowing that Hiram's will, leaving us his complete Fiesta ware, a signed (Gustav) Stickley chair and one half-mature retirement IRA, would soon be revoked by the finer law firms of our American Middlewest.

Before, I was considered very funny. Do I now sound tired? There are so many reasons. Today I muted a few. Robert's parents had acted kinder than most; their church held bake sales to offset Robert's bills. Like many of us struggling artists, he'd had no health insurance. His mom once mailed me a small costly mall-bought German teddy bear holding a note: "I am a Care Bear for You, the one who's bearing care for our boy, Robbie. We sure look forward to meeting you! Rebecca Gustafson, and Reverend Bob." Robert's parents knew just the things to say by phone, if only thanks to pastoral practice and the peace afforded by fifteen hundred miles. These folks would definitely need me by 1:25 this afternoon. Pineapples are the symbol of something . . . hospitality.

I patted one pocket of my rain-drenched jacket, touched the six keys required to open Robert's doors. My key ring, thanks to a wasting sickness, now weighed three butch pounds. Pills rattled. I kept, upon my person, medications for Robert and my others, all in separate little timered pillboxes that—day and night—went off like pocket aneurisms. Around me, other passengers, sogged by a downpour unpredicted, smelled of wool, rubber raincoat, contradictory beauty products, overwork.

Why did this medevac duty keep being mine? Why didn't others take off from their jobs? Why did I always feel so pulingly obliged? I had sacrificed the writing of six books, or seven—all that energy fed into the fire of this disaster.

Why me?   Why *not* me?

IV.

or betterer or worser, I'd adapted. Holding the subway's upright pole, I promised myself I'd someday get back to writing fiction. Once my dears were free of needing me, I'd leave New York. And I would not depart in a box; I'd find some way to make Comedy of this shuffle toward the crypt. By now, I'd ordered so many helium balloons and bouquets, I had memorized shops' phone numbers, "Wanda, Hartley. The usual. Room 198. Plain white card, no 'Get Well' on it. —Today's name: 'Robert.' Bye."

I knew St. Vincent's Hospital as intimately as my childhood home. I filched clean linen for my patients, sparing the nurses so long-suffering and short-fused. Lourdes Amy Llamos, mother of six, daily Mass-goer, kept slipping me laminated bookmarks, prayers.

She'd pierce their edges (between phone calls and bloody ER arrivals). She would then whipstitch these holes with red satin ribbon. Do not ask me why. Bookmarks showed rouged low-expectations martyrs. They grinned as they held a dish supporting their own breasts, pudding servings suitable for one, and smiling! The markers had good edges, perfect—during endless bedside hours—for cleaning your nails, freeing a pesky piece of corn from back teeth. Occasionally, in the long sleep of sick ones' tidal drift and return and drift toward perfect stillness—I would, thanks only to boredom, scan today's Prayer for Sufferers:

"Lord, give me the patience to endure what I must, and the wisdom to trust God's hard yet beautiful blueprint for me. Give me large strength equal to my little time. May I feel that, as says Dame Julian of Norwich,

'All will be well, all will be well, all will be wonderfully well.' Make me humble enough to. . . ."
 blah blah blah.

Humble, I didn't need. But shoot me an overdose of "wonderfully well." If my health was betterer than friends', my looks were often even worserer. I had narrowed my routes to a sleepwalker's Forward and Reverse. That was all that kept me vertical, still strong enough to be left holding the bag(s) of Robert's pleasure, jostling uptown before needing to rush back down.

—Even so, I would arrive only just in time to let in the poor Gustafsons.

V.

12:58 p.m. Just when this car became most crowded at Seventy-second Street, just when I'd begun to nod a bit—hoping to snag some rest before my next words of kindness aimed toward the newest oblivious Iowans—just when I felt one moment's civilian privacy for the first time all day, I readjusted the weight of both rain-sogged sacks and there came such a sundering rip.

I stared forward as, all around my feet, thirty-odd sickening thuds. *Thwunk, plonk, fwawp!* The bags' string handles heaved upward, sudden weightlessness. Then strangers' screams, the gagging started.

Penises struck rubber floor matting with hideous rubberized zest. Many bounced so. Thirty dildoes are a lot of dildoes to try and catch on the move. Yippee oh cayyah! Git along little dildoes . . .

Rods hopped knee high, others achieved unsuspecting strangers' thighs. All leapt toward/at people. Who jumped real fast elsewhere, several shrieking.

I turn: One older lady in black—lower body pelted by several humongous disembodied peckers—stands atop four to six. Hands pressed against her cheeks, staring down at sudden unleashed dickdom, she resembles someone riding a disorganized log raft right over Niagara. The aged virgin hollers those around her into early deafness.

Pink domes, large as the cups atop thermoses, plop across people's fashionable skinny shoes. One Spanish boy drop-kicks a black prick halfway down the car. It strikes an ad for dental surgery, then thuds against a businessman's shoulder, ricocheting. What this gent screams down here at me, me—already fallen on all fours, intently hunting/gathering—is extremely unpleasant. If probably accurate. All I can say is, "Yikes, little spill here, definite spillsies. Oopsie daisy, so sorry. 'S not like me, folks. Butterfingers."

I am kneeling among these many ankles. Collecting, I am so alone with loads of logs of Lincolnly homeliness and lank. I find I suddenly have much space here at the train's south end. Forty people herd off from me, quickly gather at the car's north quadrant. Strangers are united in their rage, completest sputtering disgust; they act abruptly joined, as only jaded New Yorkers can during some annoying natural disaster. "Don't we have rights? And on a workday. Do we deserve this?" one chubby businesswoman shouts.

I now assemble stray cocks by hand, spurned, an unloved zucchini worker, considering giggling, too tired to care (no, never that tired: see, there's the rub), I am mainly mortified at having zero resistance in a world so tetanus harsh.

I count the seconds till the train's stop at Ninety-sixth Street. Bent here, I seem to be farming these; I feel unzipped and peeled and sickly, for once in need of someone else's harvesting. Mother Mary, lift me, tuck me underarm, quick, gir'friend. I keep pickin' up poppas and stickin' 'em in my pockets. Pockets prove too virginal to accommodate this many.

I feel as detached, as puppet ridiculous, as the woody dorks I'm forced to hoard here. Why am I keeping them? Do I *need* these? Why not run to another car, abandon these heaped here like the Homeless? Who'll miss 'em, Robert's parents? What good are used ones? More intimate than borrowed toothbrushes. God knows, Robert will never want these guys again.

But he told me to save them. And I'm doing it. And what I keep hearing as I scoop them up anyway is a shrill half-human mantra. Repeated, repeat it. Someone not unlike myself must be shouting, even as he tries to gather peckers, stuff 'em in his britches, jam some under his belt, cover tips with spare wet scraps of Tiffany blue. As I tuck several beneath my soggy windbreaker, with the rest stacked over my arms like firewood, the point of my chin, dainty, steadying the load, I find myself calling in exhaustion something I'm not proud of: "They aren't really mine. Just carrying them for . . . a friend. Not for me! They're . . . friends'."

I must be downtown to let his folk upstairs in under twelve minutes. I must let poor Robert's poor parents through all those locks. I dread leaving them stranded on the street outside. They'll have packed too much; they'll be full of falsified optimism, trivial flight detail. The senior Gustafsons, decent people, overdressed, underprepared. As if anybody could ever prepare for this. —Is it possible to feel this tired and still stay conscious?

Why am I trying to pick up sticks, and am now dropping them? Why keep gathering and failing and stooping and making arrangements of them, now like vegetables, like lilies? Why do this?

Jeering people bunch tighter at the car's far end. Looks like they're actually passing around a petition. But, no sweat, I am by now some diva, a bit exempt, I'm really incognito—a beloved star and singer, plucking roses off the apron of her stage while spilling others, not caring, since there are plenty. Now I have slid from "These things are my friends'" to "These're my friends'"—till finally, deranged, I achieve an odd immodesty, recalling so many absent ones, the thirty or so lost already. And as I now touch each of these colossal members, cut off from a bloodstream, now apart from being anything past Artifact and Matter, now just Art—a familiar family litany surges back.

Under my either bony knee, train wheels clatter a more dignifying rhythm, I cradle and then get to name these dolls and dicks and dolldicks and dolls of dicks, these unlikeliest encapsulated friends. Sorry for being so slow to recognize you David, Hiram, Darrell, and James, sweet Tony Wu, Kit and Kirk, Paul, Ramon, Geoff, Bruce and Ansel and R.J., Stan and Roland, Bill, Gideon, John, the other Jody, Roger, Wayne, Jody, Paulo, Todd, Peter, Lance, Ernie, Marco, Jay, Jerry. And Robert, especially you, Robert, who—polite—aware how far your folks have come today, at what great cost and trouble, and with you being so kind and organized even if mostly dead, will see to it you die while they're in town, to save them a second trip, and because that is so *like* you, so like our Robert . . . and James, and our Hugh, and Deke, and our Patrick, and our Nick, and our our . . .

As my fellow passengers, understandably, fearing contaminants, scared that these are used ones, which they *are*—as strangers press against one another, dissing me and mine, it's odd to find I hold these slightly higher. I clutch with some new strength, suspecting whom I've got here. Upright before my chest, now bunched under my chin . . . A stemlike rectitude, a certain, simple, rustic Gaudí beauty, my bouquet.

Often symbols of hospitality.

"Friends." I cough toward my trapped glowering audience. I need a new logic in this, my exhaustion. "See how many? And, boy, you lose 'em, you really know it. Thirty friends are a lot of friends!"

Prologue

* * *

Am I saying this out loud, or thinking it too hard? Am I overburdening them? I do have quite an armful. I consider trying a nifty Muppet voice for each. —Instead, I'm praying for this goddamn train to stop. Pleeeease let all this stop. I draw nearer the door. Others let me. Such courtesy.

I'll deposit these; I'll take a cab. I'll let his parents in. They will be waiting. They will be seated on six blue suitcases before his place's flaking stoop, furious, checking their watches, faces pink, looking left, looking right. Irked, they are exactly that scared. Somebody's Doberman in a spiked collar will be chained, snarling, to a fire hydrant nearby. Scruffy alien kids smoke herb upwind and these Iowans, miffed by their son's illness and his friend's insolence, scan every approaching face for my flushed apologetic grin. I'll trot it toward them, puffing, "Sooo sorry. Had to rush uptown to drop some of Robert's things. But, how good you've come. Flight okay? You'll need an hour's nap, I know."

The mother, nearly a foot taller than her agreeable husband, looks so much like Robert in high heels, she will spook me. I'll shake both their offered hands. I'll try to lug their largest powder-blue American Tourister. Their features grow less irritated, my Southern manners somewhat softening their rage.

"We're under lots of pressure," she tries explaining. "You cannot imagine."

"Aha. I can only guess. —I'm afraid we still have quite a hike straight-up," I smile so; they must never understand my full exhaustion. They are still innocent. And I? Am not.

His mother lightens: "Our Robbie certainly chose a *col*orful neighborhood." Just eleven minutes late for this, now fighting with the keys while dragging heavenward a Stonehenge of luggage, I call back down the steps, "Mmmm, yes, colorful. You have no idea." Then I'll lead them. Lead them up toward the huge bed waiting, made, hospitable.

But for now, here on the train, to bear these select items even higher—scepters, majorette batons, my isthmuses worth crossing. Titanic and magnificent and clumsy, manly weapons. No one will come near me . . .
    and why?
Because they guess that these I hold are souls. These—raw, toylike—are retarded but honest, the wasted overly-male souls I am still somehow in charge of. —These, my favorite thirty.

Lord-Express have mercy on our stop-making, stuttering local. Place me expressly beyond these stares, past such terrible embarrassment. I say I do not feel it. I feel it. Credit me at least for trying to help my others. Let me trust your blueprint even though you're really succch a bad designer. Let me know how best to clean up after people other people do not want . . . Let Ninety-sixth Street happen soooooon! Say my friends are at least as safe as they are dead. And since You've done all this to them, could You please just let them go now? Just leave my boys the fuck alone.

Someday let *me* rest. Then tell me, You, O Lord and architect of suffering. Tell me, You:

Is it going to have to get . . . Betterer, or Worserer?

—Take me aside, and set me down on something soft—and, promise me just once, that . . .

—All will be well, all will be well, and all will be wonderfully well.

Amen.

Won't it?

Catastrophe and Child's Play

> Our life is based upon the mutual interpenetration of play and earnest. So long as this happens, we live in peace. In a catastrophe, the mixture is lacking. Just as it is lacking in the games of children.
>
> Catastrophe and child's play are the two poles of all social life.
>
> —ROSENSTOCK-HUESSY

I.

 don't consider myself psychic, just lucky—with friends.

Shall we start with the recent playful miracle? How fast a migraine can clarify to the buzz of good champagne. I am riding a taxi toward La Guardia airport, I'm hurrying to the old house I now occupy. My ticket to North Carolina is nonrefundable, I feel glad to be headed south. I sit studying the purple turban of a driver whose name is, according to the card depicting him, Krishna.

Suddenly my forehead—from just over the eyebrows to where the hairline once reigned—goes exquisite and sneezy as with some ice-cream headache. I look to the left of Krishna's orderly topknot, I see a peeling decal: "I (Heart) New York." I know.

"Excuse me, Mr. Krishna, sir? We must do a U-ie. I am going to miss my plane. We will now be heading back into the city. There's a little downtown street. I can help navigate. You will double-park, please. In thirty seconds I'll know if it's still there. I bet you anything it is."

"Is, is vhhat, szir?"

"One chip of paint from the back side of a radiator near our table at the coffeehouse. We all wrote on it. That chip is lying on the tile floor underneath. Piece maybe five inches long. Tomorrow, she will sweep it out. I'm this sure. —Look." And, through the open plastic panel, I shove my very-white-man-in-his-forties hand. It is trembling, that happy, wobble wobble. I feel proud of my hardearned uncontrol.

Dark eyes in the rearview mirror gauge my blue-gray ones (brown can "go into" blue more often than blue'll ever fit brown). Mr. Krishna tells me, "Szir, you are having veesion. I vill join you in showing I know what veesions are. Am off-duty. Krishna he believe your veeeesion."

I cannot say how much it meant to get a free ride, forty dollars' worth. Of course, I later paid him anyway. That's part of what you learn. From taking care of people. To accept whatever they can offer. Then you try and pay it back quick. That helps them to give more, which helps them.

He speeds into the web of nighttime Manhattan; things either flash or hide; he finally stops, he activates the blinkers. I dash into a store all new to me. No coffee smell, no crowd. It's become one of those short-lived shops selling African crafts. The entrance stands guarded by wooden giraffes, near-lifesized, spotted in darker shellac. A dashikied clerk chats up her only customer. I fake shopping. I pass bright crocheted hats you could fit over world globes. I find four bolt holes. Here our group's table once stood. Behind it, the old bowlegged radiator we sat on during our worst winters.

The owner seems occupied and I, clear of sight lines, now drop to my knees. I reach, blind, beneath a radiator still half-warm. I pull forth a handful. Paint chips, each flake no longer than a feather. My palm closes, careful not to crush even one. I thank the woman, praise her loot, swear I'll be back, and, smuggling litter, jump into Krishna's chariot. It, participatory, squeals off.

When he sees me sorting through my lead-based tea leaves, sees me tilting toward street lamps and stores' neon, Krish, unbidden, ignites the overhead lamp. "Here we are!" I call.

"You are finding, good. What exactly are finding, szir?"

"We all signed this. One night, half-drunk after performing for each other, our works about Paradise, we piled downstairs, needing caffeine, we make a pact to live forever in and out of art, to visit one another's podunk hometowns. Then each of us, using her yellow felt pen, let a single line spell all our names as one long, perfect, brand-new word, Mr. Krishna. —My head doesn't hurt now, I feel ecstatic.

"Krishna, sir? How'd I guess that a woman would sweep it away by noon? How'd I understand our name was still tucked under there tonight only? How'd I know that, buddy?"

Came the calming word. "Veesion."

II.

As one of their caretakers, I am taking care to save a record. (Somebody has to.)

By now, my nerves are shot but the news is good: today, at last, my every dying one is safely dead.

—Right now, a Thursday, for the first time in over a decade, this very morning—sunny, slight breeze from the Northwest—my dry-cleaned funeral suit slid back into its closet, I am allowed to guiltlessly ask, "So, Hartley, buddy, how 'bout an onion bagel? Sound good? Maybe squeeze those navel oranges for juice." My last sick friend found peace in this very house, ten days back, upstairs, in an antique bed, inherited.

—This might not sound like much of an achievement, but oh and oy, is it ever! Maybe my rejoicing strikes you as a wee bit weird? I know only this: I can wake up and not wonder first thing, "Has the gasping started? Will they return his apartment's security deposit? Which of his aunts did I forget to phone?"

Now . . . Where *was* I?

If you go down on the *Titanic*—the saga of your drowning becomes just one gust in the vacuum of a famous ship ending. The vessel's destruction outranks your own. Who will see your last three air bubbles rising to the surface of that much-black ice water?

We have all been upstaged by the newsworthiness of our particular disaster. This is just one of the ways History snubs us.

I now make monthly payments on this clunky, comfortable house (circa 1900); I own that dull Ford wagon (circa 1990) parked out back. Without quite trying, by default, I am hiding here. I am not quite safe, but I'm not dead, either.

This, you see, is my life's A.D./B.C. revolution. I, Richard Hartley Mims jr., am briefly returned to my home state, to bovine health, to my own care-taking. So nice you're here; you, alive, too. What a coincidence. That gives us something undeserved in common. I need to testify. The tale of them should ride one long gasp across this first morning I feel fully off-duty. I need to tell our history quick.

I want it stated in a way as literal as those guides so popular at our public libraries.

How to Tile Your Own Patio in Under Six Hours, No Previous Experience Required!

I want it rendered into mild, safe steps.

How to Survive the Loss of Your Beloved Address Book in Under Fifteen Years, How Not to Numb Every Inch of Your Interior While Doing So, What to Make of Their Remains, and How to Go On, Having Forfeited Your Pals and So Much of Your Previous Experience! First Time Every Time.

The relief today feels like this: having borne all the children you could ever want, you finally choose to get your tubes tied. No further worry about preventing other babies, ever. The perilous fertility has ceased.

My own artistic generation, gay and not—so essentially and goofily good—idealists for just as long as we could be, longer—is now, before age fifty, often good and dead.

There is one big advantage to getting left back:

Now I *know* I am alive. Turns out, that is a huge plus. It makes you concentrate. Suspecting you're fairly strong, you let cabbies rise, godlike, to your own occasion. Your duties as a nurse force you to half-medically forgive yourself.

There's another main joy in being the representative left behind: I am allowed, encouraged, to remember them. You will not believe these people I got to love for years. I still do!

I have always been so lucky in my friends.

Just tell me I am not the jinx that "disappeared" them.

A week and a half ago, right after the exit of my best surviving pal, one of the *Titanic*'s final survivors died. She had been just five when the liner sank. Last words her father spoke to her from deck?—"Hold Mummy's hand very tight. Now go and be a good girl."

She recalled everything. Considering the darkness, certain noises stayed especially real. After the hulk's immense last gasp, from one cold lifeboat where she drifted bundled with her mother in her mother's coat, the child heard many swimmers scream. Such cries.

But, she reported, what soon sounded even worse was the quickly spreading silence. One by one, from a darkness out of Dante, so very fast in water this freezing, all the screaming singly ceased.

It was, this old woman (never married) recounted, the stillness afterward that scared her most.

"Out there, floating, in the black, it became so quiet, you could not believe a single noise was being made anywhere else on earth."

That is where I live this morning.

The phone is idled. I now take messages for no one else. True, my grandmother's mantel clock ticks on. (Not even silence quite stifles that.) I tell myself I mustn't burn my only bagel.

These days, people newly sick with it expect to live much longer. Great. But not my crowd. Always pirate pioneers, we were, alas, among its first. The long-promised boat, tiny but already there at the horizon, seems finally to be coming in.

It is a boat my darlings missed.

Now everything is slowed and eased and lazied. Medications?: one daily vitamin. I have just myself to care for. I am, increasingly, a cinch. Keep it fed, keep it warm, keep things quiet. The complex loss, it simplifies you. Last night, showering, I shocked myself. I almost hummed—four bars from an old Lerner musical.

I begin to guess what has just happened—what delicate, expensive ship so recently slid under. Look, I'll squeeze those twelve nice oranges. They've only just begun to "turn." Too much juice for one bachelor, but it'll probably get drunk. A few sure things now get me through.

Today, no waiting for doctors' grand rounds, no faux cheer around my sick. Which reminds me of a tacky joke.

It was told at the start of the plague. It was told about a stunning Miss America, disqualified. The committee found that, precrown, this ambitious, hard-working girl had made some lesbian porn. A girl has to eat.

"Q: What is the difference between that Miss America and the *Titanic*?"

"A: At least you know how many people went down on the *Titanic*!"

My dead friends, see, just urged me to offer you this sleazy riddle. Departed, they can bear most anything but solemnity, especially solemnity about *them*. My circle misses noise, brass, vamping, and action for the sake of action's being pretty. Our patron saint was Saint Adrenaline.

Now I can bear everything but loudness. I live in a small village. I love its evening train whistles, its morning mockingbirds. I dread New York's career of frenzy. Now I sit here in a foursquare kitchen five hundred miles due south of Manhattan. I'm saved from the wild silver city I still adore.

Here, I feel determined to stay basic.

How to live at 6:40 a.m. How to keep your house hushed. My phone is yet asleep, if not quite dead. Out there, garbage collectors keep banging cans so loud, cleaning up after the spoilt sleepers they secretly hope to wake. —I identify with those garbage men.

Wake up, beloved litterers of my life!

O, I long to tell a Fairy Tale. It is a true one. Not to give away the end, but most of the best fairies die. I want to tell about our crowded hearty "Before." It will, I hope, outlast my pals' more recent spindly "After." Now we have floated to smoother waters, a continental divide, the "After After" of this plague. From here, to me, "Before" looks even holier. We were children. We thought no one had ever been wilder or smarter than we.

My boys and girls were gorgeous, strong-backed, impenitently sexual, ambitious, irritating, adorable, high-energy, lost and found then lost, the best hopes for our passions that now seem so antique—painting, writing, composing.

Don't worry: I can still be amusing. They always liked that in me.

Even their sadness often happened very funny. Disaster never rushed you from the direction that you bravely faced. It played too well with you. It did play very rough.

Look, I've squeezed this juice, for us alone. Such a color! Let me pour yours into Granny Halsey's only leaded cut-glass tumbler not yet broken. With your permission, and in your warming company, may I award myself a morning off? A whole one, too. No changing sheets. No dealing with the parents. No talk of sick, sicker, sickest. Let's end all emergency thinking. Please.

I inherited those crystal pendants there from Robert. I strung them in three eastern windows that'd feed them each dawn's best. I cannot say I bought this house just because its kitchen faces sunny-side-up; but the brilliance of those crystals has become, for me, our Robert's own.

I'm now an early riser. One blessing of the plague—I need less sleep. Even when I try to force myself to stay in bed, I wake by sitting upright, feeling stressed but needed.

I rest here with my coffee in night's final dark. I wait for day's first color. My hot mug, caretaken, is circled by two hands merely warm but still glad to feel useful. I welcome light. I dare it not to come.

You may think me superstitious. (Oh, by now I've grown quite pagan!) But, some mornings . . . I speak to hatching prism brilliance. There'll be a first wink, usually redness, then an almost-comical glimmer, all points. —"Well, star, hi. Look at you, back everywhere. RobertRobert-Robert."

I have a minute now my friends are finally courteously (slowly, then suddenly all too quickly) dead. All of it remembers like some inlander's tale of a great luxury liner that sank. It fell asleep, and settled on the bottom, and only a few of us woke up in time, got out.

Now, lucky, later, we are allowed to dive back down among the wreckage, gathering precious evidence. Here, a long name on one piece of paint, the magic beans—retrieved. I finally get to spill them.

Unfair, my friends are dead. Unfair, I'm left alive. And yet, here's what's miraculous:

We have only just begun to know each other!

Oh, but we thought we were truly something.
Boy, but I have really meant to get to this.

BEFORE

The Thrust of the Launch

> No one should come to New York to live unless he is willing to be lucky.
>
> —E. B. WHITE, "Here Is New York"

 here are just three days in the history of Manhattan: the day you first see it, the day you get to move there, and the day you, far smarter, much less intact, still find the strength to leave.

Seeking my fortune, I swept into the city two years before the ultimate careerist, a disease, did.

The Pastoral Symphony offered shepherds an idyll, quickly followed by a storm. I arrived just in time to witness the exuberant peasant dance, midglade, midtown. I felt those first fat playful droplets cool the dancers before lightning struck us. With malice aforethought and damn good aim.

For the next decade and more, I somehow kept myself afloat on a pure stone island overstocked with jesters royal, too many contenders for King, and a whole of lot of queens. I founded my own handhold on this piece of castle rock surrounded by moat. With friends' help, no thanks to centrifugal force, I clung there all those years and for dear life.

Everybody knows NYC is a cliff dwellers', mud daubers' generative and wondrous mess. Weaklings don't last long here. This town is reserved for what Strindberg called "the Stronger."

* * *

I unzipped both plaid canvas bags when I, newly into address book number seven, was thirty-three. I'd planned on becoming a New Yorker since the age of eight. You must hail from rusticated eastern North Carolina—its topography flat as a table—to understand how very much the erect and steely city truly means. Being so upright, it is visible, self-reflective, from a long way off. From the chem swamps of stinky reedy New Jersey. A citadel for hopefuls, it looks mainly at its own profiles in the cubistic caverns of sky-like mirror it provides itself. Open compacts everywhere.

Early in my stay—drunk on city life, glad for its free tickets and dollar pizza and standing room, I told my new friend Robert how much I really loved it here. Really. I admitted that my dingy minuscule apartment reminded me of van Gogh's simple room at Arles—bed, chair, desk—everything a guy might ever need. Robert laughed his pirate baritone. "You know what you are, Hartley, pal? Down deep, you're basically a happy person."

"No!" I said, looking around, half-shamed. I stood here, on public view, accused of having "a talent for happiness."

"Well, yes and no." The compliment seemed to undercut my serious intellectual credentials. Sure, I knew pain. I just preferred the other. Colette advised: "Be happy. It's one way of being wise."

Wasn't that natural: expecting contentment in New York after just two months here? "Happy" meant work done well, done so well that grudging acceptance, then inevitable fame must follow. How ambitious was our group? We were so ambitious, we did not know we were.

That young, we believed most every myth. We certainly believed Manhattan's. It had just drafted us.

My parents introduced me to the city at age eight.

My starter purchase was, alas, a tiny maroon paisley ascot from a tie-shop in Times Square. I recall my folks' worried glances. "I guess it's his money, Richard." Mother sounded exhausted in advance. Did my folks consider this baby ascot a prediction of my show biz queerness or, maybe worse, some indication I was finally home?

We saw *My Fair Lady* (original cast), we Christmas shopped (the old Bergdorf, the old F.A.O. Schwarz, original locations, both, like so much, gone). I stuffed my piggy bank's nickels into skyscraper telescopes. The Rockettes made me cry.

* * *

Manhattan seduces even the sternest. It specializes in the sternest.

Even my proper mom, my war-hero dad, succumbed to unlikely dandyisms. Dressed for a nightclub, she wore her reddest mouth and the real pearls. His cuff links matched his onyx tie tack. His hair was oversleek in some new way that gave his whole blond head an eerie prettiness. Dad had worked hard convincing one white pocket hankie into three distinct Chrysler Building points.

The hotel provided a baby-sitter, one swart old woman I believed would undress my kid brother and me the very second our handsome folks waltzed out. (Instead, she ordered many room service hot fudge sundaes, smoked her whole pack of Luckies, then snored like some stevedore. Disappointing.)

Leaving, Dad bent over our bed. Wanting to commemorate our whereabouts, he did the most charming thing. Eyes on his sons, he simply pointed to the white peaks of his own perfect hankie. "Boys?" he said as his pink forefinger moved, a magician's, showing how the trick is done. "One, two, three. —New York, look out!"

He pressed that same finger to his own backside and made a sizzling sound while winking. We giggled. "*Rich*-ard!" Mom, as usual, flirted by pretending to overcare.

I'd never seen Dad so worked up. It made me straighten the ascot I wore atop my blue pajamas.

I would later judge that New York City made my dad feel very (almost cruelly) sexual.

—Like father like son.

The folks soon noticed a strange expression claiming their young Hartley's face. My frown became more set each day, and Mom at last stooped before me. She brushed at the brown velvet collar of my little chesterfield. "What is it, darling? Are you scared in New York? Hmmnh? Yes? —Scared?"

I nodded.

"Scared, what of?"

"Leaving."

I had the shaming secret knack for happiness. Even as a boy, my image of perfect contentment always centered not on toys but the toys' workshop, chockablock with paint, hammers, table space. Now, full grown, arriving here at last, I imagined myself one skilled elf about to go on payroll at the North Pole's action central; I would soon meet all the other top toy-making young elves . . . or is it "elfs"? (Kinds of people in the world? Those who want to own the toys, and those who long to make them.)

First six months in town, I would climb to the roof of my tenement and watch the city's beady lights come on and remember Mom's real pearls. (She wore them "out" despite expecting robbers, even at the Rainbow Room.) I would sip my cheap Chilean champagne from the last of Granny Halsey's flutes (long since stepped on). And I would toast the skyline like some hick, to your health, chin-chin, for simple gladness. I *was* a hick. Whose life had finally begun . . .

Newly-off-the-train, I sensed I was not the only gay one. All of us were still very much guy-guys, the more so for youth's stubborn cockiness. Butch and jawed and proud and hung, our mothers' favorites. In Falls, North Carolina, my sexual outlook had been Hush-Hush. But here, on glossy streets—one glance at any other slim tailored dude was returned with interest, a brazen unharmed "Yes?" Safety in numbers. Who the hell cares? Strong, we were here now.

We had come this far to be ourselves. We would not hold back. There were hundreds of thousands of us.

And we were mostly so friggin' cute.

Why are so many writers, painters, (and hairdressers) gay—that's another story, anybody's guess. Maybe self-defense by those most longing to redesign an unfair split-end world? Camouflage got invented just after the airplane. During both world wars, the gay-friendliest of army divisions? Always the camouflagers. Born experts.

We had all chaired our high school prom decoration committees. We now met at interviews for the same job, which none of us won, being a bit too visibly "artistic." We seemed latent nonteam players—despite the blue blazer. (Borrowed, it, alas, looked borrowed.) Still unemployed, we adjourned to whine over coffee.

I lost the job (writing-editing *The Gasket*, a rubber industry newsletter). But I found Robert Christian Gustafson.

I first encountered said youth in a polished-deco-stainless elevator, going down. I had no particular feeling yet about the rubber industry. I stood behind this tall person, also studying the clocklike needle marking our descent. A smell rose off his back—the newly starched white shirt seemed worn by some kid who'd just mowed his folks' two-acre lawn. He looked gold and smelled green. Gilt ringlets blocked my view and seemed the spinning arrow's fulcrum: Cupid head.

The interviewer had told us, "Expect our call"; we knew better. Leaving through a checkerboard lobby, he was drawing slow-burn looks, not noticing. He stood six feet, but so much beauty taffy-pulled to that height made him seem a sailing ship. I followed, already noticing others' noticing for him (surely someone had to). Here I was scrapbooking for a (literally) perfect stranger.

One old guy, his mouth clamped around a nasty unlit cigar, wedding ring cutting his finger, did this comic double take, scoped out the blond's ass. Girl? Oh no, boy, oh well, a boy that young, why not look, long as you're lookin'? Sir, my sentiments exactly.

Catching up, short of breath, as if auditioning as Beauty's executive secretary, I only knew I had to stop this youth. Soon backward walked I, before his silver-yellow fire-engine advance.

"Don't tell me." I let my Southern accent go more molasses. "International Rubber hated you. For exactly the reasons they should have fallen on their knees. You've been in the city from ten to fourteen days, and you're an artist just fantastically talented, and you think nobody knows or understands about your caliber of talent, but I do."

"Because you are gifted, too, right? I mean, like, extremely."

"Ditto. —Coffee? My cheapest legal vice. With refills, if you put a lot of cream and sugar in it, one cup can get you through the afternoon." We spoke our names, told our "fields," our minor hometowns, we shook hands and scanned each other from the knees—to the telltale groin—(two groin boys) and up, still smiling when our eyes rendezvoused back at either's face, and we were already friends.

Gustafson lived, turned out, one block from me. "Lucky for you," he said, "I've been here five whole years, going on a century. I know things."

"Such as?"

"Best getting places. Certain amazing people. The ropes."

I nodded, "Okay."

Soon after we said Up Yours to International Rubber Gasketry (which never called), after we memorized each other's siblings' names and birth order, we learned each other's exact junior and senior prom themes. I still recall Robert's gym masterpiece was "20,000 Leagues Under the Sea." The welter of gym plumbing and steampipes he upgraded to being the Bakelite wheelroom of Captain Nemo's submarine.

We lived exiled to eternal bachelor pads; but we'd arrived here free of childrearing's time-drain and expense. They assign you ugly vents and ductwork? Make a line of it.

We had not impregnated our hometown sweethearts; nor had we been impregnated. We were none of us the fair-haired letter-sweater son that Dad hand-groomed to stay home and take over his Budweiser distributorship.

That was our form of luck.

Blake wisely instructs certain prudish stay-at-homes, "The lust of the goat is the glory of God." And we billy-club aficionados already knew this, thanks. Sex was among our several unacknowledged art forms. So early in our careers, most of us were still better at it than our sundry vertical artistries. —In those, we'd not yet found a way to be just natural (as we helplessly were the second that our pants fell down).

But, in New York, you could get famous even for that.

—We, barely unpacked, already painted (self-portraits, the model always being present, moody, and cheap), we wrote (self-portraits of young persons arriving in great cities that, happily, we were far too artistic to actually, like, call New York), we sculpted (torsos not unlike our own, if just a bit more "defined"), and we composed.

Robert's starter chamber works were early Straussian tone poems in which yearning Coplandesque adolescence met caterwauled Bartok car-horn cello-scratches indicating a confrontation, the Iowan Lutheran Bucolic being eaten by the Godless Urban, get it? And, barely out of Port Authority bus depot, we fucked. Actually, in the depot, if memory still services.

After one year's art school, I'd found I might just make a better writer than a painter. As with most land-poor Southerners, my family tended to mythologize its struggles, enlarge its charms and holdings. In New York, I farmed out such diehard traits and glories to new friends.

Having no money, we naturally moved into your cheaper neighborhoods. There still *were* some then. Instantly, on the street, Robert and I recognized others like us. Leashed urban dogs scout only at ankle height only for leashed urban dogs of a certain scent, size, and use.

The town then mainly seemed child artists, also freshly drawn to Manhattan's clearinghouse and open ward. I owned a typewriter. At least I knew what my work would be. In Manhattan, when you're this underfunded, even small self-knowledge can give a kid a big head start.

At thirty-three, I'd already finished grad school, worked odd jobs, taught in California and North Carolina, but somehow I still looked like a kid.

My first Manhattan night out, each new disco Robert squired me to asked for my ID. I appeared to be just what I was: new here, doggedly healthy, loaded with energy, nearly as talented as driven, a rube, if a well-brought-up one, terrified, oversexed, and reasonably fearless. Meaning: innocent innocent innocent, and not unpretty. New York, watch out! Jump a goodly distance back.

—Only in retrospect do we ever really understand how we actually looked. The young ones who learn that at the time can be rendered whores by overknowing. Whores, or actors.

For me, New York meant the chance of having fun while creating something true and beautiful, a chance at lowering my address book's bucket into the deepest, coolest waters I could find.

New York offers the twin necessities for founding your artistic reputation: one very public stage, adjoining (via long service-corridors) many anonymous Santa-workshop refuge caves, places to perfect the work you'll soon make public.

Listen to the name of entry-level Manhattan real estate: "Studio apartment."

Your art's foundry. Plus, where you go to hide from its results. "Ghetto" is an idiomatic Venetian word for "foundry"—a landmark in the only neighborhood where Venice allowed its Jews to live.

My ninth address book (I still own every one, and will show you later if you're not careful) reflects all this: a first huge forward swelling. There is red wine splashed across the *A*'s and most *B*'s—the thin, rich, membranous color that itself has now become something of a sensuous address in time.

Looking back, rereading my young Manhattan life's fine print, I now wonder who this Astrid Terboldt is. All Astrid's possible extension phones are listed, and my scribbled note to myself: "Give her father's driver at least 15 min. notice, named Griffin." How did I (and memory) lose her?   Jotted here are back-room phones for off-brand midtown galleries long since shut. There are the numbers of good restaurants' pay phones. Here's a friend of a friend in the Met Museum's Department of Education who might help sneak us into black-tie previews meant for actual adult donors. Plus a lotto ticket number that, apparently (I hope), did not win. Addresses exist in time as well as space.

You get a larger urban life; you go buy yourself a bigger, sturdier binder, industrial-strength. As soon as you've established your address book's critical bulk, Natural Selection starts to cull the ones you really love from those you just find entertaining despite their bad characters.

Then—too soon—Natural Subtraction kicks in. You adore some folks more than others, but you choose the ones who can best and truthfully adore you back. And—even there—little tiffs occur.

Three missed dates. The promised letter of recommendation that never arrives. You keep score mostly by transferring the names of the living, your dearest, to the next book and the next. Buying up, humanly. Who will fit into your narrow pleasure boat? "Finding yourself" means the ways your favorite company mirrors all you've founded, all you hope for. You, Foundry, you . . .

You assemble a community, and, in your early thirties, looking younger, you naturally assume that your assemblage will stay put.

A collector, choosing paintings, has every right to believe those works will not leave home, or fade, or burn up in their frames, right?

Welcome to New York. Welcome to the Lost and Foundry.

JumpStart

he very first time my very first Manhattan telephone rang—an old black rotary that, in memory, seems heavy, carved, and Deco-gloss-important as that movie's Maltese falcon—it was Robert, joshing. His resonant voice managed a credible Svedish accent. "Is diz Mizzter Hartley Mimzz, der writer? I haf good neeeews from de Nobel Committee! Would tomorrow be acceptable time for home delivery of yer Pwrizze?"

"Finally!" I shot back, ready for wit's first SAT question. "I can maybe pencil you in, but only before ten. 'Cause after that, I'm booked, bitch."

Laughing, he liked this. I'd wanted him to. It is hard to express, after so many years of work—after all the writing things down, then cleaning things up—how easy and inevitable our first play felt.

Fun founded itself on our assumption that great work would emerge from us. My starter story contained fifteen hundred sentences, most I'd memorized like Catechism. Fifteen hundred chances to get it right. We felt rewards were due us, if not now . . . soon. First, glamorous parties to crash. Then masked balls to legally attend, until, eventually, when we were old and forty, such bashes would be big ones thrown for us. Watch.

Robert had phoned to invite me to the opening of something called the Boy Bar. He always sensed, it seemed, the one event in New York each night that the largest number of intelligent people would, next morning, kick themselves for missing. He had wasted not one evening of his five years here. I, clever enough to be teachable, followed all his hints. Followed all his entrances. Bouncers spoke his name, looked my way, paused, then wagged their heads toward side-entrances. Came the first night I heard a girl singer dedicate her next torch song to Robert—pointing out his ringlets so the credit would accrue to her.

I fought to keep my face neutral as I sat slightly to his left, our shoulders touching. It was already at early bubble, RobertRobertRobert. And I, taking lessons, always fully along, if half-smiling, lived three steps behind, checked the coats—his fake fur and my own outmoded camel hair that made me, he said, look like the son of a Mafia kingpin newly enrolled at Andover.

I agreed to help him open the Boy Bar. "Dress down for once," Robbie coached me well, "got a torn T-shirt?" "No, but I have a T-shirt and two good hands." "You'll overdo it. I know you Wagnerians. You wear the shirt, I'll do the tearing." "Best offer I've had all day." "Oh, that again? Hartley? I've heard Sisterhood is powerful, what say we stick with that forever?" "Fine, my powerhouse sistah. Ma's napping. —Would you now consider incest?"

The fact that, on first sight, I loved this guy insanely made me in no way unique. But it just got worse, or better.

Many local boys who'd heard, "You're too handsome to waste that grade of face here, you deserve to go to New York," *had* by now. At the bar's gala opening, such a smoky din—former small-town camouflagers blazing all the primary colors of *Broadway Boogie Woogie.* I heard others say, Robert was the god, terminally attractive, and had just one competitor: that gladiatorial towhead. The guy was named Horse, for reasons beneath mentioning. Robert's hair shone platinum, Horse's mane a mere corn yellow; I felt relieved to soon overhear Horse called "the *oth*er blond."

From the Boy Bar, Robert was whisked off in a white limo owned by someone older, the surviving lover of an early film star thrown out of the movies for being too incautiously gay and so became the adored interior decorator to his fellow actors. And me? I got squired home on foot (twenty block hike, freezing cold) by one Ed, who worked in "drapery alterations," whatever that was. Next morning, Robert gave me my second New York phone call.

He told me what he'd discovered from his date: One reason Wallis Warfield Simpson had had such a hold over the former king was that she had such a hold on him, his. The Duke, just the tallest in her kennel of popeyed pugs, was pitiably endowed, apparently, and always had a premature ejac apparently. But that slyboots Wally had learned, from some madam in Hong Kong, a vaginal clamp technique that could bite right down on her lover, very severe.

"And she could hold the Duke until he achieved at least a brief reign."

"Oh," I said. (Sister, I don't think we're in North Carolina anymore. In Falls, such morning-after conversations concerned which socially prominent doctor did the least obtrusive ingrown toenail removal.)

"And what, my dear Airedale—('cause if you were a dog you'd be no pug, but a noble Airedale)—what, Hart, did you learn?"

" 'Learn'?" I asked. "Oh . . . learn. Last night?"

And then, thanks to Robert and Manhattan, I learned that learning was really a main part of it. To learn. From sex, from everything. We soon lived life in order to learn and then report it to each other, facts rouged and pumped some.

"I guess I could say I learned that Ed—Ed was the one I was talking to? Thin, with the boots?—I guess I could say I learned that Ed needs the Duchess of Windsor. Ed was overready, Robert. Ed was a premie. One thing, Ed introduced me to a term I've never heard before— 'window treatment.' Otherwise . . . back to the drawing board." I felt such a failure.

"Back to the 'Bored of Ed,' hunh? Hartley, be tolerant of poor Ed. He only came fast because you're so exciting," Robert rattled forward, saving me. He did that from the start. "There's a coffee shop at the end of your block, which is the beginning of my block. Ossorio's 'physical plant' is for shit, but his coffee is the tincture of ambrosia. He believes it's very good for you and that makes it so. Trust me. The place is all tiled like a mouthful of broken teeth? You've seen it. Go back to your writing, sorry for interrupting, but I'll be having caffeine with the silver older guy from last night around, say, six? (He was Carole Lombard's confidant and favorite fellow shopper.) He'll like you, guy's got amazing stories. Cary Grant–Randolph Scott sex in the pool stories. Then we three, from there, we'll just invent the rest of the evening. What you and I don't know, for now we'll fake. So, bye. Scribble, scribble, Mr. Fitzgerald. Oh, and don't forget the Nobel delivery, your stoop, by ten. Ciao, Airedale duck . . ."

1980: It was always a new guy, it was usually the first night. I was so new to Old New York, I kept getting lost: the avenues had names, the cross streets numbers, and Romance wore size fourteen boots.

I could now claim a friend one block away, a closet-sized apartment, some few clothes in it, a Hermes portable typewriter Swiss-made, of stainless steel baked a detached and promising pistachio green. I also had a part-time job and certain short stories I continually worked on. And I had limited bar-admission mad money for weekends spent prowling, picking, preferring, perfecting. Erotically speaking, with Maestro Gustafson's encouragement, I was already making book.

I felt as shy as I acted bold. Before entering certain doors, I literally shook. I crossed arms to disguise St. Vitus spasms. Fear, governed, made me look pugnacious, or so your Hartley hoped. I grew wilder in search of quips and news and good details for him.

Robert went so often to the St. Mark's Baths he called himself "amphibious." He assumed I knew the place. I stayed away, scared. But I was haunted, goaded, stoked, by Robert's query, "What'd you learn?"

It was always the inaugural reach into unfamiliar britches, it was the first sight of the New World. We were all brave Magellans circumnavigating the belt and what was under it, circumcised or not. We all sought the single shortcut to the nectar spices of India.

My ideal, I found, was tall, rough-hewn, silent behind his brooding. Unlike your gullible cream-rinsed Hartley Mims, Jr., here, he need not be from a good family. Fact is: Broken noses were a selling point.

A housepainter was fine; or some rough-hewn farm-owning Spanish count. I tangled with both during my first Manhattan month. I was an equal opportunity. Episcopalians need not apply. If they'd ever attended a private secondary school called "Saint" anything, show me the door. Been there, done them.

No, make it anyone as unlike my white middle-class *My Fair Lady* self as possible. The bedroom was any private chamber not mine. What room service brought up for breakfast . . . was never a dish that I myself could fix on my dive's two sputtering gas burners.

Romance was a love slap, a non–English speaker, a criminal exception—a still photo, the contrast so high, it became almost as abstract as a great dark city seen from the air by some brilliant color-blind angel looking down *on* us. A guardian angel, right? A guardian angel amused by all this healthy coupling, a male angel blessing us for providing him such good and squirmy entertainment from on high.

1980 was a great time to wash up on this rock island. Our youth plus New York's riches made a heady mix. Money was being extravagantly earned, instantly spent. Not necessarily in that order. All, of course, by others.

But, if you were young and hungry and artistic and presentable, and if you knew how to get to certain glamour troughs, the trickle-down theory briefly worked. If people had more money than sense, if they bought season tickets to every single concert series, they were always giving away their box seats . . . "Do you know any youngsters who're especially 'alive' to music and might make good use of these?"

If richfolks order too much catered food, you—poor, but ski-nosed and backpacked—get to haul away as much of it as you might camel home discretely. If you cannot afford drugs, well, they're down yonder on that little mirror-topped end table Altar to Silvery Oblivion. Three brandy snifters full of pretty-colored pills, and round hand mirrors with several ivory nose-tubes, plus six new single-edged Gem razor blades, and mounds of fine white powder that'll numb your lips.

It'll soon make you feel *you're* throwing this bash, and not just mooching off its lush periphery, you hick bottom-feeder new-here, you.

Happy happy pretty boy.

What are you scared of in New York?

Only of leaving this, him, too soon.

Robert pointed out how, in the last boom of such proportions—the 1880s (centuries having repetitive life cycles, too)—New York society offered thanks for its good luck. Thanks registered as civic tenderness. The earlier high-rollers founded the Metropolitan Museum, the Museum of Natural

History, the Metropolitan Opera, and on and on. But, during these gusher eighties, where did most of the good fortune go?

Directly up about sixty rebuilt noses.

And yet, for those of us smart, white, connected yet needy enough to wiggle into the edges of this endless feeding-frenzy party, we got quite stuffed, thanks. We made sure of that, notifying one another via pay phones or Princess extensions in some stranger's fourth guest bedroom, "Get into your best clothes and get yer memorable young ass up to Park at Fifty-second, and it's worth taking a cab this once . . . Because I don't want to ignore even one of these throw pillow–sized South African shrimps and I'll need help, carrying. . . . Here, Marco, copy down their names and address . . ."

Being so young, we didn't know we'd arrived during an economic peak. We figured New York must stay this lush. Being young, we made New York young, too.

Robert, the pastor's son from Iowa, my sermon-teacher-hymn here, attracted/transmitted at starlight's speed. I told myself, as I watched him chest into a room of folks who never gave an inch, a room he suddenly subdivided like young Moses working the Red Sea hydraulics, I told myself, Hartley? Diversify.

To seem to fall for a golden one like Gustafson might be part of the starting fun . . . But to fall, for real, for one wanted by so many, is a tragedy hatching. Look around.

But only Ed kept calling back.

Among us, being a "good" painter and being "good in bed"—soon ranked as virtuosities somewhat interchangeable. Robert Christian Gustafson was becoming famous both ways. Me? I just wanted to be.

Robert introduced me to one of his girl lovers named Brenda. Next day, I met her again and she was called Bethany; a week later, someone referred to her as Grey. I soon determined one quality shared by those of us who preferred making toys to merely playing with them: we got to call ourselves what we liked. I had started early.

There is a snapshot of my dad doctoring his own name with paint. He stands beside our yard's black wrought-iron lamppost, horse-headed at top.

Dad has just placed his paintbrush to the period ending a new "Sr." after "Richard Hartley Mims."

His "Sr." looks orderly, even semiprofessional, no unsightly drips as he creates a dynasty. He grins and is attractive, a gent lanky and younger-looking for squinting so in daylight.

What the photographer did not factor: her own steepling shadow, a woman's legs and blockish dress beside the curving outline of a baby carriage, its lid raised, an arabesque of wheels and handle. Mom and I lurk out of sight; but we've just underwritten his triumph. Till me, Dad had not been a senior partner of anything.

First day at kindergarten, the teacher took roll. "Mims, Richard, junior? 'Dick'? or 'Dickie'?" I already knew what *Dick* meant. I respected the word too much not to flinch on hearing my entire weight called one.

Mom, clutching her purse, waited at the classroom's rear. I, five, now rose from my little desk, I piped toward the teacher, "My name, ma'am, is Hartley Mims."

Teacher scanned her roster, found that middle name there. So, it was legal. "All right then, 'Hartley.' "

I saw her pencil X the name and make it me, forever.

Home that night, Mother, proud if somewhat flustered, told Dad how self-possessed I'd been. And all while other snivelers still clung to their moms' legs.

"So, young man, it's 'Hartley,' is it?" And he gave me a look so cold, even Mother glanced away. "So much for chips off blocks, hunh, son?"

I studied my napkin.

"Richard, darling, maybe it's just me, but I think if he wants to be called Fido . . ."

"No, no, it's all right. Sounds classier, doesn't it, son? This way, fraternities won't blackball you quite so fast. Oh, you'll go far, you will." The blue stare was exactly as proud as it felt withering. But I stayed Hartley.

And therefore Dick was elsewhere. Dick was others.

New York had always seemed our only likely tolerant home. Plus it was the single possible distributorship for our work (much of which—we admitted—had not been thoroughly created . . . as yet).

Like Robert and me, other pals had fled chafing little home places. What choice? There was nothing back there for nature's bachelors to discuss past other people's weddings. We couldn't, even at the top department stores, register "our" patterns (though no silver flatware would have been chosen with more care and skill).

We had nowhere local to do the sex that so needed doing. In my own Falls, sex with other men could only be had at Boy Scout jamborees or down near the Greyhound depot late on weekend nights, using the family station wagon as your portable honeymoon suite. Sex you got "off" certain drunk Marines between buses. ("Maybe a fiver before you get down there and start, pal?")

Arrived, transcendent on espresso, riven by eros, steadily loquacious if only fitfully brilliant, trapped in cracked-plaster closet apartments, Robert and I now lived like pets in the pet store—at the very front of our cages.

On display—ready to go home with feeding sponsorship, ripe for learning very new tricks from fairly old ones.

In neighborhoods as bad as ours, we nightly courted robbery. And—given our lack of cash—that could mean banter, then death. Later, muggers would hurt us. But, early on, we blazed in our exemptions. We didn't know the costs. We briefly got things free.

We were protected by our physical strength, the two of us being big boys with official shoulders. We seemed a third again larger when side by side and usually glad to be. Another help: the strangeness of Robert's velvet suit on a man so visibly in control, the zircon star pinned to his lapel, platforms lifting him above his own good six-foot norm. The outfit had already slid a bit past fashionable; but since he'd invented it, Robbie was the last to notice that or care. We convoyed everywhere. The town, you know, can be quite mean. But, curtains up, pants half down, our talents stuck clear out to here, we tobogganed through it—energy to spare. Stupid is passive; gorgeous can be too. "Out" as we were, we lived so passive in our boylike trust. We mainly didn't know why they were being nice to us. Why fate was.

For the usual reason.

It wanted to fuck us.

Instructions for Young Emperors

t the age of thirty-three, I had made $196 by actually selling some of my, like, you know, writing. One hundred came from the Kiwanis: "What Democracy Means to Me." It never occurred to my mildly prosperous folks to underwrite my overwriting. And I felt far too furious to ask.

So, needing other incomes, I soon coached Asian-American students, private classes. I dressed up for one Park Avenue apartment—its rock-candy mountains of backlit jade, its folding ancient screens were oil-black and stretched long as locomotives through shadowed dining rooms suitable for seating forty. The Wu family triplex was staffed by very young Irish servants with beguiling accents, illicit sexual glances, and—in uniforms of Pilgrim black and white—complexions pink as pink carnations. Their sullen stares at my coat and tie and only "good shoes" longed to communicate with Irish malice, 'Ye're just their servant too, so don't be goin' and gettin' above yourself.' I simply winked. Flustered then pleased, they winked back, "We got the Wus waitin', and very serious are our Wus while waitin', too."

Sipping green tea, I soon spoke of gerunds to a chic-looking, exquisite boy named Tony and, incidentally, his mother. Madame Wu insisted upon being present, maybe trying to improve her own determined, if uneven, English, maybe fearful I would take her frail beautiful son onto my lap. Stranger things have happened.

Whenever I made a joke, or mentioned some rock singer meant to impress and engage young Tony, his mother, wearing a high silk collar overly fastened as a priest's, would check her tiny wristwatch.

If I led Tony toward the letters of John Keats, she urged me back to perfecting his résumé, his overliteral preparation for the Ivy League. How, she asked, did I feel about Tony's wearing loafers, instead of tie-up wing tips, to his Harvard classes? (Tony was still thirteen.) During each lesson, my frail, beautiful student, in his rimless silver specs, flashed me two dozen glances that said, Do not blame your Tony, please, as I would also like to kill her, truly. Never to abandon your young Tony, please. Tony did not use contractions; that made him seem unearthly; it also made him royally adorable. The Little Prince. I imagined abducting him to the squalid safety of my downtown linoleum life.

I fled their teahouse of a penthouse twenty dollars richer but completely spent. There was this curious guilt over leaving Tony prisoner of his mother's understandable ideals. Did he ever just go out and play?

My first canvas suitcase contained my mother's arrival gift, four boxes of good blue monogrammed stationery suitable for the thank-you notes. "I expect there will, thanks to the world's courtesies toward my dear boy, be many!" Mom was right.

You are reading one.

I keep remembering how it felt to be young enough to place your every earthly possession in two cheap suitcases, all your writing inside one loose-leaf notebook, and the whole world's friendship in a twenty-page address book!

I recall this state with some glee and envy, but no regrets about my current materiality, the bulk of middle-aged associations. I am now both my own seagoing vessel and its very anchor. "No wise person ever wishes to be younger."

My truest address? The intended destinations, the prizes I expected would be mine quite soon. Before my old bathroom's blotchy mirror, I already practiced, "I wish to thank the Academy and all the helpful, loving background tech people who made this . . ."

Back then I could do everything but stop. That much a kid, I had just two speeds: awake, asleep.

But I do acutely recall how it felt to be poor, talented, poor, and popular and young and pretty and as lavishly talented as pitiably strapped for cash (if "poor" only in the play-dire way that middle-class kids are). And all this in New York. Before.

By now, my newest address book (maroon leather) is big as Merlin's cookbook. The thing weighs one pound and four ounces. These days, I buy a new one every two to four years. I've made a ritual around this changing of the guard. Before I transfer my viable, breathing pals onto new lines and costly clean rag-paper, I'll grab a half-sized bottle of champagne, take the phone off the hook, light a candle at this kitchen table or the cleanest of my three "textured" desks. I use a favorite fat Mont Blanc pen and Pelikan brown ink. I meditate on each person being inscribed yet again, again.

Who's new, who's not, who has bolted through hostile-takeover remarriage, who has moved to Africa and therefore doesn't write and—that far into the bush—has no phone? Plus, of course, who is dead at twenty-nine. Disappeared into the bush indeed.

I hand-copy the record of my life (best pals) into a spine of superior strength, between new covers, stubborn and handsome as leather armor.

My address book often seems to me the best book I've ever written. Certainly it contains the most complicated characters. Surely it's the work in progress longest.

Draft after draft, you revise and shape your ideal tome. (Or does it revise and polish you?) As in art, you keep trimming repetitive weaknesses, you jettison unexpected impurities. Retain primarily the protein, please.

Sometimes, dreadful, garish mistakes disappear without your even needing to banish them. Someone sulks away, hurt, for no real reason. (Good, I hate "scenes." Except in fiction, where they should be as lurid, endless, and revealing as possible.) You must, with each revision of your holy text, acknowledge the Deletions not of your own making.

When my address book slips—by accident—behind the couch, I panic. It's like misplacing my suddenly necessary reading glasses. While the book is missing, I am literally lost and mainly blind.

But, as a born record keeper, I feel thwarted. Certain thorny questions stubbornly recur. Shall I let my own dear dead remain—page to daily page— right where they stood while yet forthright, contactable?

Why not? Well, because it's so goddamn inefficient . . . to keep stumbling—midworkday—over the names of your missing lovers and coconspirators. Mornings especially, you first feel joy at seeing them recorded, still on call. No matter how often I tell myself what's happened, there's this momentary time delay, a split second as you sip the day's first cup of coffee when you decide, "Good, I'm gonna phone him. Get his advice about that mess last night."

First I flash on him at his rosy best; then he becomes the final him (reduced to soup stock). I picture his crossbone's skull still smiling so, the former lifeguard becomes a Medusa of IVs.

And finally the big "Oh" strikes, becoming "Uh Oh." Next, emotionally sidetracked, I literally forget which living party I first dipped in here to seek. (Literally. I am not making up one syllable of this fable. For many reasons, I couldn't.)

Enter: Stage Center

I met her at the VD Clinic.

Like so many health services offered to the poor, this clinic's emphasis seemed more on punishment through waiting than relief by cure. The building was a pretty Beaux Arts schoolhouse, tucked among mature sycamores at Chelsea's edge. It was now reduced from primary education to basic regret. Barred and wired like a zoo, it was.

The waiting room accosted us losers with overbright posters. I felt sufficiently ashamed without DOES IT BURN WHEN YOU MAKE WATER? IF SO, YOU PROBABLY HAVE . . . a long list of fine print followed, spikey Latin names for what now crimped our love lives. (If my parents ever found out!)

I had only lived here long enough to find one main friend and some nice acquaintances, the coffee shop, three students, a good used-book store on my block. But I'd somehow managed to become, being overly affectionate, instantly infected. (Robert consoled me: Hey, no sweat, at least I wasn't staying home. I was out learning. I must be doing something right.)

It'd been that Ed. All this, for forty seconds!

Arriving, we were each assigned a number, then handed a serious chunk of two-by-four, pinewood painted white. Its edges blackened with two lines, every side showed our freehand patient-ID digit. (Was this block so huge to prevent our stealing it?). Clutching such anchors, we—the sexually experimental, the sexually disastrous—got sardined into a single airless narrow room.

If you believe that Hell might offer jolly fellow-feeling among its sinners, a VD clinic's lobby argues otherwise. Its water fountain didn't work. Fluorescent light seemed bent on making your pores look huge, your beauty corrupt. I had played one semester of junior varsity (to please Dad, who felt only sadness at my benchwarming). Now, after waiting here one hour, I recalled the embarrassment of basketball physicals. I remember hearing other boys give their testing cough behind a curtain where our dull pediatrician squatted, laying hands on the family jewels of our whole village. Now, I peeped around at others ambushed by New York's sexual dangers.

Instead of feeling the shame demanded by poster cutaways of our inflamed parts, fellow addicts idly cruised me and one another. One painted lady, old enough to be my grannie, winked at me, then licked her lips. Please, Missus. Repent for maybe fifteen minutes?

My poor parents would drive their Buick three states out of their way to avoid any of the syphilitics sitting here (me, included). Gum-chewing proved widespread. One creased widow all in black sat beside an eight-year-old granddaughter wearing what looked like her white confirmation dress.

Across boundaries of class, race, sex, we scoped each other out, pictured each other at it. Yeah, it burned. Sure, we'd all been "grounded." —Despite that, chastity did not seem a long-range plan for anybody present.

There was just one ass on view worth—in my opinion—worship. With me this out of commission, call me a backslider . . . Said butt belonged to that young guy over there, short, punkish, built like a brick gazebo. See the one in Levi's over near the building's only pay phone? The kid under that handwritten sign reading PLEASE KEEP CALLS SHORT, ONE PER "CLIENT," RESPECT OTHERS FOR ONCE.

Ignoring this, the chain-smoker, wearer of slicked-back hair, jeans jacket, Levi's, and old battered shit-kicking boots. A large hardbound red address book was opened against the phone's coin box, placed there like some singer's portable sheet music.

One righteous ass. Very slowly did I guess that those minor unsightly swellings at its outer edges might just indicate Nature's padding, the excelsior accorded only the holy lower productive regions of, well, a woman. . . .

Against my hopes and plans for the next few hours, this bad citizen with the great backside became, as I listened harder, a boyish woman (which actually ranks among my favorite kinds).

I couldn't yet see her face. But, jotting notes, sipping bottled orange juice, she had set up office on the phone's brushed stainless ledge. Piled dimes were stacked Vegas-high. (Yeah, dimes. It was that long ago.)

Her haircut was some tough delivery boy's, a two-dollar jobbie done on Astor Place in three minutes, two per side, one fer top. The jeans jacket showed more wear than she seemed old enough to have yet achieved. Her address book might be the ledger of a prospering small-town hardware store. I shifted two seats nearer. From here, the book's crisp penmanship, heightened by yellow Hi-Liter, appeared womanly in its forceful efficiency, then downright club lady–like.

Equipment spread before her-him included a WW II silver Zippo lighter, a (sterling?) Deco cigarette case with its own built-in ashtray, a forties fountain pen whose pocket clip was a gold Cupid's arrow, and the yellow marker-emphasizer favored only by "grinds" at my college. Orange juice rested at hand; every need she expected might jab her, she'd provided for. She seemed a person as complete, magnetic, and "portable" as Robert.

Others, waiting to call home, would step toward the public phone. They'd see this short stubborn back, would note her array of gear and coins. Then they'd turn toward our crowd, dull-witted from the wait, and—making some expressive Latin shrug or comic snarl—they'd step outside to seek a street booth. What amazed me, even in combative New York, even in this ungenteel drip-ward, no soul had yet dared confront her.

Plus, so dreamy an ass. One of those taut high-riders, its either outer flank as dimpled as my folks' old Buicks. Half melons placed an eighth of the way up the back, just so. More a black boy's than any white girl's.

I had brought along my thumbed paperback of *Tender Is the Night*. I trusted its misty Riviera terraces to offset my first low-down VD holding-pen. But instead of reading, I moved closer still. To her. I could now eavesdrop on this young person. The pay phone was bolted to a plaster wall. This offered the one visible surface still bare of posters blaming us for our little mid-leg peccadilloes. PROMISCUITY POLLUTES one stated in harsh orange.

Here, across the only plaster wall left bare, generations of the sexually restless, waiting too long for cure, tried to set up something for later this evening. They had left graffiti, come-ons, insults against American health care, plus diagrams of what our room's every occupant (except the child in white) already knew too well—exactly what a dick and pussy look like, enraged, up close and personal. No two, alas, alike. No one safe.

My novel left unopened, I faced the backside of this perfect boy-girl-boy as she successively harangued, promised, charmed, appointed, and then cried some. I remembered Robert's early question, about what I'd learned from sex; I determined, as a storyteller, to shape the news of this found character for R.'s amusement later over coffee. God knows, I had time; my client number was a distant 284.

I heard her Southern accent come and go rheostaticly—as need (charm) required. While chatting, she idly touched her yellow Magic Marker to the scratched wall above her. Among the lurid brew of phone numbers and genital sketches, she'd make a dot here and, head tilting, another over yon-der, all the while taking care of business.

If her body seemed a boy's in spareness, her phone talk proved curva-ceous, spillsome, scarily and lavishly expert. Her tone reinvented itself with each call's mission. She was a woman, I could now tell plain. Head bent, un-aware of anybody hearing her, she would order, chuckle, offer wry asides, then poignant pleas. I heard her take every secretary (reached by chance) into her humid confidence. Her speaking voice could go so soprano or dive quite dusky—various—as an adolescent boy's. Conspiring, her tone dropped low enough to produce a tropism of shameless tilting among those others overhearing. Even the pretty dark girl in her doily pinafore attended to the lady talking back, now begging, now being such a tease.

Our receptionist's miked voice issued from her glass booth like some Bingo caller's: "One thirty-one. Oh One thirty-one? One thirty-one! All right, One thirty-one lost *his* place for good, so be it. One thirty-two." #284 here sighed.

The wall beyond the phone's present boss had been painted a faintly nasty coral color then gouged by ballpoint. Tangled script told what Hec-tor, at his current dosage, might be ready to do again to you by week's end. Over this surface, our girl-boy steadily made stray squiggles. As she com-plained to a photographer that he had overexposed her recent paintings, that he must reshoot them all for free—pretty please?—as she killed his fee with such ease and over his many objections, she reorganized around her head and shoulders a growing set of speckles interconnected.

Soon a yellow structure, like concentric rinds of a pumpkin, emerged, parenthecising the telephone. Her yellow marker on coral paint gave off a pumpkin's pinky orange that exuded power and, soon, an odd well-being. We all slowly saw—since half the bored waiting room had now begun to look her way—that these were huge yellow legs she'd started drawing. Drawn from the waist down, open legs, a giant's, welcoming. Crosshatch-ing, she soon created a roof of potent guardian thighs around atop this very telephone. She did it unconsciously, head tilting side to side, her conversa-tion unabated. So short, she had to go up on tiptoe to reach the navel part of it. This was like watching another person daydream, but in a thousand ner-vous yellow lines.

Now our communal phone—itself clappered directly between the most gorgeous rounded pair of legs—suggested ample male equipment. Bell Tel.

* * *

The girl seemed to take in the whole surface—venereal pleas and all—and to unify it. Her lassoing yellow pulled the coral tone forward, it forgave the nasty drawings, it laid on them a whole new scrim of form and color.

If, earlier, only I had watched her, now even the receptionist—interrupting her own fingernail painting—sat transfixed. The art rendered was no vandalism. Our group seemed to feel that. People literally leaned toward her now, as if in protection, as if dreading (and half hoping for) a security guard to come and try to bust her for malicious doodling. We'd pollute him so fast.

Instead of seeming harmed, our room (in a way, come to think of it, this really *was* ours, wasn't it?) was prettier and funnier and even more strange. But more militantly strange. Her curious wit, in taking the only hot line out of Drip Central, and clamping thighs so Whitmanesque around it—her compositional sense in letting the drawn skin not quite touch the mounted phone's hard edges, the fact that these great legs, the perfect crotch, proved sexless—offered free rein for all our venereal imaginations.

I recalled from school that the word *venereal* derives from Venus, our goddess of love. Lovesick. That sure described most all art lovers present.

Even the charming girl-child sat literally opened-mouthed, staring up at the colossal legs and, working hard between them, their boy-sized creator. Rounded via a series of short straight yellow lines, thighs seemed rendered by raw magic—less by one person's skill, more through our group will, some group dream—half-horny, half-ideal.

Only the artist herself was as yet unaware of how much acclaim her own enormous lower body had snagged. I, meanwhile, heard her book a flight to Savannah, then confirm this with her mom (the accent pitched at its lushest). Her former efficiency changed; squared shoulders bent inward, she leaned against the shelf (she left off drawing!) and her brisk boy's voice grew still and snively, so low that we were all forced to shift whole inconvenient inches closer. "I'm not. Cain't, Mom. They hate me anyway. I'd feel like a complete fool in pearls and a Peter Pan collar, Mom. If I am paying to come see you, and I am, I'll do it wearing what I fuckwell usually wear, Mom. Mom? . . ." There was a definite hangup and we watched the artist fall a bit against the cold black phone, and cry but in heaves, a bitter, tearless way to do it. I looked down at the curly child beside me, she shook her head and glanced up, sad. We both then gazed protectively, consensual, toward the artist.

I'd seen her moods swerve with each call, whipping forward, drawing back, responding to however much the other party gave or exacted.

Finally, coins all spent, red wine ordered by the crate at 20 percent discount, please, the photo session rescheduled free, a gallery owner slated for "a studio visit," whatever that was, a date shyly accepted with Moishe, an Israeli med student she had only heard about through friends, reservations secured for a Strindberg play but in discount student seating, please, and no, sir, she did not have her student ID card on her because she and her roomie had just been mugged and this'd be her first outing to try to cheer that battered lovely friend, sir. At last, collecting herself, she gathered her gear, stuffed her pockets, opened her cowgirl backpack, closed her big book, reclaimed the emptied orange juice bottle, snapped her ashtray shut, lifted the huge block of issued wood, and turned.

To such applause. I guess you can say I led it. Or maybe I just joined in after others started it—even the amplified receptionist did, beating wrist to inner wrist, careful not to smudge her nails newly red.

Now I saw that this artist girl was a definitely girl. As pert as pretty, vague as tough. I saw her face was fox-shaped and that her eyes were still unfocused, wet, from crying at her mom. The hair stood up in front, a dark cowlick like some boy's age ten, but it was overhennaed, nearly purple-black.

We, the clap-infested, clapped. Glad at having something positive to do, and for one of us!

She shifted from a facial "What . . . ?" to "Oh, that," to "Well, okay then" to "So, you noticed, hunh?" Her features did this at a speed peculiar to those born stars. Like Robert, her movement from hidden sadness to full center stage showed the unaccountable and selfless speed of starlight.

Then she did the most divine little impromptu bow. Her arms held lots of gear; but it was this clunksome bow that broke my heart and made me fall even faster for our pocket Venus with her felt pen, her oh-so-felt pen!

The bow was like a little boy's, some freckled ruffian forced to join his sister's wedding party—a kid already secretly liking the rental monkey suit but griping about it anyway. On the cue: "Bow"—forced, he places palms (front and back of cummerbund) and flops forward. Her bow was just that sweet, half-geeky, formal, hopeless—and therefore somehow male.

I decided only, Here she is. I got a sinus burning and one jet of scalding water within either half-shut eye. It is still my own sure sign of a sure sign.

She was 282. But, owing to the receptionist's interest, and with universal agreement from us usually crabby waiters, the art girl (as she was soon called) went right to the head of our line. Without doubting she deserved it, showing no surprise at all. Smiling, she disappeared into the hall of cubicles. Then 283 was summoned, and turned out not to be the grand-mother.

It was instead her formerly virginal-looking girl-child wearing white. The kid proceeded through a door with uneasy glances back at grannie. We all gave such mean looks to that lubricious old woman. Profiteering on her grandkid's chaste treasure?

We were soon left to look only at a peachy four-foot crotch exuding well-being, a benediction we all sorely needed.

I wound up in the cubbyhole right across the hall from snubnosed art girl, #282. I saw that, even waiting, she bent, drawing, cigarette smoke half obscuring the NO SMOKING sign. She sensed appreciative observation (was that the usual oxygen she lived in, thrived on?)—she glanced up. I must have been grinning, because she smiled back a crooked fellow sufferer's smirk that filled me with a troubled, tumbling sort of happiness.

Behind me, another poster. Now, as she watched—pencil in one hand, her Camel gone all ash in the other—I pointed to my wall's big black letters: DO YOU DRIP MUCH? And, from her plywood closet toward mine, she aimed the pencil right at her implied pussy and announced, "Jackson Pollock."

I laughed, as she had known I would.

It was her compactness, her coiled cowlicked snakes-'n'-snails potency; it was her outdoing boys at greaser boyishness and undercutting girls asleep in their own unnoticed power. It was her knowing the very image out there that would stir, then unify us all. She did things without planning them, but they turned out right anyway. It was how, in breaking laws, she'd already made the day for eighty strangers before she even noticed us behind her. It was her weird combination of garden-party girlishness and toad-collecting male-childness, stripes of the mild and the rude jumbled side by side.

"What?" she asked, of my staring across the hall.

"You." I pointed. And she made a mouth, but with a strange respect in it. As if I had just gotten some essential coded joke. Eyes lowered, she said mostly to herself, "Yeah, well . . ."

We were prescribed the same high number of two-toned, aptly clown-colored pills. "What a coincidence," she said very flat. "I caught my dose of it from a boy named Delbert. You, too? Well, avoid all Delberts. Name like that, shoulda fuckin' known."

On the wall beside her, the same poster asking, DOES IT BURN WHEN YOU MAKE WATER? She now jerked her brush-cut head its way (face very fair, hair tinted wound color, the nose's three freckles an actual shade of pink). "No, nurse," said she. " 'When Angie Makes Water, Angie Makes Water. But When Angie Burns, Angie Burrrrns.' "

And, guileless, she grabbed the crotch of her jeans as if there were more packed in there than there must have been.

It turned out to be her name—Angelina Byrnes, sometimes Alabama, sometimes A. Z. Byrnes. I told her I was having coffee with a friend who would like to learn of her existence and that she must trust me in knowing she would like this person very much back, and how he would change her life, as he'd changed mine.

Having talked more and faster while waiting at the pharmacy's half-door—we soon washed down first pills with street-bought papaya juice. She said her father was a doctor in Savannah, from a society family, *the* Oren Byrneses, but he'd fallen for a waitress named Fern Jewel Williams—which was bad enough, but young doc actually married her, and at the Episcopal church—and was at once disowned.

"My mother, when she worked, wore her chewing gum on the side of her neck."

"What?"

"See, the waitresses weren't allowed to chew it on the job, so, between breaks, Fern Jewel just mashed her Juicy Fruit five-pack right onto her neck, where, during smoke breaks, she could get at it faster."

"How appetizing. Say her maiden name was Delbert? She must've looked like Ava Gardner, or was your father determined to go slumming with the first exotic hash-slinger he saw?"

"She does look like Ava Gardner, actually. Looked. Now she plays bridge and wears florals only. A mistake these days, given her evermore couchy size. She polishes the silver but never gets blue powder out of all the tongs and gar-lands. She sits in their big house and wonders why she and the 'Doctor,' as she calls Dad—it's too groan-makingly waitressy—never get invited to what she called 'the top parties.' Mind if we stop over there and I break that li'l window and use its broken glass to cut both wrists? Because, whenever I'm down there, Fern stays busy trying to bully me into wearing English chintzes and cultured pearls. Picture me. Because, I won't do it. She also keeps telling me what to paint—cottages with azaleas blooming all around them, 'their flowers like drifts o sea foam,' she actually said that. Still has the soul of some bus-stop pie-pusher. Imagine me in pearls, painting cottages with dust ruffles of herbaceous borders? I cannot go back. I would kill myself first. Or them. No, see, I would do *me* first. They made sure of that. I hate that part."

I felt amazed to see her nearly cry, all while staubing along under her Dale Evans backpack, kicking at wastepaper, chin tucked way in. But when she came upon a chalked sidewalk hopscotch, she, glum, did half its dance while plowing head-down forward. We passed a huge newsstand sign for a gambling game called lotto, and she said from one side of her mouth, "Every man in town named Otto plays lotto, wanna bet?"

"So." I would now try and make her happier. "Those pearls. You tend to wear yours around your neck or—being her daughter—more stuck against one side of it?"

"You are a sick motherfucker, you know that?"

"Me? No, I'm still being polite. This *is* Standing on Ceremony. I've only lived here long enough to catch it once."

"Why do I keep thinking that you're talking like somebody else? Talking how you think you should, now you're really in big-time New York. Who is it's got you so hypnotized?"

"That's for me to know and you to beg for."

"Savannah society wouldn't let me 'come out.' " She stomped on some discarded curbside french fries, nearly slipping. "So I came up north to. I'll show 'em."

I told her, funny, hers was my same un-coming-out story.

Well, she said, maybe getting snubbed for waitress genes was good. Maybe if Angie had debbed—she might be married to some blue-blood rabbit-faced orthodontist? might live with their nineteen kids named Taylor or Tyler on one of the lovelier squares?

"I doubt that very much," I stated, sure.

"Thanks." She met my gaze. Her insecurity was the only surprise she could offer, now I sensed she was somewhat immortal. But pearls? this little dynamo Sherman-tanking forward while sulking over pearl-wear?

We now walked quickly, as we both naturally did. We would not be late for him.

It's odd, thinking back—my first impulse on meeting Angie was taking her direct to Robert. Call it self-destructive, or the simple cost of love.

I sometimes replay our lives: What if I had kept her all for me, just my friend? And why would anybody want two such stars as pals? What did that make me? A supply ship? Black hole in Waiting?

* * *

And when she saw him first, saw him even from outdoors, even through the big unwashed window of Ossorio's, saw all six blond caramelized feet of him, saw him gesturing and listening, saw his boots up on the radiator, slung near the trim older man, Angie jabbed glass with her paint-stained index fingertip, not bothering to look back at me, "That one. That one, hunh? Hmm. Hartley Mims, you do have an eye. I mean, for my eye. —Shall we have him 'wrapped to go' or both just eat him here?"

So, yeah, I met her at the VD clinic. If I hadn't been an early sexual risk taker (if it hadn't been for that fun-in-a-minute Ed), I would never have encountered the girl who'd become Wendy to us Lost Boys. All of us who found ourselves able to fly while wearing pajamas.

I noticed her ass first; but the rest, her now-acknowledged gifts, still trailed most happily behind, bass ackwards.

Later, after we were both starting to go out more, some partying sophisticate would grill Ang and me about who'd first introduced us. The questioner, now knowing Angie's reputation, expected it would be some art world bigwig. But, I believe, to our credit, we never minded stating, "Oh no, us? We met at a free VD clinic. Just dripping, boy, but were we ever sick!"

The stranger would often laugh and say, "Yes, right . . . I'm sure."

And then we'd all get to chuckle. Each of us believing what we must.

And everybody laughing at something else.

New York!

Nature Merit Badge

'd sprouted from a long line of amateur naturalists. In my childhood home, the only works of art were calendars and Audubon.

At the grandfolks' house, every book you opened showered across your hands the particularities of some dried fern. A slip of paper noted, "Pressed on August 1, 1921." Why? I mean, this plant was in no way unusual. Still, you hated to just throw it out now. Maybe the leaf was just a token of a day that had included it.

A scavenging attention to wildflowers and animals stuck with me in this new landscape—one merely mineral, mainly vertical, only manmade. My eyes kept trying to naturalize the building blocks, canals of asphalt linking them. For us hicks, nature is a habit. Hard to break.

Mom once parked our station wagon on a country road to let my brothers and me watch some huge redtail hawk talon up mice fast, then eat them slowly. We kept *North American Birds* in the glove compartment. I now set my trained eyesight loose on wild Old Amsterdam.

The first thing to register and become necessary fast? This town's variety of glorious human skin tones. Before, it'd all been North Carolina black and white. Here I'd fallen into Santa's paintbox; new color preferences, odd snobbisms, evolved. Puerto Rican boys from eleven to fifteen, the brown of perfectly browned marshmallows; Lycée girls' pink cheeks burned beautiful by costly Eastside soaps; the coal-blue ashy skin tones of ancient Haitian ladies out shopping for root vegetables whose names I still lacked. Once home at Christmas, during Presbyterian service, I felt anemic, stuck on bread and water. I now felt lost among complexions merely Scot-Presbyterian (boiled New England dinners). I craved others' color like some subtle-tasting "blackened" Cajun food, the unaccountable delicacy of wild game.

I was my grandma's heir, born a cataloguer famous for her sense of smell. Urbanized, I soon faced cataloguer's hell—"All this noticing; No place to store it."

What to do with a note jotted longwise across a page of phone numbers: "Second Avenue at 7:00 p.m. August 1, after a rain in this heat, turns the exact purple of French lilacs"? What to do with friendship, random sex, the family history of art movements, the names of the puffy Indian bread and the flat kind? Learn. Save. Save against the dawning of a personal National Debt, against the moment of your death and others'.

So I, impressionable, pressed the city. To my front, between book pages, betwixt my legs. I pressed each frond it offered me as I'd save some soft fern I knew would stiffen only into a leather lifelikeness.

Where to keep the mash notes and engraved calling cards and the cosmically apt fortune cookie fortunes? In the back of my address book, naturally.

Protestant Work

I 'm sure my bird-watcher's contentment here sprang partly from my parents' horror at this raptor combat zone.

Before I headed out for wage earning, I rose by 5:30, loading up on a generic oatmeal that could fill you, wallpaper paste, till early evening. I put in my hours before the typewriter, recasting one page, retyping it again/again, until I'd mostly committed its grudging sloggy music to memory. Saying it aloud made me feel somewhat safer in a place this ragged. Syllable rosaries.

Corrections were pasted then repasted right atop first tries. One reason for succinctness? Lower glue cost. Less typing. I must choose from among the three adjectives that barnacled in rows before every noun.

I knew a page was done when—containing so many sandwiched scar-face layers of paper and gummy rubber—it actually rested upright. Every page I earned in Manhattan, learned—like our stiff island battlement—to stand up on its own.

At the Salvation Army, I bought myself a battered writing table. Robert helped me haul the thing. I painted it a buttermilk yellow. Above it, Scotch-taped to the wall's peeling enamel, a postcard (gift of Robert) showed van Gogh's *Room at Arles*. Bed, chair, table, window, water pitcher, home. Monk's cell, jail cell, all any guy artist would ever need. During boyhood visits to *My Fair Lady*, a smudged flowergirl had sung, "All I want is a room somewhere, far away from the cold night air, warm face, warm hands, warm chair (clean hair?) . . . oh, wouldn't it be loverly?"

My boyhood bedroom (and its annex treehouse) had surveyed the golf course, a rolling green, consoling as it was artificial. But here, my rental dive stared mostly onto air shaft bricks and whitewashed pigeon dudie (what did those poor things *eat*?). Only through a gap at the top of one window could you, if you stood upon my desk chair, see an actual fragment of the Hudson shining pink-gold at sunset.

"My apartment overlooks the river," I wrote my worried parents.

To spare the cost of another plumbing hookup, management, circa 1910, had stuck the bathtub on a pedestal right beside the kitchen sink. My folks would someday try to visit me. They'd stay at some pillow-mint midtown hotel. I knew I'd never let them see this place. I knew how it'd scare them. I knew their fears would infect me. Dad already called New York "The Sewer."

"So, how're things up yonder in the Sewer?" he asked every goddamn Sunday afternoon by speakerphone.

One visit to our VD clinic would have sunk them both neck-deep into a vat of yellow Lysol, at soak for a week. My mother loved chocolates but allowed herself only Triscuits. Dad once undertook a brief costly "hobby," acquired the best German photo gear, took a single decent picture of a bowl of fruit, then sold everything to some sucker from the Club at top dollar in six weeks; Dad seemed relieved. I hated what my folks' own freon gentility had done to them. At times, I felt a wild private heat still beating from each of them. It had been strongest in New York in '56. I vowed to make mistakes not theirs. To make such errors here. I told friends over coffee, "If this boy goes home, this boy goes home in a box." That was just swaggering; that was just a facile turn of phrase I would live to rue.

I somehow lifted such a force of concentration from New York's daily chaos. "How can you write with all those sirens drowning you out?" Dad asked. Good question.

My first night here I was waked four times by one shrill woman on the street. She kept screaming to be buzzed in. "Angel? Angel, let me up. Ring me in, I'll suck you, Angel. Okay then, be like that. Cause you got baaad skin, Angel, everybody say so. —Okay, Jesus? You wake? You so pretty, you never din't want me yet. Buzz your baby up. I play wiv you then work on you good, Jesus."

I see these words jotted on the page; I know that they would stun my Republican parents. First with doubt that such things are ever said aloud, then a sickened admission that they might've been hollered once somewhere, in the midnight slums of Ecuador maybe. But certainly never within hearing of their Hartley Mims jr., please.

My folks just wanted to protect me.

From my life.

Back home, there was just one way Robert and I could have "fit in" snugly: as the dapper gift-giving adored bachelor uncle, chubbily ready with the groan-making pun, quick to recall others' birthdays, always shocked and moved when anyone remembered Unc's own. No thanks.

Free in New York, we were racing, not Biological clocks, but Mirrors. In any gay bar, a so-so looking nineteen-year-old will outrank any thirty-year-old beauty. That's the rule. —So, deprived of having children, we became ours. Youth seemed our one-time-only grant, pure capital, and we didn't plan to waste one pearly drop of it. The word "capital" derives from the word "cattle." Some said, "The New York bar scene is just a meat market." Yeah, so what else is new in the late capitalist society? —Mooo, bull.

Given the relentlessness of male animals in the first fist of the full-throttle hormonal urge—maybe our right image was not a biological clock but the hand mirror and the hair-trigger combined, pow, pop, fizzle, gaze, reload, repop, looking fabulous. —Triggers and Mirrors all kept saying, "Hurry, laddy, Hurry. —Get over the trauma of turning thirty. Get off the bus. Get you a little apartment. Get unpacked. Get laid. Get to work. Get further laid. Get exhibited or published. Get famous. Get really laid. Get out of New York safe."

Company

"Hartley? it's your newest oldest friend Angie here. I know this is your writing time, doll, forgive me for phoning but look. I'm outside this junkshop on Eightieth between Broadway and Amsterdam? And he's got this harp, it's a mess—in terms of ever playing—but it's to die for, I mean, for its Look. Full-sized, Harpo-sized we're talking, every string a different licorice color of catgut, it's American and 1810, easy. Somewhere between British racing green and celadon, with gilt decoration tarnishing more toward silver. It's painted in this crude homespun way. Three vestal virgins dancing on the wide part down near the bottom? (Sorry but my harp terminology is in the toidie today. 'Soundboard' maybe, its soundboard.) But the thing is so 'faded Southren Gothic.' Just propped in one corner of your little place, it would be utterly beyond fabulous, as Robbie says. Looking at it makes me jolly in some of the ways you do, sugar.

"I've already got the old guy down to a hundred and sixty and change, and he has not a cul-lue what it's worth, and I know it'd wreck your budget but I'm at the pay phone outside. Had to try it out on you. No cabbie would let me wrestle this into his trunk even if I lashed it shut with my new turquoise cowgirl belt, but maybe that stepvan Robert's friend's girlfriend, the jingle singer? can borrow sometimes? No? —Oh well, seemed worth a shot. How goes your short story about the effect of a divorce on the family dog? Where do you get your sick ideas? I just know *The New Yorker* is gonna scarf that one up someday. No male writer alive takes half the emotional chances you do, know that, hon? Every sentence sticks out its li'l mouse neck. —Coffee? six then? Ossorio's, the usual. Great. Anybody mentions needing a Federal harp in the next fifteen minutes . . . Oh Christ, somebody's spotted it. Somebody with his checkbook already stopping around. Probably curator of priceless instruments at the Met . . . Oh well . . ."

(I still regret not grabbing that. The harp. Somewhere in a mildewed paradise of a thrift shop, might I not eventually find the stringed instrument once predestined as mine? At the time though, even if Heaven had yielded itself whole and on a layaway plan—I just could not have afforded it.)

Remainders

yet heard from friends in Falls. I still loved them. They were often other guys named their fathers' names or, worse, locked within the straitjacket of great-great-great-grandads'. How could I compare the mellowness of such old-world bourbon-colored Southerners to the modern junk-clear pioneer-intensity of a Robert or an Angie?

My country club chums and I, we had often secretly despised each other. Only from New York could I see that. At eighteen, we'd all wanted out. We each feared we lacked the rocket force to break free of such sandtrap eighteen-hole gravity. The more afraid we felt, the closer we drew together, scared that one of us might make the jailbreak overnight alone.

So we drove family Buicks around mewses and into cul-de-sacs seeking nonexistent parties. Fantastic parties sex-drug-loud. We blamed one another for not knowing where the cooler kids really lived. There were none. There had once been, we'd heard, two. They had hitchhiked elsewhere, at sixteen. The greasers were the only lucky ones in Falls; no namesake shame. They didn't mind getting arrested if fun required that.

In New York, over coffee, I told my fellow marginal outlaw-greasers, Robert and Angie, "You know what we three are? We might not be a Movement yet, okay. But aren't we already at least a . . . Motion?" They, flattered, laughed. Yeah. They remembered this, and took it straight to heart. It was a bargain they would hold me to.

"I do feel right much more settled that I've changed my voter registration to Manhattan." I showed Robert my new card, his head drew back in the way some alarmed snake's will, neck broadening with the joy of supporting such a Greco-Roman face.

"You, Hartley Mims, are hopeless. The Apartment Finders took you to the cleaners. They stick you with that toilet-closet and you write them a nice blue thank-you note? You're so ordinary, you're extraordinary, know that? Still hooked on right and wrong, aren't you?"

"Why? Should I not be? Show me something better. Take your shirt off, Robbie. And, you—are you so extraordinary you're ordinary?"

"Dream on, clown."

"Are you a registered Democrat? Or, no, don't tell me, an Independent, right? Right?" His head was still pulled back. Gustafson gave me a look flatly mystified. Was I so simple that I puzzled him? Wasn't that, in itself, a ground-floor form of attraction? Or overly limited? —There was so much to learn.

—Odd, I figured I would write of him and Angie, of this, of now. But, like all exiles, I ricocheted through time and met—returning from the front—my own genealogy. Was I lonely for that world I'd bloodied myself trying to leave? Now stuck in the back apartment with a view of coal-smudged bricks and extremely incontinent bird life, I seemed to look out on, what? A farm my family owned.

My window might let me glimpse the Hudson. But my typewriter made a prow that crested mostly on the Shenandoah, on the surf near Sumter, the dear old River Jordan.

I had considered myself modern till a first year in New York proved me, in subject matter, if not sexual tastes, still a rube. Some mornings after partying with Robert, the fronts of my eyeballs felt sanded. I woke feeling stranded here by accident. Strangers called my lingering accent "touching." When I tried to sound New Yorky, they asked if I had fever blisters. My stories all returned to native soil: "One woman in my hometown stole things, anything, though her husband was the Pepsi bottler and they needed for nothing. One day, while doing the dishes, her best friend set her wedding rings on the sink's edge . . ." One day in 1921, a girl in love pressed a fern to mark the afternoon she first saw him, half-naked, swimming. One day a dog got left when its divorcing couple moved. The poor Airedale trotted clear to California, feet bloodied but (during the recognition scene) its stub tail so at wag. The story, written, was better than it sounds here. At least a little better. One farm boy, maimed by a cotton bailer, is carried to the house in his sobbing father's arm. The image that soon ran through all my pages was a Pietà, one boy or man holding, helping, another, fallen. Since I and my friends were all so healthy and so frisky and so chased, even I admitted it seemed strangely retrograde. Pals teased me that I was a history-buff traditionalist. (I was, alas, a closet prophet.)

"Living Up Here"

At Ossorio's, we'd long since claimed a table called Ours. Angie's handwritten "reserved" sign stayed there full-time, Scotch-taped to marble. True, ours was stuck in back near the kitchen's dangerous swinging door. But the round table rested under one shelved plaster statue called Our Lady of Perpetual Help and stood near its own loyal radiator.

As we passed the coffee shop, we'd crane against plate glass window, trying to avoid our own blinding reflection, to see if anyone from the gang was there. Arriving or rushing off, about to go to bed at noon or up and out by two p.m., you heard who'd done what to/with whom the night before. People were forever leaving things behind. Sunglasses. Her Zippo. Angie stocked her leather cowgirl backpack with her finds from The Honored Owl. She picked up odd leaflets about color theory (beautiful prismatic illustrations tipped in), works about ancient religion, or how-to guides for outdated etiquette. These were often left stacked on the radiator behind our table. This way you tended to find good reading if you got there first (and hadn't brought along your own Great American Novel in progress).

In one New York care package, Mom sent photos reproduced from family tintypes. I first stuffed these in my sock drawer. But the harder New York's streetlife got, the more often my rent fell due, the more of these images emerged. Now I typed toward tintypes. Each face (containing

ingredient-features partly mine) became a separate votive candle, perma-
nently lit. If my van Gogh postcard or one such forebear got pushed out of
its ritual place, I couldn't focus, couldn't imagine over the maelstrom flood
of car alarms, spats, and sirens.

My desktop lay strewn with gluepots, brushes, round-nosed scissors,
and the pedicure clippers I used on finer punctuation. Looking back from
our present age of the computer, a quill pen might've seemed perfectly
at home there. I could've been Santa's secretary, making a list, checking
it twice.

My great grandfather's tintype showed him wearing his moth-eaten gray
uniform. He had served under the daring young Mosby. Gramps's face was
a grizzled rehearsal for my present smoothed performance; but at least our
busy pressured eyes rhymed.

I touched the frame and Colonel Harbison Increase Hartley. Though not
born of the officer class, though too poor to own a slave, Increase Hartley
had outlived most of his division's aristocrats. The seminary boys had been
made only reckless by their learning. Field promotions and a sense of duty
helped Increase rise in rank. His name is still listed in the histories of two
major battles.

After the war, he returned to anonymous subsistence farming. He had not
bettered his family's lot via the freebie valor so generally admired on market
Saturdays. He did turn up in Mosby's famous memoir: "No officer serving
under me ever cared more for his men. From their blankets' repair to the
cuts of their hard-won bacon, he noticed all. No one else was such a very
Mars while in ire and dander. No one proved so precise a horseman nor so
ferocious a defender of his troops. We each respected and half-feared our
somber, dutiful, and pious young Increase Hartley."

To me then, this seemed damning with faint praise. A soldier's merits had
been cited without once mentioning the Enemy.

My Yankee friends, finding family resemblance cobbling every surface,
mistook me for a blueblood. Only highborn Northern folks seem so obsessed with lineage. You know, somehow I failed to correct my friends' mistake. I recalled my father's bemused disgust when I advanced my "Dickie"
clear to "Hartley." All at age five. There are many kinds of pedigrees. In our
great country, the simple will toward betterment remains a biggie. Increase
Hartley, indeed!

Quorum

wo of us always seemed to be sitting outside a building waiting for the other to show. As if my job were that of scout, making the world safe for our incoming three-way democracy, I was usually early. I hated the role; resented its necessity; but never managed being mysteriously tardy. Robert arrived—the very second you first feared he wouldn't. Angie, trailing helpers, cabbies, street kids, dragged up ten to twenty minutes late. Custom could not stale her infinite excuses. I would rise, bend into her lastest explanation, kiss her hair—whatever color. Angie's scent was that of clean feet and hot rocks. She smelled agitated. She smelled . . . late.

"God, we got caught in the Haiti Liberation Day Parade, wonderful magenta frilled shirts, I want one, but you wouldn't believe the traffic backed up midtown. . . . Before that, I was running ahead of schedule for a change but somebody threw himself under the train at Eighteenth Street. For half a block of track and the white station tile, such a mess . . . Grapeade shading off more to the color of weak Lipton tea."

"Lunch anyone?" Robert, dry, asked. We laughed.

I knew I was just one of a million kids my age trying to paint or write or compose. Compose here. Others roomed in my very building. With their outsized bargain winter coats, just the sight of them squirreling the pitiable mail from home off into their cubicles filled me with such shame. What seemed noble in my gifted friends looked only sad in strangers.

I'd wake to hear kids' typewriters clacking, besting mine in cascading volleys at 3 a.m. Other voices, worse linoleums.

I could not explain my faith in what I did. It was not yet even faith in my own work, since that was fetal. It was more a faith in the right to work. The beauty of just trying. It was, at first, belief in the option to fail magnificently (and, thank God, magnificently far from home).

Who'd need know? We'd die here, old, together, safe with each other's secrets. We were each other's juvenilia.

I had some angel-overview sense that I was, if not so beautiful as Robert, if not nearly so gifted as our Angie—then not unhandsome, never truly tineared, replete with some capacities and many a courtesy. I sure put in the hours. And I had the nervous luck of the upper-middle class to back me up.

Now I see, so much derived from the rushing horsey talents of my friends.

Their shouldering force, my flying buttresses. Others wanted their bodies, then wanted to create as they did, soon others copied them and failed, then others—feeling rebuffed—reviled them. This just made Robert and Angie somewhat more famous. (If getting imitated means anything, and it does.)

—I saw how my pals dealt with the byproduct poison of being a little too visible a bit too soon. If they believed in me one quarter as much as I felt sure of them . . . We might all do something yet.

I tried, during Sunday drinktime phone calls, to state my excitement to the folks. But—even if I had subjected my parents to the shock of seeing where I lived—no working lock on the street-level door, an elevator rarely functioning and then coffin-sized and urinal-odiferous—even if I drew them up four steep flights to my desk and reassured them with the desktop gallery of family mugs, even if I showed them draft after typed draft, mark upon inked mark, even if I convinced them I was writing about honest farmers whose prettiest sons (preferably shirtless) got bad-hurt way back when, how could I justify what I was trying here in Yankeeland? Maybe I was like Angie, banished from the beautiful town that wanted her in sight but never quite included; surely it was lucky that I had no wife, no kids, no chance of harming any family through my long quixotic try at adding, to a basement bookstore, still more mellow dust.

I knew only this: my locale, my work, my friendships all felt necessary. It was spiritual mainlining and I mostly woke up hopeful. I trusted I'd remain this lucky. There were so many beautiful people to talk to, to bed, and, perhaps finest of all, to talk to, afterward, in bed. Was learning ever easier? Was anything not possible?

My "collection of short stories," my "novel," and my address book grew. But the address book expanded far faster. Its characters sure "held reader interest" longer.

Angie hunted for a boyfriend and a gallery, not necessarily in that order. Robert sought some peace from all the boys and girls he'd made be pineapple-upside-down cake. Said he needed time, to compose music.

Before

On Gathering Content

f I ever worried that I'd squandered my first thirty-three years, I pulled out the seven earlier address books that proved otherwise. I sometimes left these propped among my kinfolks' antique pictures on the desk. Even then, they seemed one form of modern achievement.

Remember your own starter address book? Do you recall the color of your first person-gathering kit? —Mine was red. Red is still my favorite color (also Robert's and Angie's). The day I turned twelve, I bought the book for forty-nine cents under a sign MEETING ALL YOUR STATIONERY AND BOOK-KEEPING NEEDS. At Belk Tyler's Department Store in bustling uptown Falls, North Carolina. The price had been slashed, down from a dollar. I knew it was meant as mine. I was so sure, I got an erection. But then at twelve, the sight of a blooming apple tree could give me such an upsurge.

A cherry-red leatherette near-toy, Book Number One was little larger than a commemorative stamp. "Important Addresses" had been engraved across its glossy cover in gilt, not twenty-four-carat. At public pay phones, in our hometown (whose every household could then be reached by dialing just five digits), I soon whipped out my sassy reference work. Letting others see it made me feel half-sexual with my own sense of worldliness and longing and connections. One passing farmer rolled his eyes.

Needing to fill the pages, I resorted to lackluster second cousins. I did. I was so low on R's, I even listed my own Sunday school teacher, a local radio announcer with a shriveled hand, a man I would not have phoned at gunpoint to save my family's lives.

It'll sound briefly immodest but even at age twelve, I was not without mail. My one official pen pal was an ungainly older girl with black bangs and absurdly sturdy legs. Trudy T—. She hailed from Altoona, Pennsylvania, and I'd met her when both our families camped at an evergreened state park. Her father was a very gung-ho football coach. His cement-gray crewcut stood utterly on end like a gym class forced to do Nazi jumping jacks. Trudy's handsome, dark kid brother yelled a lot, hyperventilated, broke off a good-sized tree limb and, with it, beat—for no reason I could see—all four tires of his family's Plymouth. "Just, let, that, show, you," pounding, he instructed whitewalls.

Studying him, my mother told her young sons, "Steer clear of that one." Trudy's brother had been given a new red ax. Mistake. Through camp

67

one day, a snapping turtle came crawling. The thing gathered a crowd, marveling, if from five feet behind. Haltered tourists aimed their Kodaks. The creature was lead-colored, immense, quite visibly ancient. Serrated ridges like some dinosaur's stood upright along the domed center of its shell.

One crazy brother swerved from nowhere. Before adults could stop him, he'd chopped into this beast's bowed complicated back. No natural awe, no fellow-feeling, slowed him. Coursing through this kid—first testosterone, grainy and rattly as white sugar. The dying turtle looked a century old. It'd grown at roughly the rate rocks do. It was nearly big across as an auto tire. The sound of new steel severing its bony platelets, the sight of how the beast's head and legs and tail, first tucked inside, exited writhing as blade entered hidden flesh—I'll never forget. The turtle thrashed so, biting air, hissing. And I, alongside Trudy, palms pressed to our cheeks, screamed bloody murder. We two screamed as if auditioning for Hitchcock.

Trudy felt the two of us had lived through something momentous and were friends for life. A girl eighteen, she somehow fixated on me—one freckled, allergic, sweetly squeamish kid barely twelve.

Vacation over, I rolled home to find six letters already waiting. Trud's stationery was pink, scented. Such notes at once became my family's joke. "Rome-e-oleo," was my new nickname. Teasing and whipping: a loving way of life with us. In our household, the weak did not survive. You learned to laugh, because you'd better. Good practice for later, for New York.

My own jotted answers to Trudy eventually faltered, then condensed to postcards. I finally grew silent. I had much to tell someone, okay. But maybe not a girl whose attractions fell below even those of my dowdy powdered aunts. She was a girl who'd begged me to kiss, for practice, if not her mouth, then, okay, her arm? Deep in the woods of an overcrowded state park, I found myself fastened to one pale wrist of a plump girl. To indicate a deeper interest, to spare her feelings, as a born caretaker, I, gallant, frenched her wrist. She wriggled, sighing. I remember that. Anything to please. I was already a junior trainee artist.

Somehow my postcards ceased, causing Trudy's chipper martyred tone to slowly curdle. First it intensified to miffedness then starched itself toward irony. "You are no doubt busy with your other so-called 'friends' " soon became "I knew you'd leave me, as does everyone, in Pennsylvania or the Universe generally."

Twelve years old, I read her waiting letter daily, with a sickening appetite for fresh news of her pain's location. I felt a sad awe at how I'd damaged her health and self-esteem. What shady rock had those slid beneath today? I recalled the giant turtle, mottled gray-khaki-black, moving away from us through piney daylight, its shell opened, raw and glistening, grape-purple, to sunshine. The creature sputtering its final sound, pulled its weight toward woods, a red ax still wedged—bookmark—in its opened back. The thing was still alive enough to know it must use final strength to go and try and hide its dying.

Trudy's immediate pain soon crawled off too far to even attempt answering: This was my first correspondence, she—my first legitimate and romantic address. I failed her. Trudy: my starter course in unrequited (unrequired) love. I am sorry.

Now I know she loved me, Trudy. Truly. It then seemed hideous and so arbitrary for some heavy sigh-prone girl, eighteen, to actually love a skinny kid unscathed by manhood. I now know: Love is often far more surreal, far more arbitrary.

Though Trudy was someone I would never dare write again, I did need one more out-of-state address. If I ever felt bold enough ahead, I could find her. So, into my prized red booklet, Trudy's name and stats arrived, months after her own clear silence cooled and hardened into a lead-colored shell. I inscribed her—so large that "Trudy" extruded, two whole pages all her own. Homage. "There," I said. She would've liked that.

I ennobled my childish roster with phone numbers for the fire department, how to summon an ambulance. Because you never knew. There was still the shame of having no known L, and certainly—in Scotch-Irish North Carolina—no exotic X's, Y's, or Z's.

For the first two decades, each new address book gained inches as did my formerly twenty-three-inch waist. If you graduate from school a year early, if you win a scholarship up North especially, they have to let you leave. For a while, you're magically eighteen. You admit to feeling really "old." You like it when the adults moan over your saying this. Time and life seem purely additive.

Only new folks in your book. They each seem brainier, flashier, less local, and far dearer than the dreary hometown ones. This, you think, is living.

You soon acquire three whole L's, and one V (if only an acquaintance met on a train). As your school chums go forth, then procreate and sort of prosper, as work leads you, there's a need to buy another, bigger, sturdier volume; soon the folder has outgrown anything merely "pocket-sized." You graduate to a desktop address book with simu-leather alphabetic tabs. Traveling, you pack that item last, so you can unpack it first. It has now grown more essential than your toothbrush (those, you can replace at any airport).

If your book is not in sight, you pat your pockets, fearing for your keys too. Already you suspect it is most truly you. —Justifying the address book and loving its lives, that is your real life's work.

This is the time of gathering names. Unto everything, a season. This one occurs before that harvest rite called editing—a middle-aged virtue and necessity. This happens long before First Death gets your attention. Death? Isn't that a Strike Force that grabs pets and other less lucky kids' grandparents? Cartoon characters can fall off cliffs and magically reconstitute. They merely shake themselves, then road-run right back up rock-facing. At twenty, there's such reckless traction.

You can't yet know that listed friendships won't all last forever. You never guess that, with life being vapor, even good ink set into a costly high-rag-content durable book, doesn't mean that much of Forever. —Never suspecting this, how happily you assemble names. You cannot know your players without a program.

(After the disaster, you will tastelessly and giddily revise this phrase: You cannot know your players without a pogrom.)

There are two kinds of people in the world, those who'll help you automatically—even despite themselves—and those to whom that thought will barely occur. And both are lurking in your address book, side by side.

Shall we keep them all in our mulliganstew of a ledger?

How, in advance of trouble coming, might you separate the good stuff from the junk pulp? You can't.

You must first live through it.

Appliance

ully eight months after I led her to Robert, Angie admitted me to her place and, tat for tit, pulled a filthy Snoopy bedsheet off one large painting. I had not asked. It was understood how much I wanted to see.

Enroute, I'd inquired again if she were "an abstract or figurative artist" (a pat respectable opening phrase I still clung to in those days). She shrugged and, greeted by her building's stoop-sitting widows, "Ciao, bella," Ang answered, "Little dis-a little dat-a."

The painting first appeared abstract, potently so. It had so much macho energy, you needed Ray•Bans to study it long. Done very wet with almost scary certainty, it was like a 1949 de Kooning, painted fast. Colors-rude combated colors-lyrical. Only slowly, as I backed away from it, did I see a second layer filming its surface.

I was aware of her watching, not me—but, both hands on her hips—the picture itself. Its second level was rendered in a faint blue-gray of cobwebs sogged with beaded dew. This surface seemed a net, drawn in the same accomplished crosshatching she'd used to render that fine grin of an opened crotch.

I at last detected—stretched like some tangle of knitting across a maelstrom or pit—one image, corny and overfamiliar. It'd been there all along but overshadowed by its complex surroundings. A kitchen, clunky forties appliances, plaster fruit plaques climbing the wall at a diagonal, one curtained window above the gleaming sink. This scene of certainty (and constriction) had been rendered within a circle. Like the china-painting done on some "display" plate. So prim a candybox interior was made disorienting, almost obscene, by its placement above the whorl and splatter of first paint. It stitchery seemed some webbed anchorfence—keeping us back safe, as behind zoo caging—just clear of the mad lava churning underneath. (I'm not describing this very well, I fear. You'd think I could do better after all the early catalogue essays I was soon to write. These essays about her work are mostly lost now, in brochures published by nowhere galleries, the endless series of such places where her painting languished far too long. In the days before commonplace Xeroxing, I did not keep copies of the essays and, for what it tells you, neither did she.)

But if I might cannibalize from one such yellowing leaflet I do still own:

"Ms. Byrnes's 'Appliance-Volcano' is the admixture of comically male Abstract Expressionist underpaint—woolly-chested, outward, GI extrovert— and the clichéd femininity of a domestic ideal rendered, with self-conscious prissiness, on top, doilying the void.

"It is this ply, conjoining impossible versions of a single world that marks the young painter's almost folkloric frontality, that signals her gender-leaping ingenuity of imagery. In the execution, there is nothing provisional. Her dazzling technique is one that any seventeenth-century Dutch painter could well appreciate."

Bla bla blah. But heartfelt.

That first day, I looked long, kept quiet. Angie's place smelled of heavy solvents and light housekeeping. She said nothing, flats of her wrists still at rest on either hip, a cigarette burning, the smell of a bad mood. She tipped her head and squinted, time-out for a workshop elf. But my private showing felt like an excuse to let her peek at her own work one more time today. (I sensed she had a quota, to prevent herself from undoing what was good, from staying here full-time. She'd repeated Noël Coward: "Work is more fun than fun.") I remained quiet for three minutes, an eternity when the painter stands right behind you, especially if the painter is someone with Angie's edgy energy.

"The bride's kitchen painted here on top," I attempted. "It's hanging over the pit like a necklace. It has no power to protect, but it believes it's an amulet, a good luck charm. The tension you get, sandwiched, is what's unbelievable. The real painting happens on the level between the two you've actually set down. . . ."

"Something like that. Well," she shrugged. "Seemed a good idea at the time . . ."

"No," I urged her. "Don't take it back."

"Oh, I'm *not*, Hart, believe me. Can't afford to. It's just—here, now I see it, now I hear you gasbag some, if well . . . it's still too much an idea. As if I'm doing this just to make it easier for middlebrows to describe later. In my head, it's so . . . but by the time I get it out . . . it's mud."

I soon learned never to contradict, never to "cheer" her. She would later cure me of that by calling me, for three weeks straight, Hartley Hammerstein.

Now, I kept my mouth shut. That in itself became, as silence found its fulcrum, a weight of respect between us, an early lesson. (When placing my own first stories into anybody's hands, I usually turned into a babbling contortionist of apology and protective preemptive self-doubt.)

"I've never seen anything like this . . ." summarized the gasbag in retreat.

"Well," she told me. "It's archaic Angie. I know when I look back I'll see I've barely started." And she eased the sheet back across it, a hundred Snoopys on a hundred doghouses. Her short hands tugged the cloth straight with a motherliness, a modesty, I'd never seen the girl award herself.

She turned to making coffee, her back to me. I loved her back. Almost a boy's. I sensed she was upset. What'd I said? Already I was learning to read how her anger alternated with her breakthroughs, and from all angles. Through walls. "Did I do something?"

She shook her head no. She was pointing down. In one corner by the sink, a mousetrap, not sprung but nibbled clear of most cheese left on its killing clamp. "Damn Minnie the Mooch rodent," she said. "I would get a

Ph.D. one. It holds the patent pending on this fucking trap. Thing keeps me up nights. I hate the sounds of scuttlings in the wall. Savannah all over again. It ate a half a tube of my cadmium red (light). How do they know which paint is most expensive? Damn damn mouse." She acted stiff, as if I'd bashed her work.

Had she gone rigid because a very red mouse was still at large, or because one overly white boy remained too-present? I didn't know yet. I moved toward the door. She failed to stop me. I left before the coffee brewed.

Know Your Whereabouts at All Times

he city's sense of promise is based precisely on its being all blinders, blinkers, chutes. Such tunnel vision means sudden awarded views that (on a good career- or love-day) can feel designed, singly, paradisal for you. The city offers you the whole Sun waiting (surprise) at your gray street's very end. Sunlight is glittering on the godly Hudson River like some sudden fad, a fad with your name spelled dancing across it.

—So, even in the memory of my later outrunning thieves (or not), there's this glee, this wild survivor's glee that's beautiful, if quite inaccurate.

Already boastful about our bravery, we didn't yet know the ways we'd need it. Hold that off? Muggers, sure. Communicable venereal woes and age-old Heartache, fine. Weekly form-rejection slips from *The New Yorker* ("Does not suit our needs at this time") okay. But hold the other off. Please hold it off awhile?

Sure, being that young in Old New York, we were scared a lot, and as insecure as we were swaggering. But, ah, we took the art of partying to new heights. And, oh how hard we worked. Private effort, not group sex, became the deep dark secret of our circle, and our age.

Some evenings, I'd explore the used bookstore across the street. It was named The Honored Owl. Before it, a bird-shaped shingle hung. Rumor claimed it'd been painted during the thirties by Rockwell Kent between paychecks. (Someone later swiped the thing and sold it through Sotheby's for a six thousand dollar minimum.)

They let you read there in the Owl. We considered it a badge of honor to hang out and absorb without sullying our love of literature through actual cash transactions. You sat on books as you initiated other books. Some wise earlier shopper had stacked a makeshift all-book reading chair. It was made of Lamb, Amis, Lovejoy, and two complete Barchester Towers; wedged where your elbows fell, find opposing copies of *A Farewell to Arms*. Into the chair's rearmost spine-support, *A Pillow Book*, and Henry Green's great novel, *Back*. (New York is nothing if not allusive.)

About to leave, I always stuck whatever three novels I was reading into some spots hard to reach, an advantage of being tallish. You could smell the great books disintegrating; their musty glue, their bitter ink and bandage spines, all acted on me like pipe tobacco or some form of dusty opium. I'd soon sneeze myself outdoors but I never lost the scent. Since the Owl's half-blind owner was always pasting something, using clamps on leather bindings, the place retained the varnish odor of a workshop. Though decaying paper gave the air its stink, your final impression was, oddly, one of permanence. The paginated richness of others' passions, yellowing yet legible. It sometimes sent me running up four flights, to type. I'd hold a blank white page and rub it till the urban oil of my thumb and forefinger ruined its perfection. How could I explain this to my parents? New York was not a sewer, it was an archive, a new bed, a wanted poster, a grape press, a new futon smelling of straw and possibility.

Angie and Gustafson and I found we had skads else in common. The less we could control these ground-glass streets, the more we cared how our tiny "spaces" looked. We shopped alike. With serious skimming methodical glee. We boy-boys and straight girls had a nose for bargains and a penchant for extravagance and we guessed that these need not be mutually exclusive.

Poverty-stricken spendthrifts. As good a description of Humanity as any!

Once as we wandered Columbus Avenue, the stalky brilliant Marxist English actress from a great theatre family pounded Robert on one shoulder, handed him a twenty, smiled. "Never figured you'd get it back so fast this time, now did you, luv?" We walked on. I said nothing, practically rupturing my spleen, pretending that his heightened life was normal. One block later, Robbie greeted a Heineken delivery man, "Hot enough for you, Verne?"

"How do you *know* all these damn people?"

R. said he'd had five years on me here. "And it's basically a friendly town, Hartley. Give them a chance, people'll talk."

"People'll talk to *you*."

It was often a call from Robert, mostly at the last minute. "Me. Come quick. I've just met a woman who worked as a Paris runway model with Jean Rhys, back when they were both sort of hooking on the side? And she has the most complicated accent and knew Joyce, then toured with the Gish girls, and you know how I am about Lil Gish. There are radioactive stories here and my big ole Geiger counter it's a-clickin. Not to mention, she's crazy to meet you, Hartley."

"As it happens, I'm done with work today and I'd love to join you. But, Robert, this old gal? she doesn't know me from a cat's ass."

"She will. You have so much that she'll like."

"Charm, you mean?" Fishing, pitiful.

"Oh sure, charm, but . . . charm is easy. The two of us put out more charm while flossing than most people do during their entire honeymoons. You know that, don't you. —Charm? I'm told there's even one New York cab driver who has some. No, you've got something far better than charm, Hartley Mims the umptyumpth."

"Yeah? Like . . . what?"

"You have potential, Hartley. Such potential. We all see that. Problem is—you insist on writing about nice people trying to stay nice in only moderately tough test-situations. You need a higher octane of trouble. Only then will you find how decent or not they really are."

"But, Robbie? Just inventing tortures—feels so sadistic."

"That doesn't stop God."

"What's 'God'? A category on Double Jeopardy?"

He laughed, sad. "You're not cruel enough to be a novelist. But at least you found the right city.

"Assignment: Hartley must think up some dreadful things to jump the bones of his fictional darlings, by drinktime. Wild mushrooms that a family gathers then cooks into an omelette, but there was a misprint in their guidebook, see, and they picked four pounds of the wrong kind . . . And . . . what? . . . wait, some jerk's trying to get this phone . . . Lead-based paint is chewed off a crib by the baby son of a professor and his wife and the kid is left a bit retarded. But, see, it's the one thing, the boy's being dumb, they cannot live with but they must. And I'm not even trying. Meanwhile, take the A train. Meet you here in twenty minutes." He was gone.

I now know: The term Fairy Godmother has many shadings.

Never forget this is a fairy tale. Fairies make good subjects. Though they are very hard to keep around.

75

A Fairy cannot Marry. A Fairy believes in Magic, because he cannot get a credit line in anything else. And since he so believes in Magic, he really gets to practice it at times.

One rainy day, Robert, holding forth at our table, using handy sugar cubes, built a vertical white temple. "Doric?" Ang, entering, asked. "No," he quipped, "Doris. —Why?"

Ossorio's other clients soon noticed, bringing over sweet contributions. Watching Robert's steady hands, the old guys made bets about when it'd all fall down. The structure didn't, not for years yet.

Since the table was rarely wiped clean, since Ossorio respected it as Ours, a changing toylike pile of doodads often held its center. The interlocking white cubes lent our leavings an Incan nobility: Lost earrings of Angie's, a Santa Christmas ornament found unbroken on the sidewalk, stacks of matchbooks and untraceable keys. And, once, a short dildo nobody would claim but all the regulars nicknamed, made a pet of. All this got wedged into pounds of pretty, then dingy, chunks of sugar. As we slumped here—discussing life and death, meaning art—our voices raised amid the clatter from dominoes and dice, we, still such kids, barely noticed constructing it all, everybody working on another end of it.

Sugar-cube boats wore toothpick-and-napkin sails—a frosted city sprung up here, mutating amid and among us. The sandpile. Anyone's.

On Being Overly Active Sexually

oung persons, fairly new to New York, hoping to appear cool, must lie about many things. Running with my flashy favorites, I'd begun to fib, as camouflage.

Restaurants conquered, celebrities or celebrities' support staffs slept with, advances paid. Hard-bitten hipness was often faked. And eventually—just when you'd prefer not—your own pretended speed catches up with you. It shoots you past where you'd hoped to stop. And, by the time you need not fake anything ever again, you'd truly prefer to.

For several years I'd pretended going (many times) to the St. Mark's Baths. Most everything I'd heard about the place scared me. Though it appeared a hygienic steambath committed to public swimming, weight lifting, and recreation, it was actually a maze devoted to sexual stalking. No panthers worrying their cages can suggest the crouched energy of Type-A male New Yorkers set down in a plywood maze, goal-oriented, on the humid trail of Same.

(Once a week, on slow Tuesdays, they tried Lesbian Night. Then the corridors emptied. Mostly the gals just sat around the TV room, wearing towels, eating potato chips, and telling their life stories.)

The procedure for getting through the front door spooked me most.

If only Robert would go with me. His beauty friction-proofed all entrances; but then I would be lost in the backwash of that very lubricating allure.

I feared making some gaffe during the gatekeeper's questions about lockers, deposits, codes, towels worn around waists, towels tied shut with the rubberized binding on your cubicle key. It seemed too codified to let a first-timer fake finesse. That mattered to me back then.

As for parading around half naked, I was at my hunky peak and, though insecure as hell, I at least grouchily sensed that.

One night, stood up by a date at an Indian restaurant nearby, I coasted past St. Mark's stainless door and saw a line atypically short. I pulled a U-turn, then circled the block six times. Finally I vowed to follow strangers in and do exactly as they did. If cautious French-accented Canadians could risk it, so could I.

One assumed that one was, by now, unsurpriseable. But what I found at the "tubs" (can we finally talk here?) shocked me. It just did.

I had been memorizing Blake epigraphs. Now the scent of steam, poppers, rubber soles brought one to mind. "Fun I love, but too much fun is of all things the most loathsome. Mirth is better than fun, and happiness is better than mirth."

Well, you got to start somewhere.

Having surrendered my clothes and checked my shoes, I found that what really made me feel nakedest was peeling off that last black holey Orlon sock! How pale and huge and North Carolinian this foot looked. After wrapping all of me in a smallish white towel—Miss Sarong stalks Mr. Right—I set out to try and seem, not naïve but, native.

Three hundred people circled each other, seeking sex from the one person not present. I read a sign THE ORGY ROOM. I entered, prepared to see three seated elderly gents, their midriff terrycloth sorely tested, discussing the rumor that Callas died of tapeworms she'd consumed to control her weight. Instead, I found one hundred males, all young to recently-so. Each was naked, all were working on each other in a tumid smacking hellish lovely silence, nearly post-*Titanic*. In the so-called orgy room, I met the last things I'd expected: no room, an actual orgy!

I next found four to seven hands under my towel is what I found as, gingerly, I excused and, oops, unhasped myself. God knows, I didn't mind being groped; having lived a good while in New York, I no longer required extended previews, credential-establishing conversations. (Go to buy a necktie, wind up with the customer behind you in the giftwrap line who winks, "Got a few minutes, Dropdead Gorgeous?")

But I was still old-fashioned in certain thank-you-note folkways. I did not need names and school affiliations, I didn't even ask to hear the guy's voice, but I did like having one face to match each pair of hands working on and under me. Call me conventional.

Was the orgy room this dark as a gentle nod toward our older clients? Fingers felt like some web of tentacles let loose, presumed welcome, up under my rental towel, set free on home-boy home-grown goodies. You know how in a car wash, hula skirts of octopus-sponge shimmy your vehicle rudely clean, almost against its will? Like that. Would the universe allow this much wet mischief at once? My parents on perfect days told us, "Enjoy this weather. We'll pay later."

I'd grown up.

For some reason, I pictured my never-smiling father. He seeing this, would absolutely die then absolutely kill me.

I'd grown up Presbyterian, okay? And now, sobered by the image of my dad's lipless face, I sidled, smiling, toward the glowing exit sign, "Excuse me, thank you, ooops, no offense, li'l bathroom visit . . . coming out . . . nothing personal . . ." From the water fountain in a non-steam area, I drank deep. Then, having found a dime, I dialed Angie from a pay phone (they all reminded me of her), "Guess where I am and what I'm wearing?"

"First, did you mail away your cocker spaniel–divorce short story this morning? Number two—you gettin' any?"

My voice is the voice of thousands, and my towel encases much. Walt Whitman, are you watching? Because, Walter, check these guys out! Nudity is democracy. Erection, the great leveler. In here, bare young milkmen outrank myopic Wall Street brokers. NYPD detectives stake out chorus boys, figuratively then literally. All are alike only in the unlikely eyes of God.

You get reduced to your most major owner's strut while wearing the most minor of rental towels. No secrets, no closets—only timeshare cubicles where you, odalisque, recline, then beckon or reject the passing cavalcade of chest and leg hair. One boy had precisely Robert's ears. Another Angie's butt.

I dallied with a somber smoldering lad whose crazed glare bespoke a cleric freshly, wisely, defrocked. He was sexy till admitting he'd soon snag his doctorate at Columbia. When he mapped out his thesis topic, "The Ontological Impasses Implicit Between the Populists Sympathy and the Tooled Aesthetical Surfaces of Flaubert's Prose," he sent my erection toward such an impasse. "Abiento," I departed.

I felt followed and it pleased me, "Well, hello, Ed. Sorry, been busy. Yes, well, thank you. But tonight I'm trying to widen my, I was hoping to . . . you know, branch out."

What am I, a tree?

I toured a hundred open doorways where nude boys summoned me or waved one past. I remembered my own quiet horror during a student trip to Amsterdam—lady prostitutes on display, gals busy knitting in small overlit houses, wearing no underpants, wives for lease.

Here, boys made much of time-share cubbyholes. Some had brought along their own pink lightbulbs and screwed in a little flattery. They lolled, but only after oiling their very best sides. Padding around I recalled Lord Byron's description of Turkish baths: "marbled palaces of sherbet and sodomy." Might our snackbar serve sorbet?

One fellow had outdone himself. He'd draped his booth with towels of a moorish pattern, sand-colored silk softened the lightsource. Some tasteful sandalwood incense burned. Mideastern music whined from a hidden ghetto blaster and, on his person, a wide brass bicep bracelet, actual saffron harem pants. I overheard one toweled peruser tell another, "Little Turkish Delight back there deserves a big E for effort. He's not that cute really but the poor queen's done more to that room than I did to any of my science fair projects. I'm gonna give myself to him. I'll consider it a form of group thanks. So you guys each owe me one, okay?" We, strangers, laughed.

In towels, we stood here, glad for this odd sensibility linking us: our love of hopeless comedy, our appetite for outrageous effect, our honest fellowship that springs from sinning very often and extremely well.

Now I slid into a smaller steamroom lit by one red bulb. It felt safer here. This looked like the set of the newest Bob Fosse musical I'd just seen in preview for seven bucks. Only two other patrons present, a relief.

One watchful old man listened to his transistor radio (it was that long ago), scratchy coverage of a hockey game. The other person, a spectacular youth; he was perfect as any platinum Aryan poster-maker's hope for his own one son. Such an ideal specimen seemed to belong, cast in wax, lording over some glass case at the Natural History Museum. "Homo sapiens" definitive. His nudity had such fierce authority, such frieze-worthy geometry, not even busloads of Connecticut schoolkids would dare giggle at it.

We nodded—amid staticky reports of some goalie's face-to-ice despair after allowing a score. The young man soon made slow seductive small talk in a German-Italian-Britishy accent easy to like, hard to place. His naked manner was assured, urbane. Even in such red glare, his sudden white smile, the whites of his animated eyes exerted the glamour of some silent screen star. Lordy Mercy, happy hunter, me.

He sidled nearer. The long legs, easing ever nearer, gave comic ducklike suction sounds across wet tile as I felt readier. I slid my key on its elasticized band around my wrist. The light in here was blood red, poetic. The guy appeared handsome as Robert. I would later say so to Robert—my friend but not, as yet, my lover.

Here, in this tiny room, one face per customer, the best-looking boy at St. Mark's was about to be mine, all mine. I was, as usual, already making a story of this beauty before we'd even established skin contact. I asked what he did. A flight steward, he said, someone who "touched down" all over the world.

"Spreading joy?" I asked, my tone trying to sound dry amid the therapeutic vapors.

"D'accord," he responded. "Spreading, anyway."

Then his whole hand pressed my lower back, specifically my ass. "Prego?" asked the master of flight and international dissemination.

"Well," I stalled. "But . . ."

I was too recent on the scene to feel ready: getting jumped right here, before our hockey enthusiast. That fur-backed codger had, I noticed, already rearranged his sideline position so he might watch as he (radio still pressed to right ear) kept up with his beloved Canucks.

Something in the insistent touch of this archangel of mechanical flight, something in how—this close—his perfect features looked so overdetermined—hollow-eyed and masklike, something in his intention toward the one deed only, and without prelude or nicety or compliment—something in his sudden erotic sternness, his very frontal perfection—now felt offputting to the point of making me shudder.

As the red glare slid from Poetry to Poe, I could not help notice that, without consulting me, he was already turning me around, then over. Expertly as a mom about to diaper her toddler junior, he wielded some evolved inexorable strength, he wielded much implied half-surgical experience, this slickster grappling me facedown into a far likelier position. I was, in fact, being—wasn't I?—somewhat gingerly pinned, rump-up. Hello, major experience incoming.

—Sometimes, even in a world as cerebral and abstracted as our New York one—your own beasty instinct hollers at you by means of all hairs on the backs of both your hands: "NO. Not *this* one! Wrong move, wrong. Haul your sweet cherry ass out of here, pal—preferably right now!"

"Excuse me, I've got to go and see a man about a hockey bet," I said, saving perhaps my life. The steward, proving me immediately correct, suddenly cursed so. Ruddy steam sputtered cumulus, a guttural venomous Indo-European language I did not speak and have not heard since. I elbowed him, found the carved door handle, wriggled backward into open air.

From his red mist, I literally ran. True, I'd left behind my only towel, but oh, to feel unwedged, to breathe.

Even a Purgatorio like this must have a roof.

I followed three flights of stairs and, depending on the banister like someone old, found myself—naked as when my shame-faced mother bore me—on the lid of the baths. Fresh air! Oxygen unsullied by saunas, Aramis cologne or suntan stick, or the hard-luck aroma of the junior high school gym.

This roof, being gay-owned, proved perfectly landscaped. Pointy ever-greens rested in round cedar buckets. Boardwalks crossing tar made the building's top a Parcheesi board of routes that only seemed haphazard. From circular grottos set in far corners, hot-tubs released column-shaped clouds. Those rose straight up. City glare filled each with borrowed light that appeared original—original to this place, original to us—this town's un-wanted outlaw-cowpokes.

It was a warm evening for late March. Lucky for me. The bath's roof garden felt jammed right up against the skyline. From here, you felt you could reach forth one of your male, King Kong paws; you could play chess with all the famous skyscrapers waiting on their grid. Signifiers, dildoes, bishops. Who'll jump whom? Many of these lit-up structures had once been World's Tallest, former subjects of Hart Crane poems, John Marin water-colors.

The Chrysler Building glowed, fantastical, Industry's toolmaker Deco wetdream of itself. I, itemizing landmarks like some out-of-towner, tried to calm myself after that scuffle with the German. How rude. Unfair, being poleaxed by some guy that so outweighs you.

Being up high in the middle of a city this great, you could read by its byproduct light. Scraps of cloud passed over me, half ticklish. Odd, I felt safer now I was nude out here in its harsh soothing blaze. I still had my locker key! And I felt chaperoned, by Wannabe Has-been Manhattan itself.

Beyond rental office towers' serrations—a free and melon-colored moon rose.

One Moon. To Let. Short Monthly Leases Avail. Act Now.

This far aloft, light seemed a genial voyeur, half a companion.

I swallowed belated panic at that guy's scary strength. Breathing deep, I found myself near crying. Mom? Dad?

Plank fences screened nude men from nosy neighbors. You felt an ab-solute privacy out here. Safe except from the eyes of God or very good binoculars off the Empire State.

To stand undressed out of doors in the winter night of New York. I re-called my boyhood treehouse where, that hidden, my first impulse was to strip.

Emerging from hot steam, you find your wet body glossy with reflected light from the Empire State. The concept itself is Art Deco, pure Broadway in its earnest artifice. People wishing to escape the countryside band together. And, through their own hard density, they formed a carapace, an alternate, a vertical and yearned Bucolic. Five hundred thousand little towns candle forth into this one big blaze.

God, but I love New York! An addiction undying.

One silhouetted stranger, as endearingly tentative as the air steward had seemed cruel, is now circling this tub, is asking in a ripe baritone if he might please slip into the churning water pinwheeling here beside you. "How hot is it?"

"Fairly."

"Thought so."

Something to say.

You exchange first names, one dumb joke and the briefest of career résumés (Dean, a commodities gold salesman from Laurel, Maryland, near Baltimore? Owns two cockatiels, collects eighteenth-century miniatures, often up here on business). Winter air across your freckled shoulders feels brisk, but the genitals' water boils, Barbados with a fever.

Then this nice guy—who seems to hail from an large affable Maryland Catholic family—this Dean's educated right hand starts massaging all the city tension from your upper back, your neck. All the crisscrossed wire cording required to hold up yonder Brooklyn Bridge. Tense much?

Unlike the totalitarian mitt of the Eurotrash steward downstairs (he's surely found someone else to jump by now), there's this kid-brother feeling in the touch of my young Dean here. How much of his decent life is communicated through the morse code of one supple cushioned paw. Anything can happen. Soon you permit the trusted hand down along your spine and it's under the shared water and with and on your lower half, and is truly getting to know you. Hello. Is it not a joy to trust someone this brand-new to you and find you mostly can? And so follows tender Pastoral Symphony sex here in the open in the middle of New York.

The corner privacy of a most public space, the openness of a great mineral city that likes to watch the innocent gambolings of bare winter animals sunk gullet-deep into hot water behind evergreens set among towers erect full-time, year-round. Act now. Constant upright inspiration.

The prigs won't tell you how sweet and rollicking the peasant dance was. Before such accurate lightning struck us.

Oh, but if our parents had known just the half of it (young Dean's and mine, Robert's preacher and his choir-director wife, and Angie's doctor-waitress, camped forever at the edge of Savannah society)! They'd have sent thickened detectives to abduct us. And that might've saved some of our lives. But it would've meant our forever after being tied up back home in old childhood bedrooms—the Fifty Years of Aviation wallpaper, the suspended models, the tall tin horse-riding trophies—we prisoner-artists bound and gagged but safe, subjected to factory-recall on Country Club Boulevards all over America.

From Other Galaxies

ngie had a date, it flopped. She had another date, with the med student, he was forty minutes late and she hated herself for even being present when he showed, barely apologizing, convinced as the Israeli Army in which this Moishe had served, and whose funny stories he served Ang and the waitress, soon especially the waitress. Angie finally threw the contents of her waterglass at him . . . "Mainly as something to do. But it was a mistake, it just drew them closer together, Moishe and the blond blotter waitress. Why am I like honey to gay bees and Raid to the little yellowjackets I could use a big one of?"

We would see other clusters of gay men, also with a single complete-looking stylish woman in their midst; each group believed itself the most gifted, and therefore entitled to be, in all of New York's history, loudest.

Angie explained how certain subjects, adored by males, made her space out so: ball scores, cars, inner-office politics, college frathouse hijinks, mothers as saints. Chat concerning a flaking unplayable Jacksonian-era harp was, she suggested, wasted on these dateable fellows. To us, of course, the loss seemed theirs.

Angie admitted she craved male companions. She conceded being a Daddy's girl. But the guys she longed for were verbal, expressive, could dance, knew five good wines, and some art history, plus the names of colors, and told hilarious jokes as filthy as hers. Somewhere, there must be men alive on earth as self-mocking as she and therefore as self-aware? Were there fellows who saw language as a playground, not a minefield? And who lived at comic ease with themselves and who could acknowledge sex in all its comic technical details. Angie said she needed to be near men who did not view younger women painters' intense opinions as just "cute," Foreplay.

Once at a party, I expressed an emotional opinion. A self-confessed CPA, hovering at one edge of our talk, his face not-showing, half-hollered my way, after one of my emphatic clipped opinions about an overrated stage actor, "Excuse me, but would you say you're from Mars?"

He snapped it like some drill instructor, hard as my father's disciplinary voice. Angie stepped forward, tensed to protect. "No," I said first. "From Falls, North Carolina." My first impulse was to stay bland, to seem to miss this putdown. If you were emotional, you became a public nuisance, you lived as a visible threat and enemy. You never knew when such dudes might hurt you with it publicly. When you met a good straight guy, he only made you more scared of the others. They'd been getting away with this for years.

It was safer to stay around the few that you could trust. We did have some married friends; but we noticed that, if both were painters, one was always called The Talented One, and the other The One Whose Parents Bought Their Loft for Them. At dinner parties, they often seemed midfight, they were gathering votes, just putting off the final round till the dramatic cab ride home. In company, they seemed to give us only half as much as any Single one of us offered them.

So, I was Martian. Okay. In the long run, however accused, it was easier being kind. (My mom, wife to my complicated chillsome dad, had taught me that.)

Still, it shook you every time they called you foreign, not quite human. Over coffee, after the CPA, Angie "talked me down" as we then called it.

Certain guys—Angie coached me from her bitterest experience—take their sports metaphors to the metaphysical. "For such fellows as our CPA, Hartley, the sex act is Scoring. My good breasts here, pips, hunh? Signify second base. The goal? It's this. —By your last athletic quarter—you'll wanna get as many other human beings to say 'I Love You'—without ever giving up even one of your 'I Love You' points aloud to them, see? Now you understand the object of life's game. Okay. And, for them, that means we're losers because we give so much away, to our work, to complete strangers, to playing around in our work, and with each other. They're devoted to a life-time spent holding back. That alone makes your Mars-hating CPA-guy a real end-zone winner, see? How have they stayed in charge so long? Has to involve our own self-loathing. —Sad, because he was not half-bad looking, really, the CPA. —Just joking, sheesh. Don't go ballistic on me."

About Stepping Out

t was easier being half of a decorative boy-girl unit. Simpler to turn up at some East Side literary party as a conventional couple, not your usual self—gay and alone or with some person of your own sex.

All eyes turn toward the door, assessing the newly arrived pair shedding their coats, smiling greetings at the hostess—all eyes judging them—separate, together, eyes then turning back to drinks, each other, the door-entry score made as surely as at some Olympic diving event.

After that, Angie and I could split up, solo handshakers, sex-seekers unimpeded. And if I was still alone by party's end, she'd be there to leave with. We could then do a long party post-mortem (best part?) on our train ride downtown.

Awkwardness set in when one friend found one, and the other was forced to subway it home alone. It could feel somewhat hurtful, your leaving the party unasked-for. Odd, it always seemed a judgment on your work.

The two of us soon fought like longtime spouses. Knowing how to wound each other best. (References, not to looks, but work—proved most painful.) Sure, I understood I was not quite Angie's lover, okay, okay. But did any of Ms. Byrnes's one-night-standers know, as I did, precisely what her uncle (Fern Jewel's shrimp boat captain brother) had done to her, at age eight, behind a white sail at a Savannah boatyard? Which of Angie's latest married executives knew that her cranky painter mentor, Joan Mitchell, had not co-starred with Bruce Cabot in some Lost City flicks from the forties?

The intimacy of sexual intimacy seemed, especially in a girl so bodily immodest, far down the list from the candor her average good-night phone chat to me yielded—about how slowly oil paint dried during a New York January this arctic, about recurrent yeast infections, about avocado facials and whether, come morning, strapped as we were for food, you dared eat the green you scraped off the face. But how flippant came the wink "my" Angelina snapped me as she oozed out of the party under the arm of some Cromagnon. He appeared to be from Passaic, wearing gold neckchains, a doorknob-sized poly-tech class ring, trailing a store's worth of Old Spice odor. Angie later said she'd wanted the dude in the worst way, and so—it turned out—did Connecticut and Rhode Island, for mail fraud.

—Yschh. Poor child had perfect taste in art, but as for clothes and men, hopeless. Her men friends, of course, excepted.

The girls that Robert and I now met everywhere (beginning not to like being called "girls") were the same kinds of artists we men were. We all loved shoptalk. But, from field to field, it proved too specialized to bear.

Angie's women painter friends discussed solvents, a brilliant new Japanese framer, and conspiracies. "During meetings, we mainly gripe," said she, "but at a very high theoretical level. And for the best of reasons." Her crowd was often taken for lesbians: They wore men's jeans and knew what they wanted.

Our fellow artists, who happened to be female, did not resemble the sweet funny girls we'd vaguely dated back home. Friends here seemed to descend from a different species. The stronger.

They were so unlike the kind of tractable deb whose local life often meant decades of decorous waiting—near the phone for dates, then for appointments with Raleigh's top society bridal consultant, then for contractions in the maternity ward, then in the van—with its heater on—listening to public affairs radio or advanced French tapes, hoping to outlast the son's clarinet and daughter's dressage lessons. Then the resigned wait for menopause, retirement, death of husband, own death.

No, here were singular New York single "girls" in denim, who, having found their gifts, having learned their own hard lessons early, were now mostly only in action.

Reversing the gravitational field of expected ladylike passivity, their forward motion required twice as much energy. The joy boys (who liked men) and these overdetermined half mannish girls (who also liked men)—banded and—our differences transcended—male-bonded. We were similarly disadvantaged and underrated, enraged by an itch that offered us artistic immortality in place of so much else that a "real" life daily denied.

We were serious. Which meant being seriously militantly playful. (A.F. ELF of C.I.O.)

The live-in half of Angie's dive looked colorful if messy. Tonight its scent mixed turpentine and curry. There was a huge ugly Sears rag rug, "Early

American," braided like Saturn's rings. But her studio itself stayed white, cleared, Windexed nearly scientific.

Seated, I now watched my harp-finder, four feet eleven (though she called herself five two and nobody'd ever had the nerve to contradict). You could tell she considered herself "Major" but only because she had no choice. Everybody in our VD holding-pen had known so too, on sight.

I watched Ang—gossiping seven-deadly-sins art world gossip, making strong coffee, dealing with her gorgon phone and its twenty-foot cord plus our group's first "call-waiting feature"—rush all over her tiny studio-apartment while stretching a canvas eight feet by eight feet. I watched her, phone still crooked against neck, grapple this immense white canvas across stretchers while stapling the cloth in place. She fired a few staples into the air just for playful emphasis. It was like studying a single if mighty quail—ropes bunched in its right claw—captain some four-masted schooner, and sail it very well.

Nothing about Angie had ever been miniaturized. She stayed Major, despite her frequent crying jags, despite an erotic interest mostly in the guys who answered her own dad's appetite for waitresses. She was Major despite her professed insecurity that lumbered along on a scale only Cecil B. De Mille could stage if way overbudget.

Before canvas, squinting through the Camel smoke that seemed a by-product of hyperactivity, she knew everything. In restaurants, she could never decide. Seeing her, staff hid. "But how do you personally feel about the chewiness quality of clams *in* your chowder? Because I've finally got it down to that or the tapioca you described so well," she overconsulted our waitress (did she hate them all?). The woman gave Ang a look, pure blue-plate-special ptomaine.

Angie's was a character that only seemed inefficient. As I envied Robert's negotiable beauty and sexual prowess and social ease, I studied Angie's character, tenacity, her tuber knottedness. I wondered, being milder myself, if it were learnable. Might I not render her daily forward traction into my own small achievable steps, a How-to Guide for Gaining the Necessary Strength Artistic? Paranoia prepared her: She had a teaching hospital's worth of emergency generators forever backing her up.

Her paintings possessed the surest sign of early promise, an energy quite absolute. Three ideas were forever being worked out and with obsessive daily care. In bed, I'd heard, then heard from others, Ms. Byrnes was the most supple and specific, inexhaustible, and funny lover. Her eyes met yours and there was no deskclerk-negotiator on duty in between. You were already upstairs. It was a child's guilelessness combined with lessons learned from her Poppa's pals smoking their cigars and talking statehouse scandal on the mildewed side porch; while their wives, Mom's friends, weekly presided over needlepoint loveseats, exclaiming, "Welll, see? Start with a can of Campbell's Mushroom Soup, add . . ."

From her work, her lovers and friends, Angie held nothing back because, I later learned, she could hold nothing back. At the time, I thought she had a choice. Because *I* did.

She'd begun to show under the name "Alabama" Byrnes. That name out-ranked frilly Angelina; it had an edge over A. Z. Byrnes, an earlier try that meant to hide her sex from competition jurors.

One day at her place, as she upgraded to a rat trap and slathered the thing with Philadelphia Cream Cheese, I admitted that I found her new name memorable. "But, honey, how do you just pick a thing like that? True, I chose to use my middle name and not Dad's first. But, I mean, have you ever even *been* to Alabama?"

"Not that I know of."

"You'd remember."

"Thomas Lanier Williams," she answered, trap in one hand, loaded knife in the other. "Ring a bell? As a hint, I can quote you the low-on-potential opening line of his first story: 'Hushed were the streets of many-peopled Thebes.' Does Thomas Lanier Williams not sound like some fifth-rate Mid-western college teacher poet with a rat-colored moustache and cracked white cheese for skin, who writes about lilacs and cottages? Sure you don't know his stuff?"

No. Angie told me that, since her mother was also a no-count Williams, she'd felt attracted to any Major artist who had survived the curse of so lack-luster a country name.

"But 'Tom,' you see, Hartley, had the sense to do a factory recall on him-self. Of himself. Recalled himself Tennessee Williams. He actually spent more time in Missouri. But . . . preferred the other's sound. So I figured, being a Williams and his halfassed kin some way, I would join him. It's true I come from Georgia but that's already a woman's name. No fun there. Besides, Georgia O'Keeffe beat me to it. She's a sentimentalist, but a cagey one. Knows how to crop the image of a pebble, like some good photo-grapher would. Her work reproduces better than it ever looks in person. Get up close, you see that paint's just a means-to-an-end with her. And 'South

Carolina' seemed a mouthful, besides I hate double Southern names for Sweet Briar belles like me. Which left me only Mississippi (which I was absent when the others learned to spell). So Alabama Byrnes it is."

"Has a sort of Sherman's forced march feel to it—I see torches, mansions. And it does sound male. 'Gary Cooper *is* Alabama Byrnes.' Has a sort of macho violence about it."

"Male. Good. Scorched earth. What every girl who stands just five foot six needs—name that sounds like some dude with a twelve-inch dick, going on before . . ." We broke into "Onward, Christian Soldiers." I knew the most verses.

Finally she retired this subject, and kicked the loaded trap under her paint cabinet. "I do hope a person can become what she calls herself," Angie said, husky, sober. "I reckon we become whatever it is we play at hardest. Take a wimp like Thomas Lanier Williams. He would never even attempt to write a work as ferocious as *Streetcar Named Desire*. Only a Tennessee Williams could. See, Hartley? I call that self-knowledge. Which is your Alabama's favorite form of self-defense."

"And public relations."

"And public relations. Let's us go eat."

Robert, Darling

I t'd be wrong to say we two competed for him. Instead, especially when he was out of town, we sat at Ossorio's and made tireless catalogues of R.'s merits. How his eyelashes, caught by a peculiar late-day rosy light off the Hudson, glinted like silver. We anatomized his hard herbal smell. I said it resembled crushed geranium leaves; she cited nutmeg cut with fresh basil. We once tried writing down his better-known conquests but soon gave up, very hurt. We'd both caught him climbing out of some limo three blocks from here. That way it'd seem he had come home by subway like the rest of us. We said how, on the aristocratic scale of blondness, yellowblond is country tawdry; silverblonds alone truly reign.

Sometimes he'd disappear for ten whole days. No advance warning. Ten. It drove us crazy; his answering machine would be off, too. We considered phoning the cops, but a quick visit to his place showed no signs of struggle.

Then he'd simply be back at our table in Ossorio's, sitting on the radiator for direct heat. He never explained, he just resumed. "Away. Needed a change. Had to see a man about a bet." (That was one of his lines I'd copied.) He would either return to us tanned in January or else with a greenish pallor, sooty rings disfiguring his eyes. Once he showed up with his ear pierced but, as he never wore an ornament, it soon grew shut. I told him, "Either you're IRA, or still in that three-way with Mick and Bianca. Or there's a li'l opium-eating prob." The look he gave me was God Viewing a Bug.

Home among friends, within three days he grew lustrous as some nicked road-warrior tomcat, limping to ensure his lady owner will put out real cream. R. grew mainly only gorgeous again, if with a certain growing sense of the mileage still tailing him.

I now told her Robbie had just left two sentences on my answering machine, "Lord Airedale, I don't feel we've been using the word LAD enough. Lovely tartany sort of nappy feel to LAD, so do remind us, love."

But we did worry about his music. At his jumbled apartment, with Robert seated before the upright piano, he admitted to us he was writing a tone poem based on the launching then the sinking of the *Titanic*. "Oh?" I asked. It sounded like an idea so good its results'd be pretty terrible. Then Robbie confessed the piece would have two major themes, a sort of Before and After. Maybe we'd like to hear them?

We two sat clumped high on his high bed, riveted by the sight of his outward-tapering chalice of a back. He now played—with old-fashioned Lutheran Sunday school rectitude and flourish: "Bicycle Built for Two," then "Nearer My God to Thee."

Robert turned, saw our faces, laughed until he wheezed. "You guys are already too sophisticated for the likes of this simple-simon preacher's kid."

"I don't know much about music," Angie started. "I mean I'm sure you're a genius, don't get me wrong. But I personally think it's fairly cornball even when Bach recycles 'A Mighty Fortress Is Our God' in about eighty other pieces, and he wrote the fuckin' 'Fortress,' right? At Sweet Briar, in art class, all these twitty debs would clip out their favorite *Vogue* models—including that trampy girl-child you're shtupping—and they would glue photos to canvas board and think they'd actually *done* something. If I can't paint it from scratch, I never use it, except maybe some real object I'd fasten directly to canvas. But then, I'm old-fashioned. I have an aversion to quoting if it's only lifting. But that's just Modernist me. So your pop song and the hymn, I guess they were really played the night it sank?" He nodded. "Robbie, I'm sure you know what you're doing, darling. If not, there's always a place for you in Male Prostitution. Matter of fact, my Granny Byrnes just sent me this fifty-dollar bill. What can Hart and I get off you for that, you OrganGrinderMonkey?"

"For fifty? How you two feel about some dandruff?"

Others, referring to our composer, resorted to the radiant. "Robert's so bright, brilliant really, outshines others, such a fuckin' star." RobertRobert-Robert.

Usually, familiarity breeds disinterest. Just our luck, she told me, we get the one on earth where familiarity only . . . breeds.

He liked boys. Then he liked girls, then a girl'd introduced him to a former boyfriend. Conversions abounded. I reminded him, I was a boy. Ang a girlie, why not just stay home, give at the office? Why not do some Hospitality pineapple popovers for friends?

His glitzy or dorky or well-known boys, the ones he brought to an ever-busier fourposter, I only scoffed at. Angie shredded his showy taste in starlets and Carnaby bird leftovers. "Cheap," Angie judged them. "I hate to use the word 'cheap.' I do. But they paint their lips, and some I'm told actually henna. What are they, in the larger moral scheme of the universe? Buncha fuckin' whores."

Robert Christian Gustafson was seeing the post-deb daughter of a UN lady personage who'd been Adlai Stevenson's mistress, a spoilt Madeleine who now modeled just for fun, not needing the money. Her advanced makeup and tulip of a face were on every fashion mag that year, making Angie insane with jealousy and vicious jokes. (She acquired a *Vogue* subscription and a dartboard the same day.)

Angie told me my big problem, when it came to ever getting into those most ideal of velvet pants (long since copied, even by Alexander's, kiss of death): I considered Robert perfect. "And nobody is ever turned on by real worship. Fake worship, okay. But you, you're idolatrous. I find it increasingly hard to watch. Especially when he sometimes almost notices you." I denied believing in the Gustafson perfection.

"Okay then. Name three of your Robbie's very worst bad faults. Now." She stomped one high-heel boot.

"Well, he's too busy to see us often enough . . ."

"That's not a fault. That's a scheduling glitch, you besotted idiot. Now, me? I do his laundry. I see he has li'l mishaps, has certain fluids to him. Angels don't. See? Angels never sweat. Distressed angels give off a form of powder. At most. I know this from a former life. It's why I'm still so mad for Johnson & Johnson Baby Powder. I do iron Robert's jockeys, I understand accidents happen. But, tell Angie true, sugar—you've got a key, you're over there constantly—have you ever taken home his used undies, tell me true now."

I said absolutely not. No way. Then, faking shamefacedness, I hung my head. "Do . . . socks count?"

She threw a pillow at me.

We were often the only people alive who thought we were the only people alive worth laughing at. When we got going, we could clear the room. We rarely noticed.

Fact is, we were both really waiting. For our Robert to "declare." We both assumed that only a few details and the right mood-lighting stood between us and Robbie's down-on-one-knee offer of a betrothal eternal.

"But what if he actually chose one of *us*?" I asked her, frowning, shocked at the idea. "What would that do to our friendship?"

"Our what? Who are you? I've never seen you before in my life."

"Seriously, Angina. If one of us got to see and feel all of him instead of his wasting it on these inferior society types he keeps balling, then what? I mean, if I found that you'd so much as touched him twice, down there, in the powdery floury part? It'd kill me, honey, wouldn't it you?"

"But, for drill, and to take a more reasoned view (that's how my darling Jimmy Stewart GP of a daddy talks, you'd love him), might it not be better to keep it in the family? —Okay, honestly? if you 'get' Robert before I do? I'll kill you. On first hearing, I might con*sid*er killing you both. But, in the end, after careful consideration, you're the only one that'd have to go."

"I understand."

Robert Christian Gustafson was that baffling creature, someone truly bisexual. Nobody can break your heart like a bi-, babes. Imagine what a long-shot percentage true love really is. Got the odds? Now, from those chances, deduct fifty percent.

There is a *Journal of Bisexuality* with the funniest and truest title: "Anything That Moves." But that phrase feels tragic if applied to the person you yearn for most. If he doesn't phone, it's like somebody turned your iron-lung down to power-saver half speed. You try to wean yourself off the necessary sight of him, you go three days, cold turkey, you tell yourself your pride has begun returning, and you sit down with the *Times* and there, in the society section, at the center of a group of new money charity ladies with smiles like electrocutions, there between two famous old cigar-wielding comedians who've become national institutions, he stands in a tux he borrowed six bucks from you to buy, used. (He never paid you back, did he?) He pivots at the group's center and yet his iridescent smile hints, "This is not important to me, but what a goof, hey, I'll go along, I mean, after all, I'm *here*." It sets you back in your control substance battle. That instant, the phone rings, and Angie's venom at how he would compromise himself to pose with such a low-end Hollywood toupée crowd and those gals wearing diamond chokers to hide their necks' going. "I plan giving his publicist holy Hell for letting the *Times* get their newsprinty mitts on our Prince Golden."

"So now he's got a publicist? Angie, tell me the truth. You think *I* need a publicist?"

"I *am* his publicist, dickhead. Robert is overexposing. For everybody but me."

We all kept keys to each others' places, and sometimes, when I knew he was out of town for a house party or on some dreary Bloomington twelve-tone seminar, or traveling with the Stones' entourage, I'd drift over to his place. Because I could.

Alberta, the seamstress who had told us so many juicy backstage Ziegfeld Follies stories, would be working at her Singer. She kept old show-tune 78s stacked up, one crooner sounding as much like a reed instrument as the thirty saxes behind him sounded brilliantined and male. She'd sometimes leave his apartment door ajar (she also had a key, as did half the neighborhood). Her yellow alley cat called TinPan liked to stare down on the street. Alberta's place, like mine, faced only rearwall. "Makin' something pretty?" I called.

"I tryin'. But this new polyester, you need a screwdriver to stitch into it." I slid inside, I hurried to his fridge. I could open its door, see the light flash on, showtime! I could study a giant brown bottle of vitamin E, the two plates of wilted sushi, could sigh, then meander back home almost refreshed.

Only our plans that failed unleashed the little toxins. Ambitions met, confirmed, achieved, let us revert to lightness, tungsten charm. We became, briefly, sloppy sentimental messes. We gave each other gifts commemorating each advance. Small magic shop novelties. Eggs carved of marble. Week-old genital-shaped cakes from The Erotic Bakery. Because no one really ate them anyway, those cakes.

Back home in Falls, "ambitious" stayed a bad word. "The wife of that new orthodontist overdresses for the Piggly Wiggly and corners you in Deli and calls her baby daughter Crosley and seems . . . 'ambitious.' "

It meant someone not from around here, someone trying to horn in, someone too visibly seeking. The preferred WASP technique was to push, like air pressure, without ever seeming to.

We three stayed blinded by coffee and hope, while playfully working. We confided sensing, like seismologists' sublest needles, that "something huge" was coming. This young, we assumed we'd be its chosen subject. We believed it would want only our work.

We felt a strange and bracing daily fear, one all stage stars recognize as the surefire foreplay to greatness. (Alberta recalled how, in the old days at the Ziegfeld, even little Jimmy Cagney kept a bucket backstage to throw up in. —Plain terror before stepping onto that huge stage each night, the boy was pure talent, but still terrified of how unterrified he now must go out there and be. For all those paying others. In the end, he proved immortal because: He was more afraid of seeming afraid than he was actually afraid. So, he stayed on record.)

Make a Wish

As we sat waiting for Angie to join us at the restaurant, she phoned to say she'd "solved" a five-foot painting that had been driving her (and in turn, us) insane for weeks. She'd just figured how to attach a piece of wood and make it "read" as actual paint. Instead of being miffed at her, we ourselves grew briefly withdrawn. Robert and I felt suddenly overdressed and a tad shallow. Though it was, after all, a Saturday night date-night in flashy New York, we slouched here, we were not home working.

A little better known now, two group shows in, she was even more fun to be with. We were always throwing each other "coming out" parties to mark our latest little "Firsts." First time Robert had a commissioned piece performed outside a church, we were all there, one high-styled pew, holding our confirmation gifts.

Alone together in a tea shop after a great thrift shop sweep, Angie and I wondered if anybody alive is really *not* ambitious. "I think they're afraid of hoping for too much, so they make a merit of killing the wish, just stymying themselves, don't you, Hart?"

I looked at this strange woman I adored—today a choppy brunette with blond roots—and decided there must be some Cherokee blood on her Williams side. Only Indian genes could've given her Mom the Ava Gardner bones so strong that even a clinging fern-curled jewel of Juicy Fruit would not turn you off. I asked Angie what she wanted most. Right this second. She spoke over the sound of frying eggs and a car alarm that'd shrieked till it seemed routine then inaudible. How many Trojan Horses can each of your five senses drag into its gates and unload—vanquishing—concurrently, while you still sorta concentrate, urban artist?

"Apart from scouring Prussian Blue out of these stubby little Millet-gleaner hands? I use Lava and, still, look." She knew, of course. "But, it'll change next second. . . . Even so, right during this one, two wishes leap to my weakened mind. Okay—scenario this: I rush into the lobby of the Museum of Modern Art. It's three or six years ahead of here. Robert is to meet me. I am running just the wee-est bit late, shock of shocks. I bust through the revolving door. Let's make it snowing outside just to heighten the diff between outdoor freeze and indoor heat, umkay, story man? Let's make it being a blizzard because we can and it doesn't cost a friggin' cent more. There he is, waiting, gorgeous in his sheepskin shearling jacket whose cream color sets off the pink patches sunk deep in either downy cheek of him. (I'm still saving to get him that coat.) No surprise—most every eye not fixed on art is locked on him, my husband. He is my husband—since you asked. Do you respect me less for being married by then, for already wanting to? I'd even spring for babies, given a staff of sufficient size.

"By then, see, we're the darlingest, most sought-after, hottest, talent-on-talent couple in town. And our Robert (now mainly *my* Robert, I fear. Can ya cope?) adores me and eats my pussy as his three squares daily and I am so like fused with him, and this is the second part.

"When he sees me, he smiles that lighthouse beacon thing, you know how much heat the first sight of his first smile just for you gives off? Did he practice as a boy? And directly behind him, here comes the second part: (I hate being predictable but that's where my power comes from—isometrics, levees) hangs one of my bigger and arguably most important early paintings (I mean one of the ones I'm doing now, with certain 'collage elements' you'll recognize and I want you to see before they leave the studio).

"But this day at the Modern, I'm already forty, forty-one, in there. The painting is from the Bammie Byrnes raw-ore period, preceding her greater later Periclean stuff. The hits just keep on coming. But however early, all the ideas are there 'in vitro,' it's still visibly mine. In front of the big picture, maybe we can gather a small school group from, say, Brearley? Uniformed girlchild artists gather before the work, enjoying—with the help of a young lezzie teacher who has seen and liked my photo—Alabama's sense of texture, layered planes, perversity of images' slamdancing. And this is the best part of the second part . . . I see his head, his jaw, see Robert's too-true-a-blue-to-trust eyes fixed right on me. Despite every woman in there staring at him including the schoolgirls and several panting Princeton boys, his head is framed by the only picture that MOMA would even, like, consider putting out so you'd see it first thing. Not enough, being in the collection upstairs, tucked behind partitions with those uneven others. No, it has to be like this: There is the information booth, two ticket counters, some backless benches, the huge plant, the coat check sign, the Alabama Byrnes, the six chrome ashtrays, and the drop-dead husband of the painter running toward her.

"Something like that. Banal, but there you are. I didn't choose it but it's mine. More coffee? Here . . . you've got a touch of foamed milk on one corner of your lovely sad little mouth. There, got it. No more caf for you? Me? I just cain't seem to get enough today to even think half-straight enough to even *start* to work."

Same afternoon, I received what appeared to be a love note from my gifted student, Tony Wu. The week before I had stressed the utility of semicolons. His letter proved a clove-orange of them. Tony's handwriting spun along, refined yet forward-leaning.

I felt disturbed that he, so protected, had somehow learned my dive's whereabouts. Had he filched it from his mother's green-silk-bound address book, one she carried with her everywhere?

"Mr. Hartley, sir;
I feel that we have much interest in common despite our age differences and my mother; joint fascinations might well unify us at a differing more advanced personal level ahead. What you say to this, sir? I am sure your leisure time is limited; you have what seems to me a big need to be creating creating creating! Even Mother says you can teach Tony

far more than thank-you notes; I receive excitement when you speak of Literature; I also notice certain of your recent looks; remember when Brigidhe brought in yesterday's tea; remember the look you then gave me?; perhaps a moment savored or a touch of one of the hands might could be someday fun? You must not underestimate us because my father is prospering now as imports lately catch on. In ways, I am a political prisoner of Park Avenue; I long to know more working men such as you; carpenters I consider excellent. Tony is all too human; Saturdays she shops . . ." Oh, no noo, Tony, thirteen.

Then I spied my own mother's usual blue envelope and somehow it looked particularly charged and, I knew it! They'd invited themselves North—to Christmas shop, to "see the windows," to "catch several of the better current shows, though there will never be another My Fair L., will there?" and to get a tour of "your new life and your attractive young artist friends."

Oh, help me, Lord.

Our Mentors

ecause we were all variously talented, and totally sociable, because we mainly looked pretty good, if only from being kids, and because, having got here, we now scouted our own field for those non-parental elders we most admired and because, despite what many think, however famous an artist is—having sacrificed her/his life to be an artist—no amount of fame ever suffices, and no acclaim is sweeter than that from somebody twenty-six and smart and still so very new-minted, someone who sees exactly how original you are within the mechanical limitations of your form, we soon found our ways to our idols, however incognito, however unlisted.

And because no one is ever likelier to offer you a truer picture of your genius than someone newish to town and feeling only expanded by your pioneer work in personal expression, you—new mentor, old fogey—soon invite the kids over for drinks.

Angie asked me along to meet a man whose paintings I had studied in coffee table books belonging to the Falls Public Library. The size of the great one's loft impressed me; it was big as a tobacco warehouse back home. His curatorial-managerial wife, all Hopi jewelry and peasant braids, looked us over with the harsh Swiss interest of a metal detector. Their place was so perfect it might have belonged to two closeted young stockbrokers posing, weekends, as The Arts.

When the genius appeared, from a nap, still puffed, jowlier than any photos ever indicated, I marveled at how young his recent work still looked. Reverse Dorian Gray. In life, his ears sprouted ant farms of hair. His manner was easy, within the confines of his right to brag. His mind was a Who's Who address book of Legends Only. Reputation, his among others, strong-armed his every reminiscence. "So, an aspiring writer?" he asked, and then was midstory about Wallace Stevens.

I felt thrilled to be in the presence of a fellow who as a college boy had taken the train to Hartford, camped outside the Beaux Arts insurance office where Stevens worked and, twice, walked home with the great poet (though the boy was never invited in for cocktails). Still, the painter had quoted Stevens to Stevens while Stevens quoted the same Stevens back to him but better. It was, for me, like hearing that Zeus still swam Tuesdays and Thursdays at the pool of the 92nd Street Y.

I felt flattered by this artist's kindness. He'd had the rare sense to collect the very best of his own contemporaries; he'd had the luck not to need to hock them later. They were all on view. The small Rothko was the best Rothko in the world and when I said it was, when I said that it seemed painted in tears, our hosts blandly agreed. For forty years, the painter and his wife had attended every twist and turn of New York interior decoration. The design of their loft looked younger and far hipper than Ang and I. Amid this season's brushed chromium furniture, blond elm and frosted glass, our pouchy elders appeared Iowan farmers uneasily house-sitting for their drug-dealing grandson.

The artist would send Angie to fetch a cheeseboard across the quarter mile of loft, just to see her walk away from him. His eyes sensed mine, already mustard-plastered there. Turning to judge the scope of my claim, he smiled simply, "A fellow enthusiast! Excellent judgment you have, young man. Her . . . back, it's one in ten thousand, non?" And though her ass had led me to her, I watched his famous eyes return there; I joined them, feeling while feeling trepidation, strange pride, and some awe. Those eyes, Wallace Stevens, Angie's heavenly butt. The Family of Man!

Maestro enjoyed her nerve, her interest in him. (She was good for running specialty errands; she proved decorative at middle-aged parties.) I warned her he was a tailman on her trail. "Sherlock here," she shook her head, pitying.

Ang told me: The wife was diabetic. Whenever she clanked off for a doctor's appointment, Maestro phoned Angie. As inducement, he scattered a trail of breadcrumbs leading to the couple's loft bed.

The intended narcotic: dropped names sprinkled across the secret histories of his own best-known masterpieces. Ang resisted, saying she respected him too much. She felt weak at what he'd done with the color gray. "Not since Manet . . ." etc. He visited her studio and, the second he saw her work, Maestro was so struck he never groped or ogled her again. He had not known that she was also "good." In some rare cases, being good can keep you good.

What she learned from her master—in the year before he dropped dead at Brown University's commencement before a crowd of ten thousand while receiving yet another honorary degree—proved less arcane than brushwork tips or hints about his work's spiritual sources. Instead of a philosophy of aesthetics, instead of how to prepare canvas with rabbit's foot glue available only from one trapper outside Winnipeg, Angie's mentor taught her:

How to "handle" an egoistic gallery owner who thinks she's the artist because she represents so many; their shows come and go while only her name remains forever frozen in those foothigh letters across plateglass; here only she is news, and permanent. First be nice to her, and eventually do your best just once at Scrabble (she's a friend) and then ignore her. She will find you with a favor.

How to cope with a batch of visiting Texas collectors who are staying at the Pierre, and would you consider taking their youngest daughter shopping for leather miniskirts, at the hipper shops downtown? (No.) How to buy linen wholesale direct from Holland from a man who's actually van Gogh's great-great first cousin, and how to serve the cheaper wine in cut-glass decanters so nobody'll know it's Gallo, and ways to greet, seemingly by nickname, "Old Man" "*Here* he is," the critics who know you but whose names you—daily besieged—have long since lost.

Cross-pollenating across generations, Angie brought Maestro current pop recordings she insisted he must know, songs he would quote in his next show's titles, further luring the youth vote. He had remained a young Turk since 1954. (This was partly a legacy of eighty earlier Angies. Always skinny girls, almost lethally hip. Six of them had OD'd, but most of them prospered, while forever after praising him.)

During my fourth visit to his loft with Angelina, she blurted after a few drinks something she'd clearly been preparing to blurt. It sure got Maestro's attention and, even more, his ethnic jewelry store of a cost-accounting wife's.

"I don't know how you let those early paintings of yours stay nailed up all around the University of South Carolina. "They're ones you must have done during that probably-miserable summer session when your mom was dying of throat cancer, I guess. You were, what? just nineteen but already scraping on the oil paint, gouging so it'd resemble the encaustic you've since used to such neoclassic effect. I think those are about the first of your map and target works. Probably you forgot and just left them, maybe when your Mom finally died? Well, the guys in Buildings and Grounds stuck them up in dorms and they are signed by you and dated and I have a girlfriend (who's only enrolled there so she can be close to this cloddish if scarily good-looking frat boy, idiot, but humongousy trust fund), and Karen says she will gladly smuggle them out and ship all seven pictures to your dealer— if you'll just tell me your gallery's UPS account number. —Oh, you want them sent right to *you*? Is HERE good? Well, they surely are yours, okay. You starting to remember? Great. No telling how much they're worth now. —To art historians, I mean."

And if a kid like Angie is bright (and you, Mentor, invite over only the crackerjack ones who need not be told what you pioneered and why you're important)—she will keep you in the address book, as the crown jewel of that book, even after spurning your forthright early advances during your wife's post-insulin nap.

And when Angie speaks (sooner than you know) at your funeral, her gratitude, her skilled eloquence on your behalf (I helped her with the speech)—her telling the fourteen hundred present (plus the international reporters)—how you wanted nothing but to encourage a kid's excellence and to guard younger gifts, how you found her a Texas collector all her own, how you asked absolutely niente in return, how you simply wished to be a small part of art's own continuous and self-renewing community—she will prove how right you were to choose her—to quietly, of all people in all the noisy places, help this child first.

Not a dry eye, in the church, at the funeral, of you, a genius, and also, apparently, a mensch, being—for this beautiful, still-mostly-untested and someday maybe-famous kid—her saintly selfless mentor.

As with art itself, what's unique is: everybody gets something.

The Continuous Audition

long with coaching youths Harvard-bound, I became a sperm donor—thirty dollars a pop, tax free, cash and carry. No job interview ever proved so painless. Robert and I tried out the same day. I'd joked with friends that, given my endless need to please, volume one of my memoirs should be called *The Continuous Audition*.

At the sperm bank, it didn't matter that my blue blazer still looked borrowed. Alone in the concentration booth with its black chaise (vinyl for quick cleaning), its single desk lamp (in case you needed the dark), its big big box of Kleenex, its stack of *Playboy*s with one *Playgirl* slid underneath, hooray! you were not required to look your tiptop dreamiest.

I remember settling the clear cylindrical container, still hot to the touch, into the hand of a young redheaded woman at the reception desk. "We'll call you," she winked, and, for once, they did. Robert was not summoned; he sulked a day or two then turned my potency to joke. Great-great grandson of Increase Hartley, turns out my wriggler count was off the charts. "Wait," Robert said. "Something's slipping out under your right pant cuff. My God, it's the head of an eighteen-month-old boy-child."

"Very funny," said I; but looked.

Thirty dollars meant a fortune then. I still recall the feel of fresh bills in an active right hand that had just easily coaxed forth another eureka! deposit, headed right into our nation's gene pool. "Fully ten inseminations can be achieved from one male ejaculation," the lobby's antiseptic brochure explained my cum's fiscal validity, splitting stock. "The technique was first advanced by an Italian scientist who wanted the semen of every Italian soldier to remain on file. That way, if some young man were killed at war, his widow might still bear his child." —Now there is a project to administer, hands-on. —Sergeant? Atta boy, aim here, prego.

I now toyed with one definition of infantilized happiness: a state where every fluid leaving your body is valuable to someone. It will bring assured cash and motherly goo-goo congrats. There was the soothed feeling, newly jacked-up and expertly jacked-off by the in-house Master at that, the sweetness of stepping (flush!) onto businesslike pearl-gray Madison Avenue. And nobody knowing.

You snapping your baby-new ten-dollar bills, a player, a hunger artist, a hair trigger for hire.

In Solvency

had grown up the grandson of small-time merchant landowners. I once thrived in a world where particular and ancient trees gave their names to streets. Our rivers had been titled for eighteenth-century families whose great-great-grandkids I played with.

During the Depression, my father's parents and his five sibs ate only beans and rice from one Thanksgiving till the following Easter. Even the littlest kids agreed it'd be worth it—to save for that piece of fertile bottomland adjoining their own best acreage.

—Dad's folks would later lavish every Sunday after-church, dressed up like Mr. and Mrs. Gotrocks, her hat pinned into place, driving all over creation admiring green fields made interesting because we owned them. It's like a tale from Grimm—amazing what you can get for beans (especially during that bad a Bank scare!).

So, the first economic concept to seep into my young brain, even before my "soft spot" hardened?: "They don't make any more land."

The need to have our name on every deed, that surely registered. How could I explain to my city friends that these grandparents—who looked a bit like Okies, and who reused envelopes—by now owned half the county?

And I? Somehow a New Yorker, I lived from one patched-together rent check to another, lived in a leaky building I wouldn't buy if I could afford it. My grandfather's parting advice the night I trooped North for college: "Hartley, number one'd be, if you know who you are in Falls, you'll know who you are in the world. Number two, when in doubt, say so, at the top of your lungs. Number Three's a large one: Don't rent, own."

Words to live by.

* * *

And I could barely make the rent. It always seemed the last week of the month; I wasn't either brazen or good-looking enough to sell my body for that kind of cash. My parents weren't poor; but the idea of offering me monthly payments (in exchange for what?) would've struck them as unmanly and debilitating; maybe they were right. Sure they were.

I was far too chickenshit to steal effectively. It was rent I needed. It would determine where I slept as of the evening of the first. First of January. By now, the streets were sheet ice. Even diehard dogwalkers kept placing Jip in the bathtub, then standing alongside with a handheld shower unit, saying, "Go, Jip, go." —Can't have been easy for Jip, either.

I recall I had $4.13, I needed fifty bucks more, and by six p.m. It was ten in the morning and four below zero. I had spent my Tony-tutoring money on one little Federal mirror, a deal, but for me costly. I had run through my other cash during a single office supply visit—besides coffee, my favorite legal vice. I hoarded twenty-four-pound typing paper, high in rag content. I needed to keep at least three reams at arm's length from both my desk and futon. Just as some mothers of six cannot sleep without milk in the house, I required quality blank white in easy reach. I believed that anything one human being could think (about his own condition) might be set down in writing (specifically my own). What I didn't know was: Just how little, most days, most of us get to know about our present state.

I'd frequented my sperm depository so often, my jism's motile count was flagging. I'd need to let sufficient wrigglers build back up. Never touch your capital, son. I had pilfered the futon's folds twice. I even patted under it, found nothing but crispy fossilized insects that I let be. I now assumed my frantic month's-end hunting-gathering.

Unannounced, I stopped by Robert's apartment, yelling into the intercom, "Moi." I wouldn't borrow from him, he had nothing. Whisked away at night in friends' Jaguars, by day he cleaned strangers' apartments. I just needed the stamina his example and beauty provided. "A fix," Angie called it, with that word's bogus hint at true repair. He'd now become the dispensary and mascot-leader for more crowds than ours. Poor Robbie was so cool he never understood it. Is not that the definition?

Gustafson never led by "leading," more by being, which meant doing. Our homages forever surprised and flummoxed him. During good reviews, Robert averted his crystal blue eyes till praise finally ended. Coast clear. "You don't know how deeply flawed this mirror is." And yet, he needed compliments as much as we. More. Since his "tolerance" had been stretched far larger.

Robert's resistance to hyperbole just made offering Robert-praise-songs more fun. (It still is. Hear me?)

He'd paid retail for one thing only: the American 1820s fourposter pineapple-crested bed. We orbited it.

His own erotic leftovers and referrals, they dutifully seduced us; finger foods he smuggled home from ever fancier parties, verily these fed us too. His encouragement, from so far in, took note of our work's technical babysteps ("You are weaning yourself off even the occasional adverb. Good, Hart. Adverbs are the monosodium glutamate of speech. It's another sure sign of your genius flexing to become pure verb. My baby Merlin— 'You make them laugh, make them cry, get them hungry, or hard or wet' . . . You've already got the keyboard's full potential in your two-octave reach, child") that sort of Robert kindness fed us most.

His red door rested ajar, the green suit, stuffed toward scarecrowness with the *Times*, hung above a filling kitchen sink. It was being steamed for tonight's serial bashes—poor man's dry cleaning. Curled nude as Maja Undraped, framed in the huge bed, surrounded by a fanned-out score, Robert, smiling, greeted me. Clear plastic dimestore half-specs perched on his nosetip; one smudge of black ink made a crescent moon of his cheekbone. There were towers of aging scrapbooks concerning the *Titanic*'s sinking. Atop his black Chickering upright—one of Angie's smaller paintings, wildly yellow, outlines of toy cars painted over it in heavy black impasto. A gift. Your eye went right to it, amid all this stuff. (She had never given me one.) In the far corner, four sets of red Swedish-made cross-country skis and their old-timey poles. Crystals, presents from the love-struck worldwide, scintillated in each window. Lead soldiers bivouacked above the sink. His antique pen collection nested in an Easter basket. On a wire hanger, one unreturned rental—an eighteenth-century burgundy-red brocade frock coat, and its powdered wig. Upon the window ledge, a ten-gallon aquarium filled only with water supporting an exquisite scale model of the doomed liner. It was complete with thread for rigging, the correct inadequate number of lifeboats.

Robert's whole place smelled of fresh-sliced oranges, sunlight widening each white wall. Thirty prisms' rainbows seemed whole notes trying—then rejecting—various locations. The boombox (new word then) blasted Peter Pears singing an English folk about some beloved sailor drowned at the height of youth.

And I told Robert I was broke. He laughed, "So what else is new? Maybe you'll find another Queen Anne sidechair on Madison and sell it for six hundred cool ones." (That had been a major coup, never repeated.)

He suggested I phone my sperm bank, say I'd eaten oysters, swear I'd had a no-win weekend, had read the complete Henry Miller and felt ready early. Or call my Tony prodigy and ask his Mom to fund, for her son, a tour of meat-packing-district gay bars; and maybe bring along Madam dressed in leather? She'd look very *Terry and the Pirates*.

Robert was my address book's first to be tattooed. On his left pectoral, behind one forward-sailing clef sign, a five-line musical staff awaited notes. The way these crisp blue lines rode the upper quadrant of his pinky-gold chest made you want to place your own notes there, using the clear ink of your own melodic spittle.

Robert, ripe of baritone, with his platinum pubic hair, his curving rose-colored dick and its birthmark shaped not unlike a valentine heart, went on immodestly inking the notes of his own First Symphony. I marveled that he could get in at three and be up by seven, this hard at work. (And he hadn't even known that I was coming.) The harder he partied, the better Robert seemed to concentrate. I wondered why I rejoiced less, revised more.

Hand still moving over wet notes that looked, to my illiterate eyes, like some headband made of stars, he now recounted favored moments from last night's three best parties.

He had met an old starlet, a famous minor thirties ingenue, Groucho Marx's lover; she had, after four drinks, described in detail Groucho's sexual preferences, then . . . "Listen to this, Hartley . . ." he pointed to a black ghetto blaster the size of a baby coffin. Peter Pears's isinglass tenor sang,

> 'Neath this hulk lies poor Tom Bowling,
> The darling of our crew,
> No more he'll hear the tempest howling,
> For death has broached him, too.
> His form was of the rarest beauty.
> His heart was kind and soft.
> Faithful below he did his duty,
> Now Tom is gone aloft,
> Now Tom is gone aloft.

Before

"Good, hunh? And after a fifth drink, she described Harpo's own erotic likes and zoo noises. Harpo, ambisexual it seems, was mute only while 'in character.'"

"Sandwiched between Marx brothers. Talk about a circus in bed," I stood, hands testing the depths of my back pockets for some stray fiver. We discussed the song, the sailor, Benjamin Britten playing the piano as his lover so simply sang.

While Robert worked, I wandered his place, enjoying its surface comforts; like all of us, he was a visual glutton; that's part of what pulls the retinally stronger to stroboscopic Manhattan. Eye greed: five thousand faces seen at once, and it's still not enough. Where is the long-sought One?

He belonged to a society of fanatics on the subject of the *Titanic*. A smitten member had given him this handbuilt watertight scale model. During one recent confab here, grown men played at submerging this model while debating the several theories of how it broke apart, settled where. Robert told me that, till its last few minutes, the great ship's lights had remained blazing. This detail (sinking, shining) seemed significant and, as with so many facts about Robert then, I stored it away, some tenderboat provisioning itself for later, just in case.

He continued silently composing. I was hungry but didn't want to bore him with it, I longed to climb in bed and hold him, touch him, maybe sing to him, more, but knew he wouldn't like it. He would say no kindly. I never had been asked up the gangplank into that galleon bed.

So I did a tugboat tour of the apartment's snug harbor. It seemed that, in Manhattan, there were only two kinds of places: Out and In. Of the "in" ones, there were two further sorts: Others' many spaces, and your one. It didn't matter if your room, like mine, was closet-sized; it had to be this stocked with charms and amulets, just to let a guy break even in a tempest so harsh as the New York waiting downstairs.

His phone rang, Angie. I knew just from Robert's smiled "Ahh," how he cut his eyes my way, said, "Yes." He told her I was in fine spirits but low on cash. She explained that a friend who worked for a catering service called Glorious Food was too sick to waitperson a party at the American Indian Museum, wherever that was, and how his tuxedo would just fit me and he was forced to find his own replacement but couldn't till now, and if I would bus right over to his place, she would have him leave the tux hanging from his doorknob so I wouldn't catch his Hong Kong flu, and I could head direct to her place and change, and did that sound okay? If so, she would arrange it. Robert jotted a stranger's address

107

on a scrap of five-lined music paper in his personality script. It looked valuable.

"Well, guess I'm off . . ."

"Much luck with dispensing those finger foods to the Sioux, and Godspeed with the rent. If waitressing fails, I hear there's a Professor Fagin at the New School teaches a course in the undetectable pickpocketing of Rolex watches and East Side pocket hankies . . ."

I asked if a boy could pay the tuition *after* learning the trade. His boombox, set to Repeat All, had taken us clear back around to the drowned one, darling of our crew.

> He seemed so light and jolly
> Many's the time and oft,
> But Mirth has turned to Melancholy.
> Poor Tom has gone aloft . . .

"Anyway." He looked back into my looking back at him, "You'll think of something, Hardly Ever Sad. All you want is 'a chair somewhere' . . ." And Robert made a kissing mouth, so I tipped up, and smacked him goodbye on his cheek's crescent moon of ink and felt insulted he did not need more.

"RobRoy? You know how much I respect you." I risked this. "With one exception."

He heard my troubled tone, set his pen down, peered over the glasses. As Robbie shifted, his male member, formerly loungelizarding leftwardly, rolled, significant, right. "So what's my lapse? I can take it."

"You never saw fit to seduce me."

He gave me this strange look and then a smile leveled itself, angelically deranged. Sign of such satellite distance. He reached over and pinched my cheek, not quite hurting it.

"Oh no?" he said.

I tried smirking, felt broken, said "Toodles," left. He'd just told me I'd long since been "had" by him. He'd got the best of me while giving me, in fact, quite little.

Are any eyes ever colder then beloved glass-blue ones while being so mean? First I earned the needed money, played waiter, then lingered outside Angie's. I would never interrupt her painting. When she finally appeared, Ang saw my face, said, "What?" I explained. Was I overreacting? She could tell me. I could take it.

We strolled around the Village for an hour and a half. She kept glancing over at me, her face placid with a shrewd patience that bordered on pity. "You don't have a clue who you're dealing with, Sweetness and Light. I mean, let's say—conservatively—there are thirty other capable people in New York who love that boy as we do. Now think how cunning he must be to avoid the thirty-two of us, our expectations, all day every day. And yet, to find a way to keep the whole crowd interested. Miracle is, he has anything left over to write down as music, even bad music. Fact is, in most ways, he's to die for. We both know that. But it's a sinkhole, loving somebody already as noticed as a Robert Gustafson. You have to either do it, or not. But do it only if that makes you feel more vivid, Hart. There are ways of stopping it. For happiness's sake—just don't expect much of anything from him. Okay?"

So, being unrequited love, it was never solitude, more socialism. Privacy lived only in the privacy of art, which was, if not yet public, then at least intended as universal from the beginning. Promiscuity? A revolving door back into community. Our life together was not quite drudgery, since it mainly meant being so young. I had little else past this: I lived my work, I loved my fascinating troubled friends. I phoned my folks each Sunday drinktime. One stiff drink in, fortified to fake the love I only felt head-on by faking.

And since my work was mostly promissory, that meant the love alone—even love of those too booked to quite respond—was all that really held me here. Still, it seemed enough. We thought we were really hotshot something.

I was, therefore, less a renter, more someone who owned, being owned.

Ways Means

ngie, like us, lived wild on purpose. She gave "the look" to middle-aged butchers and young CEOs, and succeeded with both and later recalled each clench in encyclopedic detail. "So, how *was* he?" we asked each other the next morning by phone. Before asking, we made sure we had our coffee mugs in hand.

Though it cost her, she was very "good" at whatever she undertook. She did say often that—she had to be. I wondered if Angie might not be overdramatizing.

She kept insisting how hard it was for women to show paintings; she snorted at my skepticism. So one Saturday, dressed up, Angie took me to my own list of the ten finest uptown galleries. In her best Lois Lane mode, she asked at each blond frontdesk to see the roster of artists represented, please. It was, she said, for a "piece" she was researching. "Secret is," she explained to me on 57th Street, "*I* am the piece." Five of the ten places showed either no women, or two. I held the stacked inventory, men. I don't know why, whenever confronted by human stupidity, I feel personally to blame. Maybe being the eldest child is a disease I'll never shake. My fantasies are rescue fantasies; my cross to bear has someone else's name on it. And here it was again: four hundred males listed, twenty-six females. Eight of those, German!

"You win," I said.

She said, "If only . . ."

Our relation to New York had changed. We now walked faster, said more with fewer words, dressed down oftener, dressed up better. We each owned formal clothes—thrift-shop ones; but by now they'd been worn so often they seemed second skin. We expected less, but from our safer, lower spots—some central chambers of the anthill—we all still baby-sat each other's sweetest hopes. Though we were as yet undiscovered, the three of us now acted like guest-curators of The Getting Place itself. We watched new kids arriving, running into buildings while looking up at bigger buildings, we laughed at their ascots and cigarette holders. "Wouldn't you love to get ahold of that cute blond one on the end and strip him down and dress him right?" she asked.

"Yes," Robert answered. "If only to spare him your taste in clothes."

When we failed to find it wholesale, we knew who'd know. If we raged about this sewer-moat-and-fountain, we did so to survive it. Our gripes were no longer those of supplicating children; they were the tongue-lashings you'd only visit on your lover—the lover you assume will always be, however irritating and delusional, your lover.

This same New York allowed Robert his hidden love nests, his vices we still loved imagining; it let me patrol for "story background" in The Sequin District, on The Diamond Block, The Flower Market, where I asked questions Angie-like. Claimed I was doing "a piece." I steadily played at learning. This same quarrelsome fond New York somehow let our Angie earn a living. But how?

Before

* * *

I'd known her for a good while now, and yet the central source of her subsistence stayed a secret. She'd made sure of that. I knew she received no regular money from her parents; I knew she could still claim no gallery, though she sometimes sold things out of her studio. My great aunt mailed me a hundred-dollar check, insisting that I "spend it all in one evening on someone fun and nice."

So, one rainy night, I used the last of it for our actual cab ride all the way downtown after a good Italian meal. (At two a.m., a fluorescent subway home can really shoot your atmospheric evening.) Just as Angie and I approached our neighborhood, just when the security of one's home-slum kicked in, I stroked her short and hardened hand, "One thing you've held back—how you earn the cashola, hon. Will you finally trust Hartley with that? I mean—hooking? stealing? Because, I can take it."

I heard a twisting of clothes, I heard one long swallow in the dark. She stared straight ahead.

"Come on, Ang. It can't be worse than whoring or thieving. After all, I teach. I wank off into sterile little bottles to make babies for Connecticut. Your means of livelihood can't be no more dastardly than that, art girl." She nodded four times, yes. Hers was. She asked aloud how many years we'd known each other. She swore me to full secrecy, forever, okay?

She sighed, finally beckoning my head toward her mouth. Using cupped hands as megaphone, my Angie whispered a single sad sad word, breaking it in three. Each unit popped against my ear:

"Wait-ress-ing."

—As males, we'd been born blind to the very exemptions manliness extended us. As guys-guys if gay ones, Robert and I still somehow felt promised our own Blue Ribbon distributorships, even as we made bitter fun of those. Thanks to mother-love and daddy's name, we believed our work, if good, would naturally, in time, get noticed.

Angie, born with huge talent, ready to title the wall-sized canvases *Volcano-Appliance* and *Vortex Armor Battle IV*, often raged, freely cried, lived racked by an insecurity that her male friends found (if silently) absurd. When she fell into one of her underclass moods, any little thing could set her off.

One evening at Ossorio's, I noticed she'd spread makeup under her right eye, it looked swollen. She often experimented with clothes and excess rouge, dolled up like some not-that-smart drag queen—trying things for pure effect, rarely knowing what was "good" on her. Once Angelina tried to indent her cheekbones with powder; Ossorio asked if she had "the blisters." Robert would often shake his head: "You're hopeless. Phone me and describe it before you wear it out of your place. As a service to Manhattan's many-peopled streets."

Now, leaning closer, I saw that, despite fast-smeared foundation (in far-too-nutty-a-brown for so pink an Angie), her right eye had been blacked. "Honey, who *did* this to you? Because your baby brother will now go out and hurt them bad." I feared that Ang's sexual experiments had crossed some dicey new frontier.

"Funny. I guess *I* did. Get so frustrated. Got my slides back from another uptown gallery and you know they sent them fourth-class mail so it took weeks. And then I spilled, Hartley, I hate myself for this, but I, no one else, spilled coffee . . . on the big new drawing? That one you liked, best damn one, and I felt so. . . . I hit myself."

"Next time"— I misadapted Robbie's lessons—"phone me first. Here, let me kiss it better?" I closed my eyes and bent near. I fancied I could heal whatever they had done to Angie to make her The Heavyweight Champion of Knocking Our Own Angie Out. What do we do to our best women?

"Hey, you! that hurt. Some doctor you are, Ben Casey! Is it still covered? More coffee? Fucker's throbbing now."

Here recently, she showed only under the name Alabama Byrnes. One early collector insisted she return to his apartment and change his early painting's signature of A. Z. Byrnes. (We laughed; but I would later marvel at the auction dollar-value of his sound consumer sense.)

"One reason it's good, my 'Alabama,' the jerks won't ever get to hold my sex against me, see?"

"Yeah," I said, "like George Eliot."

"Who? He that old English guy, hermit, shows those painterly little cow and apple things at Davis-Langhorne? When is Robert coming?"

Alabama Byrnes was achieving the sort of early territorial standing that precedes official statehood. She was already being admitted to small group exhibits if only often on Long Island; she was sometimes singled out in a review. And yet that never seemed to help her titanic crippled confidence float fully upright for very long. She had started, our Angie Bama Byrnes, with strangely little hope considering the scope of her talent. She'd got her old-family doctor daddy's brains, his memory for names and dates and prognoses; she'd inherited her mom's country people energy, along with their strange clannishness, that hot-cold redneck detachment from their own consequences. Expect very little; but use all your energy almost getting there.

By the time Angie was a kid, her mother just wanted to be a serious bridge player. Her mother sulked, like the versatile Wallis Warfield, craving a better title than mere Duchess. Mrs. Byrnes must've taken out her discontent on the very child that Savannah had blackballed on Jewel Fern's account.

Even with steady application, even twenty-four hours of daily obsession, never let our Angie completely believe. Her blind love of Robert seemed, like mine, a displaced form of self-respect she didn't feel quite worthy of. She could tell you where her career would be at the start of the next century, including names of galleries and curators, but one indifferent remark from someone at an opening—where the indifferent cracks were considered kind—could send her weeping to the Women's Room or out into the blind wet night.

Boys and girls, Robert and I agreed, are more different that we'd ever imagined back home. The very thing that seemed to make our women friends so capable of empathy—the harp-scouting for others—became, they swore, their own worst enemy. Many disavowed any automatic tenderness as self-destructive.

We truly wished to offer them confidence—like donated blood we'd hardly miss. But Robert and I couldn't give Angie a transfusion of our own dick-swinging birthright certainty: Our dim belief (transferred to us by doting moms) that what we did mattered because, hey, we had done it! Watching Robert and me sit around assuming, Angie sometimes sobbed. We shrugged off her charges. Then she really sobbed. She once tried pounding our chests, overturning more cold coffee. This time, onto us. "What?" we said, as we signaled—like young lords—for paper towels over here, please. Quick, please, thank you, Ossorio, my good man. That really set her off.

But, during sulks, while racked by killer mood swings, menstrual telegraphy, throughout unaccountable rages, while she complained that, when she introduced me to a woman friend, my chair had been nearly two inches nearer to that stranger's than to hers, Angie worked. "Just to show or break even, we girls have to be four times as good as most of these jerks." She meant men, but men generally. Not always us. By then, other males were joining our small Circle at Ossorio's.

It was from Angie we all learned to work full-out. A good policy, growing twice the normal rate at what you do. It made the bunch of us—us boys willing to be oversupple and listening as girls, and us girls hoping to get armored as most boys who're born Juniors—become better artists faster.

My parents received my calls each Sunday evening, one round into their holy bourbon and my own. They used their speakerphone. This device dared personal intimacy; it had all the nuance of a junior high school intercom; the folks seemed to like that part. One-on-one calls now became suspicious, possibly divisive. A speakerphone let them monitor each other; bad Radio Shack amplification forced my own news into the spritely tone of their friends' Christmas letters: *"Fifteen-year-old Kirsten's bell-ringing group took top prize again at the Boulder meet! Congrats, Kirsten. We're not a bit surprised!"*

"So, how are things in The Sewer? Can you swim yet?" my dad, long distance, asked, chuckling every goddamn time.

This particular Sunday, after informing them I had booked their room at a hotel I hoped they'd like, after telling my folks I was still trying to learn enough to simply start to write well, "What else?" my father asked, his tone dry as some antique wheat-based dog biscuit.

"They're paying me for my sperm up here."

I imagined how it sounded, blared from their tinny speaker tucked behind the houseplants. "I mean I've been asked to be a donor." For their sake, I softened facts into seeming some award.

Silence ran right on till my dad cleared his throat. He quizzed me about the secrecy provision—how would I prevent such children, sired anonymously, from someday finding me? Then Senior asked Junior, "And if they do track you down, son, where does the Law stand on all this? I mean, would you have to pay for their college educations?'"

I laughed at his resentment of my steep tuition. Then, slowly, my folks did. But I knew I'd really surprised him. Maybe that'd been my secret-cocksman goal? True, his first concern has been for me; but mainly in protecting whatever of his cash I might inherit, and hiding that from a knowledge-starved swarm of my scattered juniors.

(After four years' doning, I would learn from that indiscreet and therefore valued red-haired secretary, "I'll hold up a certain number of fingers": I had become the actual father of, actually, six. They're now in tenth grade somewhere. Working toward those full scholarships to Harvard, I hope. Waitressing, summers, possibly. Character-building.

Sit down at your personal computers, crack a couple codes, and come find yer sassy Daddy, my pretty far-flung darlings!)

Twelve Steps Forward

 ne morning a few years into our unseemly Robert worship, Angie's and mine, I chanced to be headed home from an unloving Ed-like assignation in the West Forties. I chanced to look up at a Greek Orthodox church, its onion dome so unlikely, plunked down in this neighborhood of peep shows, musical comedy, and bus fumes. I saw our/my Robert, wearing a coat and tie, seated on a low wall, smoking, alone at the rear doorway of the church.

Of course, I dashed right back there. The side path was gravel and the sound of my shoes crunching reminded me of some eager bounding animal. I noticed a slight cast fall over Robert's face. I recalled his name for me, Lord Airedale; I understood that, though spunky, loyal dogs, and clean, Airedales cannot be counted the intellectual giants of dogdom, now can they?

After kissing both his offered dewy cheeks, I asked what he was doing so near a church so non-Lutheran and at ten a.m.?

"Hartley," he said, flipping away his cigarette, signing toward an open basement room where two old ladies in matching yellow cardigans set up folding chairs. " 'My name is Robert and I'm an alcoholic and substance abuser.' "

I looked into blue eyes. "You're not kidding, are you?"

He shook his head no. I almost blurted, Why didn't you tell me? I could have helped! But even *I* heard the presumption in this. My feelings for him suddenly seemed all wrong. Did he view me mainly as his pet, his gopher? True, I often fetched clean music paper for him at Associated. In the long line of our PO, it was I who retrieved his boxes of Iowa baked goods, feeling as wrong as honored. So, why had I not been offered a crack at easing something as major as addiction?

Perfect strangers wandered up, seeming to adore him, and he bussed them and they all talked rehab. The others treated Robert Christian G. like some young parish priest whose fine looks must never be mentioned, never held against him, simply enjoyed in reverent eucharistic silence. One smiling businesswoman now pulled a packet from her briefcase, "Last month, you said you collected these. This one was in my mother's house, part of an old gas lamp," and she unwrapped the crystal pendant that at once took fire in daylight.

"Rhoda, you're a saint, remembering. It'll be the prettiest one I have, the absolute star. Bless you."

Folks filed inside now. He gestured, might I care to join them? Knowing I would miss the first fifteen minutes of my rent-paying lesson with Tony Wu, knowing I'd endure the servants' glee and Tony's hurt and the Madam's quiet burn—I stepped downstairs. For my first meeting. I recognized Verne, the beer delivery man. When time came, I introduced myself. Typically, I nearly admitted to an addiction that still ranked among the few not really mine.

Listening, I was soon struck by what I'd always professed in my teaching. Just how eloquent people can be when telling, in their own words, their own stories. There was one broken-looking broker who confessed he had kept a flower vase on his office desk, with vodka in it "for the smell. As you well know, contrary to what amateurs think, vodka does. Smell." Having botched a national meeting while too visibly sauced, the projector jammed (dosage is fate), he got fired. One weirdly chipper bag lady then grinned and shook her head side to side, admitted she was just dealing with it daily, leaning on a higher power whose street smarts sure helped; Sterno was for burning now. There was a peroxided chorus boy of forty-five who said that thanks to rye (and, true, his fondness for it), "I haven't done a show since *Sweet Charity* with Gwen." I could see that most of the folks here didn't know when *Charity* had closed, but they nodded anyway. The most ordinary-looking people told the most booze-sogged, hair-raising, and shapely sagas.

Came Robert's turn to speak. I felt myself brace. Not just because I loved him. Recently some handsome guy had flirted with me and, soon as I responded, he confided, "I should tell you I know who you are. I mean: Gustafson's assistant."

"No, just his friend."

"But I saw you dealing with the waiter and deciding who got to sit nearest him, then hailing the cab."

"Well, but if you're Robert's friend that's part of what it means. —I'm afraid I just don't find you so attractive anymore, sorry."

I wanted to intervene here. To tell these lushes to go home. Robert, so tenderhearted, was doing this just to make himself seem mortal. He was trying to cheer these dear losers by imitating one. I'd never seen him what I'd call stinking drunk.

It's hard now to explain, how committed I was—not to his being perfect, for I knew that no one was. I simply wanted one person in my New York life to seem that way. Just for a while. If only to me. Was that too much to ask?

"My name is Robert and I am . . ."

Today he told how early it'd started. How, at age ten, after a youth-choir dress rehearsal at his dad's church, another boy who sang soprano had used the green robe for cover, shoplifting a bottle of cheap red wine, sweet wine for the Jewish holidays long over, wine now discounted. Two choirboys in full regalia biked quick toward the woods. The other kid took a single swig and gagged, swore it tasted like Kool-Aid, kerosene, and cough medicine, mixed. He then climbed back on his Schwinn and pedaled off, leaving little Robert the whole bottle. My friend was now telling his past to strangers and me, but I feared they'd heard it all before.

Was this mainly to catch me up, to let my heroic-regard down easy? Today young Gustafson didn't meet others' eyes. He sat talking to his own joined hands, elbows on knees, head slumped forward. In this basement, Robert sounded so unlike himself. Here, his voice came tough and uninflected, no usual clever vamping. He seemed intent upon offering facts only, none of the Circle's standard excesses, playful flights. The voice sounded Midwestern, monotone, criminally melancholy. The opposite of sexy: dead.

"I started drinking it. I didn't want to stop, not even long enough to breathe. I was, what? ten. From the first pull, I drank to get drunk. As often as I could. Carried a toothbrush and toothpaste to junior high in my book bag. I lifted funds from the collection plate at my folks' church. I kept on, right through college. Went to a state school with extension classes, erosion management, animal husbandry, like that. Part of the course meant students' pitching in to look after a few head of livestock kept on the campus's model farm. It was really more a petting zoo. One night I was put in charge of a Guernsey who was to calf any day. I was sent out there to sleep beside her stall on a cot they had. My bourbon, by then it was bourbon, came along for the ride. In one hand I had a battery-operated radio turned to the Chicago classical station, I was hoping for some Mahler. And in the other Mr. Jack Daniel. I made pretty good progress with Jack. We were just like that by then. I woke around three to a sound, right up on my face and warm. I turned over and the cow'd got her head stuck through the slats like trying to wake me. She had dropped the calf, without my hearing a sound. I sure heard her now. But, see, she couldn't turn around to tend it, nudge it to standing and lick the placenta off its nose and mouth and let more air in. The cord had got all caught around her back left leg and she wasn't able to turn and help the baby and it'd fallen out and, tangled, she had stepped back on it. Stepped all over it and killed it.

"I looked right through the railings into her pink snout and the mouth. She just kept making sounds across my eyes. Her breath was sweet, grassy. It felt so shaming. And she seemed to know that I should feel ashamed, but she at least accepted what'd happened. She seemed to understand—this was what went on with animals. Missteps, one animal drunk and sleeping through his only chance to help another. Come morning, I lied about it of course. But I went into such a spin over her sounds, the look. That forgiving look. Still drives me crazy—I mean when people do it.

"Next week, I went to a party at some faculty member's house. This was happening around nineteen sixty-seven, and even at Ames, Iowa, things were wild, wife-swapping and everybody stoned or drunk and all. Several faculty wives were swapping me. I never really knew why I was so popular but stayed drunk enough, enough of the time, not to really even question that. I didn't mean to be drunk so often. There just didn't seem an alternative.

"After that party, I woke up with some people I didn't remember. It was in a ranch house I'd never seen. A big place. The kitchen was beautifully equipped. There were two naked girls asleep on the couch. I walked outside just at dusk (two days after the last day I remembered). A nice old lady in the next yard was watering her rose bush. I asked what town this was and where. She said, 'Sonny, you're in Moline, Illinois. And I sure do hope you get back where you wanted. And if you people in that house are a cult, like the neighbors say, I didn't do anything to deserve being hurt. Remember I was nice to you about which town.' I had a dollar or three, and I was in the wrong state, and I'd missed four days of college classes. And my parents had come for a visit I'd agreed to. I was to be the Youth Preacher at our Campus Lutheran Ministry, and hadn't been around and had missed all of it. Two hundred people had turned out to hear me. The Chaplain'd called the police. Nobody knew I ever touched a drop. I didn't seem the type. All this should've been my early warning sign, but . . ."

And he went on. But others' stories had seemed maybe even a bit more . . . if not interesting, then somehow more personal than his. Convenience stores keep cameras trailed on the registers and, sometimes, they catch a robber on film. His story sounded filmed by a security camera it hadn't known was there.

When we walked out, the sunlight seemed particularly golden and brash. Robert slung his arm around my shoulder. "I'm afraid I've disappointed you, Hart."

"No, no. It's just . . . I get lazy about other people sometimes. Guess I don't want to think they have the same sort of . . . No, never disappointed. It just makes you more complicated, probably a better artist. No sweat on my account, please. I'd just like to have helped. Just feel bad how much Chilean champagne I've always tried unloading on you." He told me he did meetings twice a week but should go more. I gave him a warm look. "You're not going to forgive me so soon, are you, Hartley? Not the same hour you found out. You're too easy, man. Speaking as one addict to another."

Then he asked if I didn't teach the prodigy today. We knew each others' schedules and he looked at his watch. "Aren't you late? You are late. You missed them because of me. Now I really do feel great," and he hurried me to the street and, like my assistant, hailed a cab and passed a bill to the driver, then eased me into the backseat after giving me a peck. "Not to worry," he instructed but sounded very glum, as if Robert were disappointed in *me*.

Sad to say (I am not proud of this), I never mentioned it again.

She Finds Somebody

Ever low on cash, I took a part-time teaching job at a famous college that—even for those working there full-time—paid surprisingly little. I got hooked by the prestige before we actually talked figures; the charming tweedy committee had counted on that.

Three days a week, I commuted to my half-time college job in West-chester. The car pool offered a gossipy, entertaining bunch—gifted silvering poets, old Lefties as exhausted as vindicated by ending the Vietnam War. There were other socially respectable young bohemians. One gaunt woman taught dance; she forever arrived late, she usually hurried toward the car carrying a leotard, still dripping with Woolite. She would tie it to the Audi's radio antenna. By the time we hit the Cross Bronx Expressway half an hour later, the thing was dry and flapping like some jousting pennant. It seemed to prove that we were ready for another day of strenuous youthful art-making at what we called, only half in jest, "The Soul Ranch."

Given half of a limited full-time salary, I could not afford health insurance. No dentistry helped save the teeth my parents had paid so dearly to have braced and rendered civil-looking. Beyond my means was anything except a peasant's ruddy turnip well-being. But hey (we all figured), this young, nobody ever gets really sick for long anyway, right? Risk it.

Robert found two gray hairs, though only he could "read" them coiled among the platinum. I'd counted five of my own, including a single argumentative mainspring pubic one, as yet unnoticed by anyone else. Angie's coiffure by now combined so many dyes, the aging process seemed, if not halted, then perpetually upstaged.

Her painting evolved—if without any galleries yet noticing. Her beauty drew looks but—after a single audition—she discarded most applicant-supplicants.

Finally she told me she'd met him, Mr. Right. A medical student at NYU, he'd be a doctor like her dad. "Cow eyes, great hands, big Howdy Doody dick (never met a stranger), inherited farmland in Indiana, knows nothing about painting but intuitively suspects I'm a genius."

"Just your type."

"Just my type. Wanna meet him?" It was arranged, for Friday. I joined them at a Polish restaurant on Second Avenue. He seemed a good influence, they were both there even earlier than I. A first. The hostess had settled them at a candled table in the window—lovers, smoochy, handsome, customer magnets.

This young doc was a sunny hound of a boy, huge hands and a head as round and easy to read as a Boy Scout puppet's. He focused mainly on her and she seemed not to notice or care much—but I knew this flush of color meant my Angie was already so tied to him . . . "Well, Hartley, buddy"—he practiced the bedside manner of using people's names—"Angie says you're mighty good to her. That you really 'get' her work. Me, I'm from a town where art means whatever the high school kids'll paint on the water tower this year. We frame flying-ducks covers off *Field and Stream*. Still, I get the goose bumps around hers, around her. You too? I mean, just feast your eyes on her. Her pulse is faster than most hummingbirds'. Contagious, that type speed. Look, she's acting deaf. What can I do to get her attention? I've got an idea I'll try out on you little later, baby. So, Hartley. You got a girlfriend or a fiancée? Because we'll all have to double-date, what say?"

I look across the table at her. Our insinuating closeness rockets forward, leaves a geek Midwestern doctor so far below on ground. I call, loud: "You didn't *tell* him?"

Two weeks later, they fight over nothing. His taste in orthopedic Boy Scout puppet-looking shoes. She never ever mentions him again.

If, by now, I can list all that I gave up for Angie, then she surely endured many sacrifices for me. But were these forfeitures she would've made anyhow? Or was a little love of me behind her every major "no" to others?

Paradise Deferred

s we drank intensest Latin caffeine in our hangout that sold it so cheap we could afford four or five hits per morning, we jumpily admitted, three years in, it really might not happen overnight, after all, you know? It. Recognition.

We heard It took some people six years to achieve. And "good" artists, too. And yet, we all conceded, after our latest cafe latte, we still kind of half-expected It, daily. Couldn't it happen?

We were confused about our good looks, our negotiable sexiness, our social-climbing dreams and artistic talent. Where did each fit in? We felt we might be discovered right now, right here at Ossorio's Corner Cuba Libre Café. Lana Turner found herself tapped for immortality while lost in thought, drinking an ice cream soda. And we each had sixty IQ points on Lana Turner. If maybe not her complete way with a short cashmere sweater.

Early genius. Self-described. Through clothes tight enough, didn't ours show? Living in New York this long, we'd banished our inherited Ruling Class hopes by making ourselves into thoroughbred Rebels. No wonder the-powers-that-be didn't yet recognize our work. It was too new; we probably just threatened their little hard-won patch of turf. By making the older others our enemies, we'd learned to resist all we had been brought up expecting.

Robert had been saying that, for every Shakespeare whose texts got written down by his loyal actors, for every hardworking J. S. Bach with a new piece due each Sunday, there must be, what? thirty other lost geniuses of such magnitude. "Imagine that the director of music, some young redhaired dweeb, at a Baptist church in Arkansas, outgeniused Bach, what would the locals make of him, and . . ." Just then Robert was called to the coffeehouse pay phone. He grabbed his address book, known as The Bag. It was a green drawstring satchel full of scribbled phone-number celebrity confetti. Summoned, he'd been seated astride one of Ossorio's wire chairs. Robert's whole right leg now lifted and moved back then over it. With one glad swing, his generative male gear showed collectively as the bulk of a single tender eggplant. And when he turned to stride away, Angie and I sat helpless not to note his buttocks in blue-jean retreat, right buttock, snap, left snapping, right.

"You do know, Hart, that familiarity's supposed to wear it off. Most people, by now, you'd be so sick of looking. You, for instance, I can live with, but as eye food? Not that I am pure 20/20 protein, either. Just our luck, we find the only person on earth who gets more and more necessary to stare at. The saltlick. Somebody apparently took Noel Coward to see *Lawrence of Arabia*, see? And afterward his one comment was, 'If that blond actor were any prettier, they could've called it 'Florence of Arabia.'"

"—If you get to Robert," she said behind one hand though we were alone now. "If you even touch it once, first . . . I want you to do two things and in this order, one, describe it to me exactly, as only you can, Hartley. Then hand me your notarized will and put your head down on the nearest level surface because I am going to have to cut it off."

"Capeto," I said.

"And what are you two lovebirds talking about?" a familiar claret-edged baritone. We just groaned. He had spent the past weekend helping crew last year's America's Cup winner. Then he retreated to Aaron Copland's compound on the Hudson. May had turned him a deeper cinnamon-toast brown and his eyebrows were bleached half-white and it made the eyes below go a scarier and colder blue so it was like staring through his skull and out to sea through his porthole skull. "What?" Robert protested. "You two conspire against me and can just look so mean sometimes. I was only gone a sec. What'd I *do*?" And then, with his bare arms hugging the chair's back nearer his chest, he cocked his head, hummed "Hmmm?" and made the deep fold on the left of his perfect mouth go way far in, smiling forth such hard-wired wattage, it was really too much.

Angie and I faced each other, balled our fists, struck each other's shoulders over and over.

Like tortured babies offered then denied something they both so want, we could say simply, "Waaaaa!"

Afraid of being liked for only his looks, Gustafson had developed all this casualness, all this ease with the lingo of morality. Just in case. (I had discovered, if belatedly, along with AA membership, he had never ever registered to vote.) Angie held his ethics in far lower regard than I did. "Have you noticed, balls for brains, that when he snags a party's South African shrimp 'the size of throw pillows,' as you would say, he shares them, true. But he never leaves food under Saran wrap on a plate with a cute note on our doorsteps, ever notice that, hunh? He always makes us come to him. He insists on feeding us, the patriarch, out of his little fridge from whom all blessings flow. Am I right?"

"Shrimp spoil. Besides, anything covered-dish left on my doorstep, I'd never even find the empty plate."

"You. You're so moved because you've seen him get out of Aston-Martins one block from home so he won't hurt your feelings. Maybe he doesn't want his snooty friends to see his own shit apartment, ever think of that?"

"You sound like someone trying to convince herself."

"He must be circumcised, right? Lutheran preacher and all, Iowa. Knife happy. It'd be a pity. I want the chrysalis still wound around the whole butterfly magilla, wrapped as it was born . . ."

"To go."

We laughed then. And lurched on about him, with a fueling intimacy we rarely felt when speaking merely of ourselves.

—Would I ever be known as anything but "Friend of . . ."? I asked myself this while retrieving his special-order Berg scores from Schirmer's. ("The influence of Berg on the sinking of the *Titanic*, eh?" I quipped. "Yeah, several people have thought of that," he answered, sinking me.) While picking up a ruffled tux shirt from our favorite dry cleaner because Robert was too rushed to properly prepare for the bash surrounding a new Egyptian temple at the Met, it sometimes seemed that Robert did all the glamour, Hartley all its legwork.

Puppet Theatre

ust when I'd decided I had the soul of a drudge, just when it came clearest I was the muddy flower-peddler not her aftermath-princess, just when I felt that Immortality would only know me as a helpmeet, just when I'd gained six pounds, Farce, as it will when your happy-quota shades off into urban gray, intervened: all pinks, oranges, reds.

I stood buying skim milk at Mrs. Park's corner store. The young construction worker in line behind me, a splendid looking Hispanic fellow wearing boots, hardhat and a hammer dangling from the belt, leaned forward. I felt his hand on my backside. (It actually proved to be his hammer; better still.)

He said in a toothy sugar-cane accent, "You mi' could change m' mind 'bout married life, I'm tinking." Guilty as ever, sure that any pleasure would exact a tax far greater, I glanced at our respected Mrs. Park. Had she heard? No, she appeared all cash register. "I ain't no homewrecker," I tried a joke. This was Hartley's usual way of deflecting opportunity. But I saw that, thank God, this guy's English was not good enough to pick up on my campy "go away." I now wondered what Robert or Angie or other healthy normal self-interested people would do before such an offering. Learn. Grab.

So I ventured something international: I winked. He winked back so quick I heard a wet sexual snap from his right eye. Next I pointed around the corner while holding up then dangling my keyring it as if to hypnotize him. Finally I let my eyebrows lift in the possibly-worldwide sign of "Howbout it? Hubbahubba." Still wearing his high-impact yellow plastic construction helmet, he nodded, he smiled around white teeth at just the moment a cashregister pinged "Sale!" I will henceforth call him Juan.

I considered simply leaving the milk, but Mrs. Park had seen me, so I paid, said I didn't need a bag, and, moving backward—asked after her boy at Vassar, her daughter at MIT. But I kept one eye on Juan, making sure he didn't slip away. He still waited out front, smoking. Passing him—I crooked my finger in the universal signal for Get Your Sweet Ass Over Here. He, smiling an endearing lopsided grin, teeth contrasting with his beautiful skin (Angie sometimes called me Mr. Support Your Organization of American States), followed.

I was noting what I wore, which soap I'd used last night, the current temperature and humidity. I was already hoping to make history repeat itself: Why me, why not, why now? Robert asked, Why not me? Angie asked, Why me just this once?

I let Juan in. I could see he was disappointed by how much my apartment resembled his. He stopped near the door, he leaned back against one wall. Juan pulled a toothpick from his checkered shirt and glumly chewed it while giving me a brown-eyed once-over that could rotisserie a raw turkey toward being instantly honey-smoked.

I resisted consulting my blinking answering machine; I fought doing any of my usual fussy things that might sabotage the mood. (How many chances had I squandered with efficient side-errands and postscripts, returning to find I'd spoiled "that loving feeling"? as Angie liked to quote the Righteous Brothers.)

Now I tried concentrating solely on Juan and the continuous auditioning present. His looks made such focus easier. Juan simply waited. He used that wall as if he were still on the street. He would not step toward my futon; the Catholic church at work; he had mapped out a system of penance in advance. Hartley, as usual, would be required to do most of the hard lifting. But life is never easy. Today such work seemed child's play.

I approached him. Now the toothpick jutted upward at a forty-five degree angle of jaunty erectile display-behavior—I reached for his groin, itself not unready. Middle-class boys might like indirection, ear-kissing eventuality, hobby chat. But, on Robert's advice, I'd learned, with the rough guys, to go for it fast or they'd hurt you or run, or both.

I had just endured Juan's first chilling glower. It put all blame for fun on me. It said "I can't stop you if you're this sick, but I might have to kill you afterward, okay?" —The mystery of the married; the residual handiwork of those hard-teaching nuns.

I sensed all that waited uncurled and evermore uncoiling down Juan's right pantleg when there came so serious a pounding on the door, my heart lost count.

As I have told you, my downstairs buzzer system was a spaghetti platter of colored wires disgorged. "Momento, Juan," said I, wondering if I hadn't picked up the wrong language from last night's De Sica retrospective at the Thalia. I stepped one yard past my surly yet oh-so-willing builder, I peeked into the door's fisheye lens.

Tony Wu, carrying a suitcase, wore a collarless leather jacket and glanced around my graffittied hallway as if about to be mugged out there. A distinct possibility. How had he found me? Why my place, and why oh why now?

If I sent him away, if he got hurt before returning to Park Ave., where he so plainly belonged, I'd never forgive myself. (Plus I'd be out that weekly check.) But I hated his actually seeing how I lived. I also hated to ruin, even briefly, my playful rendezvous with the wonderful world of Third World Work.

"Juan? Would you mind terribly waiting in yonder closet, the one with the forties floral drapery hanging over its . . ."

Meeting only irritation and incomprehension, I led him by one horny hand through said portal, I abandoned him to stand among my exquisite thrift-shop clothes. I held up one index finger in the international sign for (I hoped), "This'll just take uno minuti," only to have Juan take my hand and stick its bossy index finger into his very warm and practiced mouth. An international sign I need not go into. I jerked shut the drapery. I (heart) NEW YORK.

"Tony, what brings you to your teacher's sadder part of town?"

"Mr. Hartley, several things require being said; number one thing is Tony is running away from the home and her in particular; number two thing is Tony waits for our time weekly and Tony thinks of you, thoughts that a man is considered to be having more often toward The Girl. I am honored to view where you work as an artist. So, this I see is Hartley's own garrick?"

"No, darling, 'garret' . . . G-A-R-R-E."

"You just called Tony 'darling' . . ." and his smile was so adorable.

"But I call every . . . person I care about . . . Downtown, we say it not un-often . . . Which in no way detracts from our cordial if . . ."

"Tony has read the signs you have been showing and hopes to 'be' here with you from now on, Mr. Hartley. I have come to study under you! 'Under.' You understand?"

"Oh dear," I opined as he set down a Vuitton carry-all new enough to still have passports and various parchment assurances dangling from its handle; he opened a brown leather jacket so chocolatey in hue and texture, so recently bought, it put off a scent like some tanner's daughter's erotic fantasy. He wore widewaled brown corduroys and a brown cashmere turtleneck and his tiny brown Gucci loafers looked like shoes made to slip onto some costly ivory toy. Then Tony, frail yet determined behind his octagonal wire glasses, all smiles, unzipped his jacket's front. Young Tony, nervous, somehow opened the zipper of his pants and pulled out, an opening chess gambit, as if introducing some ventriloquist's dummy, one full-grown, ruddy, almost Irish-looking male member. "Well, Tony, honey! Look at you. This won't do, but thank you. Really."

He next pressed my hand against it, saying "Oh Mist Hartry, teach me grammar and . . ." He craned upward and, in a burst of warm air totally thrilling, added, "All the exceptions."

Juan coughed. Tony jumped. I got between Tony and the forties floral drapery, but he slid his arms around my waist, pulling me still closer against the door. I was half-heartedly mumbling something about "extremely flattered" and "can't think of anyone I'd rather . . . but . . ." I was also picturing his mother's newly hired squadron of forty detectives, all headed this way to arrest me for child molestation. —I exercised extreme willpower and removed my hand from his thirteen-year-old-going-on-forty's dynastic implement when there came such a terrible banging on the very door he had, with no real difficulty, so recently pulled me against . . . The second wave of slamming beat so fierce, I could see Tony's fine black hair move with it. I pictured the entire NYPD crouched out there, blue and brass, guns trained on my doorknob.

First I pushed Tony toward my bed, telling him to hide beneath it. With his aid, I saw I had trendily opted for a futon flat to the floor; I so envied Robert's fourmaster then—seven could fit beneath his bed, while practically standing up, and they probably had.

Without much choice in a garrick this size, I pulled Tony by one hand toward my closet and calling "O Juan?" opened the curtain to find my first guest touching himself through stretched denim, "Tony, Juan, Juan, Tony. Play nice now. . . ." I trotted back, kicking brand new luggage under my writing desk and kitchen table.

I squinted at the lens when a loud voice called, "We see your head. Open up, it's a real Emergency, Mims. 'Cause blood's way thickern water."

I unlatched the door to find my big smooth gorgeous first cousin, Lex, down from New Haven. Behind him, smiling, a thin date. I hadn't seen Lex in four years. "Hart, buddy. Had to call my mom from a pay phone for your address." He pushed past me. "You just write here or you got to live in it, too?" Lex had benefited from my uncle's golf course heart attack at age forty-two; Lex had already spent most of the proceeds before achieving that long-sought B.A.

"Lex, I'm actually living undercover, my time is not my own. I'm tape-recording the neighbors . . ." I pointed to a wall. "A child-porn racket."

"They sure found the building for it. Look, I'm in trouble. Especially trouble with Caitlin here. They canceled on us. Six months ago, I booked and now unless I can find help, we're going to miss it, flat. They say they never heard of me. I need two orchestra seats for *Cats* in the next hour, for today's matinee. Or else she says she won't marry me, right, Cait? She's a tough sell, our Cait-kins, but doesn't the sight of her just make you wanna purr?"

"You catch me at a busy time. I've got my hands full here." Just then, as Lex and Cait stood facing me, I saw the drapery behind them flare into sudden lavish motion. I felt a strange urge to cackle and point, to rush my simplest cousin and his skinny girl to the closet, place an index finger across my lips in the universal sign of Shush, then yank the curtain back to see what my lovely construction worker and the little Prince were up to, or down on.

Instead I suggested Lex dash straight to the Hilton's tip-top-front-desk concierge ("Say I sent you," I added, playing to Lex's own bad character, the assumption that you are either known or dead). "Tell him money is no object, that your future married life depends on it, and believe me, cous, he'll have you both in cat outfits by two." This new goal seemed to galvanize them with enough of a mission so they moved out into the hall. "How about this bloodbro' of mine, Cait? Did I not tell you he'd have strings to pull and irons in every fire?"

"You have no idea," I said, and they were off.

Though my Juan and my Tony, my rod and my staff, had only been alone together three or six minutes, I now felt too genteel or nervous to actually interrupt. I did call, "Coast clear." That certainly produced no bolting toward me; instead, a more persistent buckling of said drapery. So I upgraded to, "Come out come out whatever you've done." But despite my singsonging, the curtain continued its tug and sway. I fought an impulse to peek. Looking-rights seemed only fair. Most agents get a flat 10 percent off the top.

But, odd, a new feeling almost airborne settled. It was from all today's entrances and exits. It was from the possibility of being this much in demand. (How did Robert manage the hourly energy outlay of keeping thirty beloveds dangle-dancing ever-interested, in and out of scattered floral closets?) Joy came mostly from my planning how I'd tell it. Especially how I'd frame it all (Punch Puppet Theatre) for Robert, Angie, over coffee later. So this, I thought, is stardom. Subject matter forever trying to crawl into your place, your pants.

But, instead of hogging my own center stage, I pulled a kitchen chair aside, six feet away from the suspended colored drapery. I propped feet on Tony's bag, and watched fabric's motions. I, in a good orchestra seat, felt not unhappy at this matinee of my own making. I rested here, listening to certain glottal human sounds. In the gap below the cloth, I took note of plaster-crusted orange boots, of the tiny chockie kick-offs in various placements, now bent and now on tiptoe. I was both erect and smiling. I looked around, my futon and its powder-blue electric blanket, the desk piled with new fiction, three red tulips a gift from Angie, Colonel Harbison Increase Hartley (provider of blankets and bacon to his adoring troops who had nicknamed him Saint Hen). His features offered a Confederate court-martial of my life. So be it.

I tilted due right, I hit a button activating the dance tape Robert had lent me. "I love the city, I love the nightlife, on the disco floooooooh . . ."

Everything in here could be reached from this captain's chair, as on Starship Enterprise, as in Santa's Workshop full o' spunky hunky pumping elves.

I flashed on a noun—the word that describes one evening's theatrical entertainment. It applied to most of how we lived here, to all my work intended, to what I presently watched as my maroon draperies moved, so rhythmically animated.

I was here, in my own garrick, attending a lovely, funny, wholly unexpected, full-length first-run play.

New Blood

I n off the street, we dragged likely recruits for the Circle. They surely sensed being screened—a welter of rigged questions, swapped glances.

The old Havanans at adjacent tables called us "the Keeds." They indulged us with the courtesy of Latin patriarchs who protected well, knowing that their sovereignty would never be challenged. We felt guarded by them; we were. Still, Ossorio would soon double the price of coffee.

Here, Robert introduced me to Marco, a linguist and political organizer who literally lived upstairs, partly for the love of coffee's wholesome scent. His glasses always needed cleaning and seemed flecked with boat enamel; he cut his hair himself and lost interest, midway. He was one of those brilliant people who never notices what they wear; this made him unique among us. Robert, Ang, and I tended to screen-test a new Goodwill outfit every few days.

Marco's only foppery was a flimsy armor of political buttons speckling his khaki flak jacket. Even his bike, chained out front, was bumper-stickered with anticar sentiments. The button on his collar, "I Like Ike," seemed to render half-ironic the more contemporary: "Boycott Table Grapes." "What *is* a table grape? and how are they trained?" Robert made us laugh.

But Marco really overqualified for membership by telling us, with a factuality peculiar to the highest magic, exactly what was being said at those tables nearest ours. We had studied college French, high school Latin, forgotten cold war Russian. But not one of us spoke "Cuban" Spanish. Precisely this made Ossorio's Cuba Libra Café feel so safe. Loud as we could get, we lived curiously unobserved amid other tables' linguistic music, the clatter of dominoes.

Marco hunched closer to us, explaining that the Cuban dialect was unique; it was spoken from the back of the mouth and considered, elsewhere, hooty, owl-like in its sounds. We, hungover or self-involved or both, had always assumed the older gents at neighboring tables sat discussing 1947s sugar-harvest or Carlita, an Apache dancer they'd all known from their macho heydays in chic Havana pre-rev.

Marco lowered his voice to report their true subject: these slick patriots' enthusiastic support for an attempted (if failed) CIA plot. Someone had tried sprinkling poisoned powder in Fidel's frogman diving suit. Now that plan had flopped, the force was concentrating on a drug meant to defoliate Castro's beard. Would Fidel beardless not be a Fidel unrecognizable?

Robert nodded. "Marco? I believe you. Since the CIA and the world generally is run by non-bisexual humorless white guys with the souls of eleven-year-old boys, why are we surprised they sit around boardrooms all day, funded by us, saying, 'Wouldn't it be neat if . . .' It's exactly insane enough to be true."

At adjacent tables, we'd seen large wads of money change hands. Now such payoffs seemed far more illicit than back rent. We scanned our dive with new respect. It pleased us to hang out in a hotbed of such foment. Not to mention steamed milk.

My parents would arrive on Monday. I broke the news and Marco's instant pity endeared him forever. "Oh nooo!" he said.

"Thank you, jjjes. I'm trying to be brave. I have it planned down to the second. Pray the conversation stays general. Make a schedule. Keep briskly to it. Time'll pass. Right?"

My friends swore they would help me.

Nativity

urly city workers strung our block with dainty Christmas stars, white ones. My folks would soon turn up and exercise their God-given right to shop while I waited. At the threat of seeing them so near the holidays, one memory, long suppressed, unlocked itself: the Christmas Eve when I was four.

A windy night and more romantic for that. My slender father bound into my room. It must've been around one a.m.

In their never-ending plan to thwart "the robbers"—who never stole so much as a brushed-aluminum coaster—my folks stored important deeds and papers in the nursery cedar chest in my room. Dad needed something from there (maybe assembly instructions for a complicated toy being built under the tree).

Apologizing for waking me, he flipped on the overhead light. These were the only times I ever heard him say, "I'm sorry." I awaited such moments.

Since it was the night before Christmas, since I was four, since I was expecting a bike with training wheels, since I sat wearing flannel jammers printed with candy canes, I'd been awake anyhow. As I have told you, Santa's image meant odd things to me. He was not just the usual Daddy Warbucks scattering factory-made bounty. I had transformed him into my own ideal: He was an ArtsandCraftsman, part William Morris, part J. P. Morgan, partly the John L. Lewis of the elves. He got to spend 364 days a year at home, creating; only one night involved the bore of home delivery. I longed to follow him back up our chimney and fly off to where he worked. I wanted a paintbrush; I longed to help.

My imagination was glutted with the Santa possibilities peculiar to the son of a fellow prosperous as Dad, self-made. Mother liked to say, smiling, she "went all out for Christmas." Wind kept testing our roof's huge TV antenna. I'd heard a steady pull and creaking overhead. It might've been anything. Could've been anyone.

Father now lifted blue blankets from the opened chest. He pulled forth the folded document. I watched. (According to photos from then, I had thick brown hair cut in bangs over wide blue-gray eyes and a smile overimmediate. I had been born talking [no shock, right?]. I was a pretty, smiley little boy, hoping mostly only to stay happy and to always please.)

"Daddy? I don't want to say anything, but I just heard some noises on the roof? And it sounded, well, it sure did sound a lot like hoofs or something, or a sled or something . . . I don't know but, boy, it really might be . . ."

He turned clear around. He looked right at me. With two male steps, he reached my bed, he sat upon it. As usual, he did not touch me. Through the open door, a glow of blinking colored lights warmed our living room. The unfamiliar scent of evergreen lived right in the house with us. My handsome father, holding the important papers, now bent above me. He looked me right in the eyes. Sensing that the door stood ajar, that my mom might overhear, he now lowered his voice. The tender moment had finally come. Beneath my covers, I kept floppy toys as company, things "to be in charge of." Now, thrilled, I secretly reached for one preferred lieutenant.

It all looked picture-perfect as a recent *Saturday Evening Post* cover. I could smell his shirt starch. Father leaned nearer. I felt the strange excitement of finally having all his irked wage-earning attention fixed square on me.

Again, helpful, I fed him my best hope, "Dad? It might just be . . . him . . ."

"Son?" Dad said, with a pleasure faintly sexual. "It isn't."

* * *

He spoke this with such emphasis, his chin lifted. Then he tipped back, pivoting. To check. On how I'd taken it. His smile seemed one of victory. I had opened myself to this, to the forces of realism, to the grinding brunt of commerce, to the common sense of a self-made man who believes his namesake-manchild should get tough and fast.

(In fictional terms, it might be good here to include the child's immediate facial response on receiving such hard news. But, you know? I cannot imagine how I looked. Maybe blinking? A small point in the chin quivering like some pinched nerve? What? You provide that. I still can't concoct my own face then. Forty-three years later, call it lazy, but I do not want to know.)

My father leaned on his right arm, steadied for a better view of what he'd done. I knew his deepest wish: for me to cry. I knew because: half of my own body owed itself to all of his.

Therefore, I was too much like this man to give him that. Instead I muttered, if only to my hidden toys, "It maybe *could* be. Him."

From here, I can explain Dad's anti-Christmas news in several ways. Maybe some need to prepare me for our very un-toy of a world? Maybe he performed a task he guessed would be rough now but in the long run "good for me"? Maybe he was passing along some blow his dad had visited on him?

And yet, the way he'd lowered his voice so Mother couldn't hear—Mom, who would loathe this being done to any child of hers, especially on the big night, and most especially by that child's very sire—there was something sneaky, something plain ole redneck country mean in what my father did to me on my fourth Christmas Eve.

All day, Mom had been making Bing Crosby repeat about a white Christmas in snowless Carolina. Our house was decked with a blink-nosed deer, one punchbowl shaped like the head of a red-capped white-bearded man with many little cups to match him, but, son, there is no Santa Claus.

I came to with a father trying to kill me. If not bodily, then hoping to eradicate my crazy speculative fantasizing nature. Actually, my favorite part.

The percentage that plays. It is—thank God, with much work—still the bulk of me.

Sometimes I'd dream of pinning Dad down, of hugging him till he begged for mercy. I'd just squeeze the tighter, tickle more, killing him with levity. I vowed that if I were ever a father, ever put in charge of ones weaker, needier, I would be stronger, better, kinder than he had been to me.

I don't believe in capital punishment. And yet, when it comes to certain crimes grown men visit upon helpless children, you know? At times . . . I waver.

And now welcome to "the Sewer," to my splendid world of urban make-believe.

"We're here!" she phoned from the hotel. I would deny my folks all access to my railroad flat. I knew that seeing the tub in the kitchen, seeing walls enameled more colors than one of Angie's canvases—would bring forth my father's finest belt-lash wit. The parents often told me they were "worried sick" about me, my "housing" and my "choice of company." I failed to explain that my apartment rested just across the street from Ossorio's. Still, I chose instead to take them there for coffee. After a musical matinee, we taxied downtown. As we pulled before the hangout, my dad sounded Santa-affable, "So, this where you all buy your drugs?"

"He's joking, honey. Richard has more a *dry* sense of humor."

Is that what that is?

I would buy the folks a single round at Ossorio's Cuba Libre Café. I prayed that my usually tardy friends would now be gathered inside to protect me. I hoped our headquarters would pass muster.

True, its wire ice-cream-parlor chairs were somewhat badly bent since their 1920 debut. Yeah, the flooring featured hexagonal white tiles most often seen in barbershops of the nineteenth century. "Scenic vista" mosaics pocked the walls. Blue splashes from improbable fountains read zigzag-edged as crossword puzzles. A harlequin convention of tiles, laid at diamond angles, offered eight contradictory colors, all ugly—mustard to maroon to glue-brown. Even from outside, Ossorio's interior today looked ancient, valuable, newly dug-up. A storefront Pompeii.

Ossorio himself opened the cab door for Mother. He had been put on notice and now—with ambassadorial splendor—his moustache extra-waxed, he offered hostly bests. The guy was a total saint, telling both my folks how hard I worked and right in regulars' plain view. He said he'd one day put a plaque back there on my table, he'd charge the tourists extra.

I felt almost sick with stage fright. In cookbooks you read "Introduce chopped nuts direct into pre-whipped batter." Like that. Introduce:

In honor of my folks, Robert had brought cheese-and-cherry pastries (from a Greek place he'd discovered in the Forties). Angie, present early, was all dressed up. She'd worn a shirtwaist and pearls! Her hair, dyed ash-brown for today, pulled back toward spinster bun-dom, fell short. She had maybe overdone the wide-eyed Judy Garland "Dorothy" makeup. (She sometimes applied it like an abstract painter painting, or some young boy dressing up for Halloween as "Girl.") But, I could see she'd turned her charm and accent up to full-scorch. I loved her for it.

Mother, entering, clutched her purse ("A ROBBERS' DEN?"). During the last year, her hair had gone from silver to pure white. The effect was pretty if, for me, disturbing.

Mom, in a beige suit and matching shoes, now visibly tried to make her peace with such dinge as only our crew might find companionable.

Today, I must admit, the place seemed to warrant a Sanitation Grade Z. Its every tile looked steeped in coffee like those chips of white enamel used in ads for denture cleanser.

"My my," Mom said. "What a picturesque . . . little 'bistro,' I suppose you'd call it. My. It looks like the set for last year's Raleigh Opera Society production of *Carmen*, doesn't it, Richard? Rich-ard?"

Mom surveyed the garish sainted figurines, the medallions and bright old calendars, José Martí's fly-specked portrait—all upgraded only by strong coffee's royal smell. "You know?" she told Robert, pulling out the chair for her, "I feel I'm stepping right into one of those pretty old cigar boxes my daddy used to let me play with as a girl!"

We were all entranced by this. A comparison. Grateful for anything, my friends' eyes lit. Pals flashed me a glance that said, "Your folks're not so bad." (Which is what we all feel about anybody else's.)

The Circle acted pleased with Mom's gentling drawl, her willingness to step in here and quickly fictionalize our Action Central. She'd made ours seem a clean, well-lighted place. It was not. Ossorio, having understood her cigar box remark, smiled a translation to his minions, who glanced over, eyes moving up and down the springy length of my mother, still erotically imaginable. My own shoulders, relieved, had lowered two whole inches. When someone slapped my back.

"Now you people know where The Artiste gets it from."

Everyone had been grinning when this new voice nailed us from behind. Dad's. The gilded world reduced, as usual, to lead.

We turned. He stood there, dragging one fingertip across an adjacent very sticky marble table—proof unmistakable of widespread filth here in our sewer pirates' cave. He glanced from his shifting forefinger and thumb to each face present.

"Now you people know where The Artiste gets it from," might be pronounced with charm. It might be a confiding wish to include your child's whole circle, to compliment both mother and son as imaginative, adorable, identical. But "you people" contained the Republican's contempt for anything not Republican. He had referred to his wife of forty years as a place not a person, "where." Alas, his tone had been so flat, withdrawn, and bitter. It sounded dead and, far worse, deadening.

He had taken her metaphor, so stuffed with childhood fantasy; he had just squashed it like some cigar, puffed once, found lacking, stomped out.

I felt like the true butt of his joke.

I saw Ossorio, behind the register, note our change in postures. His own face lost its hostly jollity.

But Dad smirked, pleased. He was a man of honor. He would not pretend this place was anything but a hole-in-the-wall run by foreigners who put up with degenerates in order to cadge their money, which, he felt inaccurately, was really his money.

His jibe cost my friends their grinning pleasure. They had better things to do midafternoon than meet my address book's only registered Republicans.

"Pastries anyone." Robert didn't ask but told. "Too bad Hartley's apartment's being painted, those darn fumes. You can see the river from his place. And something about watching it from there always makes you stand up just a little taller. Can I offer you one, Mrs. Mims? All right then, 'Helen,' thank you."

I noticed how my mother, though settled, had seized up again. How did her body bear a day's worth of such constant expansion and recoil? She was usually allowed one little public flourish of expression. Then she waited, till he closed her down once more. It was like seeing the iris of a lovely open human eye contract again and again to pinpoint. How had she endured four decades of this?

Mom now gripped, beneath the table, her pale patent leather purse, propping it on one bouncing knee.

She held it as if suddenly quite sure it would be grabbed.

After one coffee, they departed Ossorio's and everybody celebrated with me. From the pay phone by the radiator, Robert, in our hearing, called to cancel an impending trip his folks had planned.

On Feeling New

t happened one Sunday before that Spring when everything changed. I needed to get my ass uptown to a brunch (one meal as yet unknown in North Carolina). If the city adored more and more about the bods and talents of Robert and Angie, it still barely flirted with me. New York was lately the feel of shattered windshield crunching underfoot. The mating calls of car alarms setting each other off.

I found the subways shut; as usual, a water main had busted, flooding the station at Forty-second Street. Though I was expecting a cash influx from my sperm-date next afternoon, I could never swing that caliber of uptown cab fare. So it was simple. I would have to hike the necessary hundred and eleven blocks.

Because it was so early on a Sabbath, traffic proved sketchy, passersby scarce. The homeless still rested, cocooned in burlap, terracing the church steps. It was a bright, delicate morning early in April. The weather felt like some Carolina country Spring's, washed up on this gray rock by accident.

The clear air made me feel like a young Audubon, observing, gathering. Forgiving a little. Sides of the brownstone towers held, I noticed, dew, just the way dew glistened on tobacco plants in fields my granddad owned. Those fields had been promised to my brothers and me (plus our seventy first cousins). Down tree-lined West Side residential streets, hammocks of blue mist still hung. Yellow cabs passed through such haze and came out looking varnished, baptized. This air all felt like Sunday air.

Our city, caught in a leisure day's first yawn, looked beautiful and blank.

The sight was new to me. Where did I usually spend this hour? Oh yeah, at home, on the dark fourth floor–rear, gaping out at the world of hurriedly laid brick and quick-hatching pigeons. I spent this time writing, of course. Which meant hiding, while seeking. Writing about a rural South. But never, it seemed, about here and now. New York had lately seemed one large rejection slip.

I felt like some mole who finally claws aboveground at the foot of the Alps, who assumes the world is all this vertical and grand. I'd been in Manhattan some years now. I'd been cataloguing the place with an Eagle Scout's naturalist habits; those'd seemed misplaced till now.

Odd, this felt like my first day. I was no longer squaring off against the city, competing with it, resisting its hard mass. Instead I rested with it, parallel, eroticized, we were fellow sufferers, both sweetly puffy at this early hour together. Something oddly trusting came from waking in adjacent trenches of one island bed.

I was six blocks from Central Park. And yet a verdant smell now overtook the usual sidewalk ghosts of garbage past. Something new outstripped the come-on scents from bakeries, whorish smells of the West Side's new bubble-bath shops.

A tentative scent lifted from whatever land remained unpaved, from whatever lots were just now greening, from those weed-trees that can learn to live on soot and poodle piss.

Alleys, hidden, proved to be plain dirt, understudies stuck backstage. Your nose knew them.

Striding the West Seventies, I could smell a gray, exhausted city too newly waked to hide its sweet bitter-green heart. Some thawing creaky hopefulness seeped out, rising with first heat.

Topsoil, all one inch of it, didn't know that it existed in a zone so bartered, valued, water-locked. It simply opened to the sun. Dew found that dirt; then wet dirt dried; and such lush smells resulted, even midtown.

The City itself smelled . . . New Here!

I started breathing harder. Partly from the stress of this long silent hike. Mainly from a strange and general sexual desire. I loved it all. I loved them all. Quickened, I now wanted to possess, to eat out, to rut into this, my beloved. I wanted to know its every inch. I wanted to go to town on going down on old New York. East Side was the left nipple, West Side its right, and neither would this worshipper not nibble. I'd sublet and suffuse every inner inch of it. Each brass mail slot would unlatch, all gill-slit airducts behind buildings, I would find, rear entry. I'd have my way with every street—those one-way, and those bi.

I, sperm donor, my loaf all fishes, would fill all city vacancies.

New York, lean back!

The countryboy come North smelled his city magically organically open to him. Just when I felt grayed from all the grief it gave me daily, thankless wage earning, slum accommodations, the state of remaining unpublished and therefore feeling unloved, here it rested, avenues akimbo—aromatic, wet, and ready. Not for cash. But freely given.

And so, this early Sabbath of dew spangling fortieth-floor windows, of skyscrapers dampened till seeming sweetly edible as erectile snowpeas, while walking from its Battery to its Columbia crown, I felt myself to be some oral magician, tongue-climbing his lover's entire tensed length. Knowing it, bottom to top, block by willing cave-in block.

New York has long since ceased being merely man-made. So many dreams daily wrap and re-create this city that, it, some centuries ago, went quantum. From the sheer volume of wishing, thanks to longing of such scope, on this first satiny Sunday of each April, even before the geriatrics take those seats along Broadway's medians where only the homeless usually perch, there's one annual coming out like this. A wetness uncontrolled like spots on lower clothes of pubescent boys and girls, ooops. Too much of everything good spilling. A mineral closet bursts open into light, and the town becomes not simply natural. New York is Nature then.

And, by the time I reached my brunch at 115th Street, I myself was damp all over, and not just from trudging hard uptown. I felt the oddest sort of lanky owner's son's ease, a lover's rights, the fairy tale's slowest son returning home a prince.

My friend opened the door. My friend laughed, taking in my ruddy cheeks, glazed eyes, and wettish clothes, "Well, well . . . Somebody got lucky on the way up. Who was he/she?"

"It," I said. "And this time, for once, no names, please. Because, you size queen, you would not believe the scale of what all Hartley has just 'known.' "

Arrivals, Departures

y ninth address book charts our entrances. My tenth through thirteenth start to mark our exits.

Entrances blared, "Taaa-daa!" exits often beg off only "Uncle," gimping home to be one.

Some acquaintances left early, of their own free will, and are therefore still alive today. After a few seasons of experiment, they returned home healthy, they folded back in, safely regrafted onto their Middlewest. They are the now fathers of three, inheritors of Dad's business, and no one local is the wiser.

But most not. Most of us stayed. Until we couldn't.

Since Father had visited his dark cloud on Ossorio's, I, if only out of loyalty, practically lived there. The place was brighter and far bigger than my backstairs flat. The usuals played dominoes for major money. The sound of that game's plak-plak across marble tables was such a soothing music. Ossorio's smell of coffee made every mottled tile and granite surface seem, to me, luxurious, old world, and somehow sexual. In those days, everything (as I have hinted), seemed eroticized, and was.

Upstairs, I could finish typing a draft of a chapter then rush it to our table, settling there for forty minutes' uninterrupted work. Once, during a story's most exciting phase, I had marked three pages before noting a recurrent wolf whistle. Some man called, "Not bad, not for a boy, muchacho." He was pointing to my bare legs. I saw that I had bumbled downstairs in a nightshirt Angie had been given and had then offered me, wearing only that and my bedroom slippers, carrying one wadded dollar bill. I laughed then lifted the hem but to the knees with forties starlet modesty. The fellows shook their heads, disgusted if pleased, but all still looking—with a gloomy grudging interest—at my renowned gams.

I worked till Angie dragged past then—peeking—swept on in. She flopped down, awarding me all her fast-changing drama. Had she ever entered or left a chamber without being noticed? Now I saw her stare toward the men's room. "Is he here?" She meant Robert. She always meant Robert. And before she even said hello. I answered no and therefore got a kiss myself.

"I've been to the damnedest li'l lunch at the Cosmo Club." She was all dressed up in her most respectable drag. Today auburn-haired, she wore only lipstick and her skin showed through. It was beautifully pale. She now offered accurate clench-jaw imitations of nice ladies. Their club had just pronounced her, so she swore, a Junior Miss of Promise in the Realm of the Brush. "Oh well, I got three drawing sales out of it and one nice Jessica lady offered to pay for my apartment in exchange for certain 'hospitalities offered no more frequently than every fortnight when I'm in the country.' "

"You're kidding."

"About pay for play, yer Angelina never jokes."

At the window, Robert waved through the second and middle O of "Ossorio's" tripleheader. "*Here* he is," she smiled, touching the back of her hair. But he came ushering a dark youth. "Uh oh," she pouted, "I'm in no mood for a boy audition today, not one of *his* boys anyway. The only thing I hate worse? One of his upper-class twit Adlai-sucking Barnard cover-girlsies." But we went through our usual cheek kisses and rote exclamatories. Robert poked me, "Don't look now, Lord Airedale on the trail of Literature, but you're wearing a nightshirt."

"He is," Angie noticed, now Robert had.

"Show Gideon your legs, Hartley. I've told him about Angie and you, style leaders in the youth movement, two art history time bombs just ticking to go off. —This is Gideon. Gideon is a very good painter, Angie."

"Do tell."

He looked adolescent and his jet-black hair grew in garlands of ringlets; his skin was the color of toffee with touches of raw apricots burning in both round cheeks. His looks were so like a Fayum portrait, he did not at first appear either a contemporary or a likely English-speaker.

The youth stood here holding a satchel, one long white silk scarf trailed half out of it. I guessed he had just been wearing the thing but whipped it off before meeting us. He was short and self-possessed within a kind of unblinking innocence he'd somehow smuggled across the border of his recent boyhood. He looked both spoiled and furious. His brown eyes could go the longest time without blinking. That exemption made him seem as worldly as babyish as psychic, all at once.

Robert pointed to a chair and Gideon sat on it, obedient, silent, letting us look him over. We all freely did so. Angie now bent under the table, scoping out his lap. "Come on, Angie," Robert shook his head. "Don't be like that." The strange youth could tell he had not caught her on a good day.

Robert explained that Gideon here had been born in Egypt, then his Sephardic family—Alexandria's purveyors of the best office and art supplies—moved to New York. They soon misinvested everything through a disappearing relative. So Gideon was banished at age twelve to outer Queens. He had soon won U.S. scholarships; he soon knew Virgil Thomson, he sometimes helped the old man gather comestibles and cook; Gideon now sold Arts and Crafts ceramics as a sideline; he had exquisite taste with the luck to match it; he had found two Fabergé card cases, "the green ones, that Russian imperial pastille pistachioish green that's somewhere between lime and khaki, with the watered-silk enamel surface, you know those" and at a swapmeet in Swonsett!

Plus Gideon owned six Villon prints, a small early Kline-like Alfred Leslie abstraction, one Lichtenstein comic-book pencil drawing circa 1964, and the best (front facing panels Duncan Grant, verso ones—Vanessa Bell) Omega Workshop folding screen not in a museum.

"No fuckin' lie," she said.

"My, we are nearing the end of our month, aren't we, dollie?—And another thing. Gideon has a painting in his knapsack, show them your painting, babes. One of his. I think he's very Brahms Intermezzo 118 Number 2. I think his touch is exquisite. I put it somewhere on the Morandi–Milton Avery–Vuillard painter's painter continuum, I do."

"No shit."

Silent, somewhat shaken, this pretty boy now directed his huge brown eyes toward Robert's crystal blue ones, and met only steadying encouragement. He risked reaching into his leather bag. Now I saw that the silk kerchief mostly wrapped a little landscape. The picture had been painted very fast, it seemed—and on a good wooden panel. It was barely a foot square. The thing got passed from hand to hand, from me, toward Robert, who seemed to view it as for the first time and to evince, as usual, no doubt at all. His angel face—now aimed toward Alabam—grew determined, and, with this side's nostril flaring, seemed some young god-warrior's. It showed that today he really meant this.

We all watched Angie take the thing. We watched her consider its paint, the brushwork, its odd color, half-saccharine half-acidic. She tipped it twice, to see light move across it. Her mouth stayed curled to one side, chewing nothing, speculative. She now lifted the panel a jeweler's distance from her face so she could site along its surface, could study a lush build-up of oil paint forming scalloped clouds. These'd been done all in blues and harsh plums, in vinegar ochres and one strange pink-gray. You could see that he had studied Whistler, a painter we all kept forgetting then remembering, but never knew quite where to "place."

Gideon's painting appeared done outdoors—in a gondola on a river just at dusk, and finished only when the daylight left him blind.

Angie at last glanced up from her perusal; she stared across our table toward young Gideon—I saw her mouth half relax. It was such a look she offered him then. There still seemed a first layer of hatred in it. But something fresh had broken through. We noticed actual water resting just along the lower edge of either amber eye. Then, though her mouth, unmoving, still seemed irked and restless, she just nodded once, but with a grudged and certain emphasis.

"Szank you," Gideon said, lowering his gaze in the way a small animal shows respect before a larger one. She'd handed him his own picture, which was a very beautiful painting, we all now knew, now she'd said so and on such a Grumpy Angie day. Then he did something very simple. He passed her his white silk scarf. After seeking Angie's visual permission, Gideon bent across our table and looped his silk around her lovely neck.

Robert and I watched these two; we observed Angie's atypical surprise. Now, riveted, right in front of us, young Gideon seemed to be giving her such a look of true sexual urgency. It was such a pleading boyish "help me with this thing of mine" look, that it resembled snake charming. It was, come to think of it.

Robert, caught off guard, laughed. Then I did, but one boy and one girl kept studying each other.

Our Robert could appear with a gent one day, a lady the next. It kept Angie guessing, and kept me. But to find that this latest male of his could paint like a young master and might also like women, it seemed to've shocked Robert, and improved Angelina's day.

As if Robert and myself were not present, while ignoring Robert's chuckle—Gideon now said only to her, and in a French Arabic accent that was lavish as some young man eating a pomegranate in the public market and not caring how much pink juice ran down his stubbled chin and smooth neck, "In the lower left corner of a picture name of *Bossman IV* you showed at group show on Broome last spring? c'est ca? was a shape, not un triangle, but more like . . ." and here he held up both brown hands, long ones for a young boy so rounded. Hands formed a parallelogram through which he stared at her a second. If he had licked the air within that form, he could not have been more explicit.

"Shape like . . . this, shape. And it was half of it of the plum color, ripe almost to ze color of a man blood? Other half the orange from the tomato soup, in the red can, soup that Warhol . . . and over it one blue splash, very wet. Flaa, like 'flaa,' jus flung, you know? You paint so wet, Miss Angelinabama Byrnes, *stays* wet. How you paint it? I told my friend, said this is the best four square inches of paint outside of captivity of Louvre. I don't know how you know so much and can forget it to let de paint jest happen so and . . ."

"I think Ima gonna to be sick," Robert kicked me under our table.

"You?" I said, "I fink I'm about to projectile 'flaaa.' You know from 'flaaa'?"

"Boys my boys, do quick go fuck yourselves." Angie's eyes had not left his. "The child can paint. The child has eyelashes for miles. And God knows, dis chile gots taste."

"Come on, Hartley." Robert stood. "Hoist up your Molly Brown nightshirt and bring along your short-story masterpiece. We're out of here. Unless they want us to follow them to her place and just let us watch it happen, wet. I mean I've got ten minutes between appointments. This bored, I wouldn't really half mind."

"You fuckin' wish. I don't given lessons, except"—she turned Robert's way with the loathing only long-thwarted desire can hatch—"directly."

We left. We had to pick up dry cleaning. We both suspected Gideon was in.

Target: Heart

 upid must be a masochistic acupuncturist, his former quiverful of arrows now just rattling with needles to porcupine his own chubby legs and arms, but, oh, just look how his little pink mouth is smiling!

I loved Robert and we both really sort of worshipped Angie. But Angie only truly loved Robert while seeking aspects of him in many others. She considered herself a proto-feminist despite being the almost-deb from Savannah, but she still washed Robert's clothes for him, she actually ironed his jockey shorts. He said he preferred "roughing it," preferred not. "I don't need this from you," he said, bailing up his dirty towels. She loved only Robert who—while bringing Angie sundry Gideons—was just then seeing a Brazilian stewardess and, soon afterward, her identical twin brother, a Delta air host whose last idea had been to get out of their mother's womb, but only after his smarter sister showed him the emergency hatch; but God was he ever brown and beautiful.

Angie was drawn briefly to Gideon who, once he knew her, turned back to his first interest, Robert, who later admitted that our gifted Egyptian-born landscape painter (while enlisting many hundreds of others to join him in it) seemed to mainly love Gideon. Gideon seduced, not unwillingly, me, too. Because I was there. Because I liked his work. Because Robert's carry-over love lit me to advantage: moonlight merely being sunlight on the rebound.

Marco seemed mainly political—barely sexual at all. Our group's lascivious conversations made him uneasy. That gave him far more weight at our table, since we loved making some dear one sense how good we were getting at being real real baaaaad. Then Marco himself turned up at Ossorio's with a bruised lip, not self-inflicted, and we figured he had tried something ineptly erotic with the very person least interested in him, but the person he felt most for, politically. (A Russian ship with many sailors was in port just then.) Poor Marco confused conscience with desire. To each his own.

Even beautiful Tony Wu had it bad. I'd continued tutoring him in finer points of Southern grammar and English Lit. After his eventful visit to my dive, I worried about our first chaperoned lesson. But Tony himself seemed calm, even drugged. As usual, Madam Wu audited. She offered me crystallized ginger and Moravian sugar cookies. Now I'd touched her son's secret beauties, I found her presence less censorious; to me, her skin looked very beautiful.

"I have obtained," Tony told me, midsession, "an interesting scrapbook containing many photographs concerning the personal effects of the poet John Keats. May I show you it, Mr. Hartley?" While his mother proofread his latest essay assignment, Tony led me twelve paces away. He opened the expensive book. There, tucked atop a lovely drawing of Keats as a boy, I found one of those photobooth strips, four dimestore pictures. They featured young Tony seated in the lap of Juan. Juan wore his hard hat and Tony seemed to be demonstrating, for Woolworth's camera, through a huge toothy smile, the vowel sounds O, A, and U.

"Yes, Tony, John Keats here has been widely translated but one does wonder how effectively he might communicate with others who speak many differing languages." (I was starting to sound like my pupil.)

"Perhaps, Mr. Hartley, he talked the Tongue International!" And Tony gave me a look of such gratitude, such love, but gratitude, of course, to me for the love of Juan, probably a married father of four. God knows what confessions Juan's own priest was hearing and what the priest was doing during. "But . . . returning to your mother and our nest of split-infinitives waiting over here . . ."

As usual, it seemed that none of us loved the one that adored him/her back freely and so might've offered boring kindness in return. But it was certainly all very busy, yes. Being so young, we had energy to spare for this much wasted lovely spinning, the humping, the losing half-on-purpose, dates broken, screaming scenes in restaurants, all in exchange for the Drama and its limitless funding-source: Our very own Adrenaline. The drug of choice.

It was, after all, tailor-made for us IN us, and came free.

I never saw Angie at a party where she didn't greet me first thing, not with my own name or a simple courtesy hello—but always, "Is he *here* yet?" "Am I?" I asked. The joke was lost on her.

At one such opening Angiebama, drunkish, wearing blue cigarette smoke like a veiled hat, called me aside. "No, he's not here yet," I, testy, answered in advance.

"It's not that tonight," she said. "Listen, I have read your work. You at least know what a sentence is. Till Alzheimer's, through Alzheimer's, that'll keep you busy. You have seen my paintings and Gideon's, and we know that Marco is respected in that one-language-to-another-world of his. But how much have we heard of his music, really? I mean, I ask you, 'Bicycle Built for Two'? And do we even know enough to judge?"

I took her by the shoulders and shook her, hoping to gauge just how drunk she was. "You are doubting Robert?"

"But I mean, how can we be sure? And it's so frustrating that he hasn't fucked either one of us. Don't you find?" And then she hugged me, sobbing and sobbing, burning a cigarette hole in my lapel. "He's ruined my evening and he's not even in it yet. Did you see him wearing that faded cerulean blue T-shirt last Thursday? With his eyes. It's not fair, Hartley. Angie needs a dildo discount. About thirty would hit the spot."

What drawbacks did our four-star sex drive court? Certain Braille-sized body lice called Crabs (we kept insecticide in our medicine chest alongside the toothpaste). A urinary irritation we found was titled The Clap. (This was a complaint that serious penicillin most always quelled [see same medicine cabinet].) Such sex-life disadvantages seemed as giddy and essentially polite as we were, and maybe just as slightly beside the point. The few by-product problems sex offered seemed, like most of ours then—the woes of over-carbonation.

And, naturally, we risked the standard peril: Having your Heart Broken. That old malady, like another impending sickness nearly as clever, even today has no known cure.

Except of course, the usual. Time.

How Shall We Mainly Live? Who to Mostly Be?

n memory, from this cliff overlooking fifty, the thousand parties meld into a single auction, one catered emergency. Robert's friends alerted him to bashes, he included Angie and me. I arrived in the neighborhood first. You could usually hear it. The disco bass so loud, an aquarium half a block away could experience total fishkill in forty minutes flat. You found the rental chromium coatracks in the hall; fur coats swooned over it, black sequined evening bags lay under mink hems like startled eggs just laid there. You heard three Romance languages being shouted. You smelled the hemp and tobacco smoke, colognes in jousting competitions. You let yourself in, head held aside to fend off volume and the crush of strangers checking you out before you found a secure planting place to stand still, to gather strength, and glare back, seeming invincible because bored preemptively. Not "on the make" but "made." Not "new here," "known here."

These rooms of dancers with too little space to wave their arms, of talkers with ideas too subtle to express above rock this loud, they register in memory less as festivals than firesales. Odd, the emergencies themselves emerge in retinal memory as discrete parties—arrivals, drama-middles, exit lines— with hot foods served, dress themes observed, a young English film actor throwing porch furniture off somebody's terrace down onto cabs below and no one stopping him but everybody watching.

In this citadel of overstimulation, you can be cut off from your funding source and, for a good while, not quite notice. Reeling home one dawn, thick-mouthed and weak-eyed but somehow spiked with a sense that this was real life I lived among the doors and windows and dicks and names and streets, I came upon a flower vendor setting out his wares.

The Korean boy's bouquets were wrapped in colored cones of tissue paper. Each clump of daisies and roses was plopped into a green caddy-holder that'd supported ten thousand other such profitable decapitations. I heard a sound long forgotten, and only then did I see the bees. Had their fore-bees lived right here since Chelsea was the name of a local farm? Had they shifted their hives from hollow trees to thriving back alleys as time condensed their honeyed choices?

City bees now plundered the last nectar that such bartered blooms would offer. Bees' hive, where? Some alley chimney of East 57th Street? Maybe Fort Lee, New Jersey, across the river. These flowers, airlifted in, wouldn't last four days. But insects still fed on them. And helpless not to, flowers seemed ready for last fun, last rites. New York.

Could I call myself grounded in Manhattan, or was I, severed as cut flowers, just pretty enough to still sell myself as vital? I pulled the overcoat around me, I plundered pockets but found I lacked the cash for posies.

Oh well. Leave them to the bees and memory.

Night Class

e read the same novel then met at our table to discuss it, urgent. Márquez and *Middlemarch* were all we could agree on. We convened most nights at six. Ossorio himself presided over his homemade expresso machine, copper piping and antique spigots; it seemed the creation of a drunk Navy welder, Alexander Calder, and Jules Verne. Ossorio's prices had advanced again. He still welcomed us with a phrase I learned too late was Spanish for "Ah, here they hop in once more, my white and wounded fluffy baby birds."

One night, Robert, the boy so often called a lookalike for the archangel Gabriel that ten minutes later he didn't recall if you'd said that or griped about this recent wet weather, brought our meeting to relative order: "Have you ever considered Heaven? I don't mean as a travel option. I can't credit it as an actual place, though hearing that would kill my believing parents. I mean as a subject. We mustn't let this cynical age Novocaine all our better Christian iconography. There's still gold in them there hills. Let's hog it. We're already out of fashion, none of us is Minimal; but the trend'll change.

They're already hungry for emotion, our wetness, what Gideon calls our "flaa." —Can we each agree to do a short work on this topic (a small one in the cases of you, Angie and Gideon)? I want to know now what your titles'll be, and when you'll have your masterworks finished. We can throw a recital, reading, and studio visit one night next week. I'm partied out since that eighteenth-century Masked Ball thingum. This will be something real, something new to look forward to. No powdered wigs and beauty marks, umkay? Just 'chez moi, pour nous,' Our Blue Heaven, what say?" He sensed an unenthusiasm. "You're so bossy," Angie said. Both she and he were "only" children.

"No, reconsider, please. We'll do it as a Strengthening. Angel Calisthenics. —Okay, myself? I'll go first. Come Tuesday next, at seven p.m.? at my lovely home? I will perform a new piano piece called 'The Archangel Gabriel's Homely Identical Twin: A Tonepoem in Two Parts.' I'm just winging this, okay? But mine will be based upon the hymns of my wasted Lutheran youth. I've told you about my old organ teacher (no comment), his asking me to run upstairs and sit naked in the third-floor pipeloft and tell him how each low note felt in my . . . Yeah, I thought I'd bored you all with that. I love hymns even now, don't you? I mean, 'Seraphim and Cherubim, Falling Down Before Thee'? That can still make a thinking boy hard.

"Angie? Just one little painting maybe? and why not move more toward the blues instead of your recent burnt sienna earthtones? To see your hands is to know your palette. So what's your title? What's Miss Teen Alabama's idea of Paradise?"

" 'Santa's Workshop,' " she said. "All I ever wanted for Christmas was the toyshop. Every drippy paintpot, and to have all the little big-dicked elves as my happy slaves."

I got chillbumps, staring. Had I ever told her this fantasy? No, I'd only thought it, hard. But if anything intense happened recently in my own head, my bed, it seemed to follow direct to hers: My slapdash hope of playing well in a big big room with others, of making bright pure toys alongside those few who were really best at that.

I grabbed a paper napkin. I would try writing out some title grand enough to hold my place here at Ossorio's round table.

"Hartley Mims the somethingth? I'll need the name of your story, and I want a draft read aloud by you on Tuesday. I crave your heaven. And I want to like it. And we want to laugh, please, in your haphaphappy-talkin paradise."

"Mine will be called . . . "—I read blurred ink from the white napkin's pulp—" 'Toward a More Precise Identification of the Newer Angels.' "

"You pretentious fairy. You are, like me, destined to rise." She laughed with pleasure, and leaned right over and kissed me wet. "You fum Mars or wha'?"

"When I make water, I make water. And when I make Paradise, you'll book ahead. So eat your VD-ridden heart out, Sports Medicine."

We all now turned toward the pleasing sight of Gideon. Who shrugged. The French! The Arabs! The Sephardics! He got all that world weariness poured into a mere hundred and thirty succulent pounds. Then—to stay safe—sure of its still being reasonably adorable, he showed us his excellent dimples, but only in a demi-smile, in dimple eighth notes.

Gideon said he thought he maybe had one done already. One with gold and blue in it. He said he did not intend to create what anybody ever asked him to, never for money, and certainly not for mere childish sloppy fun. But Gideon might, if he remembered, bring along the small one he had done already. "So." Robert pretended to write on marble tabletop, ringed with saucer stains.

"Title. of. Gideon's. Paradise. 'Done Already.' "

Robert rarely went at anybody. (I once blundered by telling Angie I'd just defended her from someone's insult; Robert gave me such a disappointed [and therefore schooling] glance; Angie went berserk with paranoia.)

But this he'd said to Gideon was truly devastating. Robert knew it. Angie knew it, I did. Marco, eyes lowered, understood. But Gideon, you see, did not.

Job Readiness

Y ou can be waiting in New York a long time.

If you're lucky, you'll find how to stop expecting much or how to keep expecting everything, but with payoff postponed indefinitely.

(Given everybody's secret hope of at least posthumous discovery, you can hover for decades, more. Maybe Paradise will be stardom's forestalled "Callback.")

* * *

The lady who took in and dispersed our occasional splurge dry cleaning had become very good at her job, and at the waiting, and she stayed very friendly.

On the mirrored wall behind her overlit counter, under a stylistically out-moded sunburst clock, she'd hung a framed publicity still of herself.

It had been inscribed by her—courteous—to this very shop. It was suspended shoulder to shoulder between the inscribed glossy of Tony Randall, and one Bobby Sherman, just over a sun-faded Mimi Hines. Remember the gifted singer-comedienne Mimi Hines? Does Mimi Hines?

This cleaning receptionist had already aged three decades and forty-two hairstyles past her posted glamour shot; but, to that image, the time-span involved seemed incidental. Fact is, she had sung at the Metropolitan Opera, once.

While you were naming substances in clothes' stains—chocolate, red wine, and . . . erotic . . . some erotic liquidish substance (of the male variety), does that come out easy? . . . Nina might—after first asking rote encouraging questions about your "emerging" artistic career—again pull forth her own review. She'd got it laminated early on, got it under wraps quick, but it had yellowed to a cigar brown nonetheless. I'd all but memorized it but never acknowledged having seen it before:

> *"Stepping in for Zinka Milanov was young Nina Fouquet-Marshall, with a supple if as yet unevolved though not un-promising voice. She has genuine beauty, occasional stage presence, and is someone definitely to consider watching up ahead. The scenery, as usual, proved adequate if . . ."*

Nina was lucky. She *had* sung at the Met, once. She *still* took lessons, she *kept* vocalizing daily, she *stayed* ready for recall. She'd *got* the photos made, and at prime time. Nina always "dressed" for work. Her haircombs agented a complex French Twist. Her full stage makeup offered no concession to the shop's and the world's ungrateful non-Met fluorescence. She hostessed here, auditioning her every dry cleaning customer as part of her ideal come-back audience (and claque). Nina Fouquet-Marshall had got quite used to waiting in New York.

Me, too. I'd soon and suddenly lived quite a while in that jail-and-pedestal of the zip code 10014. I'd begun writing one slim story that became a novella, soon almost a novel and eventually a huge tome, the kind it would be easy never to feel qualified to finish. The kind that was fun to discuss but perhaps impossible to sell. But, what the hell, I could also now use chopsticks like some Chinese hit man, eating on the run. I recognized eight hundred people on sight—including my hardworking neighbors and our lady of the dry cleaning: "Nina, how goes it?" Robert said we could learn from her and called Nina "Fabulous, a sort of unicorn boarding unrecognized in our Claremont stable full of rental plugs and carriage horses."

I knew all Vermeers in hiking-distance and on terms most intimate; I lived on a first name-basis with those Dutch paintings' times of afternoon light—each highlight brushstroke, a particular if minor friend. By now I "used" the Met Museum; I'd learned to go and look at just one picture for forty minutes, not simply gorge on two thousand images for three tourist seconds apiece.

I had endeared myself to the immense emotional Hispanic family next-door. The week after I moved in, I—from my fourth-floor window—spied a cop about to ticket then tow the neighboring sons' double-parked (hot?) hotrod; I found myself banging on their door, yelling, 'Quick, cop, goin' git your car, man! Queek!" Dash made, ticket eluded by nanoseconds as our whole floor watched from balconies, the community closed around me, "tight." I might look white and set and snide, but I had proved myself "all right."

We, in this poor folks' building, agreed to be similar. Our conversations in the barely moving elevator crossed all language barriers to indicate heart-felt exhaustion at the end of long long workdays. When needed, everything essential could be mimed. A palm placed to the lower spine, a rotation of neck and rolling of eyes, the universal sign for Alienated Labor. Complaints about hard work, terrible cold or heat, always drew a nod, a smile, a shaken head. We knew to hate The Law even more concentratedly and personally than The Law yet hated us. It gave you preparation time for Justice's incoming mischief at your own expense.

The Night of the Angels

nknowns, we would gather at Robert's to perform-reveal our celestial attempts. It was July Fourth, 1984; I remember this because of the fireworks our neighbors kept setting off with such scary regularity. Our City seemed even more than usually a war zone, but a comic one and safer for that. New York summers are so underrated. You get to throw your windows open. It's too hot even for thieves to work at their brisk autumn-winter pace. The streets are less crowded and those left in town seem to have more time and emotion, and to wear fewer clothes.

Many young artists from our neighborhood, those most rabidly striving, would travel out to some Hampton or other. They crowded into insanely overpriced cottages, time-share bunkbeds. They kept dressing up and going to parties where they hoped to meet the older situation-makers from New York; instead they met only other overdressed underfinanced young strivers paying too much for the right to stalk nobody more hopeful than themselves.

Served the climbers right.

Our Circle, too poor for that, stayed put. We did our homework in town; our task? to now amuse ourselves via each other. For that, it seemed, was what we did and who we were. Itinerant Entertainers. Somehow this felt easier to see during the summers. Maybe we were working up to playing Hamlet as a group. But, for now, we'd been cast as The Players, a crew just glad for the work, and only vaguely aware of its comic drama's uses here at Court.

Tonight, still living at our entry-level, we could afford the admission-price time-share of goofing off, being the paid fun for only each other. —We were "the talent," if by default. The sole career that counted on this night of the angels was Delight.

Our company felt far less toxic than the Hamptons'. (A rumor reached us, but then so many did. About a friend of Angie's from Morton Street who'd caught a cold that went direct into pneumonia that left him so shrunken he soon looked like a pile of leopard-spotted celery, and was, in six weeks, dead. And he'd been a godlike weight lifter, so quickly overtaken. Poor guy, bench-pressed into oblivion that fast. It was just a rumor but it made the rounds and, unlike most such gossip, never quite vanished.)

Summers, New York's fire department opened hydrants at either end of our block to keep the restless street kids cool, occupied. Through Robert's open window, we could hear their splashing, could hear our own known urchins pushing each other into cold spray then squealing out of it; we heard the pop and pump of firework munitions created only to look pretty, ending. From time to time one Roman candle's overheated color would shoot past a window, trailed by that most magical of human sounds: "Ahhhs" uttered from heads lifted toward some spectacle right overhead.

White pigeons, spooked by noise, settled on the window ledge and made their pearly coos and, if you squinted, they appeared almost a dovelike product. Robert's dozens of crystals, hung from thumbtacks, strung in all four windows, caught streetlight invisible from within the apartment. The pendants proved that someone before this building must now be twirling white sparklers.

We lounged around, half glazed in sweat, drinking cold cold Rolling Rocks, bottlenecks smeared with lime to make beer taste somewhat more expensive. Robert, I noted, sipped only ice water.

Seated on an heirloom steamer trunk, Marco offered us a line from Unamuno, "The devil is an angel, too." Then we got, straight from his memory, the word for "Angel" in each language Marco knew (sixteen). Was it just us or did these words not sound especially poetic and mellifluous? They flew.

Next, I stood beside the fourposter and read my new story aloud. I tried to impersonate the chief angel supervising freshmen orientation for a new crop of winged ones. The tale met with a certain admiration—both for its proposed order of angel hierarchy, and the leisurely, conversational, getting-to-know-you quality of my intended paradise. There was applause, it held. I flopped down on a bolster at the head of Robert's bed. I felt surrounded by a second, purer, kind of humid air.

These were the only people in the world I wanted to please and, having done that, I could now relax, for maybe another six weeks.

Both Angie and Gideon had hung paintings in Robert's short hallway and, bringing over the one good floorlamp, we now admired them. Gideon was teased for not bothering to attempt a new one; but he still didn't seem to know he ought to find such charges troubling. Angie's painting showed a manhole cover that soon became the shieldlike pattern from a tortoise's shell. A convincing oval fluorescent tube had been painted all around it (painted factually as if by a medical illustrator). She had given the turtle shell its own industrial-strength halo. I remembered telling her about a snapping turtle I'd seen murdered. Had Angie awarded the dead creature a miner's carbide headlamp? You were, as ever, left with questions. But new ones.

Robert had greeted us at the door and, on turning, casually showed the homemade wings. He said he'd considered throwing out early drafts of the piece we would soon hear, plus his sketches for the *Ocean Liner* symphony. Instead he'd scissored those pages into feather shapes. Then he stapled hundreds of these, overlapping, to twin pieces of long cardboard cut in curves. The striped paper and its speckled notes looked, at a distance, strangely like the markings of some white seabird. Given the heat, Robert wore only jeans, a white scoop-necked T-shirt, wings. He had fastened the left span around one shoulder with some twine; the other stayed attached via a web khaki belt. These Xed like bandoliers across his back, as he settled before his peeling veneer piano.

He slowly lit a dozen candles and now asked Marco to kill the lamp as our composer faced his new score. Robert played the two-part tonepoem, played well if with some church training evident in a steady underpulse and maybe overmuch pedal. The first half he presented was an exquisite melting thing, rendered more exciting by the shrieks of our neighbor kids, the jets of water heard striking asphalt. Pink molten spray from a Roman candle lit the fire escape across the street then cooled to darkness.

The starting half of Robert's poem was lyrical, a sort of waking up in Paradise look-see. It had long runs and the Fauré *Requiem*'s airy sweetness. The second half reprised the first but in a manner somewhat hellishly lumbering, overdetermined. Though it possessed a thorny integrity, when the second ended, when Robert turned around, wings shifting away from our applause, he sensed that something had been lacking. The two halves did not adhere. We'd all heard this.

His right hand on the bench, his left atop his instrument, he said, "Tell me true, I can take it." His face took on a beseeching softness. He was a spectacle that night, brown from sailing and from baking on his roof, with the Swedish carpenter shoulders, and a glimpse of his chest's tattoo, plus the wings' guy-wires.

I can still see his paper feathers moving in a mild breeze while some cherry bomb echoed along our street. A great Mediterranean cry rose up.

"Number one," Angie spoke first and we, having sensed a weakness in Robert's composition, felt relieved not to address it ourselves. "One: Never take the wings off. You've hit on a fashion accessory I didn't know was missing from the world till tonight. Number two: Mother will now tell you how to fix your tonepoem. Simple. This is what only a good painter can tell a fairly good composer. And you *are* good. You're just not grown. Listen . . ."

Robert's face bent itself into a paroxysm of penitence, it looked erotic, in extremis. It admitted, "I screwed up, I made something very bad for my pals and now I've slaughtered all their future respect for me forever." And yet such hope still lived in the gaze he offered her ("Maybe I can fix it in a year? Maybe they'll forgive me when I do?").

"It's not a diptych you've written. More a triptych. You probably got too literal about your own two wings, you narcissist. Try this, why dontcha? Play the sweet one first, play the sour cubistic thing second, and then, verbatim, end with the sweet one again, no changes, no pushing up the emphasis, not even a bit, though you'll want to, Love Machine. Repeat it exactly as you did it first. Thing'll come out completely different. It'll truly seem paradise the second time. Because, by then, it will all sound completely earned."

We sat in candlelight, we stared at each other, we did not risk a single smile about our own good fortune. We were lucky, we knew it, we were not scrambling in the Hamptons and, better, didn't want to be. We were honestly entertaining each other and therefore learning. Could we make each other briefly content? Could we make this evening, through our own heavenly descriptions, indescribable? Yes, we probably could.

The hardest thing to do is tell the truth and have your listeners love hearing something that difficult to bear: You're not perfect; you're a player but you still need work.

I remember feeling my usual sinus burning. I remember hoping Robert would say nothing now. No word, please. He did not. Guessing we all had time for this, he simply turned back to his piano. To play. Robert breathed once. Then—paper wings suspended between shoulder blades as easy as male genitals between thighs hang, solemn, replete, concentrated—our wizard, as instructed, began again.

I was so glad I'd already presented my piece. Imagine following his Paradise Lost Then Corrected! Angie was the only other person on this bed. As I sat upright against its headboard, she wiggled over and—just as Robert hit the first complex chord—rested her head in my lap. He seemed to play with more rolling conviction now, as if her suggestion had given him a confidence. He settled into the work as if he had not written but memorized it, and from some source superior, foregone.

Now his playing bypassed that earlier determination. Instead, it unfurled; it oared, it wingbeat forward. And this new ease let us look around. This ease let us absorb our own scene as if looking back and down on it.

The windows stood ajar, supported by sawed-off broomsticks (or, no, what were those? plumber's friends?). Pigeons, made nervous by pyrotechnics, sometimes came to rest on the ledge and then swerved off, returning. Across the street, our pizzeria's usual neon burned, hissing; it spread fitful pink, then a humming blue across the facade opposite. Robert's crystals, intensifying colors, seemed the dripping faucets of some distillery where light is manufactured.

Tonight, rendered intimate by his music and our after-hour whorehouse familiarity, the street itself seemed so narrow you could reach its far side just by leaning off our fire escape; you could water those leggy zinnia in the windowbox opposite.

Seated at the piano, one half-dressed boy wore formal wings. Candlelight played over the planes of his dark back. Light made much of his ringlets. Light picked out separate feathers, first drafts of the very music his long hands now played.

Roman candles' phosphorous tints fired by at crazy angles. They seemed— in their rocking surge—short-lived, half-sexual, pagan in spectacle—Roman.

As our Robert ended the opening section and bolted into second's gangly turns, I felt Angie tuck into herself and enjoy his every awkward complication, knowing now that an emotional competition waited dead ahead, and all at her suggestion.

I fought not to stroke her dye-burned hair, not to whisper something childlike. A smell lifted from her like heated milk scented slightly by the saucepan's steel, a scent childlike in its blank trust. I felt honored by the weight of her good head. I judged it weighed just eight to ten pounds. What a miracle, a mind this fine should be so light!

I looked over at Marco. He often preferred to stand when others felt compelled to sit; he leaned back upright against a wall near the broom closet, arms crossed, head swinging a bit, filthy glasses glinting, locked in thoughts of usual purity.

Gideon sat slung across a kitchen chair, facing Robert but with both black eyes fixed instead on the tip of his own new and pointy right shoe. He seemed to be judging Robert's sound against the visual evidence of the costly shoe itself. Robert paused, just the correct length of time and commenced, repeating the first.

The way you know true things in your very follicles, in the basis of your next breath, from the scrotum to the inner ears and back down the IRT express of your nervous system which IS a form of transportation—we all gained what we had earlier suspected: how gifted Robert was, how right our AngieAlabama had just been. What had first seemed an exercise for friends became, with one dynamic change, a composition fit for groups of strangers. It started as gifted kid stuff then got pushed, by certainty, reiteration, playful community, to a fast hothouse maturity.

And without writing one extra note! By simply knowing the material so thoroughly, by trusting its seaworthiness to withstand this second voyage out.

I felt then—as the voices of the street built, as another pink-gold rocket feathered past, as Robert reached the arc of the gentle music's soaring—something lock into place. It registered bodily as a single isolated hiccup. Angie, head in my lap, looked up at me then. As if responding to a question with a question, which was actually an answer, at the very moment Robert finished, just before we'd pitch upright and applaud our winged one, she whispered a word straight up into my face: "Happy?"

I could only nod, once, down.

Finally, secure, surrounded, I was, that. I had felt—as completely as a work of art is art, with the brevity of a single potent wing-beat—the H- word.

We would soon stumble downstairs, kicking through party streamers and burned rocket husks, we'd head toward Ossorio's caffeine and, after vowing to visit each other's hometowns for official tours of our squandered early years, in linked inches of a single golden line from her felt pen, we finally believed ourselves worthy, this night of the angels, to give Eternity itself our single autograph!

Robert's angel triptych, written as a lark—got included in a concert that was called "Ten Composers Under Thirty-Five: A New Romanticism Afoot?" (At Ossorio's, this gave rise to foot fetish jokes.) Angie was picked for some decent juried three-person show in Houston and they actually sent her a plane ticket to the opening. Her first free fare. She brought it to our table to show us. "Round trip?" I asked, checking for her. We still didn't trust the few good things that fell our way from strangers. Marco, who'd never mentioned knowing Russian, was now translating uncollected Isaac Babel stories into English. He explained the difficulties and read aloud a story so good I vowed to quit. "But," he told me, "you are something Babel was not, ever."

"Thanks, Marco . . . what?"

"Isaac Babel wasn't born in Falls, North Carolina. Think of the material he missed."

"Great. What a vote of confidence. I wasn't born in revolutionary seaside Odessa, either, ditz."

Gideon sold his blue-gold nocturne to a famous genius poet whose dad had founded the world's biggest brokerage firm. And I, after waiting forever, heard from a magazine that mailed a check and the exact date I should look for my first published short story.

Finally a single magazine arrived by mail containing fiction of a certain length, my name claiming it. (Twice!—once in the table of contents, once hovering—a wing—below the title, above my text!)

I'd deleted my unasked-for "Jr." Which of Dad's golf partners might take this work as Dick Senior's?

Faking disinterest, I bought a copy right at our corner newsstand not thirty-five feet from my bed/desk. It felt warm as toast.

I carried it to our empty table; the hour was early; none of our Circle ever appeared before two or three.

Over coffee, I flipped through the issue, sniffing gloss paper. Its ink smelled like tea. I endured the opening ads for luxury cars, for plum-sized jewels; I then perused some town talk. And, oops, what have we here? I "chanced upon" a tale.

I remember Ossorio was watering the plants that day—tall "mother-in-law's-tongues" in brass pots. There was the extra sound of rushing wet and a bright domestic sense of calm defending me.

I read it cold, as if to judge the work of any no-name stranger. In print, alive in the visible (purchasable) world, it first seemed the product of some-one not unlike myself. But soon, this shape appeared made by someone finer, more serene, more generous. Less a bitch, not so apt to whine. Less likely to pine for loves hard-drinking and unattainable. A deeper, better friend.

Reading, I wondered: What if I had stayed in Falls? Had New York kilned me into someone harder or far more hopeful? Imagine if I'd not met Robert, Angie. How had I even come to be here at this green marble table, one that felt so populated before anybody else showed up? What force had let my story ascend into plain view of the whole world (for at least one week)?

On paper, at Ossorio's, in an toney typeface not my Hermes portable's, I seemed to learn what I owned so far. How much I needed yet to know! What I read was executed (dreadful, deadly firing-squad word) with the correct-ness of a grammatical model for my Chinese-American students. And yet, it seemed far less alive than the life we really willy-nilly led here: its squalor, its raw fun, its serious work, its temporary tiffs, and rabid loyalties. Still, even fictionalized, who would ever care to read about our ragamuffin band? Hadn't I always exaggerated Robert's beauty and virtue? Could Angie be half the pugnacious diva I daily required? All we'd earned so far was rent on floorspace for our makeshift workshops. Nothing had yet truly happened to us. Sure, some erotic popularity. But certainly not fame. Barely a head cold.

Still, reading fiction about a terrier traumatized during divorce, I experienced, as if for the first time, certain emotions that some stranger-author had stuffed—perhaps overactively—into each paragraph.

The boy writer was at least sheepdogging me through events and sensations, sentence to sentence, accountable to the end. His nips at my heels were, at times, too evident. But at least the story was traversing an ambitious cliffside path. When it comes to guarding his first flock, a young sheepdog can never be too careful.

I finished reading a story that I myself had finished writing six months earlier. Even while at work with my scissors and gluepot, I'd forgot why I put in certain things. Humor, considered eighty times, had long since ceased to crack me up. But, at this remove, in others' typeface, I could offer at least a good father's fond half-smile as one joke did its single back flip, ably, if a bit too much on cue.

I looked up and around at Ossorio's tiles, wintogreen and custard; I glanced toward huddled coffee drinkers arguing at those tables set between me and streetlight. I seemed to be recalling one of my own sweet seriously fucked-up students: "Poor struggling brat. But I do hope the kid will keep trying. A story about a goddamn dog! But, in time, the boy might really hit on something. He'll bump against some event in life that's big enough to lift him. For now, he's overly happy to just be doing it! A four-year-old boy let loose in the Philharmonic's percussion section. Oh well, someday maybe he'll learn . . ." and I put my head down on the cool pages of my first visible story. And actually fell asleep.

Most of the night before, I'd been up pacing, stage fright. I feared I would feel a total fool when it was "out." My parents would simply airmail me a one-way ticket home, no note. Our so-so family honor besmirched, fools' names and fools' faces. It's painful, to be always so visibly trying . . . you know?

I slept on it, my work. When I waked myself—no one having nudged me—I guessed by the light it must be nearly four already. I felt some movement at our table and looked up and all my friends—pretending not to notice me—sat circled, reading their own copies of the self-same magazine.

Held up over their faces. "You guys," I laughed, sitting straight. But they maintained this pose of feigned detachment, reading, scanning me, reading me alive.

Friends' faces were hidden by my issue. (Who says I had no offspring?) Instead, I studied each set of hands. I saw Marco's tapered fingers, one knuckle smudged with the exact print of one bike-chain link, fingers strengthened by hours with the pear-wood recorder he had never let us hear him play. Gideon's were dark-skinned with the most beautiful pink nails and, I noted, this close, a colorless polish; I marveled that someone like me, scraping for the rent, should find ways and means to sustain a continental manicure. Robert's hands were an athlete's or a farmer-carpenter's, fractured by subtle veins that each terrace-farmed a different plane; each hand made you want to do a portrait—manly hands like those on slender boys by Botticelli. Angie's were a potato-eater's, and the more she tried to hide them via fingerless gloves and long sleeves, the more their energy tubered forth. Today hers were marred by a yellow ochre oil paint, half coating a cheap if big-rocked "dinner ring" I'd given her.

I saw my friends had planned to hide, as in some Steinberg drawing, behind whatever masks my work made. But though they knew I was awake, they somehow kept on reading. And when this ruse finally broke, when their copies lowered to show the separate principality of each grinning face, it pleased me more than I can say to note how two of them pressed a thumb or forefinger between slick pages. Keeping their places!

Angie and Robert nodded yes. "But look, pig." Her stained finger squeaked my paper. "You went and drooled on yours. —I swear, we can get him published, but you still can't take him out. First sign of success, nods off like some junky, salivates all over his own Page One."

No! I jerked forward, genuinely sorry, trying to blot it with my shirt cuff. "Wait here," Marco said. Where, I asked, was he going?

"To buy you a fresh one, Hartley."

"Hey, they printed others?"

I had always imagined that, after the first publication in some serious place, there would be only a continual Happiness onrolling. But it's never enough, is it? First you try to make the single good good thing; then you doubt you can ever repeat it.

My new worst fear: One morning next week, in my fourth-floor rear, with a view of the Hudson only if you are an acrobat willing to mount your deskchair uneasy on four casters—I would settle as usual before the yolk-colored Salvation Army desk, I'd expect to write beloved characters through yet another layer of crisis, toward some airier moment's latent grace; and all that would emerge, my own handwritten instruction: "Go home now. Join the goddamn Country Club, get it over with. Whom did you think you were kidding, Oh One Your Dad Still Calls Our Artiste of The Sewer?"

We who'd stayed in New York, truly stayed put now. Bars no longer asked for my ID. I told myself I went un "carded"—for reasons subtler than simply looking older. (Though I was definitely aging; the city slices its fair share right off the top, directly from your face.) I preferred to feel I simply looked less "new here." I had lost that rangy glow peculiar to recent arrivals. It's the glow that makes newcomers first popular and soon suspicious. A glow that, noticed and enjoyed by very many, fades so fast. Now, my writing must sustain whatever diehard virgin blush survived.

Red, Yellow, Blue

e, assuming immortality, used all our primal energy—the primary colors of your late twenties and early thirties: Red, Yellow, Blue.

We all knew how to start works of art. Some among us knew how to "sustain" an idea. But endings, how to finish? completions emotional, the pay-offs often still baffled us. Noticeable, still part-naïve, Robert, that triumph of Scandinavian coloring, overtly ambitious for a Midwesterner, now made serious progress on the *Titanic*. His apartment grew ever more stuffed with flotsam concerning the liner's sinking. He name-dropped the 1912 passenger list. I learned that Harvard's Widener Library had been given in honor of a student drowned. Above Robert's mantel, framed charts of the ship's cross sections. Some earlier fanatic had penned in names of passengers with arrows pointing to their staterooms. When Robert spoke of the sinking now, he got this moist troubled look that made him prettier but scarier.

"You're young and healthy," Angie once told him. "Why not study the history of serving strawberries and cream during Wimbledon? Just my luck, one friend is the walking Baptist Southern Gothic Kennel Club and the other goes belly-up over *The Poseidon Adventure* starring Shelley Winters as Orca the Whale. Laugh riot, the pair of you morbid goons." He shook his head with pity (her joke no use). He said Ang was not exactly chirpy herself; she believed that being passed over as a deb placed her suffering up there along-side Billie Holiday's. But Robert went right on explaining that many families in third class, see, were swamped in their little berths belowdecks and before first-class passengers even understood how major the problem was. He said that Captain Smith had not fired the first distress flare till a full hour after the berg struck. "Mostly he seemed to feel this social embarrassment. It was nineteenth-century manners trying to deny the scale of twentieth-century disaster." There had been an attempt to put the women and children in one place and the stay-onboard men in another; but the working-class families could not imagine separating in that way and so drowned.

I've often thought about it since. Robert became ever more pedantic and fascinating on the subject of the wreck. To humor him, we all went under with it, too. Again and Again. We learned. He tried showing Angie and me how it was the earliest, the most poetically condensed prediction of our soon-to-capsize shipwreck of a century. Two years before the First War, there remained this belief that progress and development and the fruits of Industry could be so titanic as to outsmart nature. Angie told him he was overreaching. It sounded like a thing someone less smart than he said at cocktail parties. "After all, only about six or eight hundred people died, right?"

"One thousand five hundred and three."

"Well, excuse me, bean counter."

Pacing, he was not amused. "But it was *who* went down. 'Top Drawer on Ocean Bottom.' It was all the people who could afford to invest in the promise their own brochure made. 'Unsinkable.' Survivors say that what you heard as the bow went under was 'the sound of a world of china break-ing.' One crew member had to use his empty revolver to keep men out of the women-and-children-first lifeboat 'collapsibles.' Mothers were setting their own hats on pretty sons, thirteen years old, disguised as girls to save their lives. You can't imagine how it felt! I mean, even if you jumped off, the water was three degrees below freezing and already full of deckchairs and barrels, and suction from the generators belowdecks could get you and hold you against the louvers till . . ."

Angie gave me a look. It said, This child is just barely afloat here. Needs to get out more. "And what," she started, "is the name of your *Titanic* sup-port group?" She sounded strict and overhelpful; he lowered his eyes, guessing we wouldn't understand.

" 'Lifeboat Number Thirteen.' "

"Honey, we love you but you are getting into such deep . . . trouble here."

(Every metaphor about the shipwreck seemed applicable and loaded, but applicable to what . . . ? Our crew had enjoyed such clear sailing so far.)

"And who comes to it, your wreck-fest? Who has time, of a busy Thursday evening in Manahatta?"

"Three Wharton investment bankers, a sweet old gay archivist from the New York Public Library, one crew member from the America's Cup winner last year who teaches girls' gym at the Dalton School, and two ancient English women who lost an aunt on it and are as polite and frumpy and dentally deformed as most Brit royalty. Those are the regulars."

"What, do you guys end meetings by holding hands and singing 'Nearer My God to Thee'? You actually have them up here?" She looked around. I understood then—Angie was jealous.

Of a shipwreck. 1912.

Street Crime Hurts Everyone

ne night, with me carrying the "centerpiece" from a party, we waded home from Studio 5-. It was either Bianca's birthday bash for Liza, or vice versa, or Halston's for Truman's, I forget. They blurred. Even during the parties. So much beautiful blurring of so much immediate drug-bright beauty. We'd later say, "If you think you remember a party, you probably weren't at that one."

Tonight our Mr. Gustafson, the sadistic imp, had convinced me to filch this table arrangement. Because there were magnolias in it. I've always hated the sight of dignified matrons leaving some bash after pulling each others' hair to snag a $7.98 "floral spray." As usual I lacked the strength to out-argue Robert, and so—sweet smells drifting up from waxy blooms—I carried forth this Carmen Miranda clot of leaves. Like so much else of that decade, it'd been spray-painted gold.

Talking, I was a little drunk or coked up or both. Robert's high was "natural" as we window-shopped, crunching through minor snow, gossiping the whole thirty blocks. We slowly began to feel followed. I said, " 'Hushed are the streets of many peopled Thebes.' Robbie, is there an echo out here or have you attracted further admirers?" He ignored me, and we went on discussing Edvard Munch's erotic oddities. Probably our first mistake.

We were set upon by brigands; they wore do-rags, their lower faces smothered behind railroad bandannas. Two weedy kids, maybe fourteen—smaller, sourer, tighter-wound than we. If we lived "hungry," they looked hungry.

Through magnolias' perfume, I seemed to smell burned electrical wiring. My head cleared quick. I passed the flower arrangement to Robert. He was so perplexed, he took it. In my disoriented state, saving these flowers seemed the goal, along with doing something heroic for Robert.

"Quick, take off!" Having accepted flowers, he, confused, made two steps forward. They were on him.

Kids' being so whip-thin only made their single huge silver gun—held high and trembling at arm's length—appear cartoon-gigantic. They slowly explained that this was a real gun. And, in it, real bullets.

"We never doubted that, not for one single sec, fellows." Robert, our leader—being the natural platinum blond—now got pressed back against a storefront grate. He asked the gangboss (the one with the gun), "What you need, man? Like some pretty flowers? —No. Say you want all my money I got? —Spent it. Back there. Fuckin' clip joint. Cover charges, two-drink minimum. No fair to us, is it? I mean, *you* guys go out. *You* know the clubs."

They told him he looked rich. "Give us it. Don't, we pop you."

"Fellows? If I had it, you'd be spending it by now. Trust me. Can't give you cash I *should* have. Check my pockets. We are walking home, right? It is four a.m., whatever. We did liberate the centerpiece. You figure we'd risk a stroll if we had a subway token or anything to hide?"

Shifting magnolias into one hand, his other strained to pull one pocket free of his velvet pants. Soon as I saw my friend's back tense, preparing, I knew this would be a bad move. It might seem sudden. It did. Robert's confidence always inspired him to rush things to their next theatrical level, then the next.

The outturned pocket showed white as a truce flag. But the second it appeared, one boy came at me and placed something into my side. I saw his eyes choosing just where it should go. It felt like one of the long hatpins my grandmother used to secure her black hats. Having placed a long pin in me, the kid stepped back.

Then the gun swung down on Robert. It cracked a new sound loose. The word SEWER seemed to appear overhead. Magnolias did one clownish roll into the gutter. Robbie's arms flew way way out. Next phrase I got was

"MANNED FLIGHT." The pistol whipping was, in memory, just a single heavy curving blow. But it had these filmy strips spoked within it, like big feathers comprising a single silver beating wing.

I was left standing untouched except for the hatpin burning my entire left sector. Had I been less rich-looking, not an apparent leader? Robert was down. The kids ran, cursing, hurling back at us the insult word beginning F-, a description of gay men that I cannot bring myself to write here even now. How had they known? Were the velvet and magnolias a magnet tip-off? But that year everyone was wearing velvet!

Robert waited on his back, palms up and opened alongside his head. The street had grown far darker. I saw his arms and legs now moving like a swimmer's. "Back stroke," I thought. I heard a bubbling sound. It seemed I'd have a long way to bend down in order to help him. Just as I commenced stooping, a pain the likes of which I'd never inhabited (seemed I was in it, not the other way round) that pain and a gush of crackling adrenaline struck me at the back of either knee. I fell half on top of him. "Here's another fine mess we've gotten us into." I tried "wit." My left hand clutched my left side and I knew what the warmth was but remained fixed upon the one hurt worse.

He tried saying something agreeable but his mouth sounded full.

Only when I bent closer over Robbie did I see how blood hid the entire blond face. His forehead was a black fringe come all across it. But, odd, he looked so beautiful, even hurt, the damage appeared half-planned. I made no sense. I must find help.

"You all right . . . I mean basically? Still here, right?" I crouched over him as if scared they might come back.

He turned his head and the street light showed me a great gash above one eye and I could only scream then. I was hurt but alive. Imagine if they had scarred him! I next screamed like some outraged little girl, "Not the face! Not thiiiis face!"

I called it over and over to a God I did not believe in, except, during Serious Uncatered Sewer Emergencies. One second-story window lit, offered the promise of help, fell immediately dark.

I grew practical-nursish. "Stay put, darl. Hart's off for help. Don't move." As if he could! But now he pointed to his face, saying just "Our, ouurs."

I could always interpret his odd sounds: " 'Eyes.' "

"Your eyes. Yes. Wait. Here, babe."

I ran two quicksand blocks. My left side was opening and closing, a new vertical mouth. I kept my hand across the opening, scared that the second mouth, like the top conventional one, would now start yowling too. Across the fronts of spice warehouses my voice echoed as I cried for citizens to rally because . . . it was not just anybody down. It was the prettiest boy in the city now. Was our Robbie down. Eyes! Face! Storefronts seemed mammoth black sandcastles that the next big rain would melt. I found a pay phone but instead of dialing 911 as planned, I heard Angie's growl, "It's three a-fuckin' clock . . ."

"Angie. Robert and I were walking home . . ."

And just from this, from knowing my whole sudden voice so well, she started yelling, "Is he . . . is he . . . where? He okay? Where?"

"He says his eyes. Meet us at St. Vincent's."

The doctor explained that a sort of blindness can happen. The doctor explained it would probably be temporary, probably. The doctor explained. The trauma of a well-placed forehead blow. Our patient would need a lot of care until his sight came back, if it came back, as it likely would in ten days to two months. If not, we should keep the doctor posted.

Me, they sewed up like a pillow.

"No sweat about the care part," Angie stated. "He is still the prettiest boy in New York, has been this whole past decade as any fool, including you, can probably see."

"Aha," the young internist said.

"I like your lab coat. Doctooor . . . what's your tag say? 'Coen.' Where can I get one, Dr. Coen? You married?"

"Angie, for God's sake . . ." She was the limit.

"It's okay," said Robert, safe back of bandages. His mouth, without the eyes' distraction, seemed simple, upturned, and amoral as a cat's.

He could go home but required watching. We would, gladly. Watch. Him. Unable to stare back at us, and therefore to defend himself, he'd be so darn watched. Now I see what a rehearsal all this was. Now, on rainy days, when the fingertips of my left hand go half numb, I understand that I was also hurt then. But for us, the idea of damage to Robert's perfect features, his cool eyes especially—that riveted us most.

We'd never done home health care; we all rushed to be of use. We were fairly bad at it. We only wanted to try the fun parts—fresias near the bed, reading his *Titanic* quarterlies aloud to him. But oh the sight of him padding around his place, arms out, head all gauze, alive by touch, as blind as Justice—which is actually Injustice, having been blinded!

Robert soon found that he could dictate music to a girl we hired through Juilliard. I would sit there staring at his fine skull, wrapped "to go." I sat silent, listening to him say notes aloud, and name the parts "now, French horns" and I would hear her pen, a real old-timey dip ink pen, go scratching. Making something the girl called "a fair copy." The pen's nib also sounded very smart if quite quite blind.

He wrote a lot of his First Symphony like that, saying it out from his pineappled fourposter, both the eyes sealed shut. She, at the window, nearer daylight, wrote it all down.

I'd never known anybody blind before. For some reason, his odd herbal scent seemed especially strong and alluring while his eyes stayed covered. I could sit three feet from him and catch its salted leafy sweetness, now lanolin, now nutmeg, then plain ole varsity B.O.

I read him all of *Great Expectations*. With feeling, doing every voice, and making Estella, the novel's cold, sadistic beauty, sound as much like Savannah Angie as I could. He laughed, but with just his mouth. "Very funny," she said flat, when I did some of her for her.

We'd all gathered. They would unbandage him today. Dr. Coen seemed disconcerted by our whole circle Marx-Brothering into a cubicle so small.

Scissors cut through gauze. Even that sound was painful. Angie and I cried, as in some forties movie. Doc's first question, "Robert. Robert? Where is the *window*, Robert?" Angie and I bawled at that.

Sight began ebbing back into the right eye's crystal-blue, the one hit worst. But its "white" remained bloodred five full months. The contrast between the red and blue—Angie admitted working with that in her painting. She cringed telling me, as if ashamed. "No, it's good." I touched her hand. "You're using it, you're making somewhat light of it, his blindness. I keep thinking about that sprayed gold magnolia arrangement on its side. I don't know why. I feel I let it down by losing it like that."

Before Robert got so he could take care of himself, Angie and I alternated helping. We later admitted having especially enjoyed the sponge-bath part. His shower was busted. "Strip," she told him, knuckles on hips. "No, on second thought, let me. Go limp like Herbert Marshall being the noble weakling in *The Little Foxes*. Here, allow strict Momma to. She'll wash up as far as possible and down as far as possible. You wash Possible. Then she'll take some good nappy terrycloth hand towel, Lad, and she'll dry and dry and buff your big ole possum Possible."

* * *

There was scarring. To the credit of St. Vincent's, the ER doctor, an East Indian who wrote short stories and had read my one, registered the beauty of Robert's face and phoned a buddy plastic surgeon, who—for nothing, for the right to photograph this particular face and his work on it—did everything science could. Robert's face drew art to its salvation. Even so, he was left damaged.

The marks remaining above our Robert Christian's right eye grew reasonably faint in the eighteen months left. Their deepest reddest V was shaped oddly, like a bow with two streaming ends. Scar tissue bit a line into the silver-blond eyebrow of the eye hurt worst. Though the gash became less angry—a mild half-pink, visible especially when he tanned—it never quite faded.

Forever after, every time I looked into Robert's deep-end eyes, I fought my urge to see scars first.

Those Left Back Home

He still heard from the hometown. Odd, it, and not New York, now seemed increasingly exotic.

High school chums said they lost sleep over our safety—us sticking it out in The Sewer—but they still felt somewhat hopeful for us. Of course, I wouldn't tell any of them about the mugging (lest it reach my parents). "Never better" remained my answer.

"So, famous yet?" they asked. "If not now, when?" —Met Yoko? No? Know Carol Channing? Saw her once on the street? Spoke? That's a start. Why not just invite her over?"

My parents had sold the neo-Colonial Big House. They relocated to a glass box overlooking a Florida golf course and the lake that made that course both gorgeous and difficult. When would I come down for a visit and a rest?

Most of my childhood friends still lived two blocks from their own folks' landscaped houses. They did weekly laundry in familiar utility rooms. From these pals, I got mail. Here came the synthetic Hickory Farm Food packets we could all live on for days. Cheeze Logs rolled in pecan crumbs became your morning omelettes then afternoon appetizers, midnight entrees, till lucky airshaft pigeons were thrown the final nuts.

Hometown friends we'd already outgrown, wrote: they truly meant to get around to someday working on their college poetry again, they really did. News of their early divorces reached the North. We heard hints about our quarterback's probable alcoholism, a habit till recently considered somewhat glamorous—but not after his red Corvette struck and maimed a black schoolgirl as he left the crime scene. A boating accident, one unexpected grease fire at the Country Club, the usual gore and flareups. We absorbed these local disasters with an avid, shaming interest. Bad hometown news allowed our city lives to seem more clean, and—oddly—safer. We might be gunned down on the street. But at least our mistakes were not the ones our folks had made. At least we'd chosen this difficulty—this impossible, because universal, goal.

We wanted our lives to be representative; we wanted our experience to go all dramatic and to become unique; we still expected to be known as our age's record-keepers in paint, word, and permanent eighth notes, full-stops. Be careful what you wish for.

One thing we never told the ones left home: how hard we worked. They associated Manhattan with vacation, shopping sprees, Lerner and Loewe. They assumed the art we sought to create was something like a pleasing dusky odor we exuded—something they'd opted to stanch with suburban Right Guard. The art scent was simply by-product, as wasps' spit turns to wasp nests. Our sitting before some rental room's desk or easel, our stewing over a created surface, then scraping everything off to start over more perfectly, our making it daily better? That was quite beyond them.

One old girlfriend-deb-date from Falls arrived the day before my birthday and phoned to insist I have breakfast with her at the Palm Court to celebrate. She was a darling person, funny, self-effacing, generous. "I don't do lunch or breakfast out. Dorcas, I work till two or three every day."

"Now by 'work' you mean what? The teaching?" I told her, Writing.

"But, Hart, that can't be work, not for you. You're a tale-teller. We used to look for you at recess, to find out what'd just gone on in our own class. It only made sense after you told it and imitated Miss Wart-Tongue Watson, remember? Hon, it's your birthday. I've made fairly elaborate plans. Play a little. What's your idea of the perfect way to spend your birthday?"

"Work."

"But don't you like to goof off anymore? We used to. You were a master at it. Remember our treehouse and the back of your parents' Buick and how we clouded up the windows and went only so far, but far enough to at least feel very naughty? What's your idea of play now?"

"Work." "And to round this out, what's your worst fear?" She, intelligent, made a joke of it.

"Leaving work." "So we won't be seeing you at my lavish birthday breakfast for sixteen at the Plaza, which'll include every chic person under forty from North Carolina now living in New York, for you, on me?"

"Cain't tell you how much I 'preciate your offer, honey, but I really . . ." Next morning, at seven a.m., I called her hotel room; I'd changed my mind. She'd already checked out.

I never heard from Dorcas again. (If she reads this . . . forgive me? Understand.)

Finally, for such sweet trust-funded pals who took fewer chances, who believed New York to be only fun and merely a street address's difference from their own, we had no words. How to inform them?

How to explain that in the evolutionary race, the strongest know enough to swim beyond the horde, to paddle right into cornering darkness straight ahead, a darkness that is terrifying fertility itself. A darkness that threatens you with your shadow-black death while promising platinum self-perpetuating immortality. (We young mortals simply didn't know yet how little time we had to make ourselves immortals.)

The Immortal part, we worked at with endearing school-supply diligence. The Mortal, we assumed.

I.D.

ideon's paintings were all still done on boards a foot square. One of them had stunned even Angie into respectful silence, a hard-earned nod. The brushwork was broad and supple, gorgeous in its automatic certainty. Gideon's color sense was unusual and, given the prettiness of his subject matter, that reversal of the sweet and sour became most necessary. If you are going to paint the harbor at Nice, a blue bowl triangulated by white sails formal as the starched collars of some ambassadorial dinner, you'd best offset the view's calendar familiarity with a rind of bitter green at the horizon, with some bruised plum clouds so sullen in arriving.

Gideon was a slow worker, so as to always give the appearance of utter ease. He would scrape away, like a flawed meringue, one pound of pastel paint gone mud, in hopes of making the next try seem effortless, his first. Gideon destroyed eight out of his own ten pictures. As a young man his standards were so high, he'd had little work he felt was good enough to sell. So, it was his very artistic integrity that drove him to the slippery world of Buy Art Low, Sell Masterworks High. He soon spent more time at auctions than at his easel. Not to worry. He was, he told us, buying himself the decades it'd take to become a master.

Each of us tried on personae like cheap and brilliant store-bought ascots, sometimes a few a day. Angie gathered collage materials off street corners; she curated her own hairstyles and that show could change three times weekly. She also "found" Ansel, a rangy boy painter just in from Montana.

He was just some hireling she'd brought in to tear down a studio partition. Unconsulted, from the top of a ladder, he had pointed down at three huge canvases: "Ma'am? You think that one's best, because you've worked on it longest. I see all the rags and coffee cups around it on the floor. But, if you don't mind a far Westerner's far-out opinion? The end one with the least paint on it is still the most amazing. Looks like you breathed it. Dance of the seven veils. You get you seven paintings packed in one. Aren't too many painters living as can do that. It's almost weird, the pileup. The longer you 'work' 'em, the more of the play you squeeze right out. It's a heap of artists in New York City that'd try and bring off that finished one, not that they could get it lathered up to where you have, li'l missie. But, of all the lofts I been in my three weeks in New York, I'd say only you can start out like that. So, leave off there, 'd be my minimum-wage advice."

She smiled up—from his for-real cowboy boots toward the three yellow crowning cowlicks—not hurrying. Larceny lived in the grin of Albam. "Number one: I like your particular level of interest. Two: great buns, excellent eyes. Now, crucial, Numero trez: Are you, by chance, also heterosexual?"

"Welp, when it suits me to be, ma'am," he scratched the rearmost of his cowlicks—and smiled the open spaces, the scent of sage after a recent driving rain.

*   *   *

So, if this Ansel, at a flea market, picked up two bird-shaped rhinestone pins for a quarter, we considered it original that someone so farmboy butch already had "a jewelry collection." Since Angie liked to paint late, she'd become our "night person." We were mytho-maniacs, inspired by a city whose major industry that is.

If our motley circle stayed put, it was because we knew that giving up and going home would be far worse. Leaving would mean quitting our whole group ambition—leaving one another alone here, undefended. That'd be a form of suicide harder than taking the forty-one sleeping pills washed down by vodka. With a life-ending suicide, at least you need not hear others' catty remarks as they prod your remains.

But, artistic suicide was destined to be autopsied (i.e., reviewed) in your own hometown hearing:

"Guy tried to be a New York artist. Lasted less than six months up there. Came back to his daddy's big white house, and a job on the loading dock of Dad's Budweiser Outlet. Regular Rembrandt, right? They say he really drinks bad now. Never talks about New York City. Hasn't touched a paintbrush in years. Sleeps in his old room. 'Beave It to Leaver,' hunh? Eats with the folks. Works here. Dates nobody. Gets plastered every weekend. Period. They say he really basically wanted to go be queer up there, but didn't even have the nerve to get it on with even one guy. Never choked a one down. Never 'came out,' like they call it now. Instead, came back. —They say the poor jerk had some talent, too. Look at him, sulking, playing like his daddy doesn't own this joint. Acting like he can't half-hear us. Real rebel, right?"

There are worse things than dying young.

In the Midst of Your Early Blue Period, Something Overtakes You

ou can paint your cheap New York studio apartment white, and it looks great for about three weeks. Then the window sills begins seeping wheat-plasma-color, becoming brown, next black. Finally some other substance arrives—some bubbling, tarlike force, unidentifiable. It is silt, it is toxic chem-plant New Jersey drift, it is others' envy, it is the spittle of the roach eggs hatching, it is applicant Death.

The neighbors' leaky pipes, the hall's Rasta graffiti artist, something starts immediately resenting and reversing mere girlish (virginal) suburban white. And, seeing this, you will either leave NYC, or else repaint, or (likelier) learn to survive it. You've already learned to cohabit with hand-sized roaches, occasional break-ins, and a certain quota of phoned-in wrong-number "breathers." Chaos becomes a constant, like Mrs. Park's almost-always-open corner green-grocery where you score your eggs and milk and they all know your name. Chaos has a neighborhood nickname for you. Does that make things easier?

I noted that, since Robert's blinding, we all walked in a new way. Darting, taking short breaks, sitting down on ledges, checking store windows' reflection to see who followed—no longer just for purposes of stalking seduction-attraction—now, more self-defense. I had just learned what the word "tired" meant. The same ole hits of Cuban caffeine sometimes failed to pay their usual kickass magic.

While Robert was out sailing with the America's Cup crew and that gym teacher from Lifeboat Thirteen, while he weekended at Aaron Copland's up-river retreat, Angie and I tried distracting ourselves. We exchanged two bits and a challenge: Go to The Honored Owl, four storefronts down, find a one-page portrait of each other. The book had to cost fifty cents or less. We would meet back here in forty minutes and swap our one-page likenesses. There is, in the young, such a thin line between narcissism and self-knowledge.

I, being born an archive, can still lay hands on my own page portrait of Alabam. It was lifted from an aged tome, called *Certain Problems of the Spirit*, stuffed with Medieval-looking woodcuts:

Thus said Bernard of Clairvaux, the great thirteenth-century Cistercian, on the joys of bodily resurrection—

> *Do not be surprised if the glorified body seems to give the spirit something. For it was a real help when man was sick and mortal. How true that text which says that all things turn to the good of those who love God. The sick, dead and resurrected body is a help to the soul who loves God . . .*
>
> *Truly the soul does not want to be perfected without that from whose good service it feels it has benefited in every way. Listen to the bridegroom in the Canticle inviting us to this triple progress: "Eat, friends, and drink. Be inebriated, dearest ones." He calls to those working in the body to eat; he invites those who have set aside bodies to drink; and he impels those who have resumed their bodies to inebriate themselves, calling them his dearest ones, as if they were filled with charity . . . It is right to call them dearest who are drunk with love.*

Last month, trying to organize my jammed attic here (ninety boxes from this period, marked "Early Drafts"), I chanced upon Angie's curious continuing portrait of me. It'd yellowed.

As usual, she scared me with how much I admired her. The passage came from a blue book I'd also seen in my mother's daily reference library. It was always parked beside her *Joy of Cooking*

Emily Post's *Etiquette*:

THE LETTER OF CONDOLENCE

Intimate letters of condolence are like love letters, in that they are too sacred to follow a set form. One rule, and one only, should guide you in writing such letters. Say what you truly feel. Say that and nothing else. Sit down at your desk, let your thoughts dwell on the person you are writing to.

Don't dwell on the details of illness or the manner of death; don't quote endlessly from the poets and Scriptures. Remember that eyes filmed with tears and an aching heart cannot follow rhetorical lengths of writing. The more nearly a note can express a hand-clasp, a thought of sympathy, above all, a genuine love or appreciation of the one who has gone, the greater comfort it brings.

Write as simply as possible and let your heart speak as truly but as briefly as you can. Forget, if you can, that you are using written words, think merely how you feel—then put your feelings on paper—that is all.

My erotic adventures still gathered, overlapped, truncated to shorthand, and meaning to keep themselves separate—soon knew: every raindrop, falling, intends, on impact, to remain standoffish from all those other ordinary droplets. Fat chance. Lakes are made of them. Oceans.

The time a New York cab driver, one cute, toothy twenty-eight-year-old with theatrical hopes but absolutely no experience onstage, told me he liked my looks enough so he'd actually "eat" the fare if I would spend the break time he usually wasted on a piss-and-a-burger overlooking the moonlit Hudson with him making out in the backseat, since the meter otherwise kept getting in our way. The time I met a high school boy in Times Square on a class trip and he peeled off the end of a long line and took me back to his little Edison Hotel room while his class did their walking tour of Chinatown; and the pathetic gym bags of his four roommates, white socks and jockey shorts with camp nametags stitched in back by moms, exuded the smell of adolescence at simmer, not unlike piping hot school-lunch Campbell's Chicken Noodle Soup. The time I wound up with a deaf and dumb house painter who wrote me notes on matchbooks and in his palm and who simply pointed at whatever he wanted and who led me home to his rented room over a Chelsea day-care center where the silence was erotic to the point of a narcotic and the only sound he made was, on coming, a drowned scream like some strangled rabbit's last. The time I answered a personal ad and the person who opened the condo door was the married president of the college where I taught and we both laughed as I did a mock-military about-face and, wordless, returned to the elevator; and ever after he acted so kind to me, praising my sense of intellectual chance-taking and my enthusiasm that recalled to him himself when young. The time, the time that, the time I found time to, found time . . . all that matters in the end are the memories of the unstandoffish merging flood, of droplets, ours, the times . . .

Angie was already known to be as difficult as she was talented. That would legitimately make her very testy, indeed. Our women friends often pointed out: Guys who hustled in the service of careers were called "movers, shakers, comers." Girls who tried were "pushy manipulative bitches, sleeping their way up."

One snowy day, on my way to the laundromat, an acquaintance told me he'd just heard a bigtime dealer describe Angie as "her own worst enemy and the classic ball breaker." As usual, I defended Ang. But I'd begun to feel more and more tired of doing so. It seemed unfair to both of us, how people brought their worst Alabama stories straight to me. I urged them to simply look at her work. They did, but her paintings were so fresh and strange, so laden with exemptions, her art irked them even more.

My favorite laundromat stood just opposite a row of awninged Old Englishy antique shops. I had shifted my folding chair closer to the dryers for warmth. As I flipped through an outdated celeb magazine instead of the serious manuscript I now carried everywhere, I saw her. Angie stood window-shopping at an expensive little store across the way. Snow now flitted down in windblown drifts and everyone was bundled, mid-December. Unaware of being watched, her back to me, Angie had eased up onto tiptoe, kept leaning against a bay window full of nineteenth-century toy soldiers arrayed atop lead forts.

She then dodged into an adjacent doorway, pulled off one red mitten, counted her money. She'd trot back—breath all blue—and stare some more. Once, using her coatsleeve and mitten, she cleared the frosted window of her own observer's vapors. She stared up and in like some waif from Dickens. The prissy owner signaled her away. "Shoo," he said, and waved ringed fingers to one side.

I knew, to the bone, she was hoping to buy overpriced Christmas gifts for Robert and me. For some reason, she was convinced—from Robert's affection for the word "Lad"?—that we both adored costly Anglo-Scottish lead soldiers. I felt such a twinge at seeing this "ball breaker" about to overspend on us.

When I later opened my gift, wrapped in tartan paper, a note was attached: "You deserve a regiment. This year, can't afford one. So settle for my company and these McLovers instead?" And there rested two lead kilted soldiers, all softened with nicks and lovely painted plaid, two warriors like something from a Robert Louis Stevenson boyhood poem. I placed one at either side of my typewriter.

If I worked to defend Angie from others, I still couldn't make her *feel* defended. My praise, my faith, never seemed exactly enough. She expected those around her to help advance her career and when she hit a lull—as we all did, long ones—Angie Byrnes commenced to flamethrow in our directions. Even Robert caught it for treasonable disloyalty.

Playdate

was at her place, seated on her floor, helping Angie paint her studio high-gloss white. I warned her: White never lasts. We had praised Alberta, eighty-five, for her good looks, and she'd told us, "Ain't nothing I ever done. It's just: Black don't crack."

"White sure do," Angie replied. "Look at Hartley already."

The studio flooring had been barn-red; it kept souring and skewing her new blue work, and, no, she had not asked her landlord's permission. He would say forget it. Ang had been refilling her Zippo with fluid and now she squirted a little flaa of that across the red floor, to see what paint did. Then she brushed white over that; it made a moment's pink. Working, we chatted, catching up. We'd not seen each other in six hours.

"Wait one," she frowned at something I said, suddenly pointing her brush my way. "Hartley, I think my ears must fail me. Because, please repeat that. Let me get this straight. It's during the taxi strike and you share a cab with the assistant director of Marlborough Gallery, right? And you never one time mention me or my work? You're always telling me that you respect what I am doing for easel painting generally. Daily, I hear this. I talk you up everywhere. Any idea how many copies of that fucking dog magazine I bought and mailed? But here you finally get a ride from Fourteenth to Fifty-seventh with him, held captive, a silver-tray opportunity—and it's like I'm on the cattle car headed for Auschwitz and you've conveniently forgot my name . . ."

"Angie, it would have been forcing things. The man was a stranger, and straight to boot. We never even talked painting. It never came up."

"Well, *bring* it up. Here I am, slaving away and instead of friends I get narc-collaborators, I'm hidden here in this attic, slaving away, and they're off riding in stretch limos with the friggin' SS and . . ."

"Angie, darling? Captain Tom to Earth toward Angelina. Would you consider giving up all this recent Holocaust imagery? You're catching Manhattan's toxic shock. Your Mom's people were snake-handling Baptists from a county whose only beauty spot is probably a ditch. Your Dad's Episcopalian and you're from Savannah and were about one inch from having been a debutante, as you never tire of telling us, your ranking friends in the Gestapo, sweetie. You're growing solemn. Beware. Under the misapplied rouge, your face is turning the color of concrete. You're forgetting how to mess around, Goofy. You've stopped really playing in your work. Honey? it's mattering too much to you. And that makes it count less for the rest of us. Ansel is right, your best is the stuff you do with your left hand. Your accidents are better than most of what we manage with tongues pressed between our new big teeth. Remember what got you started at your grammar school? The prizewinning Fish and Birds of Georgia mural, remember? Play's still the thing."

She had turned away from me. She went on painting the studio floor. "Are you crying? Are you going to kill me?"

She shook her head no, then she shook her head yes.

"They expect too much of us," she finally said. I had been avoiding the sight of a waitress uniform on its hanger suspended from the bathroom door's hook, the awful little frilly hat. At least I'd never had to see her in that thing.

"I mean," her back explained, "with one part of your brain, you're supposed to stay this divine idiot child splashing around in a way so joyful they'll all want to try finger painting again and squish all over in perfect innocence. Then you're asked to sober up and get parental and put on business drag and wander forth and sell the idiot-savant's output. It's as seasick-making as *Lifeboat Number Thirteen*."

"Why won't you look at me?" She shot me the finger. I tossed my brush her way. Instead it struck a huge blank board, prepared for painting. I tried changing the subject. "This the biggest one you've ever used? What is it? Six by nine? How you going to get a nine-foot painting out of this rat rec-center? Ever thought of that?"

She nodded yes. Still on her knees, yet turned away from me, she thumped toward the living quarters' big ugly oval "early American" Sears rug. She flipped it back, revealing a nine-foot slot. She'd sawed directly through floorboards to the landing below, sawed right through joists, everything. The hole looked about four inches wider than it needed to be.

Still glum, she pointed to a cardboard box, and the brand-new red Craftsman ciruclar saw, still plugged in. She was the only person I knew in New York who still ordered things out of a Sears catalogue, one she'd brought in a suitcase from Georgia. Her landlord was not ever going to be happy again. I had to laugh. "I take it back. You never forget how to work hard at playing.

I'll nevermore doubt Baby Divine Idiot. If you told me you had invented a new form of competitive telephone that'd send Bell Tel into chapter eleven and that it involved tin cans and lots of string, I would believe you. You're a genius. Along with maybe Robert, but, it's his looks that make us say that. Truth is, you're the only genius I'll ever know."

I understood, from practice, the kind of crying she was doing now. Type 5. Bobbing shoulders, steady gaze, and low-grade nose drip like a cold hardly noticed. "Weally?"

"Geniusgeniusgenius. Plus the best ass downtown."

"Why only *down*town? No, I'm a fat, lonely spinster. With a tragic need to be overly often fucked." She said this in babytalk but I understood. Her babytalk was ironic, if still babytalk. I crawled over to retrieve my brush. It'd smeared enamel on her huge gessoed board. One, I now understood, that would get out of here.

"Start it for me," she said.

"Start what? your new painting? I'm no painter. I tried that, remember? At art school, I was always talking the whole time. It disturbed the real artists, my explaining to them what they'd just done with that patch of Naples yellow. Then I started writing words in silver paint right on my canvas, sentences scrolling out nude models' mouths: 'Is it cold in here or is it just me?' Like that. The teacher told me this was an early warning sign for the Iowa Writers' Workshop."

"Hartley? You once quoted something out of Blake. 'The creation was an act of mercy.' To show you that your Ang still can play? And be the idiot . . . you begin it, friend. I'll work with that. Play, I mean. Wanna play? 'Cause, me? I'm easy—I'll play wib you."

"Thought you'd never ask." I heard a sound. Across white flooring still half-tacky, here rolled one yellow felt-tipped Hi-Liter, just the kind I'd seen her use before ever I saw her face. The kind we'd picked to sign a radiator. Maybe the same marker?

She wiped her nose and mouth then eyes onto either shirtsleeve, unselfconscious as a squirrel's self-grooming. It seemed important, we were both down on all fours like babies previous to needing to actually, like, walk yet. I am not ashamed to admit that everything we said for the rest of that whole day we spoke in babytalk; but I will spare you having to phonetically weed through all that, read through all that.

I next heard the words: "You don't really love me, not really." It sounded different in baby talk but no better.

After my spending four hours painting the floor of her friggin' studio, after all these years together, she could still say that!

"Love you? Love you! If I ever create a masterpiece, it will be convincing you I do. Earth to Angie: I am already your friggin' slave. The only thing I haven't done for you is oral sex because I have no aptitude for working with that little. I do convex only. You cut your nine-foot slots but leave me out of it. Where is that goddamn marker? You want me to write? I have complaints. I have threats. I have consumer advisories to those considering being friends with anybody as insecure as you."

"Spell those out then. What will be will be. I want writing, longhand, but about twelve inches high. Use your beautiful cursive script. Yours looks like some good schoolmaster's who spends weekends chopping firewood for widows. Me, I'm going to pee. Just do it. None of your usual thinking about it, either, Hamlet BoyToy. Scribble laterally at either end. Go with oppositions. Make a mess. I won't be two shakes of a mare's tail after blotting mine with one square of 'the toilet tissue,' as my mother calls it."

Onto the floor, with a whap, she flopped her white board. Down it fell where I still toddled/dottered like somebody very old becoming very young again, or vice versa. Had I been briefly taken off her SS letterhead? She kept the bathroom door open. I could see only her pearly ruddy knees from here. And before I heard Ang yank the overhead chain and flush, I was done.

I sketched curtains, like some puppet theatre, all around the edges. Down at the very bottom front, I outlined my own hand to stand in as the puppet himself. I'd written two huge perpendicular sentences you had to turn your head to read. Then I saw her lighter fluid, and by the time she walked in, I held it to my crotch and was squirting it over my lines and words to make them beautifully "bleed."

"Atta boy. Why, it's the little fountain pisser of Brussels. P is for Posterity. Look at this mess. What do it say?"

The righthand sentence read: I AM YOUR SLAVE AND HAVE BEEN ONLY GOOD TO YOU SO WHEN YOU MARRY A RICH MAN I EXPECT TO BE INVITED TO DECENT DINNERS LIKE CONSTANTLY.

The left end read, in her Nazi fantasy mode: WE HAVE WAYS OF BREAKING YOU, YOUR FINGERS, YOU WILL SUFFER TERRIBLY AND NEVER PAINT AGAIN, NOT EVEN WITH YOUR LI'L FLIPPER-STUMPS. LOVE, THE SS.

"You are so sick!" Her head butted my side. "Even so, I can work around these. I like your drippings, Jackson. First marks are always the hardest ones for me to make. So, even yours'll do."

"One last thing. Get your pretty little blotted ass down here. Now place your hand directly beside mine front-and-center. I'll trace yellow around yours, no, don't move it yet, I missed most of the pinkie. This is permanent. Look, I'm putting a ring on your hand, a yellow-gold ring. I have taken your hand . . . not in marriage but in play-like. —Here, how big an ole diamond you want?"

"Bigger than you got."

"Look. An apple, eighty carats. —*Now,* do you believe I love you?"

"Some." She nodded, already squinting toward the fumey canvas, suddenly primed to be only alone with it. "On alternate Mondays. —No hard feelings but . . . get out?"

The Verb: To Baby

ertain built-in urges were unexpected because, unlike us, they were so slowing, so non–New York. Imagine wanting:

Babies!

We boys stayed freer longer. Can we ever say it often enough?: It is easier being a boy, it's a real good career move, from day one, coming factory-equipped with a dick.

Women friends finally commenced discussing the urge and itch. And they discussed it and discussed it.

Angie's mom had blighted motherhood as an art form. But even in Angie, Dalí's famous limp massive pocketwatches sprawled, clicking, big as wet comforters. Even our more determined girlfriends admitted being inhabited by biological urgencies, tocking, springy, and alarmist. A footrace was implied between their careers and their biology. Would they become Famous before they ceased being Fertile?

Angie soon shamed Robert and me for "not at least trying it at least once." Groused at, called "chicken" long enough, some of our pals finally ended up in bed with best women friends. I promised Robert I would not father Angie's junior if he would not; we shook on it. Then we kissed on it. Then he stopped me.

If a straight woman can have efficient sex (if not sex that's athletic-totalitarian), if she can have it once with her best gay buddy, giver of such "good phone," and her all-time-fave shopping-companion, her secret sharer, then why not weekly? Why not have at least one adorable blond kid by him soon? Get your childbearing and the drive toward it over with. A good long-range career ploy. And with none of the hassles you knew you'd have with the other kind of guys, their emotional compartments overloaded with Kapok and sports stats.

Angie told Robert and then me (in that order): "Since I trust your taste implicitly—how will you feel about 'Damien' for a son, and 'Chloe' as the title for our girl? The name, I mean."

It got so bad—if we were eating in our Cuban-Chinese place, and if a single woman brought her baby in, and particularly if it was a pretty baby—Angie had to leave. "Womb Warning. Infant: closing at eleven hundred hours," Robert chanced a joke she made him regret. For about four years, she became allergic to babies as some folks are to cigarettes.

Surely there ought to be a husband for a person as alive and gifted as our Angie. It slowly came to me: In Manhattan, a truly straight, findable, unmarried man is rare as . . . well . . . a guy who's openly queer in the little towns we'd fled.

I bought a white Filipina blouse for her, and a loose replica of Jefferson's favorite muslin workshirt for Robert, a maroon ascot for Gideon, a used Portuguese-to-Modern-Greek pocket dictionary for Marco and a 1940s cowboy bolo tie for Ansel. It was not a holiday, it was a check from my great aunt marked "I URGE HART TO SPLURGE DAY!" So I did. I delivered each to each at home. It was the day of the blizzard. Reporters called it the storm of the century, but they were always saying that.

What we knew: it had soon snowed for five days solid. On my windowsill, I crumbled stale bagels for my desperate "pet" pigeons. The silence of stalled traffic made our New York Bucolic finally complete. He said, "I happen to have four pairs of Swedish cross-country skis over here." Soon we all aimed outward, no plans past Central Park, all bundled, Robert in a long black sheepskin nineteenth-century woodsman's coat he'd found upstate for sixty bucks. Ansel's skiing outshone everyone's.

New Yorkers love big clean disasters after living daily with so many minor ones. They finally get credit; they finally most generously give it!

The town looked tidy as a snowstorm from *The Magnificent Ambersons*.

Sledding parties, snowball fights, and blissfully nothing working but the horsedrawn carriages, very popular today.

Only Angie and me—snow-deprived Southerners—felt the total glamour of this town gone white. She saw three off-duty execs rolling a huge snow-ball figure in the median. "Look," she said. "A C.E.O. man."

We skied clear down Park Avenue. We were aiming for the intermediate slopes in Olmsted's masterpiece, our whole gang, one of our last great times out in the world like this. I zipped past a familiar marquee, the chiseled doorman nodded. I told my friends: That's where Tony Wu lives and, know what? I want him to come out and play with us. I asked their permission. Though they'd heard his charm and particulars described, they'd never seen Tony. So we plotted at a pay phone, me pulling off my mittens, using teeth, seeking dimes in quilted pockets, mine then theirs. I just knew his mother would never let him out.

"Madam Wu? It's Tony's tutor, Hartley Mims. Fine, thanks. Yes, storm of the century so they say. I am near your place and believe I have a unique career opportunity for our favorite student. Certain dignitaries were stranded in town during a college admission officers convention. I've told them all about Tony. Forgive my bragging. But, can Tony come out and . . . apply?"

I covered the receiver because my pals were laughing; talking trash. "Apply his skills. I see this as an early chance to sharpen Tony's inter-view abilities. —I know this seems impromptu but I wish you'd reconsi-der. He has no school today. Well . . . let's see . . . I have a Mrs. Byrnes from Harvard, I have Monseigneur Gustafson from Yale. I have Mr. An-sel from Montana's University Without Walls. Representing Prince-ton, here's Mr. Gideon. . . . Yes, say two minutes? I'll wait for him out front."

You never saw anybody happier than Tony running in his yellow snow-suit! He knew it was a ruse to free him, he tried to keep a straight face till we rounded the corner, clear of the doorman's view. "He spies for her," my young friend told us as we poled along beside him. "You are my saviors." He smiled at everybody. "I will never go back."

"Oh yes you will."

"Hartley, he's even cuter than you said. Absolutely edible." Angie, as usual, stood on ceremony. Then Tony begged me for a favor. He said that a certain person was also marooned in town; he'd come in with his kids to see the Ice Capades, got stuck. Could we call him at the Mayflower, could we pick up and play outdoors with Juan, too? "Why not? The Mayflower's right by the park, isn't it?"

Juan had driven his four children from Fort Lee for the ice follies. Their car got lost under some snowplow's mound. We were all soon in the park together. The kids, in matching hot-pink parkas, were beautiful as their dad. We took them to the swings. Watching Tony ride the seesaw with Juan's daughter, not much younger than himself, it was all a kind of snowball fight of happiness. Created by experience, it contained an innocence that can only be understood by those still somewhat innocent themselves. The rest need not apply.

I'd skidded along wearing my cowhide backpack, the address book knocking heavy within. Legs aching, we chose to subway home. I remembered to gather up all Robert's skis but somehow, during our crowded exit, I left my holey backpack on the local. It was a shock beyond the frequent robberies that kept us, by necessity, non-materialist, in six-month purges. The loss of an address book felt different, harder. I went into a sudden depression, atypically durable. My friends actually noticed, offered sympathy. Tragic, just the thought of recollecting all those zip codes one by one. I missed it, as if a pet had died. That Christmas, Angie gloated over the gift she'd got me. I figured it would be more tin soldiers, half a regiment this year. (Neither Robert nor I ever guessed who told her that we really liked those so.)

Instead, her wrapped present had real heft. I ripped in. Here was my old wine-stained address book. Since Angie's last name started with a B—, and since many of my A's were out-of-towners, the guy who'd found the thing had finally phoned her. What's oddest—I kept listed, in my precious book, the name of everyone I knew . . . except myself.

"Lifesaver," I said. "You are a regiment," and kissed her hand.

Certain Improbable Toddlers Survive

he earlier rumor had been confirmed by a little item in the *Times* but one no longer than your finger and, back in the C section, buried. The young Japanese guy who framed Angie's paintings got sick and died in seven weeks. Rumor claimed there was nothing you could do. You would know It by your night sweats or a telltale spot on arms or legs—a spot like Lady Macbeth's, unwashable-outable.

No test, no cure, no real name for It, and no escape. You were urged to make your will. You just got comfortable, preparing for it. Only comfort was not an option.

But, hey, we daily heard so many rumors. We tried to dismiss this one, too.

After all, somebody who worked nights at the Waldorf swore he had seen the longtime director of the FBI, his face like some ulcer-suffering boxer dog's. But, this particular night, The Director was wearing a tasteful midnight-blue sequined dress, a real bad brown wig, good heels, while riding up in the staff elevator (rear), and being addressed by his longtime companion, a Randolph Scott lookalike, as "Miss Mary"!

"May God kill me if I'm not telling the whole truth," the bellhop, a friend of a friend of Robert's, swore it was dead-true. So, in a world of poison powder sprinkled into frogsuits, of G-men as B-girls, you simply could not believe in some esoteric tropical fever that had not yet happened to you. Or any of your fellow pirates. And so, hearing that a person caught it either from kissing, poppers, public toilets, or the air—knowing we were helpless to in any way defend ourselves, we ignored it. —Hard as we could, we just lived.

With Gideon's dark unblinking eyes linked to his scary stillness, our boy had stayed insanely seductive. He arrived at my apartment once, ostensibly to see the Hudson while standing on my desk chair. I held his legs steady as he craned. I then felt his rich voice hum through these tibias, "You hold zhem well. I'm wonder, are you zhinking what Iyam?" I had not been, actually. But now he mentioned it. . . . My futon, my friend, our future, my my. Gideon was the Casbah, and I didn't even exactly know what the Casbah was.

Gideon often disappeared now into the south of France. Then we got a card at Ossorio's saying he was in a borrowed beach house beside Princess Margaret's on some Caribbean isle or other. The views were surely splendid and he painted them well. Using his French love for ready-made American phrases, Gideon would later half boast of these villas that they "came weeth." Came with a staff of black gardeners and cooks and their darling kids for him to spoil with sweets and coins and hibiscus blooms that, being everywhere, meant little to them.

As if replicating Robert, Gideon partied as one of his several art forms.

When in New York, he sometimes took me along. We had an erotic friendship and were like brothers who share a room and, secretly, more. When neither of us had anybody lined up, we would phone and drop in and it was comfortable. These parties he attended always seemed at the home of somebody famous, but hosted by that person's drug-happy son, or niece, or the secretary's niece—the star was away on location. We were always late to the restaurant, but they'd held the biggest table anyway. The car had a driver but both were borrowed and the chauffeur couldn't resist letting us know he knew this. I noticed that none of the people Gideon ran with seemed to care anything about painting, or how good he was at it.

Angie took us on outings to the Guggenheim to see postwar Italian painters I'd never heard of; Gideon knew a little gallery on Madison that sold Biedermeier furniture and that kept, in its backroom, three paintings by Morandi, and the owner was in love with Gideon and so would let us take the pictures down and hold them in our laps like tawny cats. Robert tipped us off to a little Hungarian restaurant across from the Cathedral of St. John the Divine, and serving a cold cherry soup that, on scalding nights in August, was worth the thirty-minute subway ride to score, for $2.50 (a big bowl). Marco told us which lectures to attend at Cooper Union and the New School and he was rarely wrong. We heard Maurice Sendak, and an Auden-lookalike woman prime minister of Israel; we heard one man whose life was devoted to tracking Nazis; we heard another man who survived the Holocaust and had somehow made himself, professionally, into The Only One. And we sometimes picked people up at these talks.

I remember Robert phoned me, I should rush to Carnegie, this'd be worth the cab fare, we'd hear Janet Baker sing, for free. I hurried in and he stood waiting. I recalled Angie's fantasy of him as a god of the lobby. While we rushed toward great seats, Robert explained what we'd hear. Mahler, "Songs for Dead Children." It was written prior to the death of the composer's own beloved four-year-old daughter, almost a prediction. This would be my own first hearing of the piece. All I knew of it was what my darling had just told me in the aisle and whatever magic the music itself might reveal.

Baker looked like my favorite grammar school teacher, a Miss Crabtree. One minute in, I understood that Baker was a great artist at her peak and, despite my not quite knowing German, I—winded from the gallop here—seemed to slowly understand each word. I tried imagining what it would be like to forfeit one's beloved children. Having none, I substituted seeing all my manuscripts burned, then upgraded that to losing a friend.

Imagine how titanic an echo chamber this great city would seem without the noise of even one of mine.

A huge bronze bell deprived of one hidden small iron clapper, its sole reason for being, its single means of song.

I could not conceive of this—and so I surrendered to the music, vowing I'd learn instead from that.

The songs' intensities soon made me restless. Sometimes when you're experiencing an upheaval, your eyes will choose some resting spot, an arbitrary target. Directly beside Robert to my right, one old old woman wore widow's black. She had the posture of a question mark. Her collar pin looked like a Josef Hofmann piece, two black coils on a rectangle of silver. She, austere and probably Austrian, held her jawline high in a way so proud it appeared antique. Comportment. Resignation. Dignity, assumed.

The audiences at these events were often elderly elegant Jews, people who'd fled Hitler. They seemed to all know each other. You felt the hauteur of their standards, a snobbery about the only thing that mattered in this new world—what else?—one another. Over the years in New York, I'd come to admire their regal demeanor, dark clothes, courtly nods. They circulated with a warm reserve that gave you this uncanny sense of prewar Viennese culture. The face of the old lady so close by, it soon seemed the best porcelain teacup ever made to then be stomped on by the world's largest boot. In a way so simple, in a way like breathing, she now sat weeping into a comically tiny, white lace handkerchief.

Baker's voice, motherly, called to children now past comfort. Her voice berated itself for subtractions far past anyone's controlling.

> In this weather, in this shower,
> I would never have sent the children out.
> They were dragged out.
> I was not allowed to say anything against it.
> In this weather, in this storm,
> I would never have let the children go.
> I was afraid it would make them ill,
> but these were vain thoughts.
> In such weather, in this awfulness,
> I would never have let the children go out.

Past Robert, my old lady now shook with a grief far larger than Carnegie Hall. I wondered at the number of her children lost, disappeared into what ice storms, what trains, what horrors of history? Gone without their lunch money and galoshes, making her feel even worse at mothering. Decades later, her crying still came as fresh and unashamed as someone shaken by three sneezes in a row, her usual quota.

When, at intermission, all the lights assaulted us, the widow saw me notice her, she turned her face, not away, but directly toward mine. The look she gave was so frozen and defended. It showed all the unasked-for poise of Antarctica. Herded and banished by world events, her pain had evolved in an isolation so complete. A mother's terror long past shame. Would I ever deal with such agony? How had she borne the complexities of even acquiring a ticket to tonight's music? Small, wet eyes seemed far past caring what I thought of her. And yet, those very eyes remained steadied, immense in their pert, acid pride. Her pride was the pride of someone who has kept alive this high level of honored pain. If it was her children she'd sat recalling, then her dead offspring tonight seemed nearly as alive to me as Mahler's own. Her face said direct into my innocence, "Zhey are all gone. I am still here. Vhat do you expect?"

I knew that, in the conventional lexicon of emotion, losing one's children is considered fate's worst blow. But, still an untried kid myself, I guessed that, apart from the progeny my sperm donations spawned, I would never have any real kids of my own. I remember—(and I admit this with shame)—I half envied her. I felt I would never know the sensation that gave this eighty-pound woman the weight of the entire Old World, Bible-black. I coveted her knowledge.

It's one of a fairy tale's tricks—you offer the idiot third son one wish for anything—then you distract him so he'll ask, not for all the world's gold, but one glass of water, please. Anything on earth? I'd just wished for the stature of that lady's tragedy joined to my own lite-tuneful happy ending, please.

And it was that night at Carnegie, it was amid the battling perfumes and accents in the lobby at intermission, it came with Robert standing off to one side in the usual group of iron filings drawn to him and calling him by name (he would later say he'd never seen any of them before). I was leaning against one of those big columns, reading the translations of one song for one dead child. I was congratulating myself on having got it mostly right when somebody said, "Excuse me, coming through," and, irritating, a bike tire almost crushed my foot. I recognized Ed, now pushing someone old in a wheelchair. Chair and driver took a place on the far side of the lobby, making sure to stay near the middle facing outward, for, it seemed, the amusement of the chair's passenger.

I saw Ed recognize me and, polite, I waved across the crowd. I returned to studying my program but soon grew interested in the seated person. I'd never seen anyone so sick in public. He was yellow-gray and the hair was mostly gone and a bone structure was apparent, even to the way the human jaw is hinged.

Slowly, I came to understand a weird militance in Ed's stance, his placing the chair mid-lobby. It came clear to me that the chair's occupant, head held up as if with an effort, fighting to seem natural here, was not old at all. He looked like some boy freeze-dried ancient, burned there from the inside out.

They had covered his legs with cashmere tartan blankets, and he wore a sort of improvised paisley shawl and sat there, stork, anomaly. Settled like a jar lid atop his bald head, a Moroccan cap of geometric stitchery, festive. How eventual was the crowd's slight clearing from his side of the lobby. It became easier and easier to see Ed and his patient and the two other gay men, banding together yet facing outward, as if to fend off some expected insult or harsh look. A voice spoke to me so close I jumped. Robert, "See him? Know who that was?"

I said no.

"That's Horse from the Boy Bar."

"Naw. Can't be. We saw him at that Fassbinder thing not six months ago, guy still looked like Kirk Douglas in *Spartacus*. The speed is unreal. Science fiction. Robert, but what got him?"

" 'It,' Hart."

" 'It'? As in 'Check for spots and unexpected bruises'?"

"Ditto, *that* it."

"Funny, I've lived in New York long enough so I started believing I'd never again see anything really new. This, though, is, right? I better go over and speak. Just say hi to Ed. The one pushing? he's the window treatment guy in boots from that first night. 'Bored of Ed,' remember? I'll just step over there, weigh in. Look how sad they look. Everybody's playing like they don't quite notice why they're flocking away. Really should, just as a sign of . . . whatever. I don't have to say 'How are you?' or anything, just to, you know, pop over there would be the . . ." Our bell rang, lights blinked once and so, shrugging, I turned back toward the hall. "No." Robert looked my way, Robert a fraction aghast at me, I fear. "We'll step across together, 'll only take a sec, won't it?"

"That's right," I said. So we did. They really seemed to appreciate it. You could see that. Especially with its being Robert Christian Gustafson who bent down beside the chair and said something funny if dry, all charm. Stooping there, he reminded Horse of some Italian beauty Horse had won away from Robert last thing at the door one night. I was there with my pleasantries, of course. Ed seemed easier to approach; Horse, after all, had never known me to speak to. After Robert and I headed back into the hall, I saw a few others rush toward the wheelchair, just before the doors swung shut—barring us all from our mixed reward, further Mahler, songs of a wandering solitary youth—the concert's final half.

Like us, these guys had been tucked back, small among the giant columns. Ready, in a way, to be heroic—but uncertain when they'd really have to start.

Last Natural Exits

art of the fun was bumping into things that stirred you by mistake. Given how New York was all the earth's distant orange groves made into so local a concentrate, we had all we needed on our block. Ossorio's for nerve stimulation, good talk, and a little short-term credit on pastries if you had nothing else to eat.

Mrs. Park's vegetable stand stayed open all hours except between two and five a.m., and she seemed to sleep sitting up at the register with a hose in her free hand blasting the arugula: With money earned here she was putting a daughter through MIT and a son through, incongruously, Vassar. Modern Dry Cleaning presided over by the gifted, if seldom heard mezzo (our Nina—being of a different, straighter, older generation—could not be asked to do our cleaning for free: but she would put a "rush" on a suit if you told her you required it, not just for a job interview, but an "audition" Tuesday early); The Honored Owl, our basement stall where great used books could be had for coins, and it didn't matter that they were peppered with ancient cracker crumbs or stank of mildew if they cost 10–98 cents.

Robert found and forced on me Defoe's *A Journal of the Plague Year*. "It's a real page turner," he said, "you'll want to see how it all turns out." Robert explained that Defoe had not personally experienced the plague he'd put on record. He had interviewed old, old survivors, he used published memoirs and the public lists of deaths. Defoe's book was like Stephen Crane's acrid, honest account of Civil War battle; sometimes the best records get written by those listening kids born one generation late.

"Like this," he read,

> *It came me very warmly into my mind one morning, as I was musing ... that as nothing attended us without the direction or permission of Divine Power, so (the plague's) disappointments must have something in them extraordinary, and I ought to consider whether it did not evidently point out ... that it was the will of Heaven I should not leave London now the plague had really started.*
>
> *It immediately followed in my thoughts, that, if it really was from God, that I should stay, he was able effectually to preserve me in the middle of all the death and danger that would surround me; and that if I attempted to secure myself by fleeing from my habitation, and acted contrary to these intimations ... it was a kind of flying from God, and he could cause his justice to overtake me when and where he thought fit.*

Robert became a convert to Walt Whitman and, like nine out of ten young gay composers in New York, he set a few Whitman poems for voice and piano or guitar.

Angie lived on Thompson Street, but kept a studio on the Lower East Side; since the day she took top prize in the Georgia public schools fish and birdlife mural "paint-off" held in Athens (Georgia), slapping up a sunfish the size of an archery target, she had always "painted big." She'd sure used up a lot of pigment, Angie. You could tell by just looking at her hair and fingernails. Another friend, that rawboned fellow new here from Montana, sublet a crash pad far up near Harlem. At three a.m., downtown Angie phoned her uptown pal, waking Ansel.

"I'm working like mad. Pearl Paint is closed, and I'm like fresh out of cerulean blue. Damn mouse got the last good dollop. Gone, the Winsor-Newton I bought instead of paying all my water bill? I'm clean out. —Look, I know it's late, but do you have any handy, any cerulean? And I'm afraid I mean, now?"

"Unh hunh," he, half asleep. And, wearing the motorcycle jacket and boots and jeans and his U. of Montana at Missoula pajama shirt—Ansel slouched toward the subway—holding before him the new tube like a single birthday candle. The price tag was still gummed to it, and he transferred at Grand Central and forty-three minutes later knocked on her door.

"Great." Angie took it without feeling the need for a single thank you. Unscrewing the white cap, she literally ran back to her overloaded easel. So Ansel aimed again toward the street and then a train that would empty him into bed. Ansel had handed it over and—not invited in for coffee, silent, still half sleeping—headed home.

It was that automatic. A sense of fatalist mission joined us. If you made sacrifices for your art, your friends were included as your artform's own extension, its first audience, the fellow sufferers, its penniless patrons. Since "tension" or "battle" is the subject of all art, even at its most serene, your work did homage to your friends' own daily struggles in theirs. What I best recall from my present subway platform (called incoming Address Book Number Fourteen), is an unadorned idealism and how little we held back from it, and from each other.

Do I idealize our early idealism?

Let me.

The truth is, our community would meet a waiting test beyond imagining. Picture that last tea-dance in the first-class ballroom of the *Titanic*, just before the ice. Imagine how all these pretty people presently being charming and sociable and complimenting each others' foxtrotting will soon line up for too few lifeboats.

Imagine how the band now buoyant with a mindless "Bicycle Built for Two" will veer toward a noticed heartfelt "Nearer My God to Thee," then silence. String instruments (being wooden, buoyant, lifeboatlike) float, then don't. Wind instruments (like us, being vertical esophageal hollows) submerge almost at once.

Imagine that—through the ultimate life-and-death emergency—civility and affection somehow improbably hold. (Sure, there is one cad who dresses in his wife's clothes and tries to take advantage of an exemption called Women and Children First.) But mostly it is "After you." It is mainly people gesturing each other toward the single valued lifeboat: "No, you go, please. We'll clean up here. 'll be along in time. You next. Here, allow me to help you in, please. No problem. So long. Soon . . ."

Let me idealize, please. The coming pandemic "made men" even of the ones it killed, especially those. It made "men" of those men still today considered too fey or artistic to openly serve in our armed forces. It made "women" of the girls in whose Class of 1980 we'd wildly arrived. It gave us a war's casualties and a war's proud, guilty (and therefore overtalkative) survivors . . . forgive me.

It created a warfare's frontline, very isolated and quite pure. Even subscribers to *Soldier of Fortune*—those guys monthly seeking our planet's "hot spots" likeliest to prove kilns for true maleness—even some of those men slowly understood that—trench warfare requiring the ultimate testosterone—was blazing away in a most unlikely frontier called Greenwich Village Basement Apartments.

Confusingly, perverse, all this soon blazed alongside healthy career advancement.

Phantom Ranking

If our fame was still asymptomatic on a national level, we were at least beginning to enjoy it on the head-turning map of our own West Village. Conceive the joy in overhearing someone younger point to you on the street and whisper, "Psst. Don't stare now, but I think that over there looks like . . . (imagine your name here). His last story, in that little magazine, made me laugh, then cry buckets. Same alphabet as ours. But how does he *do* it? And physically, still so well preserved."

Hometown friends, having jetted in to shop or "see the shows," invited us from our downtown ghetto for complimentary meals at expense-account restaurants where oil execs fed. "Up" we came from the The Sewer's lower depths.

It was our blooming underground notoriety that these distant, prospering friends would never understand. They themselves were so Aboveground, so Mainline, and therefore so utterly out of it. The cover of *Time* and nothing less would do. Nothing else would convince them we had "won."

They didn't understand that, living in neighborhoods as wonderful if risky as ours, we'd formed an "All for One, and One for All" fraternity-sorority. We now spoke pidgin Spanish or Polish or Italian. Angie, a second-tier Episcopalian out of Savannah, had arrived in New York with lucky brunette hair. She ("Angelina," not Alabama there) passed for Italian, got herself a great bargain of a place on Thompson Street. She faked for so many years, she'd become something of an honorary "paisan" in the eyes of her vigilant stoop-sitting Italian widows. She flirted with their sentimental leg-breaking sons who so perfectly defended Angie and her naturalized neighborhood.

We belonged here now. We walked like natives, direct, unflappable, observant; our shoulders tacitly signaled other pedestrians when we were about to make a turn. I could now study our block the way I'd seen my dad scan our old backyard, with a proud and factual vigilance. I felt safe on our street while wearing my nightshirt. Summers here, I even went without shoes.

Maybe more important than any single work of art we had yet made— we'd founded this ragged-ass impromptu village. Insane, fleeing towns of ten thousand in order to found another just two hundred strong. But its unity would lead us, goad us, bully us—toward our greatest masterpiece— the nursing, cheering, burying of our own.

—Denied the cover of *Time*, indeed.

Flipping through Robert's Defoe, I came upon this:

My friend Dr. Heath was of opinion that (the plague) might be known by the smell of their breath; but then as he said who durst smell to that breath for this information, since to know it he must draw the stench of the plague up into his own brain in order to distinguish the smell? I have heard it was the opinion of others that it might be distinguished by the party's breathing upon a piece of glass, where, the breath condensing, there might living creatures be seen by a microscope, of strange, monstrous, and frightful shapes, such as dragons, snakes, serpents, and devils, horrible to behold. But this I very much question the truth of, and we had no microscopes at that time, as I remember, to make the experiment with.

I put that book down so fast.

False Positives

irst there was no test to let you know who would get it and who might live. Then a jackleg test existed but one riddled with false positives, terrible reversals. An acquaintance received good news, he threw himself a major bash, then next morning got the "oops" phone call. He packed at once, moved home to Utah.

A fate worse than death, or was it? Finally, one accurate battery of blood samplings existed. I put off even considering it. I gave myself so many excuses. Even if you knew, what could you do about it, except feel suicidal, or move south, cave in? My decision was: Whatever distanced me from my untested friends, I didn't want. If it spotted me, I'd spot the spot; I'd know. Otherwise, I'd rush until the leash ran out.

Looking back, you forget how suddenly it all came on us, how few choices it offered us. It was, as Angie said, "The Lotto called Blotto." I did urge a few others to go get tested but only because they focused so singly on the test itself, the worry was literally driving them mad. I wondered if I'd ever find nerve for that Russian roulette of knowing. I recalled my address book, lost without my own name written in it anywhere. Even as I carried soup upstairs to one friend with a cold that wouldn't quit, even after chatting up our familiar pharmacist about his grandkids in North Carolina, I somehow held off knowing. Knowing about my pals' life expectancies, knowing my own best-if-used-before date. Partly, I was being existential. Largely, I was being chickenshit.

New York had already battered me to where I was never again asked for photo ID. I'd not got laid for two months; lately I couldn't get arrested. Having eased Robert through his being jumped and mugged, I eventually took note: I myself had stitches up my side, and not ones sutured by some artful plastic surgeon. I lied that they were "distinguished," my Heidelberg dueling scar. They gathered, raw, a pink side seam on Dr. Frankenstein's rush-job humanoid. They and my address book: early proof that I had lived.

Worn past polite now, something extra had commenced standing up in me. Polite moved fast toward bold and was then getting brave, accidentally. At least our veering city's energy, to some interior hamster running wheel, let me write sentences that, unmeandering, were less badly Jamesian. They lurched more. They learned to live with interruption. They did theme and variation on the New York show tune. Their long solos shot like serum out into a world perhaps incurable.

One phrase, we'd all of us quit using overnight: No beauty ever again longed to hear himself called "certifiably drop-dead."

Bubble Reputation

ollective anonymity is far easier for a group to bear than disjunct teacher's-pet promotions. From Fame's farm team, some of us got singled out for its visible Big League. Others stayed unfairly ignored. Still others yet live there hidden; rising hours before the office opens, working daily to make art. If only art for heart's sake.

With our uneven advances, there came jealousies, a souring pettiness. Lovers and best friends fell out, and then made up. Then one prominent rave review wrecked any possible reconciliation forever. Till years and a major success-of-one's-own made contact possible, made a friendship run even deeper. No one can sympathize with a best-seller's woes except another best-seller.

Our Angie had talent, a luck unaccountable, and all the dogged ways to press both further. It'd still taken her forever. I felt personally disappointed; I'd begun to transfer my own hopes of a grand career toward her, toward hers. Angie's major mentor dropped dead wearing a mortarboard in Providence; he could've helped her; his widow would not, would not even return Alabam's post-eulogy phone calls. Two paintings of his she scouted out in the dorms of South Carolina now hung in the Whitney. She'd received no commission, no inscribed lithograph, no thanks. He never quite got around to writing that long-promised letter of rec: "To whom it may concern, never in my sixty years of painting have I met a young artist more . . ."

But, one day, sitting beside two loud travel agents at a lunch counter, Ang learned that the wife of a famous midtown gallery owner was flying to a Mexican mudbath health spa for Christmas, and so Ang (wearing pleats, shirtwaist, mouse-brown hair dye) took out a home-improvement bank loan, paid top dollar for it, learned which plane, which seat, got herself plopped right next to the unsuspecting intended friend. They were soon being mud-packed in adjacent adobe vats. Angie did not let on that she'd ever painted anything more ambitious than her toenails. They mainly enjoyed full-strength N.Y. girltalk. They swapped paperback novels; they laughed to find they'd both brought the latest trash-pop best-seller: *Why Brilliant Careerwomen Still Choose Cavemen: Those Who've Recovered Look Back.* They starved over single green beans (exquisitely prepared). According to Angie—their massage teacher insisted that they practice "deep muscle" on each other. By Valentine's Day, our talented friend, having finally admitted to "painting some, and even semiseriously every six months," could claim a new gallery, two new mentors, and a home-improvement loan rolling on at 14 percent interest. By April Fools' Day, she'd repaid the loan.

For me, the fun of her big moment finally arriving was undercut; I resented all she'd had to do to get her remarkable pictures seen. I had written and submitted articles to *Art News* and ten other magazines that are no more. They didn't know me, they didn't know her, they didn't even return my self-addressed post-paid efforts. One dealer had told Angie, "Your problem is you're not enough like anyone else. You lack context. You need a movement. Art history moves in convoys."

"You know what the Captain of the *Titanic* told those in first class? 'Don't worry, we're just stopping for ice.' If I'm not a movement, will a little motion do?" She flipped him the bird, left.

But then, hey, she overhears two travel agents . . . "Whatever," she said when I was dumb enough to act grouchy at how late her good luck finally waltzed in. I told her it just seemed unfair to me.

"Look, Hart. All I ever wanted was to get my workshop onstage. My form of stage fright has been the fright of never finding one. But from now on, from Angiebama's spot center stage, everything takes care of itself. If they try and get me off it, expect quite the catfight. Bet on my staying put. —I will never sling no hash no mo."

Ms. Byrnes's first one-person show opened to raves, October first.

"Odd that in a town called *New* York so little should feel genuinely fresh and novel. But, on Thursday night . . ."

She'd lived in the Celestial Cesspool City seven years.

And come Halloween, under the arch of Washington Square, in a witch's rite, we, the gathered, burned her waitress uniform. Plus that dreadful little frilly white Dacron cap. Its smell rose, noxious. Like so much else, in our pagan Village, it did not want to end.

Suddenly, recent best friends were saying, "She never really cared about us anyway. Was always just milking us for her starter-level contacts. Loads of charm, Angie, and great hair, a steel rat-trap for a mind, and not that bad of a flashy painter really but, underneath, pure user. Borrowing paint in the middle of the night, and never replacing it. That girl had the ethics of a virus."

But, against the odds and punishment of friends' successes, I still envision a silver paint tube, unopened, brand-new. So blue a blue is coiled in there, concentrated blood of the sky itself—the most costly of all blues. I see it in the rosy farm-strengthened hand of a Montana wheat-grower's boy on the IRT, then the shuttle, then the Lexington Avenue IRT, then back on the IND, then back across town at Grand Central where all the predawn screaming crazies would be echoing, then up to Harlem on an IRT not wholly undangerous at three-thirty a.m., and finally to bed. (A trip nearly circuitous and stressful as the sperm seeking/finding the ovum.)

I, forty-seven, know now to remember this, to honor it by listing it here, addressing its valor. Come morning, the kid who'd delivered his only cerulean blue via train (paint's price $9.98 in 1984 dollars)—would barely recall the trip. And, even if reminded, he surely wouldn't think it notable. Looking back, I—a bald(ing) to bald man of forty-seven—try and save it. A deed like art itself. Like art, a gesture made by one—yet shedding a light communal. And he never got his paint or money back!

If there is a blue paradise, he belongs there, just for doing that. Seeing that there probably isn't, this bulletin board notice will simply have to do. And since he, Ansel, our photographer farm kid with the "jewelry collection," died at thirty-one, I will remember for him. Shall I keep him in the Book?

It is a strange fairy tale, how we got here, how so many of our crowd knocked off so early, how our entire palace-liner drifted, stilled toward the bottom, then fell to sleep. The *Titanic* settled fully two and a half miles below the troubled surface.

Only a few of us yet remain alive, holding flashlights, somehow still breathing at this depth, allowed to move about the sunken ballroom—each clutching a tattered hall pass and our one trivial precious light source—each saying aloud, to them and to eternity, our only mantra-motto-logo, the names of these, our adored fellow passengers, lost.

Our voyagers lost.

Lost. But still, in us, listed.

Performance Finally

isease itself was already "in" some of us. Soon life really felt like one of those pod people movies that we'd hooted through at midnight shows. There's just one other survivor on earth, everybody else has "turned." Then your single friend, lonely as you, moves to kiss you and, yuk, the Fangs, the Gills!

Surface-wise, our days still meant pooled resources, the compensations of being somewhat young, still good looking, as yet generally desired. We waited, but while playing.

Now, there was a far younger set, all punked up in ways that soon seemed to us comic and affected and endearing if misguided. "I saw a boy today with a ballpoint pen stuck through his cheek," Angie announced at our table.

"Awful—how'd it get there?"

"He rammed it in there, dumbie. As a beauty aid. How old am I? Ask me."

I did. "I'm so old, so out of it, I still just wanna look good."

"Pathetic Retro Passed-over Bitch! Acetone off her mascara! Burn that woman's sweater sets!"

Bouncers still waved us in (though we secretly felt fairly long in the tooth)—while the silver-haired limo crowd waited, segregated behind maroon velvet cordons, sulking at our mysterious cachet. That part was nice. There was still the joy of being "active sexually," as our parents put it in their letters: "We know you're having a lovely time with your young friends, but we hope you are not, darling, being too active sexually."

Right.

Tell Niagara, "Now remember to wear your rubbers, hon, stay dry."

Just as one portion of my address book finally started—if a decade or so late—to become well known, that portion and another commenced feeling older than it really should. Sooner than we quite expected, we were grousing about undignified limitations known mainly from our parents. "My back is killing me, I never plan to leave this chair again, what happened to all my energy, I don't need new friends, can't keep up with the ones I've got." So ran our parents' gripe-fests we'd vowed never to repeat.

Robert's Symphony no. 1: *The Titanic,* had not yet heard a single note of itself. Six years in progress, it was nearly two movements complete. His beauty had been more regularly performed and praised and practiced. (Soon as I finished writing a story, I could rush it toward loved ones; Angie's paintings were nine feet across and highly colored and dared you not to "get" them at a glance. But among our circle, only Robert's symphonic work remained a mystery.)

Ned Rorem said of Robert, "Quite possibly the best-looking, truly talented new boy in the world of serious New York music since . . . well, since *me*." Now Robert had quit vocational partying long enough to get his brilliance moving. He had always worked, but now he ruddered a project so immense it called forth newer energies, wilder risks. The mugging and its months of blindness kept him home; there he began to dictate; soon a sheaf of pages became a pile.

The First Symphony had been accomplishing itself only onto copy paper. But it was created there with the glacier-inexorability of a native Midwesterner getting something done, once but well. There now seemed the hope of a eventual premiere in Hartford, through a friend of a friend sort of thing.

Thanks to Robert's generosity toward the legions who loved him, there were many friends to have friends of.

One was Mr. Copland. An all-day performance of Aaron Copland's work would be staged uptown. "Wall-to-Wall Copland," it was called. The deeply venerable, successfully closeted, and fully smitten old composer phoned young Robert with an offer.

Since an orchestra would be assembled anyway—to play "Appalachian Spring" and "Rodeo" yet again, maybe, before the doors opened—Would Robert like to hear a cold sight-reading run-through by New York's topflight pickup musicians? of whatever was completed of his First? of Robert C. Gustafson's Symphony?

Yes, sir! That meant we, Robbie's handpicked claque, had to arrive at the hall by six-forty-five a.m. Mr. Copland himself must also be there then. (He, over eighty, would conduct Robert's piece, then leave during the daylong playing of his more familiar music, reappearing only for a difficult favorite work [his Piano Concerto] at nine p.m. So Copland would be using his day's main energy on his protégé's music, not his own. He, obliging, said he had heard his own so often.)

Robert typically invited everyone. Even his parents who, if thrilled, declined, "We'll come when you have more free time for fun and us."

All Robert's prima donnas of both sexes promised to try arriving exactly when expected. "This must be major," he said as each of them, usually temperamental tardiness embodied, bustled forward, some actually early. All were overdressed, each perfectly in character.

I stood with Robert at the corner of Broadway and Ninety-sixth. Here the West Side subways all rumble and ungorge. Most of our downtown gang would arrive by train. The rest would turn up on foot, probably in heels.

Somehow I remember every detail of that day. I felt I was finally about to "have" New York. In memory, the morning when we heard the first of Robert's First remains the light-filled high point of our innocence, being the last full day of it.

Nina Fouquet-Marshall, always at the front of any line for flu shots and still on call as fourth alternate understudy to young Stratas at the Met, rounded a corner. Nina was wearing blue and white polkadots, a flair-skirted number with matching clamp and net hat (very Jackie Kennedy) from her Met heyday (one day only). Her outfit, rustling, had come right back into style. "If you don't look fabulous," Robert smiled.

"Thank you, dear. Ciao. A great occasion in the history of American music. —Your Nina's just honored to be included. On the dot, you'll notice. We pros? We can do that for each other." Eager to make an impression, Nina admitted she planned slipping "Aaron" this. . . . A tastefully gift wrapped (cowboy buckeroo paper, "Rodeo," get it?) cassette of Nina Fouquet-Marshall's own finest versions of Copland's best art songs.

"And, with the new dirge-slow tempo I've chosen for 'I Had Me a Cat,' I do not think Aaron'll be displeased."

Angie rose like Venus, from the subway's mouth, smoking. Pointing to her watch, she said, "It is six-forty-five a.m. Subways open before noon? Am I here yet?"

"Completely," Robert said, "and just look at you, beyond fashion."

She'd lately tried upgrading her usual paint-stained gear and bikeboy drag to actual, like, dresses. Ang admitted she'd not yet found a style quite wholly hers. Today, our Ms. Byrnes sported a rust-colored forties suit, boxy shoulders far too wide for someone so short. She'd borrowed one of Ansel's better copper pins, shaped as a calla lily. With her hennaed hair slicked back like some boy criminal's, her white skin looked beautiful and stark. And yet, little wrinkles, crackled laugh lines, fanned from the outer corners of each amber eye. Experience and abandon suddenly showed in morning light. We usually lurked in Ossorio's cave, or else it was night. We never saw each other so early and in so much, like, sun. Young as we were, we'd already gotten older.

Her lipstick was the darkest of shades, somewhere between rust, blood, and grapeade. It, alone, was absolutely perfect on her. Angie did have such a sumptuous symmetrical mouth.

That mouth now spoke to the composer: "Hey, History's Han'somest Prince Golden. All fer you, genius-y boy." And from behind her, two dozen white calla lilies lurched, noddish, breasty, white, so "period." She pressed these against him. She went on tiptoe to nibble his left ear. He laughed, staring over her shoulder, winking at me. He had to have all of us, didn't he? He already *had* us all.

Robbie's platinum lashes looked beautiful pressed shut for love of his darling. My feelings for him just then made me feel stricken, blanched. And still, above his shut right eye, the bow-shaped scar from a pistol barrel whose wet crack I recalled completely as some rainy place I could still visit. I should've prevented their hurting him.

As Robert's own fashion statement, he'd chosen an ancient too-large $6 Nick Charles tuxedo, aerodynamic thirties lapels. Plus my Thomas Jefferson gift shirt. For a tie, one long red argyle shoestring knotted in a bow to match the laces of those in his red Converse All Stars. The tux sleeves were too floppily long, so Robbie'd just doubled these over and folded them back at six-inch intervals—to reveal his pale ideal forearms, one knot of moon-white biceps.

When, next season, designers forced all New York men to turn their jacket arms up this way, we swore they'd seen Robert outside Symphony Space on this, his day of days.

Gustafson kept grinning, and in so much daylight.

Gideon arrived lateish by cab, another new cashmere sweater tossed over his shoulder. Broke as usual, as usual he waved a blithe "Keep the change" to the snaggled smile of a cabbie who kissed the bill and offered Gideon Allah's blessing. Since Gideon now owed several of us more money than any of us could quite afford, we stared after that departing ten-spot with mixed emotions, even today.

Marco pedaled up on his bike plastered with insults to all autos. The basket filled with pastel political leaflets, his one concession to dandyism. Waving, he set about chaining it to something architectural, anything very there.

As we faced the theatre, Ansel wandered up, at a Montana cowboy's rate, bolo tie evident, its silver tips swinging, male, and so easy on the eye in all his denim elongation.

I don't remember what I wore.

We now presented ourself at brushed chromium doors marked, "Wall to Wall Copland." Passersby, amused yet disdainful of our outfits, spared us outright sneers. Something in our solidarity today, something in our Ivy assurance must've held off their fullest scoffs, sensing we might turn up in the *Times* come Sunday, fearing we might actually someday be somebody. And (at least) collectively, we already were.

The Circle faced a uniformed guard. We all pointed to our pirate-captain, flying foremost in his baggy evening clothes. We announced, as one, "The Composer. We're with HIM." The gatekeeper laughed at such rehearsed-sounding fusion. In we swept. After our years of party-crashing, this was one time we all felt utterly entitled to the star treatment.

(At Angie's big opening last fall, the crowd had been so chilly and Uptown. We'd appeared uneasily conspicuous Dickensian in our downtown drag as she worked the room and left us in one corner.)

Our joy today was because of: RobertRobertRobert. Robert's rightful, cushy entrance, finally. And we so fully with him, as we had been for so long. No matter that it was not yet seven a.m. No matter that this auditorium felt freezing. No matter that we ourselves must, as usual, suffice as our own drum-beating publicists, then our major audience. That was mostly all we'd known.

Mr. Copland, beaky as the bad witch while gentle as the good one, greeted Robert via one rickety hug. He shifted weight from his cane to Gustafson, a fine move. Robert introduced us to "Aaron" in a gracious if general way, so as not to tire the old man. And Copland, facing us, said, "Fellow member of the boy's cult, I presume?" Such an intimacy sprang up between us all.

Ossorio and his three best lieutenants were already present and stood around, proud as fathers at a confirmation, which we hoped this would be. Angie hurried over to them, Marco interpreting, explaining everything in his solemn, sweet way.

Copland commandeered Robbie aside, a conference over the hastily copied parts, choice of tempi. Maestro was attended by a charming young woman; she showed him a few yellow Post-it reminders (those were new then). Copland's memory was just beginning its total tragic implosion. But he could still manage whatever score was placed before him. We, settled, watched his helper feed him many colored pills, offer the water glass, wait to see each tablet downed.

As promised, Mr. Copland himself would conduct. Robert had once explained to me how good the best New York musicians really are. Bad ones could not get work here twice. It was Darwinian, the high quality that orchestrates so many West Side apartment buildings into all-day rehearsal halls. Robert swore: a cold pre-breakfast sight-reading by Manhattan professionals was often better than four full rehearsals anywhere else on earth. My fear: Robert might prove wrong. My fear: today they'd be sloppy or bored. They'd see Mr. Copland's interest in our ringleted beauty as nepotism or worse. What if the string section yawned at this hour, and hurt my darling's feelings? I would hurt their hands, or bows, or both.

Somehow, this all seemed too good to be quite real, except as in a children's tale. I could not quite trust it.

Thrilled, restless all during, I kept trying to accept it, but felt like some dog circling itself before settling in high grass. Couldn't stop some inner spinning above a spot too long promised to feel comfortable once achieved.

Robert, ceremonious, situated before me. To his left, Angie wedged herself completely under one of his tapering ivory arms. Parts of massive Ansel's upper right quarter fit somewhat beneath Robert's other wing. Nina had chosen an aisle seat, arranging her skirt, rechecking makeup. (Robert had palmed off her giftpacket to Copland, pointing at the soprano, who waved, Queen Mum gracious.) Marco and Gideon flanked me. Clustered around us, two dozen others that our composer had asked, all of them wanting, even prior to seven a.m. to participate in history, to draw as close to Robert as possible. I recognized a dozen faces from AA; we signaled. There were other composers, a tight group Robert consulted and supported. The Stones' manager sat third from left, talking to Mrs. Park, our adored small-credit-granting greengrocer. She'd dressed in black, looking like the diplomat she was. Ossorio and his crew kept turning back to Robbie with winks and thumbs up. "Aren't they cute all dressed up in sharkskin vests and collar pins?" Angie leaned my way. "I'd like to fuck every one of them."

"So what else is new?"

"You say the sweetest things, dear. But I really do feel a heart attack coming on, I'm so excited. Me, I just paint the pictures, chainsaw them through the floor, ship them off. You stuff your wishful li'l fantasies into manila envelopes and cower at home, waiting. But, an orchestra wholehog? That first oboe is a definite possible. See him? The hair? Can you believe this level of prep and fuss? Or is it just its being 'early morning'?"

Today my pockets bulged with a little thriftshop jewelry for Robert, plus some one gizmo for each of our inner-circle pals. It was always like Christmas, you knew to give your every sibling-elf a remembrance of comparable value.

Assistants now helped Mr. Copland rise. He uneasily achieved the stage. His gray hair curled long in the back, eyeglasses perched at the end of a character actor's complicated finger of a nose. There was something magical about this very old man encouraging the unheard music of a boy so new.

Copland hooked both canes over a little railing, an oddly glamorous sort of walker, built up there by some pipe-fitter just for him. He appeared unsteady. Then stabilizing himself by leaning forward against pipes, he lifted a frail baton. Mr. Copland tapped his music stand three times and, both arms already lifted, half-turned back—to smile at Robert, nearly falling, not. His was the smile Robert lured from all of us, and though I could not see my friend's full face, I watched its outlines broaden from behind. I noted Robert's long neck tense, curls shifting; I felt the wattage of such joy leaving him. It aimed toward Copland, smiling, and a bored-looking orchestra, eager to just get this non-union favor over with.

Then Maestro gave a clean fast downbeat.

Robert had always told me that the greatest works begin in the middle—(we'd once sat through the first blast of a stellar Tenstedt performance, the B-Minor Mass, sat holding hands like children on their inaugural plane ride). The first tone cluster of his own First Symphony now hit us like a wind. You could feel ten emotions lean right in against you with the great good G's. Our features spread into a backflung butter of Happiness. Blast-off ripples the grinning faces of young astronauts. There followed an upsurging breath intake, a sense of comfort arriving by earned degrees, then slowly some half-mean vindication. "You see!" There had been such anger banking up in our own long hard wait. For this. At last!

If our group's first response to The Gustafson Sound was to plop back against our seats, whoa—now, as music progressed, we tipped first forward then slowly more sideways. Five minutes in, we'd teepeed shoulder to shoulder nearer each other, against. A little scared, there came this need to touch beloved familiars.

If Robert's first big work was too good, didn't it court trouble? Shouldn't he have made some moments of his work flatten into being just so-so, for safety's sake? And how did our own efforts—in our other fields—stack up? Could we ever prove worthy of such a moment? Then how, in our own forms, might we try preserving, say, him, say this, now?

We huddled closer. I noted with a curious smugness—as if taking credit myself—that the Stones' manager, a tough worldly cockney, and Mrs. Park were all but slung against each other like some old fond married couple. Ossorio and his pals sat straight as for the Pope.

The first movement of Robert Gustafson's First Symphony, unwinding, soon registered its curious authority. Somehow the brass section suggested the very gleaming engine of the tragic liner itself. You could really hear that in there. Being a musical illiterate (except for what Robert'd taught me) I still don't quite know how he managed it. You received whole waves of sound that seemed a large crowd's parting cheers. Ives-like drifts escaped at least two bands (one onboard and one ashore?). Waiting, I caught first strains of "Bicycle Built . . . ," a hymn to locomotion, one 1912 form of love. The programmatic part never impeded the music's blowing forth, stark and beautiful. It sounded somewhat wild. No Glassy minimalism here. Instead, forward-motion percussiveness. I detected moments of Edwardian craft—an Elgar swell that had the cushiness of the top liner on its first crossing. There was this tightened-stomach-muscle sweetness boiling just underneath everything. You heard why Copland might respect what our Robert was trying. There was a sensuality I associated so fully only with Robbie here, right here. The Robbie who fed people leftovers he filched, who'd fixed up nine live-in couples straight and gay, who was always lending out his bed, or tracking down free long-range cat-sitting sublets, lucrative short-term jobs. He was still every inch the preacher's kid—just that willfully bad, exactly that helplessly good.

We followed his symphony from ship's launching to certain sea-swells reminiscent of surge and surf in *Peter Grimes*, then "La Mer." You began to hear the ship achieve its cruising speed as ballroom music of the period came curling back at you in stray wafts, seablown snatches.

Six years aborning, much of this had hatched while he was blind, and all of it was new to us.

Underneath, some dark beating insistence grew even louder, a jagged figure in the strings as we approached the inevitable iceberg. Robert shook his head "No" twice, as if deciding "Ouch, we'll soon change that." From behind, I noted his platinum locks toss at some bassoon effect he must've felt he'd calculated right. He now turned left, to mug for Angie, who was melted against him, and in that flash, Robert's profile appeared to me, as I'd first seen it the elevator, some Roman emperor's, maybe the young Augustus who bribed state sculptors to make him even more immortally ideal. Aimed forward again, Robert stared at the frail conductor, arms lifted, pointing, pulling, leading. Robert's music now seemed our very anthem, its Wagnerian scale emotional and unashamed.

I felt molten I was so confirmed. So sure then—of our promise. The knowledge that we, our group, had finally wound up—the dispossessed kids and outland losers, girls unmarried and boys subject to arrest for simply making love—where we'd all always belonged. What was I scared of? Leaving New York. But what was New York? Just these, my people. I knew I'd never have to leave them. Hooray!

I have always been so lucky in my friends. I scanned these slouching loved ones—poor Nina, on the aisle, still awaiting her *other* night at the opera, and yet so cheerfully willing to wait. Angie, predestined major, having known it even as the preeminent fourth-grade Wildlife muralist in the Georgia public schools, patient for immortality even at her most fraught and engagingly insecure. Ansel, who went about New York with a leathern factuality that made it seem another (if fairly sizable) farm chore. Gideon with his luxurious tastes and creamy company, his ambisexuality, his fluent French and Arabic, his expectations of the best in every cuisine and any language. Marco—such earnest faith in human goodness, in common sense, his chest ever rattly with political buttons that seemed instructions to himself as well as warnings to the world. And me. Me, here, alive, amid, among them.

I cannot say how blessed I felt then. The auditorium was warming. A rumbling from the subway under us and it almost seemed that the whole building had lurched, like some great independent vessel cutting loose. Our circle occupied just a sixtieth of the best seats in the hall's finest forward section. Robert had accused me years before of being happy. I felt that finally. A daily quota, enlarging my daily capacity.

Almost shaming, getting this darn much of it at once. As always, during the best moments, at that age, I sat guarding most of an unexplainable erection.

Sometimes when you're experiencing upheavals of emotion, your eyes will choose some convenient target. I guess my ears were just so glutted that my eyesight needed a brief rest. Sometimes at very good concerts, I must fight to keep from thinking past the music, from fixating only on my fiction waiting back home; I resist channeling music's power toward my story in progress, letting aural energy course into/through my invented figures awaiting me on good white paper, pumping them with further drama, value, opacity.

Today I struggled against that. I wanted this to only be about and for our Robert and his work. Maybe that's why my eyes came to literally alight on him—a familiar simple spectacle, one whose grace and sex and tone I never tired of: Robert's shapely arm, the left one nearest. Its light hair silver-gold, more like pinfeathers than any coily manly tufts. The left arm still curled around Angie's rust-colored rayon shoulder. Robert's skin looked springy and supple, a pink tone overlaying the shade of old ivory. You could see his arm's every ligament and swell.

Black cuff rolled back, his skin's tone was, as ever, coral and butterscotch with a translucent wash of flat burnished white. Now, with my own head rolling to Robert's rhythms, I, slowed by the emotions his music demanded, half noticed then slowly fixed upon what my overstimulated eyes had found before my mind quite did.

Four inches from Robert's wrist, indentation, a mark no bigger than a tuxedo shirt stud. His skin had sort of sunk in there, like the purposeful perforation atop some bisque salt-cellar. Indented, tinged an angered purple-red-black new to me, this was not a scratch, not quite a bruise. It was a . . . hole. It seemed a sign of odd corruption, the body's slight and temporary inability to heal itself.

It's nothing. Listen, instead. —But, helpless, my eyes kept darting back to the thing, just eleven inches from my nose, eyes kept denying it then reworrying what was, after all, just one tiny tiny flaw. A first.

The mark seemed to have befallen our darling from his inside out, not the usual outside in. Friends around me—joined to the music—sniffled,

nodded, communed. Robert's grin at some triumphant passage of storm
and impending shipwreck, rearranged his curls and I let myself tip even
nearer the perfect arm's sole stain. Here was the one body we all wanted,
comically loving even our own futile longing after it.

Odd, the better his music now grew—the harder and meaner did this vacuum dent appear.

I must ask Robert about it, after. Point it out. Soon. But not now, of
course. Not today. Certainly not this week.

I recalled the ominous birthmark in one tale of Hawthorne's. From a fairy
tale, I recalled the curse that some blackhearted witch hurled at a baby during its own white christening. In milk, black ink dropped, blossoming.

I cannot say I knew what I was looking at. I mean, you heard about The
Spot. But couldn't this be anything?

And yet I no longer quite listened to Gustafson's First. —Instead, I'd
started making sentences. They are my own vice, after all. My own poison.
A more interior music.

These sentences all began with dares—"If . . ."

"If somebody this good and generous and talented . . .

"If after hearing only this much of it, he goes and gets in any way . . .

"If our group, after everything we've been through while trying to start off
right, if if, then I will, if . . ."

To now sit here, my hand resting in group-hands, to hear the stick-thin
big-headed Mr. Copland pull this orchestra through the cataclysmic finished parts of Robert's work, it was so thrilling. But music had abruptly
come to feel titanically sad. (I didn't really know what the hole in Robert
meant—but some of it, I simply felt, as any healthy animal must.)

I saw how the musicians, capable complete professionals even just past
seven a.m., had slowly grown half-involved with the score. Some of those
not playing had ceased studying their watches or sipping coffee from Styro-
foam. Instead, not wholly uninterested, they followed along, even scouted
the development a few pages ahead. The harp player kept staring through
her strings out here at Robert. A wind machine had been tracked down, left
over from a David del Tredici concert. The gale now started building
toward storm's own yodel howl. The ballroom oompa-rendition of "Bicycle Built for Two" was breaking up, metamorphosing toward hymn

played soon for real, for keeps, played as art, not just distraction, "Nearer My God . . ."

Ushers, off to the sides, placing the usual nonprofit fund-raising brochures on seats—had slowed to a halt. They soon stood facing just the orchestra. I saw how their eyes cast upward with listening.

When it was done, a musical offering that seemed to stop midnote, all ushers and some of the players applauded. The first violinist tapped his bow to his stand, then aimed that bow our way, seeking the composer. Mr. Copland turned with the help of railing and, beating his stick onto the metal crossbar, signaled Robert to rise. Our boy did. Those of us brought to cheer, we so surpassed ourselves that, next day, we found ourselves hoarse. Ossorio and friends soon made it a standing ovation: "Composer, composer!"

Robert's arm, the small angry hole in Robert's otherwise ideal arm, those were briefly almost lost to me. As I, crying, clapped like mad. And kissed everybody, including an old lady usher.

I cannot say I knew what I was looking at.

Robert, settled, turned around, studied us each in turn. He took my hand. "And this one," he said of me to all our others. "What would any of us do without this one mothering us to death?"

I'll never forget his oval face then. Its glow, I swear, just radiated, heavenly. Robert pulled my palm forward and he nodded, moving to kiss my hand. But, for one split end of a single second, one interior alarm went off; I resisted, preventing my own pulling back; but knew I'd feared . . . contagion. From him! It was a dumb creature response. That's when I first guessed how large a thing all this was going to have to be.

He pressed my palm to his cheek and the consoling thought came: I'll know every inch of him forever.

Warm face on my chill hand, I felt one cheekbone's magic ledge—Most Beautiful Boy. The meat of my palm met the cool bone in his violin of a face.

Everybody patted Robbie. "Well," he shrugged, "for a beginner . . ." Then laughed, ashamed of his own pride.

Odd, I sat wishing his parents had been here. Maybe I should write them. But how ever to describe a day like this?

When he finally stood, I saw Robert reach into the seat beyond Angie's and lift, what? Those white calla lilies I'd forgotten. The sight of him holding those scared me. He offered half of them to Mr. Copland.

"A really quite momentous launching," so the *Times* announced just two days later. The conductor had invited a critic to come sit, hidden, in the balcony. We never even saw him. After our years of scouting for a real reviewer at our circle's hundred off-brand openings, we never even guessed the guy was tucked up there. We never even knew what hit us.

It would be one of two times Robert Christian Gustafson ever heard performed any of the symphonic work (of Robert Christian Gustafson).

Because the musicians were union, because this was an informal and indeed unscheduled rehearsal, because the union local's rules protected players' concert rights and their talents' value, no recording could be made. So no proof exists of that morning's power. Except, of course, in the memories of those alive who still remember it.

After he accepted Maestro's muttered notes and headshakes from the stage's edge, after Robbie was told by elderly ushers just how good he was and going to get greater, we could all troup off to a bistro that—through a landlord of an ex-lover sort of thing, Angie via Ossorio's brother, had talked into opening early—and, by ten a.m., we were drunk on my favorite low-cost high-impact dry champagne, Chilean.

The great inevitable vessel, christened. Maiden voyage.

And it was during this endless festivity, we established another fact that joined us all for life. I can't remember quite how it emerged. Maybe someone was saying, defensive, we can't all be geniuses. Marco stated Harry Truman's famous edict, "The world is run by C students." And somebody else, Angie, started quoting the Georgia public school's evaluation of her own rotten character. We all laughed, amazed. It seemed their view of her was precisely our own schools' vision of us.

Across many state lines, far-flung bitter teachers had described—and therefore created—our circle:

"Though she talks too much in class, plots constantly, and works far below potential, and though we have found her to be a terrible troublemaker when bored (easily is), she does seem a 'creative' if messy child, and plays well with others."

Perhaps . . .

obert, at last coming into his own artistically, had finally conceded he was mainly gay, after charming and confusing Angie and ten more chain-smoking hennaed girlfriends (who each finally guessed before he did), and after steeping himself in Ravel's suave dewy orchestration, he'd grown somewhat surer of his own idiom and inherent decent force, reading John Stonewell of the *Times* call him "possibly something new under the sun. We find a true melodic gift at war with and finally overriding a more astringent atonal expressionism. The subject of the liner *Titanic*'s optimistic (not to say arrogant) launching—also on April fourteenth (but in 1912)— provokes young Gustafson into a brilliant synthesis of nineteenth-century tuneful grandeur soon swamped and eventually sunk by a fatal cacophonous twentieth-century weight. Gustafson, just 33, a Curtis graduate, also studied agriculture at the State University of Iowa! In this single piece, he has seemingly used everything that ever happened to him and to the U.S.A. generally. That is both the unfinished symphony's triumph and its possible problem. Gustafson turns out, as Mr. Copland privately predicted, to be a prodigy of some scope. If one has reservations, those stem from the composer's rushing to try all effects at once. The piece sometimes displays an 'everything but the kitchen sink' inventory. As with many young composers, Gustafson must learn to trust the long career that so clearly stretches before him. No doubt the crowdedness simply indicates how great a fertility will serve him ahead. Though he has been a feature of New York's music scene for nearly a decade, his piece seems written elsewhere. Under the Midwest's landbound rectitude maybe just this opulent will for voyaging has always burned. We look forward to hearing whatever might next emerge from this season's decided novelty, young Robert Christian Gustafson." This same Robert admitted he did feel tired here lately.

He had been on the road a lot since the great launching.

He was out of town so often that I had to gather his mail and take in the gift champagne and floral sprays that kept arriving late. All his Café society friends—"Nescafé Society," Angie called them—seemed delighted to have found him first and then to discover him discovered! They gave themselves full credit, as if his musical gift were what had first turned their heads. They sent Robert orchids and chockies and huge ridiculous stuffed toys, a shop's worth of vintage bubbly. I settled it into his fridge, worried I'd finally corrupt him. In there, I found two half-empty amber vials of cocaine. Gifts, too, I hoped. Used by guests, I trusted.

The week after the review, along with seafoam drifts of pink flyers from Empire Szechuan, the hallway outside his place remained an obstacle course of gifts. I passed the canned macadamia nuts and two good bottles to his loyal neighbor, Alberta.

Just after the *Times* piece, his usual invitations tripled, but now he was asked to speak at colleges and seminars on The New Music, whatever that was. *His*, I guess. Robbie toured with a string quartet that spiked its hair and played as well as the squares did but chose far cooler things. They commissioned hip comers like Gustafson to write the quartets they soon shopped around at concerts for our sleeker universities.

I knew Robert would be arriving home in the next few days. Having a key of my own, I chose to wander in his place, a sedative, and work there. I was nearly finished with a memoir about my father's parents and a touring gospel singing group they joined. It's the oddest tale—my farmer-merchant grandfolks wandered into Falls on market day, heard a traveling choir so good that they clambered up onto the flatbed Ford truck and rode off for five months, leaving their chickens and their children. Joined a cult, come to think of it. In some attempt to match up my life's work with the tragic face of that Austrian woman crying at Carnegie, I'd now revised my own list of suitable subjects. Instead of focusing on my mother's faintly aristocratic Scottish forebears, I was fessing up to certain trashier aspects of Daddy's redclay clan. I sensed that my work's lovely surfaces needed more difficulty rubbled underneath. Robert's shipwreck had inspired me. So did the depths implied in Alabama's lyrical yet scratchy pictures.

Her belated good career luck held. A Southerner had recently been elected U.S. President. His wife came from Alabama. One of the First Lady's pet projects was extremely visible, and comfortingly uncontroversial: bringing the arts of that underrated state to national attention.

Neither Angie nor her dealer had seen fit to trouble our young First Lady with any geographical tedium about the painter hailing from Georgia and now living, actually, in New York. So, it was in this way that, not four weeks after Robert's stellar review, Angie, alongside one of her best and largest paintings, shoulder to shoulder with the President's blond wife, appeared in a famous supermarket celeb magazine. It is rare for serious painters to become mainline notorious. The last one to do so had glued cracked dinner-plate settings for sixty onto his pocked pictures. He had an ego the size of his weight problem. Angie seemed the next. My darling was not caught unprepared.

Wise, she commissioned Alberta to make her a beaded top, one patterned to resemble her namesake state. The bodice map featured favorite sequined crops and cities of interest. Angie later made fun of the whole White House opening; but she admitted enjoying her caustic informed Powder Room powwow with the First Lady, who had attended Wellesley with three great girls Angie knew from Savannah. So, again for reasons other than her major talent, Alabama Byrnes's paintings were being reserved before she could complete them.

"My problem now is how not to hurry. Interesting switch," she told me as we both sat, pining for Robert's return. "I am despised enough these days without pressing too hard on this Alabama statehood stuff. 'Hush, ye many-peopled streets of Tuscaloosa.' You should read the vicious letter I just got from some three-named lady who 'spearheads' (her word not mine) the Alabama Arts Council. She wants my pedigree. She hinted I should send along my birth certificate to justify myself. I plan to make a goodly donation—two drawings—to their Arts Council, just to smooth their feathers about my real nationality and get them to shut the fuck up. I wrote her exactly what I told them at the White House when they asked point-blank. Said I'd spent many a happy summer in Montgomery with my grandmother. I claimed my grandmother was a second cousin of Montgomery's top deb ever, Zelda Fitzgerald. Hartley? Wasn't Zelda's maiden name Sayre?"

"Think so." Of course I knew.

"I should have brought over that letter I wrote and showed it to you first, so you could make it stylish and check my waitressy spelling."

"Ahah. Well, thanks for thinking of me, but I'm actually working on something of my own . . ." And I nearly added, sudden bitch and grouch, "believe it or not."

" 'Believe it or not'? Well, I see." And Angibama gave me such a look.

But it was their picture in the *Times* that really did me in. After the review, the Philharmonic asked to play an excerpt from Robert's *Titanic* and though I attended (it was strangely less thrilling than that early morning, the first time. The orchestra was more technically capable but . . .) there was a party afterward but they'd only sent him a couple of invites, so naturally he took Angie. It was the week her White House magazine pic came out.

I'd grown used to finding Robert depicted amid society dames and those patriot comics who tour for our troops abroad. It'd even been a pleasing shocker to see her, with the President's wife. Like Ang, the painting behind them photographed so well. But discovering my two best friends alone together, my darlings, beaming, she in her Alabama top yet again—that was different, that felt somewhat harder. They were no longer the decorative young lions asked into the shot. They were the event now. Both of them appeared, arm in arm, absolutely made for each other and . . . happy. Plus, the picture rested equidistant between the Society page and the Arts section, so you didn't know if it meant fluff or news: "Composer Robert Christian Gustafson, whose Symphony no. 1: *The Titanic* was previewed last night by emeritus guest-conductor Leonard Bernstein and the New York Philharmonic, enjoys a light moment with companion, the young painter Alabama Byrnes, whose work was recently featured in the First Lady's White House ArtsAlabama Talent Showcase." I got out Scotch tape, I dutifully affixed my best friends' grainy image alongside the postcard of van Gogh's retreat. But every time I sat down to type, my eyes flew right to them, I lost the power of speech.

Their Clipping Service

e had a cold snap that May and my two-hundred-dollar-a-month apartment felt freezing as I sat looking at a clipping from the *Times*, my two closest friends at a party I had been such a good sport about missing.

I would not say I was feeling directly jealous of my friends. Not exactly. It helped to know that each person depicted was carrying his/her address book. The roving photographer must've caught them as each was headed to the bathrooms where the pay phones lurk. Robert was shown holding "The Bag," a green brocade sack that Christmas liqueur had once come in, one he stuffed with scraps of paper, names and numbers of the mythically unlisted. Under Angie's right arm, the same red cookbook binder she'd worked from when I met her, a work long since revised, since the thing had binding rings and pages could be replaced, as the entries' quality rose. Anybody else, seeing such objects in the hands of these two handsome productive youngsters, might have thought he held her purse and she the score of his symphony. I knew better. But this offered me not all that much consolation.

When my parents phoned from Florida and left a message on my machine to say they'd chanced to see the picture "because the Albertsons subscribe" and to congratulate me on my friends' doing so well, I breathed deep, and tried to write fiction about the traveling gospel choir that was, for reasons now lost on me, my current pathetic subject.

I was glad for my pals, but I would've felt somewhat more happy if there had been three in the picture. Three is such an interesting number, don't you find?

I'd hardly had a private word with Robert since the great event. I'd certainly never approached him about the matter of one spot no broader than a collar button. I told myself that bringing it up now would look like latent sour grapes. Besides, since there was no cure, no health regime that helped, what good would it do him to worry about this during these first days his ship had finally come in?

The morning after their *Times* photo, I'd stopped by Ossorio's, expecting no one. Through the window, I saw Angiebama alive and in person. It was such a delightful shock, I literally ran toward the table. But she was giving an interview. At our table.

She introduced me and asked if I minded waiting. The journalist and the photographer and their three assistants were all hip humorless unwashed young Germans. Cigarette smoke formed a minaret above our table. The Germans were really "into" her, I was now told during some attempt at inclusion. Angie informed them I was a coming young writer. "Really," the journalist said, looking critically at my shirt. I hung around only because it would've been too rude, dashing off. Grouch that I was that week, I soon had to admire the way she managed them.

In one of her Honored Owl finds, a book on optics, I'd scouted out a brilliant phrase, one I quoted to her. Now I heard her say, "My color? I deal in oppositions. A hard battle can make a good marriage. As our great Goethe teaches, 'Colors are the deeds and sufferings of light.' " In the way of journalists, I saw the shaggy young reporter flinch with joy, cut his eyes at the photographer during the erogenous word "Goethe." I sensed she had just given them the headline for their Alabama piece, and from the epigraph that I had given her from a book she'd first shown me. When they turned away to pack up gear, she flashed me one collusive wink that made me feel almost human again, partly included.

When alone at last, we spoke of Robert's return, how drained he felt from all the travel, how she feared he was involved with at least one half of the

Smug Quartet, how all he wanted to do now was come home and hide and sleep and finish his First. I was still awed by the review he'd gotten. I'd memorized it. She smiled, "Number One, it was mixed, extravagant but mixed. Of course, you're too fuck-witted to notice. Number Two, in each department, each reviewing wing of the *Times*, you get twelve reviews like that per year. It's just an IOU, Hartley. The amount they claim is owed, that's what's attention-getting. He's still got the National Debt to make good on. That's different, honey, from the actual payoff."

"Oh," I said. "You've clearly thought this out."

"What else have I been thinking about for the last few years but work and him. And, you, too."

"Why are we always talking about him, Angie? Last Thursday, I saw a young boy, a young young young blond, who was even more beautiful. Why Robert?"

This time, she looked startled.

"You're not suggesting we be de-programmed and leave the cult, are you, dickbreath? It's too late for both of us. Some matron at that Lincoln Center party said Robert looked like a park statue come to life. If you call such a statue 'Honor,' that seems true. You name him 'To All Fallen Soldiers,' who'd argue? That's our whip-wielder all over. He's whatever anybody needs perfection to be. Once at a disco, I saw him by accident. He was with those idiotic fashion anorexics he used to fuck because they look more like eleven-year-old boys than eleven-year-old boys and a lot easier to get into without a can opener. He was with that coked-out watercress and cocaine coven. He was making them laugh tough. How? by doing the 'funky chicken' and his James Brown imitation, with a tablecloth as his cape. And not one of them looked stupider just then. And they loved him for it. I fell for Robbie because I thought he was as ruthless as I, chile. Turns out, I was wrong. About me. Hartley, the way you see him, he's a face like a jonquil and his pedestal says 'Virtue.' You make Robert good because you can't think of anything else *you* qualify to be. I'd follow him to hell and back. You, too. I know how much you love him. Well, so do others; it's *Titanic*-sized with others. Fifteen hundred people have loved him as much as we do. And instead of turning us off . . ."

"I don't think I want to hear this . . ."

Okay then. She told me I would probably be inspired by the new Francis Bacon pictures at Marlborough; Robbie loved the work; she'd stopped by the opening last night, had actually met Bacon. "He's like some little shrunken-head cherub from hell. Like his paintings, a face the color of groundround. Very funny, caustic, bad to drink. We wound up giving grades—one to ten—for every waiter serving." She herself had to rush off now to what she blithely called "a shoot" and, after . . . (I saw her hesitate to tell, but our habit of candor still proved too hard to break) . . . In a rushy urbane way, she complained that, vulgar as it sounded, her four o'clock might be fun: A famous woman clothing designer, always wearing black, erotically obsessed with her lookalike teenaged daughter, had asked Angie about her Alabama beaded top and when Ang admitted to making it up herself, this commercial wiz saw a possible "new line."

"She imagines I am going to do, either under my name or no, but better, yes, forty-nine others. You ready for this? 'Tops of the States'! I ask you. She goes, 'Bama, if I may call you that: It's personal, it's vernacular, it's zappy mappy JasperJohnsish—and like you, I'm sorry, but it's just so fucking NOW!'

"Of course, I wouldn't touch such a project, of course, but still the ride is funny, it's . . . just . . ." And, stalled, she bent, placed her forefinger to my mouth, as if seeking to hush me, and not her own talkative self. "Hart? You musn't mind Raggedy Angie's enjoying all this for whatever jackflash fifteen seconds it lasts her. You know it's only fashion. I'd pull for you . . ."

"I know," I said, even while deciding, "You'd pull for me if I had any talent or acclaim or one scrap of your unbelievable luck."

I wanted to talk about Robert's spot but I saw it'd queer her playful mood today. And when she, looking so great with the best haircut ever, a two-hundred-dollar job, rose, gathering all her gear, when she bent to buss my either cheek, I smiled up at her. Something made me say, "To quote Cole Porter, 'You're the Tops.' Maybe they'll let you handpaint a special department store edition."

"Ouch-ette," Ang pretended not to mind, and I longed to call it back but she was already passing our window as she luffed my way a customary parting kiss, my friend was gone.

Now, the evening of that same day, road crews kept tearing up a single patch of street, the fourth time in six months (graft, Union and Mafia controlled). The night work crew had been driving me mad with its jackhammer noise. Otherwise, hushed was our once many-peopled block and I felt restless for my pals, for our old days, "hungry" and hungry. I nearly felt the slightest bit sorry for myself. Who on earth was ever going to buy a hard-hitting documentary piece about some tapeworm-riddled Baptists singing all over Carolina from their yellow truck painted almost black with scrawled Bible scoldings?

After the chill, May had once more grown warm as May should be. Summer again. By now I felt so at home on our block, during hotter months, I left off wearing shoes. The pet-do scooper law was being enforced; only that made this old pleasure possible. Just as I'd worn a nightshirt downstairs by accident, there was such comfort padding along a city street, your feet nude. It can feel like suede, the nighttime pavement, cooling. Summers at home, we kids wore shoes only to church or doctors' office visits. (Looking back, I see this urge to run barefoot in Manhattan was one early warning sign of homesickness for North Carolina.)

As my solitary dinner, I'd eaten almost a pound of cherries, just come into season. Cherries, especially the first ones each year, always make me happy.

I was in a strange receptive jumpy mood after eavesdropping on Angie's interview, hearing her detached medical version of our communicable RobertRobertRobertitis, then seeing that show of new paintings by Francis Bacon. Angie had insisted I go and, as usual, damn her, she was right; it was incredible, upsetting work. Bacon kept depicting two nude white men humped over each other in some excess of erotic greed. They were usually eyeless and their pose showed a leaden suet will to do only what each did, with no more love than dogs show while fucking. I remember thinking these figures must be based not on photographs of lovers, not even on Bacon's personal memories. No, these guys seemed painted from life, done very fast—of the people in some low-rent apartment just across the way, rutting people who do not know they are being watched or preserved, even by each other.

Letting myself in downstairs, I saw that Alberta—across the hall—was up late working as ever; it must be around one or so. I thought of going in and complimenting her on the beaded Alabama top, championing Alberta as the unacknowledged creator of the thing, but, this bushed, I decided against it. Robert had known to ask her to whip up his New York cocktail tweed, and Bama commissioned a state map in Ziegfeld bugle beads; and who would I be, as clothing—a blazer made of Baptist choir robe, and Confederate gray, what? I was so friggin' sick of talking about all this. About them. Alberta's music rolled on, scratchy, Rudy Vallee doing hits describing midnight terraces, a cottage for sale. Waving her cigarette my way, she signaled that her cat was over visiting R's place.

It sometimes pleased me to just wander up to Robert's apartment and take naps in the mythic Ludwig-gondola of a bed. I had never plundered any of Robert's drawers or trunks or closets, even though I longed to. I wanted that too much to actually indulge it. No, I had standards; I only read those items left right on top!

God knows what-all lurks in a park statue's pedestal closet.

Alberta's yellow cat slipped out of Robert's half-cracked door as I slid in. Barefoot, I wandered to the bed and, using his short ladder, clambered up onto it. Feeling somewhat better already, I sat on its side nearest half-lit windows. Across the street, our pizzeria's neon; the pink word "Slice" became a blue pie-triangle then returned, a pink if violent word. Four windows' suspended crystals—gifts mostly, now hung plentiful as icicles. They seemed to burn with a green light; odd, since I'd just left the street and had seen nothing there that color. Green also burned in the fishtank supporting its little balsa wood and canvas baby *Titanic*. The ship floated there in perfect silhouette. A scale model good enough can convince you that the room is giantized, not it, condensed.

I was feeling, not exactly blue myself, but certainly wistful, more than a bit left out. He would be back in a day or two. Once he was composing here again, maybe things'd calm back down, our old schedule regained. Increasingly to me, that in itself seemed paradise.

It usually helped to scuff over here, check out his place, then head right back to my own, smaller digs. He'd been gone for ten whole days. By phone three nights back, Ang and I reinventoried his merits—finding a few new ones—then, as ever, we sighed, made the kissy sound, and hung up, each of us still alone.

Tonight I'd brought along my manuscript, I moved to turn on the crook-neck lamp clamped onto his hospital breakfast tray. I felt giddy, sinuses burning, then heard something in the corner by the broom closet. Floorboards creaked twice, stopped, continued. My eyes had at last grown half-accustomed to the half-dark.

Just then a police car passed, its red flasher spinning, and—with that—I slowly made out two forms. Caucasian, they were somewhat crimped atop each other, right down on the kitchen floor. The two were stretched out not fourteen feet from me. Maybe I had been so silent in arriving barefoot. Maybe the kitchen counter blocked whatever view they'd have of me. This place was often lent to whatever couples Robert currently promoted. Maybe that was how this pair came to be here, certainly making good use of Robbie's floorspace.

Came a louder thumping, old planks all but croaking with greater pressure and fixed grunts. It sounded like the usual wrestling had overshot even a particularly good athletic fuck. I considered tiptoeing right back out. I couldn't really see them, be they guys or girls, could only hear their strain, could just squint toward bareness, an act quite unmistakable. "No, not . . . Daaaddy, not *that* one . . ." the voice, some adolescent boy's, half-known, and then, I, driven, sick, reached for lamp and met—in its bleaching light—two faces turning this way.

Their mouths hung open, one just above the other. A totem pole of grimace. Each mask varnished in sweat. On the floor, near her splayed palms, a small brown jar, two emptied bottles of champagne. With such light in their faces, their heads looked big, rounded, somehow ringed—jagged cutaways of great tree trunks newly felled. Though I already knew, I told myself I couldn't recognize the couple. Though they aimed my way, though half the kitchen chopping block shielded them, I—like a kid, determined to deny everything while missing nothing "good"—scampered to the bed's far end. I clung to the pineappled upright due Northwest. Suddenly slowly it registered.

Their eyes were like the only four red vents they had to breathe through. Under Robert was not a boy he was so seriously fucking in the bum, but a person distinctly Angie-like. Yes. Mine, ours, her, it, us. Them. Doing this. He's the tops, she's bottom-feeding, really truly getting it.

On all fours beneath him, she was stuck as in some doghouse. His right arm crooked just under her neck. Both of them frozen, as in some superstitious form of visual prevention. Stay still perfectly, you'll disappear. And both, I knew, were still too far into the force of it to quite pull back, to quite snap out just yet.

Though light stayed hard on them, I saw his lower body unstopped, helpless as an animal, getting in a few last good ones.

Okay, this seems to be happening.

Okay.

I always figured that Robert fucking would appear to be some hovering archangel. I'd always pictured him floating in this bed above me, "a human form" made of light like spun fiberglass, no, white cotton candy. But never resembling the beast we all of us are. Not my darling. But Robert, drunk, appeared just another Bacon raptor. He looked made only of the male, only all of beef.

Weight pivoted on one vexed arm, his face hung listless, blood-filled, spongy, ruddy as a cow udder.

"You started playing without me." They, blinking, still engaged, tried so hard to contort themselves invisible. "—Since when? Since . . . in the beginning?"

How must my own face look right now?

They both acted as if, being a single two-backed cretinbeast, by remaining deaf, they could make me disappear the fastest. I dearly wanted to. Be dead. I still held my manuscript but it had somehow rolled itself into my single weapon.

I recalled my father's face, how huge and raw it looked when he'd nearly finished whipping me, when first guilt set in for the jolt my little barebutt dance had given him. Their horror had not yet fully overtaken their desire. It had been blighted at the peak of being sated. The sight of them, all sweated into each other and right down on the floor without a quilt or towel, and his braced arm (the spotted left one) filthy from our city's grime, and her below and still engaged, still hooked, the sight seemed to roll on at a length unendurable.

I saw their faces, invisible to each other, run through so many separate emotions for me; different explanations, his plain contempt, her honest excuses; a dozen changes pulsed across both sets of liverish features. I moved to reach for the lamp, to put it all out. Was then her voice said to me, regaining a certainty sufficient to the moment, said calmly to me while his whole beautiful birthmarked rose-colored stake was still in up her back.

"Hartley, baby, listen . . ."

I pointed. And the word that belted out of me was like some glum Old Testament prophet's: "Baaaaadddddddd!" Instead of rushing out, I ran at, past them, helpless, joined. I grabbed the only water that might douse them right, I hoisted the wobbly weight of an aquarium and sloshed its full wet across them, gasping. The soaked piano sounded as the boat struck keyboard. *Titanic* bounced against broom closet and promptly failed to shatter. That alone seemed right.

I jumped fell backward, ran downstairs, losing pages everywhere, molting. As I went, I somehow threw up those cherries, out and all over myself.

I do believe some howling was involved. On the street, me racing barefoot, stragglers sure got out of my way darn quick. One employee ducked clear of the pizza place ("Slice"), said "What the . . . ?" and bobbed back in. I heard my name said. Ossorio's was closed or closing, no one saw me do this dash. The shrieking was unmanly, childlike, girlish really.

When I rushed into my fourth-floor rear, me filthy, stinking, and groaning like some ox, my phone was ringing but of course I didn't answer. I could picture them nude at the kitchen table now, postcoital, having finished the act off anyway, sharing one cigarette and talking strategy. I was now their problem child, the loser.

I yanked my receiver off the hook and stuffed it in a pillowcase and trailed the cord into the closet, slammed the door hard. I lay down on my bed and made those sounds you're glad nobody else will ever have to hear. But sounds *you* must hear, as someone grownup and nearby and concerned would; and it only makes you sadder for yourself. I laughed because at that moment what I most wanted was a little dog, a terrier, a loyal clean little terrier to welcome its master. Marse Hartley Airedale is Home! And it'd be frisky, and it didn't even have to be all that clean even. Messy could be good. I knew *I* would be, for a long time.

Hearing me made me worry in all the ways you wish those others would. There, there. There, terrier, there.

I told myself in a Carolina twang, "It could have been you with him." And then a New York voice snapped, "Yeah, right. Fat chance, you no-talent scar-sided nonentity. The only way you'll ever get into the *Times* is with your next self-paid 'Needs Work' ad."

I kept remembering our vacationing together, once in a hurry on hearing we could get a rental car for nearly nothing, we just blazed right out to P-town, where we took lots of pictures I still own, and those two stars sat, automatic, in the front seat and I wedged—just as immediately—in back, between them, my head almost in line with theirs. Were they doing it even then? After I tomcatted out to stalk the bars, and after Robert seemed to leave with some French Canadian guy beautiful as a new red Swiss Army jack knife featuring all attachments, was R really stealing back up to her pink gingham guesthouse room? I did know I had been happy as their Airedale, if that is what I was. I was learning. I was their darling, I was potential. I was still perpetually a junior, theirs. They, maybe the Stronger. I, though, surely kinder.

I know that I loved them for how they protected me, without knowing that they did, how guarded I felt as I most guarded them. I always felt safest when they were both within a four-feet reach of me (or due shortly, as one or the other of us sat facing the restaurant entrance: "Are we all here yet?").

Before

I was between, I, pressed quite snug against two flanking sets of ribs as good as their ribs were. Celebrity Father, Notorious Mother, invisible li'l ghostwriter me, a triplet, a fit.

Oh but, all along, we had thought that we were really something!

And now so did the *New York Times*. At least them!

Back there on the floor at Robert's, I would have taken sloppy seconds, on either one of them, thirds.

There's the final closeness that two people can have, with nothing at all between them, having gone as far into another body as your own will fit. But, getting shut out of it, knowing you're just extra and aside, that kind of isolation can do many things to you. Including save your life.

Post-Op

Even with liquids running from my eyes and nose and mouth, it was their health that I fixed upon the most now. You know I never hated either of them, not even when I'd just caught them at it, I never hated them enough to wish either of them hurt. Much less dead. She, at least, would now need better guarding. That alone helped resurrect me out of the spittle sewer where I swam. She'd sure need me now.

If I had warned him of the spot, would he then have been more cautious? Did Robert go near the members of his traveling string quartet? How could anyone so beautiful have become so difficult, dangerous? "Careless" was a word to now upgrade. And if I had been braver and louder, might not my dear ones have waited? might might might . . . ? me me me.

After ten days, extinction lessons, carbon monoxide intake, blue-gray dustballs gathering in a kitchen bathtub unused, it was in exactly ten days I understood I was, as an addict addicted to both of them—"my name is Hartley and I crave . . ." —was in no position to do without the two of them at once. Maybe one at time, maybe him, but at some slow-boil wean, please. Give me a placebo to suck on, or sit on, or talk to three hours per night by phone?

But don't make me go cold turkey, quitting them both. It would be killing, considering the scale of chemical dependency, to give up both my gods at once.

Who else believed in me? Surely that's the control substance most needed by most people. I had written nothing in this time. The sight of my own handwriting was like studying the traces of my filth spread across the finest paper and left piled, defilement sandwich, on someone's desk.

Oh, they sent flowers, they came by, they each pounded on my door three times a day, making jokes out there: "How is our defrocked Miss America unlike the *Titanic*?" Saying the usual adorables, they knew not to slide any more of their good reviews or glamour shots under the door. They never roused me. They each had a key and could have come right in and found me naked, a pillow to my mouth, for dignity and silence that seemed my one defense, if not much of a refuge.

For a second, I considered flying to my parents' place in Florida. Overt death wish, or what? And, of course, what mainly filled my vision was the spot on Robert. It was always a bad time to find out, but now, after finding them, doing that, and factoring the spot in, too . . .

He had left town just after the concert, I hadn't wanted to bring him down right then, and then he stayed gone so long, and the very second he got back, this . . .

It'd been the sight of them like that, like two sneaky boys, or far worse, yes, much, like, yeah, some long-married couple . . . and if it had been going on all along, with the game of my wanting him and her seeming torture from the same desire and his professed indifference to us both.

If it had been just a ruse that whole time of my life, I could not bear it. But, considering the spot, what might it mean to them and me now? We knew so little. It was too early in. Either way, for either one, I still felt something. Therefore, I felt needed. They might not know it. Not yet. But, even if I had to play the Sancho Panza role for both of them forever, well, I'd imagine how Spencer Tracy would create his Sancho; with maybe Kate as Quixote; I'd be the scar-sided plump peasant leading the burro; hell, I'd play the burro— Best Actor in a Supporting Role with saddlebags. I knew I'd play. I'd play along. What other game was there?

There must still be some use for all this love left souring (mousetrap food) in me.

So I got up.

I walked half-dressed into Ossorio's around two o'clock the afternoon of the eleventh day after it. They were there, okay, she lost in smoke, and everybody gathered around, seeming somewhat mopey, mooning, with no good talk going on. I was glad to see repentance or that they missed me, if that's what it was. But maybe I just arrived at twenty after or twenty till when the silence-spreading angel passes overhead.

They all looked up, shocked. Like I had died, but had stumbled back in here for my caffeine allotment anyway. I guessed I looked like hell. That, at our age, was becoming more appropriate, far easier. Part of it today was inevitable, part an effect I'd planned.

I just stood beside their table, ours once, my face quite white and large and hard. Said, "I'm new to New York and probably a big hick—but the guidebooks all claim this here is where the very best sluts hang out. That right?"

"You should know," she said. "You taught us all gave us . . . lessons, or . . . oh, honey, come to Momma." She sputtered, her girl voice. Then Angie rose, ran around the table, grabbed me, flung me back against the tile mural of a fountain's too-blue edgy zigzags. She pinned me there, front bumping mine so hard, and almost hurt me with her force. It was like she pressed the water and the bile clear out of every hole of me, and we just leaned there, she sort of pounding her body against mine, to show me something. Some old velocity, some tomboy tie that held us, no matter who we each fucked, even him.

When she flopped back to sitting, she kept her hands circling my either wrist, and I made fists so tight, facing her but not daring to meet her eyes, my head hanging and hers hanging and our scalps meeting, a little touching comfort right on top, one warm spot of that.

It was Marco who slid a chair under me. Robert looked my way, and it seemed almost funny but not quite, because big Robbie was like some water god, these tears like jets down either cheek, like some classical fountain that is built of composition stone to shoot musical water into your very own garden. "Wouldn't hurt you for anything, Air," he said. Marco had settled me between them, but I was facing down, mostly facing the green-gray marble tabletop, like someone very ashamed of something he had done.

Marco, who knew what'd happened, now acted so upset that we were doing this to each other. And after all we had endured together and won— he rose and (darling darling shaggy boy) moved without asking, returned with my usual cafe con leche. "On Ossorio. But Ossie says you owe him for what you haven't been spending in here lately."

For six weeks, it was creaky. Stiff. Like mountain climbers who've returned to flat land safe, but are so sore from the heights, they cannot walk to the store to get bread. They risk starving on flatland for their overexcellence at cliffs.

And we never mentioned it—we, who'd told each other everything! Or so I'd believed.

I remember when she'd blacked her own eye. Now I somehow wondered even about that, who? And had the others in our group always known what was happening? How could I save my friends if, so far, I still seemed to understand so little about them. About people.

She'd once told me people are far worse than I ever guessed, plus some better, but new ways stretched in each direction. People were usually mean *about* something, but good because they found sometimes they truly could be; and soon the virtue felt narcotic. Its buzz lasted longer than mere wear-off bad. She told me I expected people to do right, but me? I waited in the wrong places. (How to argue with that?)

Lately, given the publicity, those admirers first meeting her called her only "Alabama." She hid her real first name now, or rather it hung back, in natural eclipse. I myself had always held off changing it; or else I alternated between "Angie" and that entire state for which she'd titled herself.

Henceforth I vowed I would only call her that third-person geographic name, invented. Never again "Angie." I couldn't be that personal, not after It.

A few months later Gideon took me aside and asked, in his divine accent the following phrase chic then, "Why get your bowels in any of ze uproar?" He sweetly tried to explain that I mustn't blame them, that, champagne, cocaine, good fortune was a flammable mix and I was a prig to mind, though walking in on them like that could not have been so pleasant. Was it true I'd dented Robert's precious boat? Hadn't its luck been bad enough pre-me?

How could I explain the extra sadness? About the spot. Everybody betrayed feels killed. You feel that the turncoat loved ones are now dead to you. But, loving them as I still did, how could I tell our friend here how literal all that Love-Death duet stuff might really be? So I shrugged, acting as "adult" as our pal the philosophical French-Egyptian. How could I tell him when I myself was still unable to say aloud how wronged and small and sad and underrated and left-behind it made me feel—their doing it or anything without me? Even dying, if that was ever required. And since we were mortals, certainly probably, it would be.

At least, they could have called me in to watch.

All I'd ever really tried was seeing them both.

So, after It, to me, her name was only "Alabama."

Nothing more than what everybody else called her. Nothing older than the brand name.

Strange, that helped. She heard and knew and sensed the difference, and uneasily accepted. It kept Angie, my old love, back safe, and for myself. It saved that time when we both sat groaning, joking, wondering about him. But Alabama would never again get to be, for me, plain Angelina Renata Byrnes, co-hick, another troublemaking player, my fellow beginner.

And at the same second I vowed this, I learned something. I learned that, all along, my real passion had not been Robert. (That'd all been cupid arrow ricochet.) It had not ever been Miss Alabama Famous. No, I most yearned for that freckled missing person.

It was li'l Angie that I'd really loved.

But we stayed together; we had too many years on record not to. I had never before understood my parents' marriage, how—having got this far in—they could neither of them just admit a mistake and bail the hell out. Happiness might demand it, but Mythology—the myth of their being a handsome couple made-for-each-other—would simply not permit that. Myth outranks any single person's little Joy. We're all continually upstaged by the scale of our own times and tragedies. In the end, the name of the ship that took you down is better known than your name ever will be.

Mother had sent me photostats of two letters Colonel Hartley wrote his wife after the Battle of Shiloh. (My aunt, recently remodeling the family farmhouse, found them tucked under dining room wainscotting.) I read the things hoping to understand my great-grandad's character. But all he really ever mentioned were the awful conditions, his boys losing their teeth from simple malnutrition, his outrage over all of this, his feeble attempts to make things locally easier. That seemed the single thing he thought about. Rare mention of a Yankee. Only the salutation and endings of his bulletins threw her scraps, a sentence or two of something a little personal, stray emotions for his worried hungry wife left home, fending with six kids. It was always only The Front, only Care and The Cause.

"They cannot do this to us, Julia. This loss of life shall not be permitted to continue. What must our boy recruits think of such a God? He is surely setting, Julia, such a poor example for our young. Pray without ceasing for my charges and your too obdnt. husband, . . . Increase."

Results

told Robert he would have to go and have The Test, and when he asked me why, I gently turned over his wrist and pointed to spot. It had now become two. They were black.

The look that then passed between us, the questions filed like knives in it, would take the rest of this lights-out fairy-tale story to unpack and catalogue, longer. "Who knew what when?" The Watergate hearings tried to answer. An impeachment followed. But the rushing questions still abound.

So, how did I become Emissary of Testing? And for them, not me? Hurt feelings? If it'd been a three-way on his kitchen floor, who knows how long we might all have drifted, unchecked. A busy bee erotically, I was not likely to accuse. My first simple impulse was to just save them both. If that casts me in the role of school monitor, well, they'd always considered me somewhat fusty, slow, and square.

I knocked on Angie's door. I had not, as usual, phoned first. She bobbed out, but wearing a swipe of red paint across half her face; and I could see she didn't much like being interrupted. "Call me Mr. Butt-insky, witch at the wedding. But it's this—we have got to get you tested, honey."

" 'We?' "

"Yeah, I think 'we.' To be so short, it's a right crowded word, ain't it? I saw a thing. Before you two were together, that one single solitary time, ever ever, right? . . . sorry, I saw a mark on our dear one. I'm not saying just because you . . . I don't know, if things're not done the usual way with guys and gals, if that's better or worse or counts more . . . Nobody knows much of anything anyhow but . . . I will only ask this once. Did you ever wonder about it, your health, while you were with him? They say these days you should be careful . . . It was in the *Voice*. Warnings you've probably started seeing stapled to phone poles, Bama. It's just, I love you both. Shouldn't we go find out? If only so we can all relax, at least about this part? I am not being spiteful. This is the reverse of Bitch, girlfriend. These days, most of what I want to do is run from you two. But I'm right here. —Your Hartley here'll do the legwork. Now you go right on back to making art, my wizardgirl. —Test or no test? Just give me a nod."

She backed up. She backed into her studio. Disoriented, looking for some surface to sit upon, she moved in reverse and fell back, settled, butt-first, on her palette. Surprising me as usual, Alabama laughed at this. She stared over one shoulder and down at her own still-perfect backside. "You know? Using a mirror, with linseed oil, I could daub color right off. Most palettes have the thumb hole, right, hon?" I told her I'd find out where and make the appointment and, if she let me, I'd come with her.

"But what are you saying about him, Hartley? Have you talked to him about this?"

I shook my head yes. "Only just now. He'd worked so long, he's been having such a good time (or that's what it looks like from out here) . . . I thought it could wait. If I'd known, you . . . I didn't know. Maybe it was selfish of me not to corner him earlier. If only for some stranger's sake."

Then we stared at each other. We'd once watched a TV wildlife show. It ended with two big animals battering heads. They lock horns in the wilderness. They die out there—with only each other's eyes as their own fond, sickening, final sight.

Promises, Promises

e had just some scribbled Chelsea address; I told the cabbie to slow down please; it must be around here; I saw a grove of sycamores and started laughing. "No," she got it. "The seminal VD clinic. Where history was made. They've got more serious things to deal with now, huh? But, hey, they cured us before, right, son? Must've been a grammar school at one time, don't you figure? I can hear the ole halls echoing now, 'Row row row yer boat, life is but a dream . . . I mean, discharge.' "

"A dream of a discharge."

"Ever the optimist, Hartley mine. You're incurable, know that?"

"Nice work if you can get it. I do feel a bit rustier at it lately. But I'm fighting that."

"Like your ancestor Colonel Increase?"

"You scare me sometimes. We're all going to be all right, I just know it."

"How do you put up with us, Hartley? You think you understand Humanity. You might. Unfortunately, it's people that are the bitch. Certain ladies in Savannah still believe that folks from nice families are literally made of different flesh and bones. You think our circle is."

" 'No shit?'—attributed to Alabama Byrnes, circa 1981."

"You ever going to say my name again?"

"That is your name. We get to pick, remember? I chose not to be called 'Dick,' like Dad. But you went to a globe for yours. Look, the meter's running, let's get out and go on in. I'm here, I love you. One thing at a time, okay?"

This was our last cab stop in a day of calculated pleasures. The joys were all intended to be lucky. We'd seen our Vermeers at the Met; we had different favorites but understood each other's reasoning and today the arguing came gentle and felt as close-in as those interiors with their sleepy perfect afternoon women. We taxied to the Morgan Library and studied nine of their best Rembrandt drawings. "How could he do so much in such a fraction of a second with single reed-pen? I wouldn't even ask that my work be better," she said, "Just faster."

"You were always pretty fast."

"Up yours with a Quickie," and we laughed our sore, sweet hardened laughs and got in a final cab to head toward finding out.

Robert was out of town again on another glamour junket with the Hip Quartet and he said he would "take care of things, make my own appointment, in my own time." Prima donna. Did he now believe his own publicity? There are only two kinds of people in the world: positive and negative. Whatever. That was up to him. For my meddling and much else, as for helping him, it seemed too late. I told myself I'd learned everything I could from Robert. I told myself the rest'd just be disappointment.

She would have her blood test today. Then there'd be an eternity. The two-week wait. I was glad to find they had at least dispensed with those huge blocks of client-number lumber! I said I'd lurk out here in the lobby. A black woman all in white walked over and smiled at us, asked Alabama, "You're 'fifty-four'?"

"Hasn't she aged gracefully?" I said. No one laughed. "Sorry. Nerves."

"And would your husband like to come in, too?"

"Yes, Hub prob would." Bam winked. So I settled in for the speech I'd learned through my phone research. My palms were soaked, I kept blotting them on chinos. I continually grinned, feeling sick, as if I had forgotten something. "Have *you* been . . . ?" the woman asked me a second time.

"Been . . . ?"

"Tested."

"No, but I didn't . . . Probably *should* know, shouldn't I? Funny I didn't make an appointment for myself. But . . . we've . . ." I pointed to Ms. Byrnes. "I mean, not lately . . ."

"Typical male pig thing, hun?" Alabama confided to our counselor. "Double standard or what? Drags me in here. Takes no responsibility for himself."

"Sir? Mutuality really is the beginning of . . ." but Angie interrupted, "Yeah, Hubby Sir, thanks a lot for joining your little wife in this. Two's company. I mean you are not exactly keeping it in your pants now, are you Mr. Slut at the St. Mark's Baths? And he only likes the very very young boys, that's what's really been hardest."

Our watchful interviewer, concerned, sensing either turmoil or a possible joke, whipped out a second form.

"Do I understand that you two have an . . . open relationship?"

"WIDE," my wife amended. And somehow we both cracked up. She was still the funniest person alive. What I can't convey, her timing.

To spare our interviewer's feelings, I said I'd get my test now too, if they could fit me in. But might we learn our results the same day? I was told yes, but not in the same room. Patient confidentiality. They were using blind numbers to assure anonymity. Protecting the Positive against Insurance discrimination, job bias.

Alabama said she had a superstitious feeling they should do my blood-work first. "No sweat," I said. "Whatever magic . . ." I got done fast and while they finished hers, I wandered the place. Today, everything seemed an omen. I was scouting, for nothing I could name. Some story to tell her later? Some sign I would know only when I found it.

I guess, being back here, I wanted to meet somebody exactly as lively as she had been then, somebody still very young. I'd bring that kid to Bama this time, and not, dog dutiful, trot my find clear back to Robert.

I recalled my body's warning of a sure thing on first seeing her—that burning in the nose, jets of scalding salt behind the lids of either eye. Patrolling this clinic, poking through open doors, hands in pockets, feeling on the verge of a hymn or a scream, I made certain vows. If she was okay and if I was okay, I'd . . . what? Become a better person finally? Leave Manhattan? Discover a good non-Southern subject at last? Forgive, what? And would I, no matter her status, now sign on for whatever portion of a husband she required? Which part of one? There is so little concrete that The Law lets guys like me offer others legally.

Her fantasy had been of Robert's perfect head seen before her best huge early painting. By now, MOMA owned two of her charcoal drawings and they were negotiating to buy, over time, one of her big recent oils. Alabam was not lobby-ready. She had told me, she would have to get clear up past her retrospective there, clean into her mid to late forties, even before she got her shot at the lobby.

This clinic had been gutted and revamped since we last needed it (for kid stuff caught from playing around). All the old warrens of classroom-waiting-areas were gone now. Everything looked both sleeker and sadder. I missed our youth's poster funkiness; industrial carpeting now outranked and smothered scuffed linoleum once as marbleized as bowling balls.

I tried to get my bearings and peeked through the door of what looked like a nursery. Low chairs enameled primary colors, a few battered toys, one easel featuring a daubed ideal house, smoke howling out one chimney, and over it, in child's script: "Everbody Should Get to Be Heathy."

In one corner stood a brown cardboard fort. On the far white wall, a fire extinguisher painted pink, a concession to the nursery atmosphere?

I walked in and, feeling worked up yet listless, seeking security, settled in one child's chair that looked sturdy enough to hold me. I still wore my overcoat. The sun came out. Yellow lit the wall behind my head. I felt like sleeping, I felt like crying. I felt almost old. My cheek touched chilly white enamel and it was from this low angle that I noticed a blurred image peeking through hard enamel above. Around the fire extinguisher, faintest golden lines. I laughed aloud, I almost thought I heard a child humming.

I rose and backed away and saw it, still fighting to emerge around the glass case. Here it was, now in Santa's junior elf room. Finding it made me feel far taller, somehow buoyant, giddy. If ever there were a good sign . . .

I moved forward and pressed both hands to cold paint. I saw how her yellow had bled through coat after coat of institutional enamel. You could still make out legs' rounded forms. Where her pay phone had once been clamped, they'd placed this glass-fronted fire-douser.

Thighs still formed a strange consoling tent. Though this was a kids' room, adults had penned up little comments. I was reading when I heard my name behind me.

I turned, said, "Look, you little totem-maker. One of your familiars has outlived us here, you little totem-maker. Is this happy news or what?"

She came forward, still poking a gauze pad into the crook of her right arm. I settled mine around her so we could study it side by side. She said, "Somehow I thought this room was at the other end."

"But isn't this great?"

"Great? They painted me out, asswipe."

"Yeah, but it still shows. You thought maybe they'd frame it? It's still here, isn't it? We've changed, it hasn't, and God knows a lot has happened since." Sun now flooded the wall and little checkmarks from the pin she wore made nervous feathery curves, moving only with her rise and fall of breath. The building seemed far quieter than in the old itchy drippy VD days of our curable glory.

"See what the critics are saying?" I pointed to wiseguys' jottings. This being a nursery had not restrained them—comments rested above the five-foot level. One ballpoint arrow pointed to the genderless juncture of massed emerging legs: "Will she or won't she?" Someone else's red ink had made a dotted pleading little line where one small vagina opened to this huge being. "Best offer I've had all day," she did her Donald Duck voice. The third mark was the work of some kid who'd probably stood on one of these midget chairs. He (or she, but probably he) had added a black blimp shape that swerved off to the right, intending to show an erection, seeming based on one he'd glimpsed. I felt myself, below the belt, quicken to brief life. "Nothing like good reviews." She half-smiled, fingers tracing the words, her lines. We heard a sound and started. The small head of one dark living child poked out the crenellated window of the cardboard fort.

"You like my lady?" he asked. Ordered to, we looked again at the wall's image, both nodding back down at him. "My name's Jamal. I kept real real still, didn't I? My mother gets off soon. She helps sick people. I am going to be in here from now on, but play like you don't know, okay? Okay."

And then his brown face retreated into blackness.

We two glanced at each other, shaken but grinning. "Sick people," he had said as we stood looking at our only form of proof and health.

"Hartley, what are we going to do?" She straightened her bent arm, studying the cotton's sample of her own blood. Head tilting, eyes going in and out of focus, the painter gauged, "Not half bad, this color, hunh? Dried like this especially. Take a little Mars Red. Use Permanent Green to cut the sharpness, really take it down toward flat, almost to khaki-ish. If," Alabama said, "if . . . if he . . . or you . . . if I . . . —Hart, maybe you're contagious, ever thought of that? Maybe I caught your Wannabe Happy bug. Maybe all along, I've been closet-case Happy? I mean, hey, I've finally got a Fifty-seventh Street gallery that puts my name onto its second-floor window in letters as tall as . . . that fort with no boy in it. I'm just beginning to like it here . . . My twenties were Jaws, my thirties chewed every mouthful of me a hundred times. Who knows how custardy and nice my forties might feel? —Honey, if it gets us, what are we going to do?"

We stood here, looking at her art for lack of any vista finer. "Best we can. At least, there are several of us. It'll just have to play itself out."

"If only we could've fallen for a nice dull clean little four-inch CPA . . ."

"Ysch, I'd rather be . . ." Then I changed the last word . . . "I'd rather be *us*."

Robert, home, glad for that, vowed to never pack another bag. His second night back, he nearly stood us up for a dinner at Rocco's. He was rarely late. She and I were splitting our zabaglione, table still littered with mussel shells, when he wandered past and chanced to see us. Robert came rushing in, turned his chair around, settled there, his head at rest on his crossed arms. Staring at us, silent. He did not appear talkative.

"Uh . . . dearie?" she started. "Welcome home to you, too. You hate my always being late, so what good are you? You had an appointment with us."

"Did not."

"Did friggin' so."

"Sorry—did? Forgot."

"Forgot! So," she gave him a chance, "what did you learn on tour?"

" 'Earn'?" he asked.

" 'Learn.' You taught us that."

"I caught a cold. Walked to Mrs. Park's for milk yesterday? Had to sit on two stoops. Nina let me rest on her cot she keeps for beauty naps behind the steam presses in back. Can't seem to shake this chest thing. Feel so out of it.

Last night, shivered my nuts off. Sweated like it was the Tropics and I was Joan Crawford chewing scenery in . . . (don't even tell me, Hart. Because I know you're going to try to act it out) . . . *Rain*. Shook to where my bed squeaked. That bed, even with a crowd, never squeaked before."

I advanced a theory. "Maybe it's been loosened up by all the recent floor activity." And we all laughed, but out of Robert's mouth a goodly sample of his chest cold, one corner piece of gray-green phlegm—shot, hit, then slipped down the side of one glass Parmesan dispenser. Our waiter, seeing, looked prissy, then solemn. Robert alone laughed at the projectile, laughed quite loud, pointing. Two candlelit couples at far tables turned, romance offset by his sudden braying, peeved.

"Honey," she said. "Honey?" And I saw her hand scoop forward. At her touch, he set his head down on the checkered cloth before us, good jaw amid rattled mussel shells. Bama's palm pulled back as from a lit stove.

"Hartley, feel him."

My hand now met his heat. At this temperature, it felt unlike a human surface.

"What?" Robert awarded us a dazzling out-of-sequence smile. "Because is it something I said?"

"I'll pay." I signaled for our waiter. "Robert, sweetie, you have a temperature, a brain-cooker temperature. Robert? We're going to get you fast over to St. Vincent's."

"A saint lives in the Village? I don't feel my absolute best. But, where is there one? Can we walk to see the Saint?"

"Yes." She held his right arm. I took his excellent left one.

It was among us.

AFTER

That Ship Left Already

How're the Folks?

A Highly Unlikely Love Poem to My Parents

y father has lost our car. He's way out there, wandering the mall's vast lot. He disappears behind a hundred palm trees lit with Christmas stars somehow sickening at noon. Mom and I strain to see him. There, white-haired between vehicles, his golf togs overbright as educational playthings, a thin man keeps waving something side to side.

A compass? Some pocket dowsing rod? No, she explains, it's that thing, his latest toy (four hundred bucks)—"a no-key remote-entry device" meant to unlock the trunk, flash headlights, activate the alarm of a much-missed Buick Park Avenue. Among the thousands of cars beaded colorful to the horizon, my old man is trying to flush out his. He hopes to force his own to dance.

I am, of course, in Florida. I've left Angie and the others in charge of Robert's latest hospital stay. Beside me, on this backless bench set just within mall glass, my gaunt chic mother, 80, clucks, shuddering. Feeling responsible, she acts as ashamed for herself as for poor Pop out there.

"I told him where it was." Her voice has grown deeper, sexier and as she's aged, I guess, past sex. "You heard me, honey. I said, 'Dick, it's in B-2.' Because I remembered that by—'To Be or Not to Be.' "

"Isn't a liberal education a wonderful leg-up?" (Hartley here is really working to be pleasant.) I flew South to relax. I have lived in Manhattan so long I'm good for nothing but. There, if you have cash, and if you don't look like a Harlem fare, you can just lift your hand and make a cab appear any hour, day or night. Here you get assigned a single car. And you can lose the thing, apparently.

As a favor to my parents, I usually arrive wearing a jacket and tie, to set myself apart from the airport's rude Hawaiian shirts. Not today. By now, this far into rounds as a friend-nurse, my new motto runs: Why not look as tired as you feel?

It comforts your patients, if not your parents. Isn't it dishonest, appearing too natty, in control? These dark rings under my eyes are now countable as those within some redwood's trunk—and like the tree, I'm not unproud of them.

My folks failed to meet me at the gate, first time ever. They forgot to tell me in advance. I fretted till, outside Baggage Claim, I spied their gleaming silver car. It rested in a Handicapped Zone. Had they fudged? Embracing Mom, I spotted, on their interior mirror, the Blue Permit hanging, a little white stick figure in its little white stick wheelchair.

They smiled so. Even Dad. He tried imbuing one firm handshake with a hug's velocity. I, overbold from swashbuckling hospital emotions, moved to embrace him. He waddled backward, nearly fell against the car. In his cool blue eyes, I saw a man who'd just escaped a sexual assault.

Muzak now offers us carols; I've lost sight of him. Dad drove us direct to this mall. Dad said I had to see the new Bloomingdale's that, he swore, "is way better than your one up in New York."

"Aha," said the backseat diplomat.

Soon it'll be Christmas. I do hope we find the Buick first.

I'd planned this trip as an escape from disability. —Working with a disease so wicked gives you a false sense that everything not It is easy.

They are shrinking, my parents. Odd but my own love for them seems to roar suddenly open—the mouth of the MGM lion—just as they go whittling kittenish into air. The more I see Robert turn ancient so damn fast, the more I long to keep these veterans here in health.

They still look luxuriously pink and silver.

Poor Dad—way out there—hoists his remote device. To reassure us?

These days, Mom risks more. Only to save face for him, of course. But how competent, dry, and witty this woman has suddenly finally become— she who agreed, at age nineteen, to use the leading lady's energy in a supporting role.

"Mom? I'm gonna chance sounding tactless here. We, uh, both do know where the Buick is, right? I mean, we've been sitting here going on what?

Three hours? Maybe I've grown pushy from my years in overdrive in New York, and maybe I'm not respecting the terms of your agreement, yours and his . . . whatever. But how about I barge out there and lead him to it? Tactless, right? The car is on the other side of this place. True, he's getting 'warmer,' but that asphalt's heat might kill him first. Our car is due east, Mom. Dad's due west." I sing along with one carol, " 'We Three Kings Dis-Orient Are.' "

"On that, you'll hear no argument from me. But, honey, you know how he gets. And, during your first visit in a whole year, how would that be for his self-esteem? You come and then you leave. I have to live with him. He'll find it eventually, trial and error. Patience. That's become my full-time job. Why, just last week . . ." And she wraps arms around herself, leans forward, shifting from the sight of him.

She's about to offer something she feels is disloyal. I urge her on. "He won't know. He's quite a distance. I can't imagine what it's like for you, watching all this happen so fast. We're going through it with Robert, but at least I have Angie and the others, though the others're none too well. The worst is having nobody who'll listen . . ."

Mom lowers her eyes; the toes of her good shoes draw even against the mall's blue-gray terrazzo. "Last Thursday, the fourteenth"—(I sense a boastful mnemonic virtuosity in this flourish—forgivable, even adorable) "at three-ten p.m., he did this, too. Lost it. The car, I mean. And as usual, he took his new car-door-opener thingie, and was aiming it at anything even vaguely . . . Buick-like . . ."

(I grin, and know I am my mother's son.)

"Finally, I carried take-out lemonade over where he'd got himself to. No judgment on my face, you know, no impatience, just happening to wander up with a cold drink. Then I see, see he's . . ."

I sidle one inch closer. This familiar conspiracy between us started at least nine months before my birth.

"See, honey? Dick was using the remote, from our television set . . . Richard Hartley Mims the first, my hero, out in the heat trying to find our car by changing channels. Back at home!" She covers her mouth, takes a great fish gasp then makes a smile of it . . . "But, tell me about your friends, about our friend, our Robert."

I wish I could rush her with good news. Of Robert, I mention only his loss of weight and widening of delusions. I do not tell her he now believes that a high school musical is about to go on, that its whole cast is still waiting to learn the show-stopping song he has yet to compose. The cast stands anxious around him. Cars are pulling into the school parking lot—parents, arriving, especially his. Robert seems to sit at the piano before reams of blank paper, the actors gather, sweating through their makeup and cowgirl costumes, eager to see if they can't learn a whole song real darn quick. Nothing comes.

This fact and others, I withhold.

But I fear I'm letting her down, even by informing my sheltered Mom that a boy thirty-four might be in worse health than poor Dad out there. "Mom? Look, now he's pushing a shopping cart. What's the cart for?"

"The cart, darling, is to hold Dick up."

"Oh. Oooh, boy."

"That it should be Robert seems particularly unfair," she goes on. "I don't know how to ask these things—Yours, it's a world whose forms I . . . But, were you and Robert ever . . . ? Did you two think of yourselves . . . as more than . . . ?"

"Just friends. If that's not a contradiction in terms these days. No, he never found me interesting, in that way."

"Lucky you," she whispers, and this shocks me, but I see her point.

She, dreamy, adds, "Someone as beautiful as he, there's no telling how many . . ."

"Mom? Did you know that Robert and Angie were 'a number,' as the kids are saying now?"

"But . . . Oh, it's beyond me, Hartley! First, growing up, I thought there was only one way, ours. And then you've taught me over the years to . . . accept, or try, another. And now he and she! . . . It's past me. Or I it." We sit here, silent. At this moment, I feel as close to Mother as I did to Angie when—free of any topic but art, poverty, sex—we once sat shoulder to shoulder for hours somewhere, with a view of the entrance, waiting for him.

"Your Robert always had lovely manners, and such a striking boy."

I consider telling her he now weighs ninety pounds. I don't.

"How is your own health, darling?" This is where our newfound intimacy has been leading yet again. Poor thing has asked me my status three dozen times in that many roundabout ways.

"I'm still assuming I'm negative. One way of saying something positive,

Mom. If anything changes, I'll call you first, okay? Assume the best. You've got enough on you. I'm fine but I'm learning. I keep a postcard of Walt Whitman in one corner of my shaving mirror. He was a caretaker during his whole war. I thought he must be ancient till I turned the card over last week. Year younger than me. I'm not that jollied or spiritual. But I'm all right. Sleepwalking, trying to get everything done. Sure am glad to see you— Mer' Christmas."

"Yes, you too, dear. —But look how white my own baby's hair is getting. I don't dye mine but I certainly wish a person's children would!"

She redirects a curl around my ear. I pull away. "Tickles. I'm not a baby and it's not white. Just silver, and only at the temples. 'Distinguished.' That's Nice for 'exhausted.' "

"Please don't mind my continually asking. Things change so fast, healthwise."

And we both stare out toward Dad. Who waves. We—polite, conditioned—signal back. We smile our set and wasted smiles however invisible from that far. "The time your father and I visited you in New York City that December five years ago? Robert had something waiting on our bedside table at the Stanhope. Your Robert gave me my first box of Godiva chocolates."

I never knew he'd sent Mom candy. At the time, Robert, writing his *Titanic,* earned most of his cash by cleaning people's apartments. As I sit here, I reconsider my pal. I imagine how my mother sees him, his undying sense of luxury. Robert, even when most broke, a gift.

"Those days, I still thought that Whitman's chocolates were tops. I soon started seeing Godivas everywhere and I did let myself say to Mimi Albertson, 'Yes, Godiva. Little gold box? Yes, I was given a box of those in New York City. Aren't they delicious? Rich but not too sweet, is what I like.' "

Everything today makes me cry.

(Angie insisted that I needed this trip, a break, some sun. "By now," she said, "You're yellow as sweet Robbie here."

"Thanks bunches."

"Besides, if you have Florida at Christmas, I'll get to go to my opening in Berlin come New Year's. Fair's fair? Okay.")

* * *

Mom sounds tired, "Honey, maybe run fetch us some lunch from their food court. I'll stay here and wave. You never know how long it's going to take. —Oh, and I'd so hoped your visit might be fun for you, and now look what he's . . . what we've gone and . . ."

"Chinese? What's least hideous here?"

Just then Dad, from a flashing mall security car, gives us the V for Victory sign. "Found it," he mouths, grinning like a man inviting us to come and view the huge gold nugget he has just lifted from some California stream, changing forever the course of American history.

"Eureka," I say in comic monotone. Laughing, she covers her laugh with one hand. Rising, she says, "Now now." Her new tone warns me: Once we're physically with Dad, all true and intelligent intimacy between us must stop, change, hide. One benefit of the lost Buick? We've had three and a half clear honest hours right at the start before she must mostly withdraw.

"Oh, son, so glad you're here. Even if that's selfish of me. —Can't imagine."

"I'm beginning to . . . Great!" I mime through massive glass. I hoist Mom's elbow as she mutters, "Was it in 2-B, or was it not 2-B?" but only just under her breath. And all while waving, flirting her best bent geisha thanks toward my old man. My suddenly old, old man.

Orientation

Having found our car, he actually drives it. *Should* he?

Bound home, breathing hard, he smiles so. "These days, swear holy God, never know, quite where the." He does drive oddly well. That he can do it at all seems as logically illogical as certain combined improbable tasks in dreams—say, walking a tightrope over Niagara while setting a huge brass alarm clock.

I soon see: He is competent only if everything stays predictable. Suddenly one rusted station wagon full of migrant workers swerves across three lanes toward an exit, no signals. Dad panics, honks; our tires graze median as he lets loose such a blistering list of racist epithets. Ones new to me. I mean: New to me out of him.

I see my mother's neck muscles lock. I receive her coded plea that I, the liberal, not call him on it today, at least not till this vehicle is stopped. —No problem. Hey, whatever, it can wait.

"Yeah," recovering, he finally says to no one. "I *thought* it was right around there." He means the car. And invites us to join him in beaming at his own vast male efficiency. I simply sit here, numb already. In the back seat. Glad at least for safety belts. Practicing my own homespun form of Zen. Trying to invent it.

Home Safe

y parents' is a spacious pretty glass box overlooking a lake. Sun browses, touristy, intrigued by this much daily beauty. Cathedral ceilings look steep in a white box this unsmudged.

The sun's interest gets further split among many beveled mirrors. My mom started collecting them while still in North Carolina; she swears she only knew why once she'd hung all thirty in lakeside tropical rooms. Mirrors enlarge the blue-green view, they enhance property value and bespeak our family's breeding and very good if oh so conventional taste. I myself feel sick to death of it. What help is it?

Their common room overlooks a lake with its own mascot alligator. Soon as we arrive, soon as Dad hurries to mix our drinks, Mom points to a stripe floating loglike. "This one, he's called Bosco for some reason. They change over time."

The lake can only support one really big one. When the latest grows six feet long, a game warden will be phoned to come fetch it. Why? Visiting dogs and grandchildren are not safe within eyesight of a wild gator expanding past that size. At Sun City Center last month, a cocker was eaten and one grandkid lost her leg. Retired folks must feel titillated watching this beast grow huge. Comforting to know that just by lifting a "bone white" portable phone, they can banish the creature, death forestalled. Still, they feed it.

I now lean out over my parents' deck, I see many an old Melmac plate, emptied, around the muddy lake at clocklike intervals.

Using my credit card, I dial our circle's hospital of choice from the kitchen-wall phone; my parents stay close to overhear key words: "shingles," "higher dosage," "nightsweats."

"But Bama, how about you? Still standing? He betterer? How worserer?" Mother finally mimes something, pointing from her chest to

Dad's. I interpret, "Bambam? Tell Robbie my folks send love and Mom re-members the Godiva chockies." My father's face narrows, he hears private references. He'll sulk now. If betrayals abounded during his dry-land prime, how many must be lurking amphibious these days?

Robert's conscious. Marco's about the same. Gideon holding. Suddenly after years of house parties, he's back to painting all the time. So many sick, and me in Florida!

I can finally settle on one white couch as my parents appear decorous on its mate. Drinks in hand, ice creating its own civil music against leaded crys-tal, we're safer for these; we can now properly face each other. "Well, well," Dad ventures, hearty. "We got us at least *one* son home for Christmas."

Thanks a lot.

"Cheers," I lie. We sip, pretending—with hands fused around clinking cylinders—that we three can take the booze or leave it. Right.

"So," Mom says, smiling. "You're really here."

"No doubt about it. You both look great." The visit has commenced. The box step, three-quarter waltz time. No fast moves or sudden stops.

They do look great. It is commonly considered desirable that a person's children be good looking. But rarely are you told how helpful handsomeness is in parents. My own folks' longtime tidiness and glamour have made their countervailing tensions somewhat easier to bear. Maybe I was drawn to Robert and Angie for a simple reason: My parents are better looking than I. Odd, but that's actually been quite disappointing for my folks and me. At least I'm smarter. But, of course, this has also been disappointing for me; since it's invisible to them. Except during *Jeopardy*. Which should come on in, what? Twenty-one minutes, please? When that game show's rolling, I alone answer. Depending on the category, I get about 83 percent. And my parents, having paid for my education, gloat like couched Boscos fed steady spaniels.

"Darlin'?" Mother starts. "We feel you do look a bit overworked. The color is not good. You push yourself so, like *he* did, really." She swings her white head toward a neutral man beside her. "Why not take it easier? Come enjoy our sun more? There's Robert, of course. We know you'll want to do right by him. But mightn't you be struggling too hard with all those other poor sick fellows? Aren't you helping lots of people you barely knew so-cially? Weighing on you, are they? Why not cut back some?"

I shrug. I fight down an emotion. "Number One," Father says, cryptic, but we know he means look out for . . .

(Between these visits, I recall my folks' charm. It's their uncomprehending Republican opacity, I block. —Just as the pain of childbirth is programmed to be forgotten between required screaming bouts of ouchly recall.)

Her rushing to this subject, their wordless agreement about my evil looks, it feels like yet another betrayal. I'm too tired to protect myself. I've already given everything away.

I sigh. I only seem to sigh like this around my folks. I take two longish bourbon swallows. Dusk is making outlines of the royal palms across my parents' lake. They say they want me to try their clubhouse's new Olympic pool tomorrow; I fear they'll see my knife scar.

"So"—it's Dad—"you writing a lot, I guess."

My parents still work as a tag team. First one gets you around the legs, then the other piles on.

"Some. Robert gave us an assignment six months back. To try and figure out our own idea of Paradise. I called mine 'Toward a More Precise Identification of the Newer Angels.'* I imagined how new angels might get recognized by older ones. But no magazine'll touch the piece. Maybe it seems strange, coming in without a context. I brought it with me, figured maybe to reread it on the plane home. I think it's good —But, writing? Less than I'd like. I guess it'll be there. I certainly won't lack for experience, will I? But right now, my book feels like less of an emergency . . . than this other."

"Earning a living is always an emergency, son."

"Fine sunset you got going here." I take the coward's way out. I haven't the grit for a brawl tonight. Not while feeling this beat, not after his star-search for our Buick.

"Howbout another drink, kids? Anybody else?" I dash to their club-worthy wet bar, its bent chrome faucet, green marbletop—the niche, our local altar to that favored Episcopal household god: a full undiscounted bottle of the very best.

I study sky. My folks remark on today's postcard sunset. Their lake doubles its lurid beauty. Large waterbirds are flying over in blackest silhouette. Dad compares this sunset unfavorably to the one in October: "Less yellow tonight, purpler south-southwest."

"Aha," I respond, nursing further bourbon.

*See Appendix following page 338.

Dad explains how that one in October was truly "a red-letter day . . . literally, come to think of it!" Then he laughs toward more ragged laughing unto coughing into redfaced shock. I know this. Mom, fighting for the casual, smiles, pats his back. He lifts his right arm, now his left. Poor guy's lungs are shot. Fibrosis. It killed his father; it recently killed his older brother.

Dad chain-smoked during WW II and most of the fifties. After one of his hacking spasms, I, concerned, once asked about those Chesterfields' effect on his wind. He only blinked; told me he had no idea what I was talking about, and why had I been born such a goddamn pessimist? That shut me up. Was I unconsciously gloating?

I need a third drink. Or would this might would be maybe make the four, fourth? They watch me, their eyes look light if concerned as I chat toward their bar again. I'm blathering too much about New York, non-plague art-world gossip of no interest to them; but I can think of nothing else to say; inwardly I panic at their lack of ice. I find it hard to believe my intelligent father could misplace his whole car; I find it easier to forget. I start again to understand my mother's plight. Some life sentence, a "happy" marriage.

We now discuss my brothers, my young nieces—their latest test scores, accomplishments at soccer, leading roles in school musical comedies. "Though I must say I can't believe that kids these days still want to do *Oklahoma*." My parents wince at my disloyalty toward the forties that spawned me.

"What time does the news come on here? I mean national." It's my fall-back position. But a smell intervenes. Hidden beyond the golf course vista, a single distant orange grove must remain yet "undeveloped." We know it is still there because, this evening—through huge windows—a smell drifts across their lake. I turn my head, as toward a sound. Here comes a scent so delicate you doubt it's genuine. —Can such an evolved sweetness exist this side of paradise?

"You see?" my father says. "We got it pretty much made here. They cut our grass every other Thursday. But if you plant anything extra, you tend that. We've planted. So I do have a couple outdoor chores for you tomorrow. If you're willing . . ." I nod.

"And, of course, able."

"Willing, yes. Able? that's always been *your* call, has it not?"

I didn't actually say that, did I? A glance at Mom hints that yeah, I probably did.

"Sure." I try. "Sounds good. Bet we'll have the weather for it, this being Florida. Is *Jeopardy* right after the news here or must we slog first through *Wheel of Fortune*?"

"We like it." His bitterness—briefly hidden out of shame over the car loss—now marches fully forward. "After dinner, we tend to like our *Wheel*, son."

"But the game involves no skill."

"Just shows how young he is. 'm I, right, Helen?" He gives Mom yet one more chance to show her loyalty, and disown me. "How are we for ice?" She rises; I see how much ground he's lost with her. I avert my eyes, and proceed with usual cruise-control courtesy. "So, what else . . . ? How the *Al*bertsons doing?"

Task-Directed

y father says, "You must be tired from traveling. Big day tomorrow, work to do. Best turn in." He goes to stand. Then Dad decides he can't get up gracefully, can't rise at all, so he shrugs to indicate a change of mind—but, hey, he could if he wanted to. Mother and I watch. We try not engaging our usual literary-critical match-set follow-up after-glance.

With me somehow this silvering and not sick yet, with me here at Christmas, I note how the decorations are returned verbatim from last year; they were merely moved upstairs wholesale then down again, and the tiny artificial tree rigged and ornamented, once. Mom's former deck-the-halls rituals feel, by now, too much like work. I face a seated white-haired man and, rising myself, smile, "Sleep well, all."

"So," Mother says. "But, darl, do wait, not yet, our favorite news show'll be on in no time. They catch people doing things. They take the camera right into the stores. Dick, where's the thing, where's the remote thingum, sweetie? I know that *I*, given my sieve of a mind lately, just cain't keep track of it or much of anything else anymore." Her Southern belle accent thickens, as she stands, efficient, caught in another geisha act. She gives me a look begging me not to mind how she flatters, trying to save him with one more "poor little me." Same ole same ole.

* * *

After their Eleven O'Clock Roundup, after brushing my teeth, I run into my white-haired father. He is wearing a terry robe, is stooped in the middle of the dark hallway, mumbling, enraged if contained. He has dropped the remote control onto thick white carpeting. In trying to bend and fetch it, he's lost his breath then his balance. I see that he is pinioned here, one arm to the wall. I recall Robert's arm, his weight on it, him hunched over her.

"Let me. Please." I bend, agile. And as Dad straightens, the robe flips open. I, in rising, find myself confronting nudity. His body is still his; everything's lowered two inches if still right there. But his genitals are precisely my own. Mirrored, I avert my eyes. And he risks falling, to tie the belt.

I let him scramble back toward modesty as I palm the unit his way and hurry by. He flashes me a look, radioactive.

"Sleep well. Merry Christmas, Dad."

I know to leave him. I'll let him hobble off at his own rate, gasping, unseen. I'll wait just inside the guest room. Only if I hear him fall will I run back. (But, wait, surely, the living room's remote doesn't work their bedroom's smaller set?)

He's like some child too tired to admit the world's one true fault just now is: he himself feels far too exhausted by it. I know the feeling. A child this worn out, instead of hauling himself to bed, will do literally anything to resist inevitable sleep.

During my good-night peck her way, Mother promises, "Mornings, he's better." She's doing a last science-lab wipedown of their kitchen. I try and give her a hug one beat longer than our usual, one meant to prove I see, I sympathize. But Mom breaks it off and veers away from me toward the dirty glass I left in their sink. I blame her pride. It's the pride of a person willing to sit three hours allowing another proud person to find an unlost car. Her pride grieves me like some molar hurting because it is, precisely, my own—throbbing.

So let's see, I got Dad's big prick and Mom's huge pride. Thanks a lot. Stand back, world.

Window Treatment

I stagger, literally, stagger off to bed. Their guest room is decorated with scallop shell motifs, rancid coral pastels. Only a decorator could've perpetrated this. Tonight the whole scheme strikes me as impersonal, then sinister. One entire wall of family pictures stretches floor to ceiling. At first even this appears arbitrary, like those silver-framed images you see scattered across the mantels of model rooms in finer department store windows.

Here is Dad, wearing his Army uniform, being kissed after a USO show by Betty Grable herself on tiptoe. Here again is Colonel Increase Hartley, but blown up and oil-painted beneath excessive Angie-like rouge that he plainly resents. I bend over one photo in its certificate frame. This is the single picture of my father as a child. A sepia record of his own dad's grocery store. The image is half obscured by one corner of this dresser. Half-hidden on purpose? It's the single unclassy blot on this escutcheon of a wall—all orthodontia, great legs, horse events, staged garden parties, award ceremonies for us.

This one boyhood photo of Dad must've been snapped at the Depression's lowest ebb; maybe for some grocery store newspaper ad? Because I can't imagine people so poor hiring a photographer to memorialize their plight. But maybe they only look poor to me, from here. Maybe, for them, store ownership was a first mythic step toward the riches they achieved, a first step-up that now lets me look so far back down on them?

In the shop, one blond cur is shown scurrying from the flashbulb seeking to save it. There's a butcher block; its unrefrigerated side of beef gives evidence of being hacked at; the meat is mostly covered with damp cheesecloth meant to minimize the flies.

Between pyramids of canned beans, my grandfather poses. He wears wireless specs hooked around big ears, his hair is parted dead-center. Instead of making him looking like some Princeton math professor of the period, he resembles a Grand Ole Opry backup banjo player—way too proud of today's fresh-laundered collar. One big hand rests atop a toylike silver cash register. His children, all under age twelve, man four counters. All stand on produce boxes. Something in their will to do this right makes me recall my threatened friends. A now-stylish aunt seems to have just bobbed her own hair at the butcher's block with those same greasy tools. The family's expression is uniform, efficient as their aprons. It is set and lipless. Duty makes a mouth. Duty films the eyes with owners' suspicion. The kids' faces are, for me, the embodiment of a dour yet prideful phrase, "The working class." Santa's infant elves as alienated labor.

My father, the youngest, is shown at maybe four. His platinum hair is worn in a charming bowlcut. But features underneath pinch themselves into a scared country look. Would such a child ever be allowed to believe in Santa Claus? Would such a child ever let another child believe?

Most striking: the adult-sized aprons on all the children. On the youngest, the apron's skirt seems folded up and over four full times. Then its strings get knotted hard behind. However scared of the flashbulb the kid appears, he wears this bib with such pride. It could be armor in how he presents it: "Just like Dad's. We own this whole store. Can I help you, Mister?"

As record-keeper, as sudden caretaker to my pals, tonight I feel weirdly identified with this solemn, unthanked kid. His sense of duty is already mapped out, it will be the death of him, and yet it's the single way he sees to live.

At my most charitable moments (which seem fewer lately, given epic woes waiting back in boobytrapped New York), it helps to recall my father's long climb, his dreary playless start. Instead of a treehouse, a grown man's apron origamied to diaper size. No childhood, a Depression.

This might've convinced him to let his own sons have more fun. Instead, almost from our first efficient steps, he set us all to work. A witty older neighbor liked to call our house and its sons, The Works Projects Administration.

My first memories of Dad still involve his impossible commissions. Such chores would tax the stamina of a strong man twenty-five. A child aged three just cannot fake the manual skill required to wield a man-sized hoe. Concussions bruise young palms so new. The principle of leverage depends upon a figure standing at least five feet tall, not twenty-six inches long.

The tasks Dad assigned us seemed created to baffle and shame sons born lucky in a richer time. If the world had grown tail-finned with postwar luxury, handwork with old tools stayed baseline mean, and would always be instructive.

We lived in a beautiful house with a two-acre yard. The privet hedge that guarded it from neighbors was fully eighty-four feet long. (At twelve, I bought a retractable tape measure just so I could know this. I still know it.) One ideal home became our Parris Island. Dad only stepped into the yard with us, evenings after office hours, to check on our completed labors. We'd forgot one hula fringe of grass left undisciplined down the middle of the drive. Wasn't that a one-inch dip in the hedge? Our work never really proved quite right. There seemed to be some high tax on a Dad's ever uttering, "Good."

Even as he grew more prosperous, his impatience with our country club friends (the kids next door) cast us all as softies, spoiled brats, the very crowd that must have sniggered at his homecut hair and outsized apron. I can see them, Fauntleroys in green velvet, peering through the gold letters of his family name across store windows showing sawdust, a clock advertising a starch, flypaper clogged with its own regretted successes.

Now sure only of insomnia, I sleep at once. Immediately I dream of medicating my parents. They each stretch out on pink shells that are, I slowly recognize, alligator-shaped soapdishes, only huge. My folks have shrunken to fetal size, their skin is sticky, sticky but drying. I must feed them each milk. I squeeze it through an amber glass eyedropper—old-fashioned as Madame Curie's gear; it is the forgotten eyedropper our family used to sustain baby rabbits found in the high weeds of rustic North Carolina during the early 1950s, centuries ago.

Daylight Comes and I Wanna Go Home

"We've got your whole schedule planned already. Some work, more play, makes Jack . . ." Mother greets me over the sound of bacon frying. "Excellent," I say, as Father often would, when he was better, younger.

We now glance at him, a frown, the official bearing. He's outdoors already—trying to fill the birdfeeder. His movements were once so precise, so torqued. Now, spilling blond seed everywhere, he scowls at us, then tries to bodyblock his small mistake. A blur of millet in the foreground while, beyond, a sticklike floating gator seems to idly watch my dad. Plans, Bosco?

During breakfast, a tiny white TV blares news, gives cutesy handicraft hints. After the Tampa Trib yields local football scores, Dad asks if I am sufficiently coffeed up to maybe help with those few chores? Since I am *here* after all . . .

He'll need a hand in trimming the lower fronds off that fast-growing palm tree out there. See the scrubby one past the feeder? Darn thing keeps blocking part of the lake and golf course view. Quickly, I agree.

I change clothes.

I dress down.

Mom, already fixing lunch salads, hurries outdoors first. She opens a folding lawn chair then helps Dad shuffle forth and settle. Yesterday's car-search robbed him of so much. She retreats. And Dad, just from this exertion, is huffing. He tries pretending it's intentional—one form of chuckling. "So, best get, this done, ha, huhn, ha, yes, ha, yeah, good lick, work, har."

He will supervise me from there. Ten feet nearer the house than this shaggy five-foot Sego palm. My father is a former tyro of the golf links. For me, he was once the sound of a lawnmower after dark. He now admits he has grown too winded to even use a saw: "Disgusted with myself, but there it is." I appreciate this admission; a new tenderness? A tenderness?

—I vow to myself I'll try to do my job here with real medical precision. Whatever residual rage I feel, I'll put away. There are two kinds of people in the world. I want to do right by him. Because it seems I can.

My father founded an insurance agency. My father made major money and never lost a big-time client. My father taught Sunday school and tithed and was called a true gentleman by most persons in Falls, North Carolina, black or white. His unwed prettyish secretary remained in love with him for thirty years, and he never took advantage of her, never let us joke at her expense. In public he still acts sunny, always ready with the latest joke, a back-slapper, speaking to everyone at every party, including all the help.

His truest life has involved, not any one philosophy, but a day's head-long listlike physical activities. My father can announce his admiration for thirty-year-guarantee roofing-shingles and with a passion that lets you participate, then marvel. What a great idea, shingles! Were bird feathers or gator scales mankind's first shingle inspiration? He is a literalist, which makes him—if heard correctly—a metaphysician. But Dad, of course, would argue against this. Too fancy. Too much my idea, too fey, Ivy, and "brainy sounding."

He is accustomed to giving orders factually and then he's used to pretty much getting his way. But a major general's role depends, of course, upon his being correct most of the time. Or at least some of it. Now, Dad can't catch his breath; and what's worse, he cannot hold a memory. He could never tolerate sloth in others; he always drove himself so hard. Bad luck was something weaker people chose. Dad seems shocked at all he's lost a grip on. Fact is, he forgets he forgets.

Poor guy keeps exposing himself to ridicule because he can't quite believe a brain as good as his might fail him (and his followers) and in ways so public. But instead of retreating, instead of letting my always-subtler Mom take charge, Daddy creates daily showdowns for his own mind, forcing it. (Forcing: His solution in business, childrearing and, for all I know, sex.) But his mind now balks. From his own mind. Just as I and my brothers forever balked. From our sire's direct orders.

Whenever proved wrong again, the old man blinks around, seeking someone else to blame. For minor infractions, he once beat his sons, each in turn, using his own doubled cowhide belt; now, while I, stooped, prepare to again audition as his yardboy—a job I failed for eighteen straight years—I picture him, whipping it, using the belt, it curled like a grey tabbycat on one of those white couches—whipping his own brain.

He studies me hard; he wears sunglasses, long sleeves, a planter's hat. Its floppy brim means to block a sun that's given him—thanks to golf and bright Florida and Nordic ancestry—nine skin cancers. "But the good kind," he likes to say. Amazing what we all can get used to.

As a kid, I grew so klutzy under this man's critical and freezing glare. But, today, following orders, I do not hurt myself. For once, I've not even dropped the tool yet. Helping him, I understand that every time he has looked out at this lake, Dad has seen only the one spreading raggedy-ass palm, spiting him, so needing a man's taming discipline.

He now calls which dry fronds must go, "Not that, lower, yeah. More like it." As he becomes excited over work finally visibly achieved, his voice does not grow easier—but cross, more the distant monarch's. "Forget that one. I already told you."

The tree feels splintery, nasty to my touch; it feels Floridian, more reptile than vegetable, more stucco than stone. I do loathe this state, their Elba. But I hack at offending branches with regular motions I would never use if doing this for me alone. I smile, pretending I've become a "How To" book. I am the butch brunette model in the black and red checked shirt, a young Rock Hudson teaching the patient millions "Proper Palm-Pruning 101."

I'm uneasily aware of joy at forgetting ailing friends left North. And, miracle, today, for Dad, my work seems acceptable: for the first time in nearly half a century. I am implementing the exact orders issued by this decorated war veteran.

To Dad's credit, he resists his usual withering "helpful hints": what blade angle might be *just* a little better.

Today, my heterosex brothers with their bored pretty wives and hyper country-day kids are staying far away, states safer. "But we understand that," Dad said last night, "After all, they have responsibilities." What am I, chopped liver?

Today, with Christmas Eve dead ahead, only I—the queer one—am here, doing for him, hanging out. I do feel glad not to be busying that corner room of St. Vincent's Hospital, fluffing Robert's pillows yet again, reading aloud to him (with expression) all today's music reviews from the *Times*. Whether he can hear them or not.

Now that Dad can't manage, I must appear far abler. Lumberjack at last! Moi? But around his sudden weaknesses, I feel mainly sad. Alive and well, he still had a chance to figure it all out. As for his finally accepting me, thanks only to pure default, I am both touched and quietly, jaw-grindingly, enraged.

Across the lake, a golfer small with distance approaches one flagged hole. Spying Dad, he waves. "Ed Albertson. Wave." Dad waves, then I do.

"You must miss it, golf." I try again.

"Sure. But, pity like yours really only makes things feel worse." Okay. That's it, forever.

But I turn, look back at him. He appears some guy deciding, finally, whether to go ahead and be a kind person for his last few years, or not. Dad's white hair stands out like fluff on a baby bird. He rests baffled under layers like some old-timey lady movie star resisting Hollywood's sun.

But, finally unjudged by him, I cannot begin to hint how male, how dexterous I have at last become. (My brothers and I used to laugh at Dad, out in the yard, practicing his putting, his face all pilgrim agony, no joy allowed in him. None of the willing easy sexy New York foolishness that literally means Life to me!)

I have always tried to make my work a form of play. Even at this palm-tree haircut, I'm managing. —With what ease does this butch dude move today!

Kneeling, my handsaw moving, I marvel how his early squelching hid from me my own deep carpenter's capacity. Dad's present weakness, ruined lungs, might afford me one moment of shamed glee. Surely forgivable. But, instead of giving me some heady rush: "I told you so"—there comes a brown and melancholy seepage, not pity but some real sympathy—unpredicted and the more powerful for that. How much friends' suffering has already taught me. I have already seen what everybody must endure. The Sewer, he called it. In a way, my dad was too correct. And what's Florida? A drainage canal? Can I swim yet? My way of keeping up? —A dog paddle with intervals of deadman's float.

I so want to say to him, "Poor thing. You could have had it all. What held you back from the enjoyment? From cooking, tussling, joking, playing with your healthy kids. You skipped the fun parts, Dad! Why?"

But behind me, now, my driver of hard bargains actually says, "Good." I cannot tell you how I'll treasure that. I cannot tell you why my father and so many other dads found it so compromising to send one word of praise toward kids so fully starved for it.

He keeps coaching. My dying father indicates just one more pesky frond. "And snag that one, too. As long as I'm at . . ."

"As long as *you're* at it? . . ." I cannot help myself. Some whipped childish part of me wants to yell, "That's really the story of your whole sad life, isn't it? Putting your pronoun first, the chore second and we, your supporting actors and feeble worker bees, clear off your chart . . ."

Instead, half jovial, I risk: "Err-ahhh, Dad? Can't it at least be, 'As long as *we're* at it?' Maybe one 'We' at least the once? —Hunh, Pop?"

He blinks. His lipless mouth, more old-ladyish since the dentures went in, purses its irritation. I have again become his overschooled pedantic grammarian, his hair-splitting hysteric. Not incidentally, the family faggot.

" 'We,' then. Happy?" His voice all edgy. " 'We' should take off those next three fronds. And this time, maybe *you*, if I'm allowed that as your father, maybe you will trim clear to the exact bases of those stems? Because, I thought I asked you to do that earlier. Because you're not keeping them cut close enough against the trunk. Please, if you're not hurrying off to make another important career phone call to New York, make sure your trimming . . . becomes . . . somewhat . . . more uniform." He gasps.

"Somevat more uni-form. Yezz, zir." I svitch to mock-German-military, recalling Robbie's Swedish. He snorts to prove I am not even worth getting upset about. A gnat. I hear another cough fomenting in him. Let it. Let it brew and spill. There's some pleasure in this altered balance of authority.

"Dad, sir?" Using a brain surgeon's precision, I sever one frond's inner edge. "Dad, why do you think, for you, it's always . . . so hard for you to . . ."

I am about to finally ask the question. One that, bullied daily, we all have wondered all these years.

"Because my lungs are giving out, is why. That's why it's hard, that's the reason . . . everything's so. . . ."

"Hard," I provide, now I hear him start to gasp.

I feel I'm taking advantage of him. My mother, parting venetian blinds, keeps peering out, worried for him, feeling excluded the way she does if the two of us ever get five sentences together unmonitored.

"Hate having to ask anybody for anything. Always have, son. Provide, provide, do it your own self. They taught us . . . that."

"Aha," I say. And a son finishes his work for the son's dad.

Retired

om stands at the screen door saying the phone is for me, "Long distance!" As if I'd get a local one. I take it in the guest room, dim because they've stuck green filters over windowglass. "He's way worse." The voice quavers.

First I literally don't know who this is, and which "he"? Then, I remember my life.

Knowing it's Angie about Robert, I feel such unlikely disloyal gratitude for amnesia in Florida! During one brief span of hard labor, Dad driving me, I've slipped up briefly: I have been living only in the present.

"I would say he's worse from missing you, but Robert's past that now . . . he's drift, all drift now. The nurses try but nobody has your touch, babette. How're the folks?"

I open my mouth but hear a tapping on the window opposite our wall of family pix. I see one huge beak, a white bird. Its shape is repeated in the glass of every family photo. Is this The Stork? Has Dad called it to return me for exchange? The creature stands man-tall and is peering in at me. First I'm sure I'm having an acid flashback and say to Angie, "You're not going to believe this . . ."

"Wanna bet?" New York City answers.

"Mom?" I call.

She hollers right in, our psychic tie almost too healthy, "It's a sandhill crane, son. They see their own reflections in the Mylar your dad had put on the windows. They come every afternoon at four. That's when the Albertsons feed them the garlic croutons. You really aren't supposed to. The birds get used to treats and when we snowbirds leave, cranes starve. They're considered 'endangered,' I think."

"Oh," I call.

"For the want of a crouton . . ." I tell Angie.

"Are you drunk? 'Be inebriated, dearest ones,' as says the monk. That how you're dealing with all that down there? Look, you'll still be back tomorrow night, right? Because I have a meeting with that boy curator from the Berlin show. He's brought me the final model of the exhibit, last chance for us to shift a painting. Robert or no Robert, I cannot cancel on this guy again. Verboten."

"Roger, over and out. Oh, and my father lost the car? And I just pruned a palm-tree solo? And there is a bird as tall as one of Robbie's runway models tapping on the window right this second."

"No shit? Whatever. No matter how dried out and weird your parents are, we all still love you to pieces. It's killing us you're gone."

I find myself gulping. How does it come so easily to some folks and cause others such pain. To do it, just to even say that, Love, aloud. I sit on my bed watching a five-foot crane groom itself with amorous honking sounds. Its yellow eyes very observant yet truly stupid. It keeps admiring its own image. Only it could find itself attractive. You can tell it is a male one. I think of beautiful friends. Somehow, I'm turned on. To prove I still can, I undo workpants, I jerk off.

Let tropical Nature take lessons. Yeah! like . . . dis.

Tempus Fugit: The Battering

ow, blue evening of this same long orangeish day—his chores done, if imperfectly—my father is stretched out on the adjacent lounge chair. Using both pink hands, he clutches his big black and silver TV remote. Resting on his slight paunch, it looks like both a beak and baby rattle. Across the screen, *The Tampa News at Seven Wrap-up* struts its usual woes, bombings, child murders, and comic relief (but involving only baby dolphins). Dad now lightly snores. He is shrinking just as I seem to be filling out to my full mature size (and, truth be told, beyond that some. Do I care?).

We've had quite a day, yardwork, then later a quick mall car trip. I volunteered to stay with our Buick. That drew odd yet differing looks from both parents. I waved them back toward me. Each was carrying four prescriptions in brown paper sacks I recall from penny-candy days.

At the Cineplex, we choose a costume movie. In the credits, I recognize Ed's name: Period Drapery Consultant. I tell my folks I know him. My best friends have been celebrities for months, and here I'm dropping some old trick's name to impress my parents. Pitiful.

Bound home, we're duty-bound to visit all four couples that consider themselves my folks' best friends. The four conversations, four homes, four sets of attractive couples Dentu-Creme-ad-handsome, seem nearly interchangeable. The Ambersons, the Bermans, the Mangums, the Albertsons. Two of the women are named June, two of the men are Rays. Is such sameness what they all wanted all along? It seems they sacrificed everything to become, and then remain, this alike. Allowing, of course, for minor market fluctuations. An unlucky lucky generation. I think of my little Circle, how we pride ourselves mainly on differences: "Our Night Person," "Our Farmboy Jewelry Collector."

I admit to wondering why my folks didn't invite all their pals over for a single conversation. But, hey: Florida is where, when you go there, they get to show you off.

I leave tomorrow, Christmas. The perfect travel day, everybody else is there already. I'll be back in New York in time to celebrate whatever of it Robert notices this year. Angie says she's phoned his parents. They must see him once more. I'd best be there to greet them, make things easier.

Snoring, Dad is zonked. I did his work but wound up feeling strong; he, just from watching me, grew quite bushed. TV's customary babble cannot block true sounds. Under usual snoring—heedless, animal, selfish-sounding, the grunty essence of the unapologetically male—I hear a newer rasp, a whorl, the sudden hole.

This is a noise I know too well from all the days I've spent beside all those beds of all those boys I've loved, kids slipping off into a learnable habit called un-breathing.

I hear another beloved body start to wean itself off a control substance known as oxygen.

My father's body now forgets to do what healthy bodies always do: Always take the next breath, then gulp the next.

Instead, one faltering inhale. "To breathe or not to breathe?" I hear his inhalation wait, pivot. "I know I left it around here somewhere." Leisure seems abounding. Breath turns there for one moment, on its axis, for seconds, some particle of a whole minute, it spirals, an autocrat and nonteamplayer, it twists as if considering itself, its crosses its arms, it rests its chin in the palm of one braced palm. I shift to see if I must lurch to standing, pound this fellow's chest? Then, a glottal gulp, and Dad's life moves forward one more notch. Breathe—at least—the next breath does.

But, something in this usual impaired intake seems new to me, and strange: it's this: I have never before heard these signs of coming death befall a person over forty-five.

To receive such signs from someone nearly eighty, even someone I obliquely if cantankerously love, softens, even sweetens the horror.

To hear dying set its sites on a guy who's had nearly a century, who's engendered one junior and the other sons, who's given a fortune to the church, who has made about a million bucks, it half relaxes my dread of the process, somewhat lightening these facts. I look over at this man who sired me. I don't think the usual enraged "No!" I'd feel toward some expiring friend, age thirty-four. Instead, observing signs of dying from a man whose age predicted it, his son's sigh comes just. . . . "So."

So this, at last, is Natural Causes. Well, well, death on time. Hello at last.
—Practice. Practice.

Dad, as if feeling my eyes on him, now clutches the black remote so tight he changes the news to the Disney channel. The living prairie suddenly achieves its unlikely time-lapse bloom, cacti pop forth petals and on my father sleeps. Robert pronounced after their first meeting, "An attractive if somewhat remote man?"

Mom makes dinner a room away. Her usual practiced stirrings. Dad groans. How gigantic he once seemed.

Looking over, I study this gentled-looking pale-haired gent, his face blotched from skin cancers removed, his clothes so tidy and simple, his hands clawing the remote, crablike jerkings, even asleep—anxious about ending, trying to grab hold, and stay put.

I smell dinner. Blackeyed peas for an early New Year's—the borrowed African-American custom—assuring our prosperity. For every bean at least one dollar. Dad—though sound asleep—now reaches up to scratch his nose. Such comic finicky precision, then the arm flops down. I laugh. For him, I feel a sudden wash of fellow-feeling.

His abrupt helplessness makes me want to scoop Dad nearer, touch his forehead, pat his upper back and say, as I have to Robbie, "There, there. I'm here. It's okay. Go on down wherever it's easiest. Love you, do. If need be, go, go now."

But Mom walks in. Oblivious to my father's usual open-mouthed and unattractive sleeping, she says at her normal volume, "See what the weather is for your flight tomorrow."

She stands holding one carrot, a peeler. She scans around, then nods down at the remote in Pop's pink fist.

Instead of grabbing it from my recliner (the one usually hers), I rise. Passing her, I stop beside his larger chair. I move to gingerly lift controls from Dad's close grip.

She watches the transaction with a strange, tired disinterest. (She is ready for me to leave.) Even asleep, my father resists me. Comes one stubborn grunt. I explain to our sleeper in a half-whisper, "Just want it one sec, so we can see the . . ."

Daddy jerks me hard around my neck. With a wrestler's "Ha!", he's pulled me down on top of him. Wheezing, he pins me so damn well. Surprised, I yell, "All right all ready!"

Mother, watching from above, afar, calls down, disgusted, "Well, for Pete's . . . you two. Will you boys ever grow up? There are other ways to solve things."

Fact is, the old coot's got me in a fairly solid headlock. And—even while fighting him some—I admire him for it. Call that male of me. Did I startle him? Is he even really awake?

"Daddy, pul-lease, only wanted the remote."

Mom calls, "Dick, we just need the weather channel, to see, Dick, about tomorrow, Dick. His flight, Dick."

"Ask!" my father screams direct upright at us both.

His stringy biceps winch around my head. Now he's giving me what we kids once called "the Dutch rub." (With as little hair as I now have, it truly hurts. This is insane.) I jerk toward the remote, but he holds that in a fist bobbing far aside.

My cheek presses his chin's stubble, then bumps down against his breastbone. He's forcing me toward belt buckle. Where will this end? Not a pretty sight for Mom! From his passing chest, I hear the rage and the disease, a single force snaffling up and out at me.

I'm lying half across my dwindled father. This is so weird. My big feet are now completely out from under me, the lamp's kicked somewhat cockeyed. Upset at first, I soon find I don't half mind. This is the longest physical contact I've had with the guy since my infancy, if then. Have I not been touching him now for around forty seconds? Let's try for two minutes, go for the gold. Contact otherwise? Decades of handshakes.

"Don't tell. Suggest! Ask. Ever hear of it?"

And I, scalp burning, nose close to bleeding on him, discover this grotesquerie can be fun. I burrow in, take full kid-advantage. Nuzzle Dad to Death. Great game. When else will I ever relearn my father's lap, and chest, and sweet slack neck?

Under us, the springs of his stressed chair ominously ping. Factory dust releases toward lamplight. "This can't be good for either one of you!" Mother's veggie peeler clicks behind me. I laugh. Do I just imagine, or is he enjoying this horseplay too? Wasn't that a power-chuckle? But Dad only tightens his grip around my head, literally tries to twist it off. "Don't! That hurts, you motherf . . . you mother!" I groan like a bride faking first orgasm, I just wriggle in even deeper. Mom's peeler tap tap taps along my spine, sandhill crane. "You, two, roughhousing. You'll break something. Warned you. Something always gets broken!"

How do I know how not to put too much weight on Dad, how not to hurt the guy? Why, from my long amorous career with all those boys below me, taking it, of course. Me, learning how to make the most or least of my bulk as need requires, their egress permits. This flash makes me laugh. I just stay put. Story of my life. Get happy in your headlock, pussy boy. I hate myself I love myself.

At least the channel button yields to his pressure. Still face to face with him, I hear scraps of forty shows reel past—wok cookery tips, cartoons involving whistling cliff falls, *Bewitched* laughtrack, panda birth news—all amid the smell of orange blossoms from nowhere, and Mom's jealous squeals. "This minute. Will call the Albertsons, I swear." I cling to him through a question from actual *Jeopardy*.

Host Alex: "Former President of Princeton whose idealistic League . . ."

Me: "Woodrow Wilson!"

And under, my sire growls, " 'Who *is* Woodrow Wilson?' Must be put in question form."

"Says who?" I call. Dad pounds hard on my back until, outstretched, obedient, not meaning to, I burp. I laugh, she laughs and finally even he does, but . . .

He's finally shouting, quite clear, "Somebody get the geek off me." Even that doesn't hurt at first.

My one mistake was letting him suspect I half enjoyed this. Always a tactical error—sign of any overt joy derived from him.

"In future"—He takes a breath, my mother gaping down at me with disgust, some horror—"future . . . Don't take. Ask!"

I struggle hard to disengage. It's tougher than you might expect, learning to climb down a last time off your dad. His big chair threatens to jackknife, slicing both of us, sandwiching layers, genital identical genital identical—a ply of two men playing at killing.

Dad, now confused, finally fully awake, so embarrassed at my present size, tries working the joystick of his lounger, eager to spill me.

But I only holler into his tense smell rising, aftershave and fear of losing your car at inhospitable mall America, I yell childlike straight down at him, "You win, Daddy Daddy Dad. No contest. 'Ask!' Junior's asking."

"Okay then. More like it," and, kingly, Dad yells, "Done!"

As I stand, disheveled and chagrined as someone rising from a semi-coerced sexual encounter, shamed but only seeming so, he hands over the control. Declared Winner, Dad can now.

The remote is passed. Awkward, I feel winded. Standing, I bat around the dial for the weather. It pleases him, rebuttoning his collar, to say the weather's exact channel, loud. I am pretending I'm not shaken; I'm shaken.

Standing just past his view, I look over and down at him, still allowing him to decently collect himself. I find a weather woman saying, "Sailing conditions, fair and hot."

I can still feel all the places where his big hands grabbed my upper back, a slight oil left burning even through my shirt.

"Dinner, Jack Dempsey and Joe Louis," Mom soon calls. And, after the grappling, after several quick drinks, we three regroup. Three, an underrated number. Tonight, released by all this physicality over absolutely nothing, we enjoy a joshing, boisterous, early New Year's feast, exactly drunk enough. We again speak only of old times. Mom and I try remembering names of all our former neighbors' dogs. Dad's gone silent, as she rattles, "Ginger, Pinto, and Sweetheart, the cat.

"A calico," Mother, pedantic, adds "spayed," then laughs at her virtuosity. But now, as usual, with one hand's speckled back, she stifles her own pretty sound before it even half unfurls.

It's only as I'm preparing for bed later, standing in the salmon tile bathroom, shirtless, making muscles toward the mirror, the way I did at age fourteen, only then do I hear her swerve bumping along the hall as she, without knocking, throws open the door, looks shocked—to find me posing shirtless. "Come quick. It was too much for him. You don't know what you weigh now. You two were always too much for each other."

"But *he* pulled me down . . . *You* saw . . ."

Since dinner, he seems to have lost thirty pounds. He's half on the bed, shirt off, still a beautiful man—but face up, arms out, he's like some North German crucifix. I see he's just a mouth gasping and, spying me, also shirtless, he tries pulling one corner of the white chenille spread over himself. He tries saying something, keeps pointing pointing up at me. "What's he yelling?" I ask her above the tortured red face snapping open/shut between us.

"He"—she hands me the portable phone to dial the rescue squad—"he's saying, 'Him! Him!' It could mean anything. Maybe one of those times he doesn't know who people are. I mean, you haven't let him see you in a year. You have to keep him used to you these days! —Please, Hartley, not to get your feelings hurt again now! Call!"

It's 911, then finding the closet's oxygen tank. (I need glasses to read fine print; she sets hers on my nose.) It's the messy exit and the neighbors all in robes under red circling light outside. Somehow, dizzy, I imagine the crane, the floating gator, what will they make of this odd show? Nothing.

This means extending my visit (Gideon will try to take over, I'll miss Alabam's departure for Berlin), it's the guarantee that Dad's much better, a simple matter of thinning the blood, avoiding further exertions; it's my living on the phone with those in charge of Robert, who is worse. His parents are arriving even though Angie's gone; they cannot change tickets. Everything's unrefundable.

Mom herself Buicks me to the airport, a beautiful smooth driver she is—she who never gets to. "Thank you for spending your holidays with us," she says. And only in saying something so formal and flat and partial does she finally give way an inch, she cries, hanging onto the wheel, she lets me—still fastened to the passenger's seat—hug her wherever on her I can reach.

Three days later at two a.m., Mom's voice by phone: "Honey? So sorry to wake you. You need your sleep what with everyone up there depending on you so. —You've guessed. Your father's gone."

"Gone?"

"Dead. What'd you think I meant? Lost with the Buick?" and she laughs a toxic little laugh that is, uncannily, his.

"I found him in his big chair. It was after the late news. Since about eight, I'd been just letting him sleep there. If I'd known, maybe I could've helped him more . . ."

"Mom, nobody ever got better help than Daddy did. Next plane, I'm there. Don't meet me, please, I'll rent a car. Hang in, honey. Who's with you? The Albertsons? Good. Let me speak to Ray, please. What? All right then, 'Dave'—whatever. Whichever of them is there, let me speak to the male one of them, please? Sorry, Mom. You think the La-Z-Boy wrestling, or my falling on him, set him back, whatever. . . . Dave? This Dave? Well, Dave. Yeah, well, thank you, Dave. He thought the world, too, of you and . . . your wife. How is she? I mean Mom. How's my mother taking it?"

A Remoter Control

ell, he died two years ago, or no, come to think of it, it'll soon be three.

I do see my Mother more often now. She's freer to travel, excellent company when here, somehow much clearer these days. Times, she flirts with the plan of moving back to North Carolina. She has grandkids, friends there. My folks only picked Florida for his golf.

But, while our connection feels warm and we do tease each other more, she's still holding something major back. It's not quite what I'd hoped for, our tie. Either she's saying, "You have such good taste. Not just safe like ours was," or she keeps trying to enlist me as my dad's belated P.R. firm. "He tried so hard, didn't he? Finest looking fellow, Dick, and such a good provider . . ." I look at her and wonder whom she's fighting to convince.

It's like she's scared he'll walk in on the two of us. He might find her having a wee bit too much fun, he might find her laughing and without him. I've tried, but I just can't help her with this part. There's a way a son who loves his Mom as much as I love mine can never quite forgive her choosing him, her choosing that. Which means, in the end, her having me. Go figure.

Last week, on impulse, enjoying a sense of her I trust more now and act on faster (no speaker phone insuring mass psychology), I phoned Mom in the middle of a weekday, "So, what's up? Something is new, because I feel it. What're you most looking forward to, kiddo?"

"Wellll," she said, and I knew there was something. I knew she said this through a smile and I could picture her face and mouth so vividly, it almost hurt me. My newfound kind of joy in her. These days, it is a pleasure I can sometimes show.

"Wellll, young sir? Since you asked. Your ole motherhubbard seems about to possibly be, how you say . . . 'dating'?" And she laughed, laughed her beautiful, her most sexy, laugh. I felt shocked. The sound was old yet new. It really was the laugh of some unimpeded, privileged young girl. Her whole life yet before her. The laugh failed to intercept and police itself, no hand clamped over mouth. It was, I knew, her laugh before the marriage. She was returning to some state of carelessness pre-Him and, of course, alas, prior to me. I caught such a sweep of joy from clear back then, I even felt a second's jealousy.

What a lucky man my dad had been! And yet, with him dead, she's laughed more yards of playful laugh than I can ever recall drawing out of her at once. By phone, laughter came toward me, golden and at shimmer. A great luxury, her permitting me to hear this young pure spilling silliness of hers.

The widowers down there on Golf-Vue Cay are lining up to squire her now. I do believe those widowers have been waiting. I think those widowers are very smart.

* * *

Do I miss my father? Well, my father was a decent man. There were moments of real sweetness: "New York, watch out!" Like so many guys that age—with the Depression and the War each landing a different kind of sucker punch—Dad was also a very very conventional man and a hard one. Remote. He grew up poor, wanting to make a million dollars. And he did! He made his cool million, if the hard way. He went to work on a Monday when I was about one year old and—in many ways—he never really came back home.

Hard to explain how much of him ended up Missing in Action. Did he choose which parts to sacrifice, and why?

I mean, he got to live in a beautiful house with a beautiful woman who loved him and with healthy sons who loved him or, at worst, really wanted to. Then he was a retired millionaire, and all of it was just as he had planned, just as any kid wearing an apron ever wished. Still, it all had to be stated in question form. (No simple joyful assertions: "I have always been lucky in my friends.") He seemed some hard-earned capital, proud never to have ever been "touched." Severe penalties for early withdrawal.

Fact is, Dad didn't really want other people to have any fun, you know?

The truth is—(and you are asking for the truth, right?)—most days, I don't actually miss my father all that much.

And yet, even now, evenings especially—I feel it. Some chronic low-grade longing, still.

So, yeah, around office-closing-time:

I do at least miss missing him.

On Whether to Purge
the Dead from One's Address Book

"It R US"

If my life began as an essay, it was ending as an opera. Alabama and I, assigned anonymous numbers, presumed a couple, had chosen to retrieve our test results in tandem. Somewhere inside a New Jersey lab, salaried preoccupied people (parents, stamp collectors, cat owners) had spent weeks doing things to samples of our blood. A state law kept everyone (even your spouse) outside the room while your news, good or bad, got passed.

Only three days before our long-arranged appointment did we mention actually planning to keep it. Hard now to recount how much felt at stake.

Our concern for longevity focused mostly on our work; personal health became a metaphor for that. We'd been learning to be artists for so long. I had been blundering through, just trying to assemble my profession's alphabet. I had only worked up, say, to the letter J. Imagine dying before achieving the essential noble elegance of S!

We both overdressed. "Is that your wedding or your funeral drag?" she asked. Success had not softened a certain bluntness in her. Bama climbed into my cab wearing the same copper-colored suit last seen at Robert's concert. I felt a moment's hurt. She had not scared up a new outfit for this and me? As if getting your blood test results constituted some Date of Dates. But you know? for me, that day, it did.

We would now take only taxis everywhere. All those hassles that were still in our power to avoid, we would dodge today. Luck cannot be planned and yet we all keep trying.

She said she had forgotten something, then rushed back upstairs, reappearing in a fifties hat, a clamp-on. False violets frothed all over it. She'd put on the pearls and now, stark eyes square upon me, kissed them. "As a sick sort of charm. Why not? Hartley? —My mother loves me. My mother is a pathetic social climber eager only for those parties where they'd sneer at her the most. If I got sick, a mom like mine that just couldn't have me in Savannah. Picture what it'd do to her dicey social life. Funny, I wouldn't even blame her. She cannot succeed. True, she told me if I came up here and tried, something terrible would happen. But Jewel Fern basically loves me. She wouldn't wish real evil on me, Hart. Of that I'm sure."

"Here here." I touched her right hand, today very clean. Luck. She lifted the bottom strand of pearls for me to kiss. I told her that, if either of us turned out to have . . . trouble, we could move to North Carolina. I missed it more and more. You could kick aside a million Carolina doormats, you'd find a million house keys. It was pathetic. It was becoming just our sort of thing. If we slowed down, gave each other space, we might be roomies. She could find a tobacco warehouse to paint in, they were cheap these days. What held us here except the cobweb ties to Robert and our others?

"I'd only go if I got to fade away in the bed."

"You think his mom would let us have it? Doubt that. Still, I'm learning to ask. You know what pineapples stand for."

I settled against the cab's backseat, fighting sentiment, resisting memory.

"The Metropolitan Museum," I told our driver. "And sir? This young lady I'm with back here? Has some of her own paintings hanging in the Met's collection." Strictly speaking, this was not yet true. They did own two charcoal drawings. The headguy had put a reserve on four oils but he'd never quite committed. Still, this seemed a day for accentuating the positive—I mean, the upbeat.

"No shit," the driver said, making us laugh.

Then he adjusted his rearview mirror. Bama, feeling the beloved curative warmth of being watched, sent one chaste if lipsticky smooch his way. She had perfected the whore's trick of innocent convent eyes—unaware of the lower mouth's solitary freelance sluttishness. The combination proved a classic killer.

"Wow," he said "And here I been thinking all lady painters were dogs. But you? You have way more fox-type blood in you, hunh? —No offense, Mister."

She batted the amber eyes, touched one corner of her mouth. Her voice came out all starlet breathiness. "Dri-ver? Don't mind this one back here. He's just an old queer that pimps for me. Usually he tries to get guys to give us subway tokens, but me? I'm ambitious. I moving on to cabfare. —You free, sir? Later?"

We soon stood before our Vermeers, saying what we'd each said so many times before, but gaining rosary-strength from refondling our own tired, informed opinions. We taxied to the failing Bendel's and bought Bama a sterling pin, biomorphic. One salesgirl (smocked, silksleeves, face all Kabuki paintbox ceramic) must've recognized my friend from the White House spread. "You?" she flirted. "You've just been *in* something. Don't tell me. You're either *on* a soap or did an article *about* somebody ver' big. Where do I know you *from*? Isn't this, I mean, aren't you, like, very very *recent*?"

We arrived at the clinic early. Too recent. I could tell it made my darling nervous, overmuch time to kill. Promptness was my style. Careless, I had not adjusted it for her, hers.

Now we were stuck here; there was nothing but warehouses in Chelsea then; you couldn't invent a short wandering errand to spend money. So while Bama smoked out under our ancestral sycamores, I paced these too-familiar rooms. The young woman who'd first interviewed us nodded greetings. I could see she remembered. That seemed a solid sign. Right? I was still scouting everywhere for harbingers—but only happy ones, please. I had become, as my friends now put it, "The Omen Queen."

I volunteered to go first. I showed my paper number. I recalled my fifth-grade teacher's story of Walter Raleigh throwing his cape across mud to spare Elizabeth's hem brocade. But wasn't he imprisoned or beheaded anyway? Oh, well.

I visited the bathroom, I'd been pissing like a racehorse for days. Was this pre-results jitters or some lethal health sign? When I returned, I saw Bama alone indoors. Under her violets, the face seemed locked. Beneath their NO SMOKING sign, she sat wrapped in fumes, sat rocking, an autistic in her corner. She appeared about seven years old. Then, as I drew nearer, about seventy. Soon as she spied me hurrying to help, both hands flew up. "Don't, touch, me, right, now, honey, okay? Just . . ." Right then they called my number. "Either way," she whispered as I turned to face my news. "In his magic bed. Done deal? Be it you or be it me, or both. Let's go down with each other. We never never got around to going *down* on each other; let's give this other a try. In any State of the Union, even a Southern one. Okay, Best Thing Left Me?" I nodded.

It only takes one person in your life.

Moving down the hall, I felt so very lanky. A mantis Hartley. Whenever I'm terrified, as when poor Robert got mugged, I'm always sure my legs are made of hollow guttering material. But this hall did seem narrow enough to catch me, a disciplining splint.

They say at crucial moments, your life will fan like face cards splayed before you. Highlights. A movie's "coming attractions"; only it's "going attractions," outgoing, and your own.

Some of that happened. Odd what reached me. I felt a baking soda taste at the back of my mouth, it was Duty. A taste like putting your fingers to your lips after you've handled someone else's house keys. I flashed on how my father used to stand out back after work. With only a little evening light left, the old man (young) would linger on our flagstone patio. Arms crossed, he'd just stare for whole minutes at nothing but the yard. "Look at him." My brothers made a joke of it. "The hawk expecting mice." Odd, till this clinical moment, Dad's stillness, his concentration, had seemed mysterious. But rickety as I was today, I now knew—he had been guarding. Dad, his day's work done, stood out there trying to become our own Good Sign. He was staring at whatever fertilized green he had achieved. Even while doubting his continuing success, Dad was bodily warding off the end of it.

My parents lately had felt so vivid to me. When I gave Robert a sponge bath, I got these odd flashes of two young people bathing me, an infant. All this weary sudden tenderness toward a poker-neutral father and his chipper sacrificing wife. Why now? Learned where? Arrived too late?

Into the room veered that same pleasant black woman who'd first led us through our chances. On her desk, I recognized a photo of the charming kid from the cardboard castle.

She settled, holding my file. It looked too fat for my own short history here. A lousy swollen omen. I started, "Must be hard all day, giving out the news, hunh?"

"Yes, well. The good feels good and the bad it never is exactly a cinch. But thank you for thinking of me."

"So, worked here long?"

"Yes, but I believe we should just go ahead and do this, if only for the sake of your 'wife' out there, whoever." So I handed her my fatal number. I remembered Angie's piece of pinewood painted white and black and 282.

Seated at her desk, the woman accepted my digit. Then, inhaling once, she placed mine over its sticky-backed replica just inside the folder. I received a stuttering vision, all our friends, lives lived so all together. By now, I could only attach my mortality to theirs. In lieu of a Distributorship, considering how tentative and "early" my own work was, what else, but them, could Hartley rightly claim?

On my bent right index fingerjoint, I bit. I made this hurt some. I studied the top of the woman's head, her neat modified afro, the globe; I considered the shape of her face aimed downward. There, I saw a vexing outward, mask of comedy, face of tragedy? I never before felt how close they were. A grin requires more muscles. After she looked up, I dully understood it was a smile. Her mouth moved. I heard nothing but sound's subsequent music. I could read her hand signs, I could tell that I was being urged to keep my rubbers on. I deduced all symptoms of good news but as a deaf person might. "Thank you, thank you." I took her hand as if she had originated my verdict, not just conveyed it.

"God, but I feel . . . not exactly happy, but very . . . present, you know? Never want to lose this."

"Good luck," she opened the door for me. Alabama had exercised her spousal privilege; had taken the plastic chair just before my cubicle. When she saw my face, she knew, she hid her mouth behind two hands. She bowed over her knees. One eye seemed undergoing an oil change, only her right eye's mascara blurred all down her cheek. The idiotic hat, so frilled and purple, got knocked at a slight angle that made it far more darling and much further hers. She had, I decided, never so overtly demonstrated her love for me. She was seated in a little white safe plywood corner, and I felt, standing, bending over her, that if I could just keep my darling co-survivor here, if we could simply spend the rest of our lives in this nook locked within this schoolhouse eating brought-in Chinese food, everything would be okay—really. She kissed me, then kissed her own pearls, and we were all over each other. But as in the old days when we yet pretended that each other was a boy and therefore still forgave each other everything.

"Well, your good health sure don't spring from any tendency to stay indoors and keep your pants up, do it, tramp? If *you* got away with it, maybe there's a slender hope for your way more virtuous mother here."

The same woman who'd offered me my good news—who did this all day for a living!—stood waiting, stood looking after us. She was smiling if in a neutral way. I still saw such tension in her face. I loved this woman's involvement and marveled how she kept herself open to such daily kindness, daily torture, and for complete strangers. It is shaming I cannot recall her name. Jean? Grace? One syllable. Then I remembered her kid saying, "My mom helps sick people."

Alabama asked if I'd wait out front "and not right here at the end of the high-dive." She said she didn't want me to see her face so soon after her finding out, either way.

"Whatever you wish, Princess of my particular life story. Anything." I settled in the waiting area, no fishtank, no magazines, but at least no scolding posters. I pressed together the butts of my palms. I dug my elbows into either knee. A little intentional pain might keep my head clear. I wondered why it was taking so long. Then saw that maybe only ninety seconds had passed. First I told myself I was doing some sort of forearm isometrics. One hand somewhat strengthening the other.

"You prayin' too?" a rich voice spoke beside me and there sat a young Hispanic man in a red sports coat, his moustache so trimmed it looked drawn on. "Who you waiting? Wife?" I just nodded. "Is it Take the Blood Day? Or Big News Day?" I told him. "My ole lady too." He shook his head. "Me, I've done some crazy shit over time. If she's got to pay for it, I'm . . . I just don't know." And then he pressed his own hands wrist to wrist as mine were. I guess I had been praying, if in a gym-based West Village sort of way.

His eyes closed as he said aloud. "Let both his and mine be okay, Lord. Don't take it out on them, what should have grabbed our sorry asses, right, Lord?"

I said, "Right." Thinking of Robert, I amen-ed that last part, too.

Came a blurred commotion, his wife ran through the lobby on noisiest high heels, did a little seeking U-turn, then piled atop him. "HomeplateSafe, babes." Laughing, she dropped into his lap, arms laced around him. It was a joy to see them gyrate deep into each other. I found myself dissolved, just watching strangers. The waiting room's other omen-queens (everybody) smiled, wagged their heads. "You *see*?" one boy encouraged another already visibly sick.

I was so caught up in this couple's drama—even the toughest of the nurses half-grinning—I failed to notice someone else. She had to tap me on the shoulder. It was her first entrance or exit I could ever recall missing and I didn't know if that was a good sign or a bad.

Turning, I saw she had applied new lipstick, powdered her nose. "You'll just have to put up with me a while longer. Hartley? Now I'm even more immortal." I hugged her too hard. The other couple congratulated us—not wasting time with names or details, our situations being identical. It did feel wonderful. Air whistled over ear openings. I felt like the tail of an Airedale, wagged.

On the bright street, I was determined to act on our good news. I kept walking backward before her, the way I'd first pursued Robert. I kept explaining we had to do something, something fun and right now.

"You're such a literalist, Happy Burger."

"But we're required to commemorate. No waiting, either. I took a correspondence in being Pagan. Presbyterianism had a headlock on me for the longest dern time. But us two? We just got our Ph.D. in Happy, BamieGirl."

Just to be out in sunlight holding hands! Look how yellow those damn cabs are! So I pulled her into a Baskin Robbins ice-cream place and ordered us triple scoops. She had a little lactose intolerance but that could not be helped today. I flashed the young clerk a big bill; and it was only after we'd strolled a few blocks south, pastel cones already dripping before us, I understood I'd been shortchanged. He'd stiffed me about fifteen bucks. But, I told Bama, instead of my rushing back and making the usual New York scene, today I would have to let it pass. That was part of our deal. It'd certainly be the best fifteen big ones I ever spent. Imagine: For that amount, Alabama Byrnes and Hartley Mims jr., would get to live and know each other into ripe (even rotten) old age.

We talked about whether to rush our good news to St. Vincent's and Robert, sinking fast into his own un-news un-knowing. I favored cabbing straight there, though maybe we'd deliver the news obliquely? She voted against—said that, however glad he'd be for us, it would fill him with such a backwash of understandable sadness. And we mustn't put him (or ourselves) in the position of having to *see* Robert feel all this, you know?

We'd planned to head out for a high-calorie dinner, but she said the excitement-torture had been a bit too much too much for her, and could we just let the Rocky Road ice cream—expensive as it'd been—be down payment on some later feast? I agreed, knowing I would go home and phone my entire address book. I had all this joy I planned to bounce around. Nothing could break my speed. I mapped out the next nine books I'd write, maybe ten. I couldn't sleep for the relief, hang-gliding. Then the stuttering emergency-brake questions. What this meant. Which role would the mixed blessing of surviving demand and provide? Was I up to it? Could I choose not to be?

As a boy, I had imagined faking my own death, attending my own funeral incognito, escaping to St. Kitt's, dyeing my hair silver-blond, starting life over as a tanned good-listener bartender named . . . Chip. History-less, fun, cheap. . . . Chip.

Or to stay?

Rearranging the Deckchairs

Strangely early in Robert's sickness, just after that first scary fever spike, he turned my way before any of it really showed (beyond the spots, two periods, full-stops), even before first wasting made him briefly even more ethereal, more planed and perfect-looking. It was during coffee at our table. (Ossorio had just bought a huge Italian copper espresso machine, brass faucets and a chickenlike eagle perched wobbly on top. Must've cost him everything. Gone, the boilermaker's Cuban gizmo all jury-rigged and soldered. Ang pronounced this sudden yuppie upgrade "the kiss of death.")

While our other pals gathered at the counter to admire this new caffeine laboratory, Robert asked me offhand, "When I fly back to Cedar Rapids?" (the rich baritone by now sounded mothily bigger than he) "you'll be going with me, Hartley?"

" 'When you fly back . . .' " I started, knowing he'd never return there willingly. Oh.

So I rushed in quick with, "Yeah. Count on that."

"Good. I know you'll know all the scenes of all the childhood crimes. Like our leaky red brick gym where we put on . . ."

"The 'Twenty Thousand Leagues Under the Sea' Junior-Senior Prom . . . "

"And the organ loft at First Methodist where . . ."

"Professor Tilman, ancient bachelor and Minister of Music, asked you to climb to the third-floor organ loft, where the big pipes and the little were all closeted, asked you to hide there naked and feel his highest and lowest notes played from downstairs where he couldn't even see you. And said you must tell him later how (you were about twelve, right?) each note vibrated within each and every part of your body, all . . ."

"And my dad's and mom's church . . ."

"Yeah, I'll see the Gustafson family sanctuary up close and personal . . ."

"My mother is a good musician. Her choir is solid. She's sophisticated enough to write her own vocal setting of the Barber 'Adagio' but she's sweet enough to believe she did it first. I've been savage about them, but you'll like my parents. I'm glad you'll meet them. End of subject. Another con leche, baby?"

"Gracias." I watched him get to the counter. Our friends made room for him, the other ones Ossorio called "my poor hurt white baby birds." Friends' arms closed around Robert, half holding our six-footer. I sat here and forced myself to know what he'd meant. So now he had his passport stamped. For his comeback to Cedar Rapids, called C.R. by Iowa insiders. Return fare. His visa of reentry, with me upright, riding in coach, riding shotgun to protect him far better this time and—in the unpressurized cargo hold, our darling Robert, boxed . . .

After his second and last pneumonia, Robbie's speech slowed so, muddied by the warring drugs. In looks, he first grew even blonder, was soon thinning toward an altar candle's very vertical if very transient beauty. And in one month he'd gone nearly as transparent as Venetian glass. People whispered around him. A squeal might shatter him. Our voices and fond looks, excelsior, elaborate packing meant to soften the inexitable shipment.

Studying Robert, seeing how he made a home within the cave of his receding event, I wondered whom I myself might have become without this knowledge. I'd always been lucky in my friends, and if the friends proved unlucky—did that make my own luck greater?

What if I had just stayed home, got myself into a long engagement with some solitary decent rich girl of many interests but teeth somehow too plentiful; if I had taught junior high school French, and just partied on weekends with the better gentlemen florists of society Raleigh, or maybe saved and finally bought that profitable local Ethan Allen distributorship?

To this city, I had lugged my hometown. It was in my luggage, in how I still considered pigeons (family *Columbidae*, order *Columbiformes*) a form of wildlife, it lived in my replete seersucker swagger, in an accent that persisted like my own stage-motherly ambition for front-page rave-review happiness. However much I'd failed in New York, however young I died here if my next test came back bad—at least I wouldn't end where I had started. At least I'd found some people.

James Abbott McNeill Whistler, from his pinnacle as the aesthetic king of Europe, said, arch with bitter ashy understatement, "I did not choose to be born in Lowell, Massachusetts."

But I had picked my nationality as a New Yorker. I had at least got here, got started, got to love my dear ones starting, too.

Not to mention, for the six or seven years when I looked my all-time record best, I had got to fuck my brains out.

New York dance performances of this period soon abounded with men carrying fallen men. Critics—heartless and therefore easily bored, easily bored and therefore heartless—complained of the excessive Pietas everywhere. "How 'tired,' " they said. A new movement cliché was being done to death.

At about this time, a "civilized" conservative columnist named William F. Buckley proposed in hundreds of American newspapers that every person HIV-positive be tattooed on the wrist, and again upon one buttock, and then deported to some compound in the far West, so as to spare the rest of us. May I quote? I've kept it. "The next logical step would be to require anyone who seeks a marriage license [to have] an AIDS test. But if he has AIDS, should he then be free to marry? Only after the intended spouse is advised that her intended husband has AIDS, and agrees to sterilization."*

If you doubt me, look it up. May he remain eternally known for mainly this, his civilized high church-vision of troubled others. I read this column (Lourdes warned me of it, very upset) on the very first full day Robert was hospitalized. —I sure did hide that paper from my friend, Bill Buckley.

Shame. Shame on you forever.

How to Do All This?

 here are the simple skills you feel proud of. There are hard-won abilities you'd rather not have.

Skills I've hated developing? A half-psychic ability to hear in the breathing of sick friends how long they have to live.

*The *New York Times*, March 18, 1986.

I also despise my newfound gift for closing the apartments of my dead. I have learned which brand of black garbage bags to buy, in gross. (Always grab four twelve-packs more than you expect you'll need.) Learn, learn.

You storm into the quarters of the newly deceased, your latest beloved. Even friends who were very tidy in their prime got surprisingly sloppy by the end. (Blindness can sure impede even a neatnik bachelor's housekeeping.)

It's important you first sense the stowing spots of his checkbook, will, journal, and deeds, and especially the address book (that'll be the start of his funeral guest list). Once you've set those aside, you can become privately and truly ruthless. You must. It's the only way to survive such purging.

Tip: Put on an Aretha CD (try her hit "R-E-S-P-E-C-T"), or, failing that, go with Stevie Wonder. *Songs in the Key of Life* is always good.

If your dead host was too Eurocentric to own anything African-American, then use Glenn Gould's "Goldberg Variations." (But I mean the version Gould played and hummed at twenty, not the other, done at forty-nine just before he died; I mean the wickedly fast show-off version, the very young one.) You'll need every scrap of borrowed youthful speed.

—You must move through these alien rooms like some otter, a swimmer-dancer. The moment you stop to read one of your dead friend's lively letters, the second you bend over photographs of yourself and the deceased shown together, honey-baked brown in P-town and both of you more rangy and desirable than you ever knew, you're done for—a sloppy mess. —Efficient, think efficient.

In the very center of each room, make three piles:

"Stays." "Goes." "Maybe."

The ailing hardcore careerists among us soon felt cheated of that payoff arc "mature work." So cruel, not to get the mother-lode of one's own middle period (I speak from the cowcatcher of my own midcentury jalopy-juggernaut, a lovely downhill ride).

Those who had dallied, hurried now. Those who'd changed fields switched back, fast. Oh, to see oil paint, and an easel set up near the bed of some hospital room. This, in the final quarters of Gideon.

Gideon now suspected that his work had gotten hurried, perhaps merely facile during these last few years he'd become somewhat popular. A gallery on Newbury Street sold most of his landscapes. His clients were often Beacon Hill dentists; they now vied for his next painting. They each had "a

WolfKahn" and "a Gideon—V." But he wanted his pictures seen by more than the prosperous and impacted of Boston-Cambridge.

The early tension in his work, always flirting with the beautiful, had succumbed, at times, to being merely pretty. Since he was often in France, he ceased using varnish in his paint thinner, hoping that the pictures'd dry faster. Now, reverting to slower-drying sticky stuff, he worked so hard. Gideon had always painted small and that proved quite convenient now he was this thin, and sitting up in bed.

He held out one painting, said to me, "I'm getting better again, ça va?"

I nodded, "Never better, darling," and quietly hoped, in the relay of help, that someone would still be standing, if need be, to eventually catch me. Or at least to rockingchair beside me and—decades hence—go on discussing our glamorous Lost.

We all took whatever energy was left us into such overdrive.

Days when Gideon was strong, he carried soup and silly astrology paperbacks to Marco. Then Marco, better, attended Gideon grown worse. The cruelty of the disease allowed such swing shifts. Came the time when fourth-floor walk-ups were a problem, too exerting for anything but friends' emergency entrance-exits; Marco had once visited Emily Dickinson's home; he'd noticed a basket that she lowered, by rope, out her second-story bedroom window. A young niece and nephew who lived next door would fill it with wildflowers and biscuits. Her reclusiveness was, it turns out, not all that bad, not quite terminal. (I remembered the amorous neighbor my first night here, crying up to a window, and Angel, then turning to Jesus instead.) We soon created comic balcony scenes. I bought my pals two nice baskets and some hardware store rope, almost too-new a yellow. Then "Coming up" could mean, even in Manhattan, flowers rising to them in wicker on a rope. Taadaa!

How might I characterize my loved ones' subtraction so you won't become jaded or feel bored? I do not want to rush. Nor do I plan to recount the play-by-play expiring of young friends that you know now.

I used to tell my students of creative writing, "When it comes to the death of your fictional characters, you cannot remove what you have not yet provided the reader. A general death is a contradiction in terms. —All deaths must be the death of a specific person if the reader is to feel involved and possibly even moved and, in being moved, changed, enlarged or instructed."

The mystery of creating a character on the page means providing him or her with an appearance, a hobby, a country of origin, the love of one color especially, a pet way of saying hello and goodbye, a few physical quirks, one lucky number, maybe a sexual preference or its denial's confusion, a secret love of chocolates, and, necessarily, some endearing faults.

It's odd that admitted faults should make invented character live most fully. This surely springs from a constant, renewable sense of falli-bility, our ready admission to any shortcoming before we concede, even to some stranger on some train, a single of our own true merits. What makes us mostly expect—while idling in neutral gear—not paradise, but plague?

Well, for one thing, visible plague does.

So, how can I convince you I am not a sob-sister merely? Since we are talking of say, thirty-odd close friends and ex-lovers, is it even seemly to number them? Doesn't that smack of war veteran braggadocio? . . . "I took seven minié balls and still lived to see Appomattox."

The hierarchy of suffering sets in too soon. What starts as your own self-armoring way of surviving can soon (esp in NYC) become The New Careerism.

Manhattan Person A says: "I've lost most of my friends to it."

Manhattan Person B: "Only 'most'? Lucky you. For me it's total. Twenty years in one neighborhood and, suddenly, we're talking *Stranger in a Strange Land*. For me, unlike you, a total rout—sorry."

Ten years earlier, on the message chalkboard of a Columbus Avenue gay bar called, yes, alas, The Deadwood, I saw this. Somebody had scrawled, in a self-conscious "autograph" handwriting:

"Just Fuck Me, and let me get on with my career."

A second, more direct, script added:

"That *was* your career."

Alabama would hand me the pink-covered volume of Whitman poems, bought for fifty cents and consecrated by stray drips of much strong Osso-rio coffee. She said he'd wanted me to have it; and only afterward would I find his notes to me in there, tenderly penciled, precise as musical cues and intended dynamics, the order he planned my reading which poems, a sequence, a last musical sequence he'd worked out to help me through the lost chord.

The first I found was this, from "The Wound-Dresser":

> . . . I stop,
> With hinged knees and steady hands to dress wounds,
> I am firm with each, the pangs are sharp yet unavoidable,
> One turns to me his appealing eyes—poor boy! I never knew you,
> Yet I think I could not refuse this moment to die for you,
>   if that would save you.

Gideon kept inviting me over to see still more new work; true, he was belatedly, at record speed, getting uncannily more skillful and subtle; I held the paintings now like fine small plates of food that I feared spilling; Robert had been going down fast, then leveled off and was trying to compose again; Marco was becoming even more a hermit and, since he still lived right above Ossorio's, we kept knocking on his door till, thinning, quieter than ever, he stopped answering, ceased even pulling up the basket. Two days later, I would find unretrieved jonquils dried right there. Ansel had gone home at once, the day he found out, back to Montana, and our frustration was that he never wrote and rarely came to the phone of his parents' farmhouse. "He's out with his dad checking the fences," a woman said over and over, and you could hear our bass-voiced friend in back of her, muttering instructions, telling her to write down numbers anyway. It was odd, we felt he blamed us. Maybe he did; we were as likely a cause as anything in this new Medieval zone of magical thinking.

My address book's listed facts subdivide, unhealthy cells, under Gideon's name: Two new hospital phone numbers and the exact street locations that florists require, though they know perfectly well where a whole damn hospital is. Here's how to reach his room at NYU Co-op Care where we friends took turns staying overnight in the bed beside his. And finally "Hospice" (what is the word "spice" doing there, so promising and scented an end to "Hospice"?). And at last, his sister's number in Queens, plus a note to myself, her husband's name and ages and majors of her two sons at Tufts and even their dog's name (keep it personal, Hartley).

In health, he'd had one address—the little inexpensive 1980 apartment on the Lower East Side that Gideon, through illegal subletting, parlayed into a steadying source of income. Dying, he was everywhere. As his T-cell count dropped, the phone numbers and addresses exponentially enlarged, doctors' home phones, antiques dealers busy selling off his hard-won collection a few treasures at a time. His teacher, Philip Guston, had given him a small pink and gray painting; it showed one large boot smoking a cigar; Gideon sold it via friends of friends to a little family museum in Texas. "But I got practically niente for my Piranesis, and not restrikes, either. In good late Empire frames, too. Alors."

Finally here's the phone of the cemetery office out in outer Queens, and, ending, the number of a person put in charge of the art colony memorial fund we set up in Gideon's honor.

Last Shall Be First

ur fathers were the victors of WWII; they felt justly proud of their sacrifices. They always regretted aloud that we boys hadn't been granted so good a war as theirs. They wished we had "gone over," not "come out." "Would've made a man of you," we each heard from old guys who hadn't a clue of how the world had changed around them. Even by our dads' hard standards—AIDS—another undeclared "policing action" like Korea or Vietnam—would soon make us, their gifted linebacker nelly-boys—"Real Men."

Compare the survival rate of footsoldiers from the Second World War with that of any cute young gay guy sashaying the streets of the West Village during his summer of love, 1980. Odds are . . .

The new disease had complicated and crowded our once-stupidly-simple medicine chests. Nudged out were our crab-lotion called Kwell, our bootleg penicillin for The Clap. Now the roundtable at Ossorio's became the site of staging operations. We'd turned into our own pharmacists, bureaucrats, wheeler-deelers, shameless string-pullers, accusatory screamers extralegal. We subscribed to medical journals out of self-defense. The competing lingos—of tenant rights, immune boosters, diet supplements—we learned, updated, relearned. And without meaning to, we became pedantic as the very doctors we were trying to second-guess. Nomenclature does that to you. We read aloud the news of Ronald Reagan cutting AIDS research because Haitians and the wrong sort (ours) kept being neatly taken out by it. Robert suggested that, if any of us had strength left to make mere art, the followup Hell assignment was in order. If only for Misters Reagan-Bush. No Fort Leavenworth of a Hell? Well, quick, somebody build a small good white-hot-collar one! But, by now, we were wired for something past mere rage. Rage became the starter kit that energy required for taking care of one another.

Our imaginations came to rest, in neutral, on test-pattern Pietàs.

In church basements visible from our coffee den, we, the sick and not and not-sick-yet, meetinged ourselves sicker. We were being called rude. Now, in mortal trouble, we began at rude, and upped the pitch, the volume, toward an outrage operatic. Has a human voice ever really shattered glass? Why not? Is a scream ever singing?

Meanwhile, it continually seemed that a mistake was being made. Some invoice misdelivered. Maybe we should carry Marco downstairs and ask him to interpret properly. Wrong address, surely.

How could Death have decided that it wanted, and be gathering so effectively, us? We felt right off the bus, still negotiably golden from last summer's lifeguarding. We were literally overflowing with promise and with talent, and with jism unlimited and, even now, still crazed with such a wild blind hope. Surely goodness and mercy would follow us all the days of our lives and our paintings'd wind up in the house of MOMA, like, forever. Right?

The disease itself suffered Attention Deficit Disorder. It would drag Robert once more to the edge, and then lose interest, take its own long vacation, let him scurry loose. Such hideous cat-and-mouse. You never knew whom you would find. The skull or the dimple. A stranger would be bedded in "his" corner hospital room, scaring you to death. "Released?" You'd find young Gustafson back in his own big bed, joking, hyper, entertaining you for real with every inch of wattage left him. He made you forget how he looked now. He was making you love him in new ways. (He had all but adopted one orderly's nine-year-old twin boys.) And yet you knew that, in one so weakened, love is an outlay. Even habitual seduction is exhausting. Odd, it proved to me that Robert'd never really faked it.

Good days, his mind was so perfect it seemed perfectly eerie, then it went so wrong so fast. Again I encountered him, as alone in bed as Crusoe, waterbound, rereading Defoe's account of that earlier sickness. Robert was, whenever possible these days, safe in the bed that came to seem bigger and steeper as the bulk and starch of him went. (Went where?) Holding the book, he marked his place with a single translucent finger.

"The parallels, my Airedale dear, are often amazing. But I prefer his plague to m . . . ours."

"Why?" I asked.

Robbie pointed to a faded gilt title, "*Journal of the Plague Year.* Singular." He smiled his stone-washed tiredness. "The one in here, it ends."

I daily checked his arms and shins; then, hidden at home, shamed, scanned my own. Masochistic, I bought myself a bathroom scale. Every three pounds dropped took me to the bottom of the ocean. I became Prussian with efficiency, hating to waste time. Even two minutes squandered felt . . . pornographic. (The futility, the going nowhere human.) I already felt so indebted to my undeserved good luck. My health made me feel not virtuous but sleazy. When my friends were out getting sexually sickened, where had *I* been? Home, retyping a single, sensitive, sterile paragraph for the twenty-eighth time? Home, beating off? Little else so concentrates the mind, so purifies the address book, as the certainty you have six months, tops. And your friends, six weeks.

I now felt far readier to say to sloppy acquaintances, "You've got your reasons, I'm sure. But my life's become too short to fritter away in restaurants hanging around for fifty-eight, now -nine, minutes for you to maybe show. Time is freedom and you are abusing mine, plus yours. The corn chowder is fairly good. I started without you. Never let this happen again. I could be doing something useful. Sitting here helped nobody, least of all me—No, I just don't think I *can* now. Sorry, friends waiting. I am out of here, you selfish little shit. How dare you do this to me considering how everything stands now. What world are you living in and wasting? Oh, waitress? My total." They had closed, as a hazard to public health, all the baths where sweet rough sex was nightly had and had. Insomniac, I sometimes did the math; I imagined my one night at St. Mark's, I imagined how many of those beauties still breathed this dear polluted air. The trucks parked on West Street and left wide open for nocturnal adventure were now either bolted shut or parked on the far Jersey shore where they stayed safe from trade, contaminants.

Management was worried for the trucks!

Gideon finally introduced us to his family from Queens; heavy, dark, polite, and shy, they looked like immigrants. You could tell that he, maybe our circle's laziest, was their tribe's only "success." Their glances his way were worshipful.

We kept seeing Gideon try to paint, in bed, trying to paint very well once more; and improbably recovering much of the old joy—but all while rigged with catheters and IV lines. Partying these last few years, like a minor-key Robert, he had rushed his work and we, ashamed, all knew so.

Now, once more, our darling Gideon was slaving at play as all real artists do. Life and death, one "what if" at a time. Our darling Gideon was once more hurrying to paint slow.

I saw so much I'm trying sparing you. Why? Okay, I won't then.

A certain citizen who had lived safe and untouched till the month of September, when the weight of the distemper lay more in the city than it had done before, was mighty cheerful, and something too bold . . . in his talk of how secure he was, how cautious he had been, and how he never had come near any sick body.

Says another citizen, a neighbor of his, to him one day, "Do not be too confident, Mr.—: it is hard to say who is sick and who is well; for we see men alive and well to outward appearance one hour, and dead the next." —"That is true," says the first man (for he was not a man presumptuously secure, but had escaped a long while; and men, as I have said, especially in the city, began to be overeasy on that score), —"that is true," says he. "I do not think myself secure; but I hope I have not been in company with any person that there has been any danger in." "No!," says his neighbor. "Were you not at the Bull Head Tavern in Gracechurch Street, with Mr. —, the night before last?" —"Yes," says the first, "I was; but there was nobody there that we had any reason to think dangerous." Upon which his neighbor said no more, being unwilling to surprise him.

But this made him more inquisitive, and, as his neighbor appeared backward, he was the more impatient; and in a kind of warmth says he aloud, "Why, is he not dead, is he?" Upon which his neighbor still was silent, but cast up his eyes, and said something to himself; at which the first citizen turned pale, and said no more but this, "Then I am a dead man too!" and went home immediately, and sent for a neighboring apothecary to give him something preventive, for he had not yet found himself ill. But the apothecary, opening his breast, fetched a sign, and said no more but this, "Look up to God." And the man died in a few hours.

Consolidate Surviving Acquaintances

ow dare I synopsize their suffering? How can I bear not to condense it?

And yet I'm going to hurry now, okay? Okay. Others' accounts will focus on the changing of the diapers of those once-strapping men you wanted or you had. I reserve the right to keep my hand firm on sweet Fast Forward. You just imagine those other parts. I don't care to see them twice. This go-round, I opt for dignity, because—alone and clean and so enraged for them—this time through, I can.

I go quick to what I "learned" as Robert taught me. And if that sounds hokey, if you think I'm moralistic and too proud of them and me with them, you are probably the one who kept me waiting one whole hour in a restaurant with others restless in line for our table. Well, almost an hour. If you're determined to undervalue what we crazyquilted together in our exit mode, please leave, do.

As I stood beside their beds and opened greeting cards and held inscriptions down so they could see, I no longer felt merely brotherly toward them, nor "sisterly," as when we camped it up on the street and risked having beer bottles thrown from passing cars.

Now, friends, weak, strengthened all in me that was most Fatherly. How proud I was to find I could. A whole new verb tense, "To Dad." It'd, all along, been latent. A closet case. I'd always, secretly, wanted kids. Not just Connecticut statistics, but real, needy, honest, children all my own.

Soon, I was finding my dad's own temper; it was also mine. Mine had been a closet case of rage. I'd never really needed it before. Except, perhaps, in resisting him.

Anger charbroiled to the surface during this, My Own Catastrophe. I saw how it had worked during his Depression, then his War (with its eighty thousand soothing lethal Chesterfields). Hard events "cured" Dad's fury up of him and into view where his wife and sons tripped over its tentacles biweekly. Now his Hartley yelled. See Hartley rant. Note Hartley kick stuff. Try not laughing when Hart breaks his big toe, kicking. Literally. Against the baseboard. Having watched my money-crazed absentee dad get so much wrong, *I* wanted a continuous audition now—at Fatherhood. For *his* sake, too!

I was yelling, demanding, not for me of course, but for my boy waiting at home, for his medicine please, if you, the pharmacist, could stop selling friggin' cherry Chapstick long enough to help my friend through his PAIN, much appreciated. Thank you. No prob.

I know the efficient way to tell this—combine characters. From the thirty-odd dead-letter files of friendship, I should create a single narrative address, "Occupant." I might then trace his single typifying history, his ascent, then his cliff-wall Roadrunner's drop to the canyon floor—I should combine Gideon with Robert—with Ansel, the abstractionist–photographer–construction worker, with. . . . Someone wise said of the Holocaust, "Six million Jews did not die. One Jew at a time died. But, six million of them. Singly."

Dead soldiers in a war get tallied as one daily impersonal digit; and this disease unified, then flattened individual difference among my address book's most determined, memorable individualists. 2 dead, becomes 15, becomes . . .

Heaven's password will be, I stake my life on this: "Hello."

I'd be dishonest to claim that my friends stayed—throughout their crashes—citadels of charm and thoughtfulness and breeding. Oooh, dear me, no. I could tell such tales. When tired enough these days, I occasionally let myself remember them at their worsts. It cuts through cheap, fudged sentiment so fast. I forever toy with the notion of intentional forgetting. But it's one of many things I'm not good at.

Even Robert, after I'd forgiven him his recklessness with Bama. Even poor Robert had to beckon me closer to his hospital bed. I hesitate, even now, to "tell on him." But then, part of remembering a person whole is just such a jagged, various completion. Besides, by now, you're probably so sick of hearing the exact color of his pale eyelashes, or of his pistol whipping's bow-shaped scar. Ill as he was, might not even my true love be entitled to a little cruelty, if he made it brief?

The crown prince waved me nearer. Compared to his Federal fourposter, this hospital bed looked so low to the ground, it seemed beneath him—so gleaming, hi-tech, and essentially demeaning. Robbie beckoned me over with the spindle finger, a single Hollywood Halloween crook of it. He, how-ever in and out of his head lately, had something to say, something he'd meant, he insisted now, to tell me for the longest darn time.

"It's about . . . your writing, Hartley. Lately, for a lot of us, it has gotten very hard to foll . . . ow, duck. Not always, but people, when you're not around, do say so. It's jumpy, undercuts itself. Needs more time to bake. Oh, you'll get better. Think of the years you have ahead. But maybe try and put more straight lines into it maybe? Good, though. Comic, they like. Still, nobody wants to read much more of the Southern stuff—choir practice and magnolias. No question that you have the 'chops.' And yet, you are way fun-nier in person. You talk better than you often get it down, but maybe that's true of . . . our lives. We've each always offered each other the most charm, hunh, Hart? *We* mostly got our very best, hunh, Hart? Ahead, there'll come a subject big and dark enough for you to chew on, hon. An all-week sucker. People are not very good. People never stay real happy very long. I don't know how you missed out on that. It's a first rule, really. Your weakness is this hero worship. Gets in the way of your characters' seeming real. You've still got your thank-you-note expectations, lad. Some people want to be fa-mous, some just wanna get fucked regular; your fault is, if you have one, you deepdown hope to be—don't get mad—thanked. You wanna get thanked. I wanna get fucked. She wants to get famous. Literature? It never says thank you, Hartley. Good books they just eat and go home. But . . . main thing is, babe—you keep at it, hear?"

"A-ha," I said. "Yeah, I thought maybe I *would*. Gracias, I guess." My hands felt suddenly unbusy. "Guess I'll have to work on all that. Suuure will. —But listen, after the talking just now . . . you thirsty, darl?"

He nodded. You cannot make a scene. You cannot have that be the last thing Robert remembers saying, regrets saying.

Most Classical and Romantic Composers lived long enough to complete their Ninth Symphonies, even their Tenths. He got half of one.

I now lower the clear glass straw into the clear water and watch him strug-gle, choke, to bring it to himself.

"Good," says a dadlike voice. "You *were* thirsty, weren't you?" The voice sounds like a pederast kiddie-show host, like God the Father Almighty, like healthy healthy Hartley cheering Robert who is so sick that he says things he doesn't really mean.

* * *

Shortly after my ideal one scolded me for immaturity and professional ineptitude, this (water, drugs, treats, Ensure food supplement, turning the patient in bed, the doughnut foam pillows needed to shield inevitable bedsores) started being what I did with days.

Hard to explain: First I was doing it because it had to be done. My friends could not afford paid attendants. Then I did it because I was one fragment of our Circle still left upright. Next, I told myself I did it because I *could* do it, do it as well as most and better than some. Then, old hand at rigging Hickman Catheters that pump nutrition into beloved boys' chests' centers, I got almost too good at it. Compassion can become a form of legal ego.

Next phase, I lived these rites and cheerings merely as a journalist: I planned to someday "use" it, as a feeder source for fiction. Of course I'd first have to antique it, improve it into something far more shapely, and shortly. To use it someday, in the disguise of a novel, I'd probably need to roll back the period, make myself better looking, make them less gallingly articulate. Placing the struggle in a prettier age that might retroactively give meaning to my chores as all these gifted lives were ending everywhere around us.

Nothing helps cheer a brilliant thirty-four-year-old dying so unjustly. Not your wit, not your will, not the best that medicine could offer us then.

You just keep him warm and comfy and supported, and wait. You give up any plan or hope that gets in the way of anticipating what fluid or solid or joke your dear needs next. I'd somehow stopped writing. I kept tutoring. But I gave up sperm-doning for fear I'd shoot my present sadness into some new life form. Jinxing junior. Finally, tired past gray and on toward clarity (once everyone but me and The Bama had finally come down with it), I tired till I hit an ersatz wisdom, the cult of Only Now.

I gave up the eventuality of ever having a writing life again, even AFTER. AFTER, too, was a prop I quit leaning on. By then, this was a job, looking after was simply what I did, and then it stopped being a duty or a job and it was just a Tuesday and the things that needed fetching, washing. On the back of my apartment door, I'd thumbtacked a list marked "Do Today." It had just three categories:

Must. Should. Might.

Must was a column I never quite got out of. I admired the waiting rectitude of *Should*. But, oh daydreaming ran mostly toward ethereal and skyblue *Might!*

Finally, after fantasies of all those books I'd write dissolved, after the pride in a squeamishness overcome fell away, this was all that any of us managed. Caretaking could only take care of itself. There was a whole pack of us, mongrels, defrocked priests, unwed, with time to spare because we made time, with secret missionary temperaments. The tendency to want to think well of others—certain evidence not withstanding; this tireless try at, if not happiness, then not constant screaming either. The will to do the best ourselves. *For* ourselves. So, if we lived, we could live with ourselves. Even alone.

One day on the subway, I stood reading how Reinhold Niebuhr, asked to define Sainthood, answered, "The *spouses* of saints."

I laughed aloud. People moved away at once. It'd gotten rarer, laughing aloud when alone. I so welcomed the sound, I barely noticed the fear it always stirred in fellow New York strangers. Happy=crazy.

Angie and I worked split-shift. She lunged at saving our friends in just the way she labored at the play of making art. Her toughness, I aspired to. It outbutched and outclassed us all. That she might be around to catch me when I fell, that kept me standing.

Finally, our Robert and Gideon and Marco were not just those we loved but what we did. Not as a rehearsal for some Walt Whitman story ahead, Walter nursing fallen pretty boys, becoming indispensable and then learning from it all.

Partly, my friends' quiet bravery pushed me, teaching me, beyond my own peevishness, my own inherited hotheadedness, my cheery bogus "goals," my early selfish self.

One day, filing through the piles of insurance forms that now littered a desk where I once wrote dog stories, my hand hit something cold. It was glass in a picture frame. Increase Hartley, his somber face had once seemed comically forlorn during my smiley youth. I now recalled Mosby's praise, the Colonel's concern about blankets and bacon for his "boys." They called him "Saint Hen" and the name was truly affectionate. I remembered my own early snobbery at having a kinsman praised solely as a good provider, not as Terror of the Yankees. I had known so little two years back. "They taught us to provide, provide, son," Dad had told me that last day.

Now, resemblance meeting resemblance, I pulled the oval frame against my lips. Glass now felt all grimed with New York's dust-grease. I kissed the great grandfatherly image, pulled it off a ways to study. My mouth pursed, I touched the lip. Blood. I'd cut myself on him, too. Then I coughed back a sob, put my head down amid Blue Cross–Blue Shield forms and knowing I might might might cry. Did. Oh, but a good cry, at the right time, is like shitting when you really really need to. A good cry is so good.

Regrets, second thoughts, career frustrations?—you could either deal with those, or this.

This, of course, meant:

Them. Meant: Mine. My Boys.

I received the usual blue envelope from my mom. (The exact color of that thank-you-note supply she'd sent with me to New York.) Mother explained that, without Dad, many of their favorite Florida couples could no longer ask her over; not even the Albertsons! "On group things, I can see their cars leaving without me as I now seem to throw their numbers off!"

Therefore, she was considering, shock of shocks, moving back to North Carolina. She had begun asking my brothers, the two who lived there, how crowded this might make them feel. Then she added, in her schoolgirl handwriting,

"I have been picturing buying an old fixer-upper type of home. Two stories. A back garden, private. Is this too trite of me? Big repairs would drive Dick crazy. But I personally like the idea of improving such a place. I want lots of rooms for you all to come visit whenever. And listen, you. Should you or any of your friends ever need to come down and get better from anything at all, or stay as long as you like forever, you know that I have had a lot of experience in this line. Nothing would make me happier. I am buying the house in order to get ready to entertain in a manner I would like to grow accustomed to giving away! Best to Angie. Nuf said, I remain, with love, Mother."

On one of Robert's last two good days, he barked, needing me to come closer. I dreaded hearing his next assault on my, what, what next? My remaining looks? But I could see my friend had been fretting, sad at having put a hex on my work, and last thing before I left that evening. I would lie if I told you I hadn't felt it, to the quick. (Not that all he said was inaccurate, and not that, in replaying it a thousand times, I have not really tried to learn from it. Because I swear I have.)

After

Returning from the corner newsstand, I'd just bustled back into room 282, my face burning rosy from that stinging cold wind off the East River.

I was wearing something tweed and something silk and both were colorful. Saint Robert the Gaunt appeared oddly like Quixote now; he beckoned me nearer. "Today, m'Hartley, you look fabulous. Health itself. A Dutch still life. So pink a fine boy. You always were a table full of such good things, ready."

"What you're really saying, Robert, is—your Hick Hartley here is getting just a li'l bit fat."

"Call this fat?" The ivory hand came out. It pinched up two sample inches of my sudden middle.

"That ain't fat, kid. It's luxury. Just more of your potential."

During the siege, even if she was out on the road showing slides, out bucking up the young and the visual, she still sent perfect flowers, she mailed our sick pals art books (some now about her, her work). Bama was a "name" generally known and therefore specifically lighter in bearing, even better company for that. It let her gather bigger better taller tales for us, her being major. She was producing something called "mature work." Most people who stumble into what others term "the arts" get only sweeter with their own hard-earned successes.

In the beginning, we boys had sometimes been a bit prettier and usually better dressed than our gifted blue-jeaned women friends. Back then they valued our stylized talk, sought our advice about their paintings, plus the right color for so small an apartment. Angie, having scouted Federal harps for me (I let the one go, and only a hundred and sixty bucks!), had advanced from paint-smeared denim and makeup like fingerpainting, to the sculpted worsted of a glamorous vaguely-French cosmopolite. Our Angie, a respected woman of a certain age. Her notoriety suited her. Literally.

In she swept with bundles. No backpack now. She wore three beautiful deco silver bracelets (long-ago gifts from Robert—shoplifted, we suspected but never asked). These baubles clanked as she embraced the sketch of a beloved former boy she'd fucked (once?) some years ago. Who knows how many times over how many years? I'd never learn that.

No hard feelings. Mostly, none anyway.

* * *

She now wore her best gray Chanel suit and the beautiful bone-colored Italian shoes. She trailed just a memory of scent and made the visit feel so glamorous a distraction, a blessed one. The broadness of her humor and its killer timing had grown even more refined. New York had robbed us of so much; but it'd given us all Jewish humor. The essential flotation device. Yiddish inversions, "You should be so lucky." The low expectations and high hilarity of Borscht Belt jokes. Ghetto humor helped us goys survive the ghetto, and each other.

We three sat on his bed watching some dumb TV docudrama about a dad molesting his little girl; the father was played by a dent-chinned Hunk of the Moment and the child actress was washed-out and snively. And when sexy Dad admitted to his girl, "There's good touching and there's bad touching," Angie begged him, "Promise?" I cannot explain why her tone and sulk in saying this was so hilarious. But almost fell off the bed and Robert laughed till he gasped until, for a sec, we feared we'd lost him. By now, we were such experts in New York Jewish gallows humor, even *that* seemed funny. Robert dying laughing? He could do worse.

Angie brought us personal clippings—about her big show now being hung in Berlin. She had wrapped up a scale model of the exhibition gallery with all the pictures we knew, reproduced two inches square and hung in this scale model dollhouse of art. It seemed a magical toy from the hand and workshop of careerist Santa himself. She held it out to us. "Couldn't you just sprinkle a little salt on this like so much celery and just eat it?"

"No," Robert, a scratched stick, said. "But I'll watch." That we were playing, like the *Titanic* orchestra, playing right up to the end, it showed, I felt, we'd learned a thing or three. That made me momentarily happier.

I was about to head South for Christmas. She now arranged the flowers she'd just brought Robert, most of a lilac bush that smelled almost too good and must've cost a fortune on the East Side. She would spend the night and, though mostly glad, I felt somehow uneasy.

When he remembered to, Robert could still dispense the usual 100-proof charm. His quips that once pealed forth so effortlessly, now rode stray ungoverned barks, voice breaking like a boy pubescent's. His former languor revealed what work had forever underwritten its nouveau curls, the swoops most cavalier. His drawl sounded less indolent, more brave.

It was not an effect he had ever let us see, and you could tell that it embarrassed him.

Bama suggested we should change his scene. Given Robert's weakness, it took two of us twenty minutes to get him toward, then into the wheelchair.

Co-op Care left friends in charge of loved ones. You stayed with them, only summoned nurses for a code blue. The ward proved ideal for folks with lots of pals who'd sit round the clock. I soon found: scheduling others' half-reliable visits was often harder than just camping here myself.

Bama came across a long white nurse's coat hanging behind the bathroom door; she now modeled it for us, joking, "But, you know? I worry about the length." She showed off her gams; with gym work, they were now nearly as good as mine. "Oh well," she said, trying to entertain a listless Robert, "hems up one year, down the next. As Cocteau says, 'We must forgive Fashion everything, it dies so young . . .' "

Then silence. None of us would touch it for one whole second.

"Good thing you finally got a decent gallery, kid," he was merciful. "You never would have made it as a Savannah club lady."

"Thank you doubly, Robins. I always did put my foot in it. Trying to get better at that but, you know me, I'm hopeless basically." And she met his look.

We joshed throughout, while shifting him from bed to chair. But finally the three of us just shut up; we simply did the chore with whatever grunts its facts and physics demanded. We were all now old enough, ripened enough with wear and love, not to need to lighten every little bit of pain. You could do either Charm or Efficiency. We had all grown wise enough to alternate.

Given Robbie's leaflike frailty, we settled for eating downstairs in the cafeteria. At this end of life, a change of scene could be mean a change of floor. Miss Byrnes now handed our patient a bundle from Bloomingdale's. He tried to break through stubborn tissue paper, then, frustrated, struck at it.

"Here, let me," she said. "I love ripping things up."

"No lie," said I.

It was the latest in pajama loungewear for persons both rich and richly ironic. Some designer must've collected, then copied cowboy patterns from the bedspreads and boys' room draperies of the 1940s. Cacti, mesas, auburn broncos at full buck. A freckled blond sixteen-year-old cowpoke, grinning in his huge white hat, wearing spurred boots endearingly too-large, recurred, bowlegged. "These patterns arrived just yesterday. As usual, darl, you're cutting-edge," so she told the man she wheeled, Robert all done up now in cowboy robe and matching dude ranch jammers. (The pants were more than any of us could bear to bother with right now.)

We rolled off the elevator into a mealtime traffic jam of thirty other rolling Giacometti men. The age of mechanical reproduction seemed to have Xeroxed one skeletal spectre into these many identical chairs. Each replicant was pushed by a healthy rosy person whose own face showed a cow-catchering all-purpose smile: "Ain't we got fun?"

The patients themselves sat stern, hair gone wiry thanks to lethal medicine and the disease's own ferocious coarsening. Each sick boy, yellowgray-whitegraphite-colored, feeling himself uniquely beloved, being so sick it felt gravitational, ignored—with queens' unlearnable grandeur—the sight of any others, similarly ending. Thirty Elizabeth I's on wheels "cut each other dead."

Meanwhile, those pushing them grinned, to compensate, emoting gratitude for two. Emerging from the elevator, Angie and I loomed. We beamed down on others' sullen boys in passing chairs. Kids who sulked, too sick to play, their parents urging them on. I felt such claustrophobic panic and I knew Robert must.

But what seemed worse than this rush hour of the ill? Ten boys wore his same flannel cowboy pajamas! (Comes in pistachio green or beet red.) Bama had sworn that these were "hot," unseen till now. And so they were. But other friends of others dying had rushed that same counter not two hours back.

Bama, always a speedster on her feet, old medical hand from the clinic days of our mere-VD innocence, now did such a quick reverse into the elevator with our Robert.

As we rose, he said with effort, "So much, if only I, for the fashion individuality of we . . . the clone-prone." And we laughed, at least *thinking* we had followed his drift. We'd gotten pretty good at it, but the circuitous logic required ever more.

Returned to his room, relieved, Bama phoned out for deli fare, making quite a production of it. "Now when you say tapioca, you mean the old fashioned big pearl kind, with lots of cinnamon on top, and is it worth the cals to have a whole trough of it brought up here to us. And, honestly, Cal? 'Cal' was it? —Now, Cal, m'dear? Where would your own grandma rank it on a scale of one to ten?" She winked our way. Robert smiled his now feral smile and appeared, as she had planned, entranced.

We soon enjoyed a picnic on the bed. Ms. Byrnes made much of her nurse's coat as we settled, shoes off. She laughed, pointing to her sterile garb: "Déjeuner sur lab!"

Here, safe alone together again, his pj's seemed playful, a very good if overcute idea, free of others' having—the sheep—rushed out to be the first to "copy" him. Clear of eyesore strangers in the same big leaky family rowboat—we felt ourselves regaining our own old consequence, our pique.

Her bad pun about the Manet released us into irreverent early days. Like kids just off the bus, fresh meat for this carnivorous town, we became kids with nothing to lose, at least nothing that the kids yet knew about.

Three, saucy, on a bed. Our lives soon seemed all before us, along with those lives' aftermaths: Careers become reputations become memories. We were talking ourselves into everything again.

We talk talk talked, about old times. What else? There had been the insane Rasta man, his dreadlocks drumsticks, who lived in Robert's building, who made an altar beside the elevator on the third-floor landing and left lit candles and food on paper plates, food that spoiled though it was jabbed with toothpicks wearing handwritten paper legends that read "Immortal," "Metro-Goldwyn-Mayer," "Bob Marley IS one pupa form of Pope."

We had known dear Nina, the woman who finally got called out of retirement to sing again at the Met because a Hong Kong flu epidemic felled two alternate substitutes and—judged crazy all those years—for her studying every alto role for every Met performance— "working up my Hungarian" to perfect her incipient "Bluebeard's Castle," all those Health Department flu shots and the epic vitamin C she'd taken had finally paid off. Nina, fifty-two, stepped in for Carol Vanness twice and got an excellent though single sentence in the *Daily News* if not, alas, the *Times*. Still, she'd now sung at the Met repeatedly.

We talked about abortions, about one of our old friends who now regretted sacrificing Mick Jagger's child because it'd come at a bad time for her, a girl who'd had the goods but went home to Idaho anyway. There were others who had little visible talent but who stayed put, politicked, persisted, and got semifamous anyhow. Famous enough. Prose and cons. Team and variation.

Four huge works by Alabama Byrnes were still the hot topic from the last overly political so-so Whitney Biennial, where they were said to have been "the only real things in it." She was now collected by the same museums we'd sneaked into with borrowed student IDs.

Bama sat crosslegged in stocking feet, toenails professionally polished, and we were soon puppies again, snug on the bed (not a downtown floor-through's futon this time, not Robert's busy fourposter, but a hospital adjustable upright, with hidden hydraulic motors we toyed with like a motorboat's controls). We sat here downing whole containers of the tapioca just as good as Cal had promised (and warmed by him for us, special). I dragged over the phone and my textured address book ("You got some miles on this," she said. "By now, Robbie, doesn't Hart's address book look like The Dead Sea Sc . . . I mean, St. Peter's ledger . . . er . . .") and we called people all over the world, and she'd smile, "Guess who *we're* with?" and Alabama still sounded proud of it, of him.

After dinner, bored of the sound of the TV, the three of us eventually sat facing the door. We agreed that, belonging to the last generation to recall a world before TV infested every house, having explored actual woods and fields, we were the luckiest of all. We had been born at exactly the best time. We now sat, in fitful silences, as if awaiting the arrival of someone important.

Maybe one of our old regulars we didn't feel complete without. Someone big, with perfect naval ensign posture, and not hair so much as locks (like Goldie's, Harpo's), some kid with a jawline like the best Pirate of Penzance juvenile lead, ever. Even the thin courtly minor man slumped here with us, gone all wristbone and eyesocket, he too sort of faced the door, as if he was also a big fan of the missing party's. Every passerby's footsteps in the hall made us hush, half-turn. We were waiting for him. Before. We aimed in the correct direction just in case our mutual true love appeared for just a moment, popped in with party food leftovers, stories, stage kisses so enlivening, "Ciao, ducks."

Alabama and I sat swilling low-cal frozen yogurt, and Robert slumped among pillows, eating real ice cream for the weight gain, and we kept rough-housing, teasing and touching like people barely twenty will, and not folks slipping unbidden into their forties. And beyond.

And a last, loud, good old New York time was had by all.

Alabama fetched her overnight bag and prepared to sleep in Robert's room, the extra bed. You could still hear a foghorn, boat traffic chugging up and down the East River. I would crash on the sitting room's foldout couch. I stripped and got comfortable quicker than I'd figured. I knew this ease came from having her here. It made him so happy.

Around four, I heard Bam's voice. First I thought she'd muttered out of a bad dream. I sat straight up without knowing why. "Hartley? You 'sleep? Hart?" Something was wrong.

I jumped up naked and rushed in, arms wavering before me in the dark. I found Angie's bed empty. Then I saw, by moonlight, the two of them together, curled on his. Robert, in the middle, held up the covers for me and I knew how strenuous even this'd be for him. So I slid in there quite fast.

"Couldn't start playing around without you." She leaned over him and she kissed me and gave my dick a little playful harmless tossle.

"Here we all are," he said, hoarse, straight up to the dark.

"Alone together at last," I spoke, mostly to mark my place, make it real.

She groaned, " 'Bama's Back and Two Buggers Has Got Her!' "

We still found each other funny. That was lucky, if only for all it spared the rest of the world. But, hey, we three weren't hurtin' anybody.

To be naked as in the old days. (Though, of course, we hadn't ever really been, not concurrently, not as a quorum. It just remembered that way.)

To be simply warming him, this fellow so recently still the prettiest boy in New York, and to be warming him from either side like this. We all touched each other all over each other. And as for his ID bracelet, these little clips and nodules and lines tea-potting off him, she and I, we learned to work (and play) around them.

There came a moment about twelve minutes into our threeway when it really could've happened. Everything. Something. Groping each other, we found each other at least technically ready. Lowering my hand over Robert's hard dick, unshrunken, Oh Death, where is thy shrinkwrap—the very act put me into such a sweet fraternity-sorority. Membership in the collective love of him, that, as much as anything, was what I'd mainly always wanted.

By now, for us? hey, The Act itself would've seemed almost academic. Redundant. We three were such past masters at it, we now felt beyond even needing to demonstrate all that. Just to be here safe in the blessed smells of those best known, three scents mixed under a single tenting sheet, that felt almost erotic enough now, thanks.

I could tell—for Robert, it was just the chance that everything might start up again. I had not brought a rubber, and certainly not two of them. Angie probably might keep a few spares in her night bag; but to fidget with prevention, here and now after everything, it would've been oddly awkward. We never had protected ourselves from each other. That'd been the joy. That, I guess, was the problem.

So, for Robert, it seemed better that we might've. It would be wrong to say that nothing did. Happen. After all, it was us, all nude, still here; so what little happened, in a way, was really everything.

We would talk and sleep then drift, speak over the one sleeper, and hold on. I could feel her hips, the nubbin breast most north-facing, my hand struck his many many ribs, almost cold as piano keys. On the river, a ship's whistle sounded three times. The horn was airy yet magisterial. One of the last great liners leaving port? I woke at dawn, my arm curled under his head, fingers resting against his neck. It felt, the neck felt, I decided—plumper, potentially better. Then I noticed how, as we'd slept, my arm had slid, cradling, beneath the pillows of them both. And the neck I touched was, just past Robert's, hers. It beat with such life, life enough for three.

But to bundle there with them, sleeping in that second innocence, it almost felt a truer, finer form of happiness. Darkest honey is best. I can't explain. We knew much more. We forgave, not It, but most of each other's playful careless foolishness. Even our cruelty was human after all; try as we had to be merely superhuman.

I try and try explaining. I get close, I feel it, I fall back. I fail afresh. I can't explain. You must help me out with it. Please, provide a little of your own, from your own rich life. I'll count on that. You had to have been there.

Thank you. You have been.

She soon flew off to Los Angeles; she stayed in close touch with those already installing her work in Berlin. She kept posted about his temperature, R's vital signs. She had won a fellowship that was, she joked, perfect for a father's girl, coming from an outfit called D.A.D. She also joked, Now she'd had D.A.D., but would she ever get MOMA? The prize meant a residency, but she told them that sick friends would prevent her really living in Germany those six months. They still gave her the award and the big-time show at its end. She'd brought to Robert's room that little German-perfect model of the gallery, showing us where each of her pictures went, in miniature. He loved all that, holding it. He lit up as ever and was soothed for days after her visits. It sedated me to see him far far calmer thanks to her. That made my work easier.

The rest of us, without her, tried to keep him entertained, then merely amused, then just distracted. And, finally, warm.

Before Robert's eyesight faltered, we borrowed gorgeous objects for him. On approval, I'd spring beautiful things from antique shops so he could study them up close. Even with my favorite receptionist presiding downstairs, this hospital felt so fluorescent and blank. Robert's room itself seemed a sure first step off the cliff, a banishment from every visual pleasure.

So, even for us, we overdecorated. And lavishly admitted it. Our aesthetic fallback position—like that of the long-lost Moorish Princess odalisquing at the Saint Mark's Baths—ran to automatic excess. A damned good thing, considering the Operaticness of late, these death scenes were so hard to stage correctly. Familiar patterns soon set in and, if you weren't scrupulous, the same Latin-fusion-jazz combo was heard playing the same few selections at identical memorial services in the similar splashy lofts.

"We can't go on meeting like this" was our jokey funeral greeting of the moment. "Or *can* we?" came the follow-up zinger.

With us, it was reverse Bauhaus. Less Is More? Less ain't, girlfriend. Mo' is! —And Curly. And Larry, too.

Our golden rule: "When in doubt, toss in those two extras with the fringe."

So, to Robert's basic shell of a room, we added more Mercury glass spheres, further Victorian beaded bags and geegaws, old tin wind-up toys a faded-Christmas red that was his favorite color, crumbling coral-colored nineteenth-century paisley shawls slung over the shower-curtain runners that circled his bed to ensure any impossible privacy. It soon irked his favorite nurse, finding her beside table, reserved for medicine, heaped with mangos bought mostly for their lurid shade of green, plus a pile of magazines intended for thirteen-year-old girls, covers featuring this TV season's pubescent boy–heart throbs.

To the room's ugly orange plastic form-fitting chairs we added little gilt ballroom ones where chaperons once sat knitting while young ladies whirled through waltzes on lower Fifth. We told ourselves we were giving Robbie something to look at.

But now, I guess we partly did it to distract ourselves from the sight of him. He had always looked so unlike everybody else, handsomest boy in his time slot. Now that word "time slot" had a final ugly click to it, and we turned his music up to drown out everything but music itself.

He appeared all but identical to fourteen others Lincoln Logged along this hall. Only the eyes, still a shade of swimming-pool "aqua," pulled him forward from the rest. But gazing into those eyes soon made us feel neutered, boring, erased. The Ouija board had all the answers; you hardly needed to ask. The less he said, the more intricate and interminable his looks became. By the end, he was transmitting through those eyes. For the first time ever I read "Bored" there. That shocked me more than his sickness. What if I was now seeing clear through to the primer coat? What if Bored had been there, basic, all along?

Marco brought in a slide projector and we settled the thing upon its own ballchair, locked on Automatic. Random. It projected continual images toward the white wall at the foot of Robert's bed.

I included whatever jumbled images might have meaning for him. Van Gogh's perfect bachelor-artist pad at Arles. I commandeered a paint-stained Pentax that Angie'd once used to document her work. I took slides of the stage of the concert hall where his First Symphony had been so recently heard; I got shots of the front doors of Robert's own apartment building but, for some reason I couldn't name, dared not venture inside, though the keys still hung heavy on my ring.

Too much had happened there. I pictured its shipboard coziness, its secret recesses. I already felt exiled from those stacks of *Titanic* clippings, the four windows prismatic, and that yellowest of Alabama Byrneses. At the Met Opera's new gift shop, while acting like some high school music teacher, I bought slide portraits of his favorite composers. These got scattered throughout my media event for him.

If we had to leave Robert—and sometimes we did (late nights, we sometimes trusted him to his nurses' care)—we made sure he had his favorite music clamped over his ears—he could rock through the Mahler Fourth, its culminating soprano solo making such a sweet and surfeited paradise promise. And he'd have the projector rattling through its catalogue—group shots from Ossorio's, the owner and patrons waving and holding up their fingers in peace signs or devil's horns behind Ossorio's head. Some singular dictionary definitions I'd Xeroxed and then got blown up. Pictures of us, mugging at the round marble table under our Lady of Perpetual Help—a failure. Here were street characters we knew by sight though not always by name. Paintings he loved, Bonnards, early Alabamas, a Duchamp urinal called *Fountain*, corny shots of his own family, plus the composers he loved best. Godlike Schubert, dead at thirty-one, of venereal disease and then typhoid fever, after being weakened by his tendency to drink.

I remember one Thursday, running late. It was the day before my trip to see the folks in Florida. By then, Marco was down with it and I had taken sweet and sour soup by his place. He never really let us in, and therefore it was necessary to wait a while for him to get to the door. Even hauling up the rope had become a godlike chore. I dropped off a magnifying glass at Gideon's, he was trying to sell his Villon etchings, and wanted to have a lens there to assure some visiting Japanese dealer that the things were authentic. Gideon appeared, birdlike but elegant in a blue satin robe I'd never seen before, he asked me if I could lend him another couple hundred till the end of the week. As an IOU, while I waited, he did a charming little ink drawing, a caricature of me, I think it was meant to be. But it showed an Indian deity with all the arms, one supporting a magnifying glass that had suddenly grown big as Sherlock Holmes's. Gideon handed over the drawing confidently as Picasso would, that assured of the work's value and character. I thanked him, I wrote out another uncollectible check. Only Southern gentlemanliness prevents my stating the full final amount.

And so I was, as usual those days, frazzled when I pulled at last into Robert's room. It was often the last stop, and maybe that was unfair to him. By the time I arrived there, I sometimes yearned to climb right under the covers with him. (What else was new?)

Instead—my duty seemed to fortify my long morning of earnest homely errands into something frothy, a comic meringue worthy of Noel Coward or Cole Porter. I recalled Robert telling me way back that the two of us exerted more charm while flossing our teeth than some poor suckers put forth during their whole honeymoons, and I remember wondering what charm was exactly?

Some willingness to exaggerate? To live in continual innocent relation to the world's outsized joys and shocks? I had actually looked up the word. Or had I meant to and was I, in my exhaustion, just recalling what I'd expected its meaning to be?

No, wait. Not only had I got to the dictionary, I'd photocopied the definition, had a slide made of it. I'd scattered it among the sundry other images: the head of Brahms, the jewel-like nudity of Madame Bonnard's floating iridescent in her bath. I recalled more now—in the jumbled fatigued way that only let me move cerebrally in such short staccato lurches like those follow-the-dot games I once loved in my boyhood *Jack and Jill* magazines.

As usual, I entered Robert's room talking. I had peeled off my coat, had plucked a dead lilac from Angie's otherwise still-lovely arrangement, I tugged down one corner of his bedclothes, then slowly registered new retinal evidence, changes in a room that had begun to seem eternal in its sameness.

The projector had jammed between two slides. These images (held there all night?) had burned. One depicted the upper half of Schubert's face, his tiny glasses seared clear through to whiteness but the wavy hair and the whole scorched forehead remained, a brown zigzag husk. Atop this, superimposed as in some Alabama image, black spiney letter, projected, big.

Charm, a noun.—based on Middle English for a magic spell, derived from the Latin word "carmen" meaning incantation. 1. The power or quality of pleasing or delighting; attractiveness: "The breezy tropical setting had great charm". 2. A particular quality that attracts; a delightful characteristic: "A mischievous grin was among the child's many charms". 3. A small ornament, such as one worn on a bracelet. 4. An item worn for its supposed magical benefit, as in warding off evil; an amulet. 5. To attract or delight greatly. To bewitch.

Light in here bounced images off the wall and back down onto our patient. He, unsupervised, lay naked atop his sheets. He'd noticed me; I'd never felt so watched by him. When flourishing, he had never liked direct stares; but the more silent he grew, the more legalistic, dubious Talmudic, and resigned these long looks grew.

He had incidentally pulled the IV from his arm and the milky nutriment line was dislodged from a catheter inserted midchest. He was naked and elongated as any El Greco saint. His arms, thrown open, rested to either side; his features were set and bits of the projected image played over his bare form. Part of Schubert's nose lit one shoulder.

Robert's face had shaped itself into a question, one addressed, it seemed, to the projector's light. I saw that my monologue (never able to cure him) would never again even cheer him. I sensed that he'd grown finally blind to whatever might now be offered to beguile or charm him. Nothing held him to us now. He had no interests. The continuous seduction, it'd ceased.

I saw that the surface of his body, once so pure and supple, was mottled and pocked and scored as if by some terrible recordkeeper. Robert's tattoo of five-line musical possibility forever awaiting notes had shrunk, as he had—in the way a balloon, broken, renders any words across it illegible.

I climbed up onto the bed beside him, got both arms beneath his back. The crushed geranium smell of him rose so intense it threw a little clear-glass greenhouse all around us. His arm freely drained, the milky substance of the feeding fluid seemed to pour from the hole burrowed in the center of his chest like some nipple wasting nourishment that a suckling child might use. His genitals looked huge because they, having stayed their same size, contrasted with such wasting all around them.

I held Robert, nothing horrified me now, because it was him I had here. All the protection that his beauty had once offered him and us, that was now lost. And yet, the lowering of its spangled curtain, let me in, in closer, and right up against him. He now appeared as interchangeable with others on this hall as white eggs in a single carton. And yet he still smelled like Robert: Now he looked green but smelled golden. I could feel him looking up at me, dry lips forming half a name, whispered. It sounded like "Tension." Or "Tennyson?" It couldn't be. He kept staring. I got a better grip on him. If he was messy, I would be. And his long hollow look itself let me know what a construction it'd all been. My Robert—the altarboy who was both boy and altar. I had needed that, needed both. Now, him naked in my arms, we were finally equals. If what had first moved me toward him had been his looks that finally surrendered to his gift, what held me here now was simply what outlasted admiration. I still loved. He could be dead but never ugly. Because I could still love whatever of him was left. He saw that. He saw that what the nurses cleaned up out of duty or union obligation, I cleaned because it was him and his. And therefore, ours.

If loving him haphazardly had been misguided, masochistic, then this part finally, it at last felt proper, reciprocal.

His meanness and fitful coldness to me, his making me a mascot-hobby-gopher, even his exposing Angie and the others to latent harm, none of that could lessen what he'd given us. Love had always helplessly left him. I'd left him helpless. He dispensed it like monoxide and we gathered it, his archivists, his orbiting bees and jagged minor moons.

I patted one side of his face, I looked up at the wall, read part of the definition.

"Robert Robert Robert. Still charming after all these years. How do you do it? Can we bottle it? I could drink you like honey and Ensure, forever. What a strange pair we've made, hunh?"

And he? He said that last part of a word, "ension"—I got it.

" 'Potential'? That still your nickname for me? Potential *what?* But thanks, love."

And, no longer angry at the inept nurses who had not looked in on him, had not kept him covered; no longer worried how many days he'd have or if I dared go South as planned; feeling nothing but how immense this attraction still was and how much of my gratitude still held, held both of us, I cradled him. Now, as he looked up at me from far out of nowhere, I could freely rock rock rock him, singing in my only voice, the froggy and untrained one,

> *"Daisy Daisy, give me your answer do,*
> *I'm half crazy all for the likes of you.*
> *I am too poor for marriage,*
> *I can't afford a carriage,*
> *But you'll look sweet upon the seat*
> *Of a bicycle built for two . . ."*

I don't believe in Paradise.
I do believe in Address Books.

Time of Departure

ideon died first. Locked in the room with jumpstart heart-shockers, unsuccessful—a pretty gifted dark kid who'd always been only lucky (till this), a boy whose new cashmere sweater was often a green as sweetly acid as the colors in his pictures. He assumed that he alone would somehow be saved, by friends with connections, saved because of all his genuine unrealized promise.

At his funeral, twenty mourners held on to each other. Angie, determined to push Marco's wheelchair, kept bumping into drainage slots and tombs, half-blind from our week's crying.

Gideon had had the goods but often used them up, on splendid times. He maybe figured he could finally "apply himself," could become fully superb when he was old and homely, and getting no better offers. (Who on earth can blame him?)

It pained me, his being buried here, in such a cut-rate sort of Jewish cemetery in far Queens. The boneyard rested, pummeled by screams, direct on the flight path of La Guardia Airport. We tried saying our goodbyes out here; the few of us gathered were little aided by a dwarf-sized rental rabbi who had never known our friend. We screamed, "Gideon liked . . . Gideon could always . . ." beneath the howl of jets that swooped so low we might jump up and nearly touch metal. Gigantic silver planes (so close you could count their undersides' rivets) swept over this squat ghetto, gray stones somehow urban. We, already stooped by mourning, we ducked even further. Jet noise seemed a new part of the diaspora's old humiliation.

Here lies a beautiful boy who painted boats and houses, who, though forever broke himself, still managed to give his nephews refurbished forest-green Volvos to take to Tufts. Here lies a boy who caused the world to fall in love with him, and who allowed us to forgive him for never quite solely loving us back enough, for never playing at work quite hard enough at work. He had other gifts and he gave all those away, with a generosity that shamed the smallmindedness of his fond, loan-holding survivors.

I tried, the day Gideon died, to get his obituary into the *Times*. I found I would pull all sorts of backdoor tricks for friends, especially sick friends—tricks I'd never once considered for myself. I was told that the paper's art editor must approve the listing of any dead artist. The obit editor explained, "I'm afraid I never heard of him myself. We only have room for major painters. Your friend, what was his name again? Yes, nice name. I'm sure a fine person but didn't have significant New York representation. A Boston artist mostly. No important museums. Just not well known enough for us. But I can give you the extension for the notices."

"Do, please. Now, the Notices? Because all this is new to me."

"Yes, the paid-for obits. 'The shorts.' You ready to copy?"

So I at least got Gideon on record. For a mere two hundred and fifty-nine dollars, he finally arrived into the *Times*. Though below, of course, and in smaller print. It didn't seem right, Gideon's only staying down in the Personals. He'd never graduated, never became—above, free—News.

—Gideon, we still talk about you all the time.

* * *

But here's the question . . . here's the question once you multiply our darling pal Gideon by ten, by Robert, by Marco, then four times ten . . . toward the two million. Here's the question. What to DO with a decade and a half of their phone numbers and street lore? What's to become of this now-pointless information?

I must decide: Shall I leave these loyal dead in my address book? Of course, I want them there. But bumping into them daily, each hooked to his final comet trail of medical 800 numbers, still stops me cold.

It's a minor yet momentous choice. There are memories that cannot be refiled, cannot be surpassed by contact with new people. I want to send a petition somewhere, to get my circle back, to settle them around that table for one more cafe latte, one typical, ordinary between-things day. A partly cloudy Tuesday might be good. I would send this petition direct to Management, were there one.

Do I sound bitter? Do I care? Well, *yeah*, as it happens. But, one problem with surviving: you risk seeming either self-congratulatory or somehow, your own lucky self, very wronged. Instead of being left here grateful, you're stuck with a brittle sort of veteran's pride. It's like those folks who did not name names to the House UnAmerican Committee; it makes you recast yourself as Joan of Arc and all the rest of them—cans of lighter fluid.

Cleaning out Marco's apartment felt strange. Both because it was right over Ossorio's, the site of so much action, and because not one of us had ever been invited in. It was almost scary, finally barging in to pack him up. Happily some of the guys who worked with Ossorio volunteered to help me purge. They acted more superstitious than I. Looking back, I see they feared . . . contagion. But, thing is, they forced themselves. That's all that you can really ask of anybody.

By then I needed extra pairs of hands. Gideon was gone, Robert so seriously down with it, and now Marco dead. Marco had been a birdwatcher. His place was covered with reproductions of the big Audubon prints. And dozens of bicycles being taken apart and reassembled. If I didn't know him better, I'd have considered this a chop shop. I later found the list of names of friends, and phone numbers where these bikes should be returned. But there were just gears, loose wheels all over. His mother and sister arrived, articulate warm people—not quite what I expected. In organizing, they found a hundred lists tucked everywhere. Marco had remained so clear and annotated to the end. I recalled his sixteen foreign words for "angel."

One such item was read aloud at the funeral; his sister handed it directly to me after the service. On a yellow hospital scratchpad from "Billing and Insurance," set down in script so tiny and pain-contracted it looked like a modern dance troupe of Martha Graham–trained ants, Marco Eisdorfer had written a list of over one hundred WORDS THAT RHYME WITH PAIN:

butane
Bahrain
birdbrain
cane
chilblain
cocaine
Citizen Kane
Dwane
Duane
Dusquene
deplane

And with his wit intact, the suffering surpassed even sounding like anything. He'd got clear to the S's when death, which respects only itself and is therefore humorless, shushed our boy.

(His mom and sister gave me that list to "use," and now I partly have, and therefore can rest easier.)

More and more, these deaths recalled my father's, my father. "He seems to have a fair-sized chip on both his shoulders," I'd once felt glad to overhear a neighbor say. Why did Dad feel singled out? Born poor, he got sent to work the counter as soon as he could stand and speak; he came of age during America's worst financial rout; he'd outlived that just in time to be stuck into uniform and sent to mind the store in France. How can you perfectly corrupt one whole generation?—First you take all the money away, then you explain that money is what mattered most; then you ship them off in uniforms to ensure an even greater conformity and, once home, you give the money back. And more. More than those aproned kids could ever have imagined owning. And you've perfected a group totally addicted to succeeding, at their own expense, and at their loved ones'.

Now I had my own disaster. It let me know how little my own dad could've managed in shaping his. I, assigned a sewer, perfected water acrobatics on its unlovely surface. But like him, you sacrifice form. But you get ashore alive.

And, later, after the next to last of my friends died, after I escaped New York, didn't I, moping around the hardware store of my new village, show both his affable surface and his overpressurized triggerpoint? People acted kind to me but I saw they felt they couldn't really count on me, not yet. They whispered around me.

In a shed behind my North Carolina house, I bent over some old windows. Each pane reflected the silhouette, stern, bowed, manly yet thickened toward the tanklike—and it was so much *him*, I had to rush indoors and sit somewhere and miss him.

Did I earlier say I didn't, that I only missed missing my father? What a flippant, queenly, overelegant and quite inaccurate revenge on half my being. I recall his three-pointed handkerchief as he headed to the Rainbow Room: "Watch out, New York!" I remember his saying, "Provide, provide, they told us." I recollect the sight of him, having dragged my mother's vacuum cleaner out into the garage, him down on all fours purging sand from the Buick's backseat carpet, and looking so intense and playful squatting there, using the screeching as something to hide in, his face grown childlike, rapt. Doing good, doing good well.

Oh, Dad. I never even "interviewed" you.

Would you, asked, have answered me?

I will go on record. I still don't exactly know why you were so strict with your young son. Did you fear that my emotions, my drama, would cut me off from seeming serious enough to be, say, anybody's dad? That's not true, Pop. I've several friends and children.

I sometimes miss you, Sir.

AFTER AFTER

The Company of Spirits

I can never write any sort of story unless it contains one character for whom I feel physical desire.

—TENNESSEE WILLIAMS,
Introduction to *Collected Stories*

Naming of Parts

It is here, to be observed, that after the funerals became so many that people could not toll the bell, mourn or weep, or wear black for one another, as they did before, no, nor so much as make coffins for those that died, so, after a while, the fury of the infection appeared to be so increased, that, in short, they shut up no houses at all. . . . All the remedies had been used till then were found fruitless, and that the plague spread itself with an irresistible fury; so that, as the fire the succeeding year spread itself and burnt with such violence that the citizens in despair gave over their endeavors to extinguish it, so in the plague it came at last to such violence, that the people sat still looking at one another, and seemed quite abandoned to despair. Whole streets seemed to be desolated, and not to be shut up only, but to be emptied of their inhabitants: doors were left open, windows stood shattering with the wind in empty houses, for want of people to shut them. People began to give up themselves to their fears, and to think that all regulations and methods were in vain, and that there was nothing to be hoped for but a universal desolation. And it was even in the height of this general despair that it pleased God to stay his hand, and to slack the fury of the contagion in such a manner as was even surprising, like its beginning, and demonstrated it to be his own particular hand.

I still use the one book for recording my friends' whereabouts. I'm averse to a Rolodex or computer screens for my own pal-tracking function. Books somehow appeal to me. Blame my love of the antique. I must now purchase new address ledgers at those serious office supply shops that rest between the solemnity of medicinal suppliers and the useful good cheer of hardcore hardware stores.

"I am merely Society's secretary," Balzac's fake modesty proclaims. But all address bookkeepers become novelists of sorts, charting entrances, chronicling exits. Divorces register; incoming newborns warrant the listing of full names. Wars and epidemics only heighten the hindsight drama of the role-call. This is the DNA "material" of life and, incidentally, of narrative art.

Those years I spent attending, nursing, celebrating, thirty-some waning boys, my straight friends spent having, nursing, teaching one baby. It's a lovely baby, mind you, and my godchild. It has golden curls and is, of course, a genius. The parents' engendering and then "changing" said baby seems laudable to all. My own loved ones were not brought into the world by me, but only, in my company, let out of it.

I know that my obit will read, "Leaves no immediate survivors." And I know my friends who're parents will be squired into their afterlife with the ennobling proclamation, "Leaves a son, Gaines, a student at New Haven . . ."

And yet, I feel I've earned a family, too. It's just not a family of survivors.

Now I understand another peculiar fact of physics: It is possible to sit before Love—even the love of someone dead—to sit before it as you would before a brand-new sunlamp, and to become, over time, quite tanned by it.

You can be bronzed toward health by the love of your missing. I still feel irradiated daily by the playful wit, even by the stubborn petulance, of absent friends.

—So, I've decided: I will keep them in the book. But they will be spelled in capitals all their own. The living, any possible new ones, will get only lowercase. The living friends will have their jumbled data entered and then changed in pencil. But inked, changeless now, my darlings are rendered bold, right where they left off, all caps, all stars, and honored there forever.

Please, though, tell me. Tell me that I managed to love them enough.

When they started getting sick, I feared I wouldn't do enough for them.

When so many were down with it, I feared I'd done too much. Now they're
dead; I'm shamed by all the chances missed.

I am just figuring out how to do it right next time around.

You hear of something called Survivor's Guilt. That's less than half the
story. With it comes Survivor's Pride, Survivor's Glee, Survivor's Fear of
Having Survived in Name Only. Add to that, a Survivor's obnoxious tendency to work every topic back around to a Survivor's survival. You can, if
you're lucky, tell yourself you're living for them, so they can better live via you.

I hear there's hope now. These new medical regimes can sometimes keep
the sickness beaten to one place. The procedures are expensive; the sickness
is still dreadful, but it's becoming something you can mostly live with. Pray.

And yet, a pro at this by now, I feel somewhat teased by the protease in-
hibitors. They just make the struggles of my loved ones feel even more early
early. Friends seem stuck even farther offshore that long night when our
beautiful boat went down. Till then, we sure did think that we were something.

This, my ledger record, is a huge debt only partly repaid.

Only now am I just starting to begin to know them, whole.

"Hello"—as I begin my second life.

With them.

Friend?

You have already written your brilliant, funny, and immortal autobiography. It will prove, in the end, your finest and most complicated work.

It is your address book.

Just after my father's, then Gideon's, then Marco's funerals, I went a bit
awry and fell over into a swerving sort of sewering grief. Looking back, I
think my dad's death cost me far more than I knew then. I was so fixed on
the injustice of my young friends going down to it. I almost took Natural
Causes for granted.

You can only postpone the self-pity for so long. And when it jumps you
all at once, it hits you like the beast in the jungle. Jugular, it goes for.

With them dead, I found that basically I did not care to caretake myself.

You cannot simply reach down now, tickle yourself and expect to laugh. Takes two, though three are even better. You can only bear to lose so many in a row. You keep turning for help to your next-to-last one down, keep expecting he might help you with this loss most recent. Missingness cannot support you. Soon, that steady whistle is the wind tunnel you live in. Soon—you can barely sit up on your futon—(and why do futons suddenly seem so passé? Why live in a city where everybody sleeps on the same sort of furniture in the self-same trendy season?).

Then I truly could not get up off my outmoded mattress. I lost those marginal unwanted fifteen pounds and then dropped thirty-five and people began avoiding me. But it was not That. At least, not That, directly.

Only Angie hung right in there, with awful jokes and flowers almost too perfect. "Just no white lilies, ever," I begged her. She laughed her best bad witch imitation.

She was the only one who kept on teasing me alive. "You have work to do. Potential, remember? That's where we all came in."

In the literature of sailing there's the term "becalmed." To us, these days so driven by speed's imperatives, it can sound desirable. It was actually a sailor's nightmare—to be left floating on a sailing ship far far from even sight or thought of land, with only windpower to push you, and then no breeze for weeks. I felt like that. All dressed up and no place to blow, anchored yet only in some void. My sails aloft, waiting for the only locomotion something so passive could count on . . . a push, a jump.

In those months before I fled New York, I still passed Ossorio's. But crossed to the street's other side, fear of who would not be visible there at "our" table, one reclaimed for the general good, dominoes now played there by the dapper older Cuban gents.

Then, if I can chronicle another change, and I am trying trying—several things lifted, a breeze had pushed me somewhat forward. As happens at the breakup of a depression so complete, I was moving before I quite noticed.

One thing that helped—an accidental stillness. How to survive? Do not remarry at once. Don't rush out and find "new friends." Some folks will foolishly buy a pet shop puppy the day they back over their beloved old beagle snoozing deaf in the sun-warmed drive.

"Give it a rest, Hartley." So folks said to me, touching my silvered temples and strained face as if these were geological formations that deserved their own postcard. I wondered what "it" meant. I've begun to know.

With assistance from the lady real estate agent who helped Mother find her place one village away, I came upon the very house I had long pictured. My expertise at packing others quickly came in handy. I learned to unpack, myself, so slowly.

When I leave this house here, I'll be crated out (by others).

Living in this little town, owner of two birdbaths regularly filled and used by multitudes for free, I do not go out more than two consecutive evenings. I linger with my missing ones. I have bought a porch rocker apiece, as the portraits of Marco, Gideon, and Robert, and six more of my missing. By the time I lured Angie down here to see my new-old place, she walked around the L-shaped porch and, poking a chair, announced, "Your rogue's gallery. A circle, the old familiars, hunh?" Placing her hand on the back of each rocker in turn, pushing it to see if it wobbled somewhat in character, she named every boy, a chair at a time.

She scared me, smiling. Got them all. "Perfect Double Jeopardy score," I told her but felt half undone. I settled on Gideon.

She next played musical friends. "Marco sits most comfortably, but Robert's throne's the prettiest by far, just not built for the long run, is it. Showboat."

As someone always lucky in his friends, I'd daily rush to our table for company, today's gossip political and sexual, consumed like more caffeine. (I all but got a headache if I missed two days' good trash and bustle.)

But now I was past forty-seven. That age in itself makes it easier to sit alone here for almost fifteen minutes. My sex drive—once the Indy 500 every weekday—has recanted to mere spirited Sunday drives. I remembered my grandfolks' weekly puttering tour of all land they owned, no rush, it'd be there.

If I could not spend time with my Robert, Ansel, Gideon, Marco—and if Angie was off traveling more and more lately—it might as well be me here. I would be interesting, at least, for having known those mythic others. This whole house had cost what one ghetto studio-apartment would. Now, suddenly absolved from nursing duty, I was free to relearn writing. But what to write about, but them?

I cannot bear, by now, to explain myself to strangers. Spelling out afresh my number of sibs, how many parents dead or living, my childhood ball-room dancing lessons while wearing those little white chimpanzee gloves—

the very prospect of my issuing charm toward some "date" (i.e., a total stranger!) makes me feel ill and worried, fake.

By now, such an inventory of my life history must include my friends! It'd take my whole remaining life to tell it, tell that, tell them all.

And who, new to my address book, would willingly learn so endless a yarn? Prom themes of Dead Iowa Boys. No one should indulge me.

So I would sit now. In portrait rockers of my dead. I would now learn to sit.

On the big porch of an old house in a little town, there's a semi-tubby man rocking, not reading a paper, not writing a letter, not doing his taxes, not doing nothing but setting there, listening to birdsong, and that is me now.

Am I lucky, or what?

And if I did not change the pandemic,
Q: How did it change me?
Answer:
    B.C.—I did not know anything.
    A.D.—Then I sorta did know I hadn't, known.

And post A.D.?—Now I fully know I knew almost enough. If Doing ranks among the crudest yet more honorable forms of Knowing. I pretty much did. Know.

Of Robert's ending all I'll say is that he understood we were in the room, that we'd drawn up close around his bed. Don't ask me how I know he knew. How do any of us know anything about the rest of us? Trust me, there are signs too subtle to leave even one overt smudgy stain. He knew it was I who held that bone rake previously considered the music-writing hand of an artist formerly known as Robert. He knew that Alabama had been forced to leave for her Berlin show. Those two had already said their goodbyes (just in case). I did and didn't want to be there to see the terms, the scale of it, but I suspected.

He knew I had just emptied his apartment of the kiddy porn and bigboy love stakes, coast clear now for his folks, so they could sleep in that most hospitable and proactive of fruit-topped beds. Before I phoned them there to grab a taxi and come fairly quickly please, I tried to tell him a tale, to make the subway mishap into a comic story for him: of a blue shopping bag that split on a uptown local. He was past speech since his last direct orders, "broom closet." But I could see a ghost of an eighth of a smile still hammocked somewhere in him. I knew that it—a joke about some vice of his made overly public and therefore comic—had reached our boy last thing. Amen.

Robert's was a genial, a stammering halt. He waited, dutiful, for his parents to rush in, without wanting to seem to rush. "I've called them, honey," I had said. He waited till they wrestled their coats off, then half collected themselves. I could see they had been napping or more (the magic bed's romantic effect?) and that the Gustafsons were flustered on account.

You watched him take in the room as does some swimmer waiting for the signal, the contestant strong and flexed in starter position at pool's edge, eyes still busy, playful, fixed just above water level on those loved ones waving, eyes busy and glad to be working a last time before true work begins, work mostly underneath.

Then it was that starting pistol, the determined if slowed movement as through water. His mother got on his right side, his father prayed aloud (eyes lifted) with such sweet faith, on his left. I wedged in at the feet. Surrounded, he knew he was. His eyes opened wide a last time, and he took in the room and I wondered if he looked for Angie and I fought feeling jealous of that, even now! He saw me at the foot of the bed and I, silly, waved, but it was all right because he gave the slightest nod and tried to lift the hand to his mouth for, I knew, a last blown kiss, so social, then put his head back on the pillow and began the ending of it in earnest.

He was no sentimentalist; he only attracted them. I stood tearless, taking note of how he managed it. His parents must be professionals at such scenes but that could only help so much, considering who we had here.

A perfect blond pebble skips three times across the lake's surface. Then, the next try, it skips just once. A third, in every way identical, it only sinks. But it settles right where you can—in water this clear—see it go straight down and rest upon its side there on the very very cold very bottom.

Porch Angels

esterday morning, years after most of the funerals, rising just before dawn, seeming to wake at some sound half-heard only in sleep, wearing a nightshirt Angie gave me, I wandered downstairs to make the necessary coffee. I've long since learned to drink mine black. Why? Ossorio, with a third-world cavalierness about refrigeration, could never keep his cream quite fresh. Daily, you would pay for the black addicting brew, you'd glory in its potent heat, you'd pour white into the dark disc and see a sudden irregular world map evolve. Here was the separation of the land from the sea and you saw it and you saw that it was not good. The cream.

I carried my mug out onto the porch of this, my Carolina clapboard claptrap. Such a porch was bound to be a selling point. It's almost U-shaped; though the left upright of the U has been lopped out of respect for an ancient magnolia towering there. My side porch overlooks an old graveyard and, beyond that and its church spire, our village's single busy street. I had settled in the one rocker that looks most like Robert, an Eastlake beauty if not that cozy for that long. I bent, nursing my coffee, listening as earliest birds got cranked up. Our third-grade teacher, Miss Crabtree, taught us: Birds don't sing for joy; they do it to insist upon their territory, to make themselves erotically attractive to their own tiny kind. We're eavesdroppers, turning guardian peeps into "music." So it was war and love I overheard in those trees. But surely, at this hour, some joy must seep in too.

This far from New York, this many years later, I've learned to distinguish every local birdsong, and not just by species. I mean I know which song comes from which actual bird. I have my faves, of course. Hear that? The brilliant male cardinal with a nest in the left-leaning sweetgum tree out back. The female jay's cry, in half-light, sounds urban with its nasty metal edge. My Carolina wrens make their sweetness felt—each bird no longer than your finger puts out a costly amplifier's worth of volume; the mourning dove repeats itself, a certain energized self-pity. And all piled up among the chips of mica-sound from silly English sparrows.

Light was just coming clear among the tree limbs near the silhouetted church. I sat rocking, thinking of my dead. The word "my" so warms that cooler noun, now doesn't it? I sat here feeling full yet robbed. I sat alone, longing for further news and texture from that missing quarter of my heart's address. I rocked, and drank my coffee black, a person clear and neutral, if hidden. At forty-seven, I'd been rendered further invisible by thinning hair, by the long lull in my résumé. Who was present? Just me and thirty casual acquaintances, the birds.

Then, from a few blocks off, from our volunteer fire department, a clanking and three shouts. The sirens started. Their noises built, needlessly, terribly, loud in a burg so hushed. Red light, drawing closer, stained many trees. Being pulled from my defenseless reverie, yanked to such modernity, I felt the clamor and light to be violent, half obscene. Sirens in

New York, I'd cease hearing. But in this village, everything soft even sounds loud.

Red truck headed right by here, I'd braced. And it was just then I heard the secret transaction.

I heard the birds—still tucked into dim thickets, the birds that send out cries not just for joy, but to state their claim and make lives felt by their own kind—adjust their volume upward. They planned to go on being heard above the fire truck's din. So, the rheostat in every little feathered throat turned up a bit. I felt I had just overheard some secret of the universe.

Birds' transparent sounds—till now so permeable and random, competitive—knit at once, shot vertica in stripes, defending this, my acre lawn, their home. Their sounds shielded me, and before official sunrise. I recalled those foreground webs in Angie's pictures.

How automatic came this impulse to defend—one's tree, one's young. However solitary I felt here, I remained an animal among other living animals.

Of course, I knew "my" birds did it just to keep on being heard, by other birds. But, in half-light, alone, it seemed to me their voices raged a bit for me, too. Friends on duty, guarding me now; thirty friends are a lot of friends, especially at dawn.

Soon the siren faded, soon our yard sank back to mist and hush. But, settled here in my RobertRobertRobert rocker, surrounded by an implied fortress that'd just ascended to some feathery Celestial City, I found I could finally tilt forward, I could breathe. With gratitude, which was my potential.

I said aloud to no one, everyone, just "So."

I nursed my still-warm cup. I held it closer to my chest, and some stray steam touched annex chins. A strange maturing chord change fathered forth down both my arms. Then, simple as a whistled three-note song, I understood:

I was on my porch alone. But I remained in chosen company.
I was in my life.

Rite

uring the long flight toward Iowa to bury him, both of us transferring into planes of decreasing size, I had felt aware of myself sitting with posture intentionally as good as his—him, a horizontal now—below me. And I held up fine. I reread "The Wound-Dresser." I told myself that my own mourning for Robert had been so long and gradual, there would, at the funeral, be fairly little left to do. Oh these necessary lies.

Even when his parents waved from the gate (father short in clerical garb, the mother Robert-colored but in a blue floral), even as I descended this primitive outdoor gangway (be careful going down careful), I was okay, really, glad for my recent time with these folks. It made this at least half a homecoming.

Odd how close I'd grown to the parents of many friends. At Ossorio's, our circle had pretended we owed nothing to our hick towns pre–New York. We behaved like a stable of young centaurs—amused by the rustic dray horses who believed they'd sired and foaled us.

But now, hungry for any proof of Lost Boys, I found exceptional evidence in these older faces—their genetic address books. The parents mostly showed such kindness, an odd grace, now the worst had happened.

—Cedar Rapids Airport requires you to use the outdoor ladders. These get wheeled against the side of your cropduster. I felt troubled by this detail from early aviation; had our pilot worn goggles? Had the crew left Robert back at O'Hare?

The Gustafsons and I would now wait for Angie's plane—San Francisco via Hawaii from Berlin. I'd reached her with the news just as she was getting dressed for her big opening at D.A.D. I hated the timing but it couldn't be helped. For once, I tried not blaming myself. The beginning of wisdom. Nothing personal in any of this.

The German press adored her rough name and the confident supple work, so colorful, so easy to discuss thematically. The Institute was showing everything, including a fragment of a childhood wildlife mural (it was amazing, the colors from the start were hers). This show would be a big stride forward in her International reputation. It'd help her chance of getting into the MOMA lobby someday.

* * *

While we expected Angie (late as usual, but this time not her fault), Robert's parents led me to the snack bar. Without saying why, we all sat along one side of the big booth, each facing one mirror with a view of the plane I had just left. We needed to make sure he had been on it. None of us acknowledged watching, as we made rueful formal small talk.

When, finally, the crate (fuckin' plywood!) came ratcheting down a rickety conveyor belt too narrow, we stopped midsentence. We sat here, all lined up, then somehow were holding hands as simply as kids will. We stayed hushed. On the runway, a hearse appeared from nowhere. One plump young man in a gray suit climbed out, carrying a clipboard. After he'd gathered the needed signatures, with help from airline staff, he eased the box into his deep black car. Then I saw him bound back around to the front of the plane. He stood facing the sun and, in exactly our direction, this mortician gave a single index finger salute.

"Ben. That Ben! Saw us." Robert's dad waved. I understood how small this town must be, how closely preachers must work with funeral directors, how suddenly visible we all were. Oh, when all this was done, how I would welcome village life again in North Carolina.

"We have gotten the most amazing flowers, from all over the world. One gigantic spray was made up by our local florist who tries hard but Val is not . . . New York. You see, we think it's intended to represent a ship. From something called *Lifeboat Number Thirteen*."

"Yes, he was in it. I mean, the group," I explained, and added (do it now, Hartley) there was actually something of Robert's that I wanted.

"Oh," she said. "Oh?" She warmed the word.

I dared not look at Mrs. Gustafson, I studied instead the winter horizon, "Just one thing. But, I warn you, it's big."

"The bed? The bed. Good, because we have only nine-foot ceilings in the parsonage, it'd never fit. Imagine chainsawing the legs off that, below the pineapple line. Yours. Done. Never quite understood what our boy *did* in a bed that size . . . I mean besides sleep." I told her he composed there.

"So, just to say a word about the service later, Hartley," she went on. "I will be leading my choir in a vocal transcription I've made from 'Barber's Adagio for Strings.' Bob has some remarks that he is enough of a pro to get through. In the bulletin we just put 'Reading by Hartley Mims, friend.' Hope that was all right. I copied the spelling from your magazine stories Robert always sent us. He was your biggest fan, as you know. And now we are."

She asked which poem I'd chosen. (They had said they would not impose on me for a eulogy. God knows I was willing, and able, but I sensed that this was a father's right. I understood. I had no official role here, past "friend." Which surely counts for something.)

Robert had asked that I read or speak. I now pulled from my satchel his own well-worn peach-colored collected Whitman.

Seated in the airport diner, they asked, "Would you consider. Now? —Her plane's not here for another twenty-three minutes. Would you, as . . . practice, to see if you . . . how it feels. It would be a favor to us really. Our small talk today feels increasingly small. Be nice to some poetry he liked."

I nodded, feeling uneasy, but why? Then I heard almost a laugh, and felt him breathe over my shoulder, amused, even by the awkwardness, especially that, since, among us, awkwardness is often what's most alive! That's why it scares us so.

So, here goes, over sounds of flight announcements and Muzak's arrangement of "Strangers in the Night," I cleared my throat, I leaned a little more their way:

" 'In Paths Untrodden' by Walt Whitman, from the Calamus poems, *Leaves of Grass*. Okay . . . here goes . . .

'In Paths Untrodden'

"In paths untrodden,
In the growth by margins of pond-waters,
Escaped from the standards hitherto published, from the usual
pleasures, profits, eruditions, conformities,
I know now a life, which does not exhibit itself, yet contains all the rest,
And now, separating, I celebrate that concealed but substantial life.
And now I care not to walk the earth unless a friend walk by my side,
And now I dare sing no other songs, only those of lovers.
Was it I who walked the earth disclaiming all except what I had in myself?
Was it I boasting how complete I was in myself?
O little I counted the comrade indispensable to me!
O how my soul—How the soul of man feeds, rejoices in its lover, its
dear friends!
Here by myself away from the clank of the world,
Tallying and talked to here by tongues aromatic,
No longer abased—for in this secluded spot I can respond as I would
not dare elsewhere,
Resolved to sing no songs today but those of manly attachment,
Bequeathing hence types of athletic love,
I proceed for all who are or have been young men,

To tell the secrets of my nights and days,
To celebrate the need of the love of athletic comrades."

They nodded, held back. It seemed okay. "That'll preach," the father said. Then we could, till Angie arrived, pick our way amidst the flat earlier conversation about weather, urban blight, my fantasy house search, how many square feet I'd like, comforting, nothing.

We soon stood at the gate awaiting her plane. This tired, I found myself feeling briefly miffed that Gideon, Ansel, and Marco weren't coming, why always me? Till I understood they were also dead.

Ansel's mother had just mailed Angie his obit in an envelope otherwise unmarked. I recalled the other two's funerals. I'd once heard of an athlete so fast he could throw a ball up and over the roof of his cottage and, by bolting through its open central door, catch it as it rattled down that roof's far side.

If it weren't for Angie as my fellow survivor, insanity would've seemed the likeliest of available bad options. To be in a nice white room of rest, a chamber decently padded, to be strapped in safe with a certain Mr. Whitman as a baritone male nurse read to me. The real Santa, and Santa's small would-be helper, fastened down here, me, safe.

It was good to expect something alive coming down out of that same sky that had brought Robert home.

Beside me, at the low gate, with two haphazard boy-guards to keep us off the field, Robert's mother said, in a girlish voice that made me recall my own mom's recent unruly youngish laugh, "I just feel I *look* so discomposed, Hartley. We ladies have our days when we appear acceptable and these other days. Of course, as I told Bob, how *should* I look? I've kept feeling ugly since he died. I am clean at least, right? Ask Bob."

"You're far from ugly, Mrs. Gustafson. You look just like him and we all know what he looks . . . like." Her husband gave me a glance that meant, She is upset, don't mind, most natural thing in the world, really. And man to man, my eyes responded.

"Yes, but it's strange, you know, that if I had just bought some new clothes, ones I believe Robert would've adored and called 'fabulous' whether he truly felt that or not, it would've helped me. Not to boast, but I was the one who taught him that word, you know, but in the original sense, as in a fable. So, to say fabulous means that something is really worthy of a fable, or a fairy tale. *He* was, of course. By the time we got back home from New York, sixty greetings and messages from around the world were waiting. People seemed to know without being told. Surprising, the scale of it . . . There're days I believe that Robert's great gift was to make us love him and, through that, to find each other. I did sometimes wonder if he received half of what we all sent him daily. He seemed to inspire more love than anyone, ever, but to need it less. Is this awful, I'm saying? Do I shock you, shock myself? I think not. When he was about two, I remember going in to check on him. Afternoon nap. It'd sure been quiet in there. My baby was sitting in his crib, just waiting for me, and then he smiled. I saw he'd planned to. Hard explaining. At times, the beauty of him then was almost spooky, even for me. You'd catch him with his thoughts. When I was pregnant, of course we didn't know whether to paint his nursery pink or blue, so I chose a pretty yolk yellow, and what it did to the color of his hair and skin all the time! That day, his eyes were bigger than they'd ever look again but I felt he was testing me.

"He was seeing what he could make me *do* by smiling like that. He had been spending his whole nap time practicing smiling, lying in wait. He didn't need a mirror. Robbie knew exactly how he looked, from when he was eighteen months. Our darling knew too much, and at the strangest angle, from the start. Seeing how much could a smile like that get him! The answer, of course, was—anything. Hartley, you might not know that he got into a little trouble way back when. Had certain scrapes, unexpected as it was, with drink."

"Yes, I heard him talk about that."

"But I've had no shopping time, what with our just getting home two days before . . . this day. Anyway, it's not like out East. We don't have one shop fine enough to sell me a dress that's good enough for Robert's . . . taste."

"Beka, you don't have to talk, sweet. Young Hartley here doesn't need to be entertained all day."

"I know. But I like to now. You were very kind to us in New York, and even before we knew what was going to have to happen. I hope we were all right back there. When you were so late, meeting us at his place, I hope we didn't seem snappish . . ."

"I was running just eleven minutes behind . . ."

"Yes, it's all right. Now I wish we'd flown out East for his concert, and with Aaron Copland, too. It was so foolish of us. You get busy and cannot see past Wednesday choir practice. Was it . . . really good?"

"Yes, ma'am," I said.

"Where is that plane? —I know young Angela will look fetching today. She looked so well when we last saw her in New York. She wore old-fashioned pearls out to dinner with us, very smart against her dark clothes. Very old-fashioned and tailored I would say. She seems so organized. Unlike me, she will know just how to do all this. I mean, to be in Berlin one day, and here for his service that same long day. In New York, she seemed so 'put together' as the fashion articles all call it now. She was Robert's ideal, really, wasn't she, Hartley? At one time, I'd hoped they would . . . But I'm not modern, I never understood all that much of what was really going on, I guess. But I think she's like the young Audrey Hepburn. She will be collected in a way I want to learn from. You see, that's it, I am trying to enjoy and learn now from his friends, Robert's. Our boy was always fortunate in his friends. Good judgment. Good judgment, right, Bob?" She touched my shoulder and I nearly leapt. She was trying to straighten my jacket collar, which I think, did not strictly need straightening.

Mrs. Gustafson now moved around before me and bent in very close and centered the knot of my one black tie. She, with her husband's smiling approval, pressed right up against the front of me, and let her fingers stray over my ears to coil my hair back neat (did I not look my best?). When I stared, in broad daylight, at the same long platinum lashes that she had wisely never sullied with black paint, and when she, chins appearing as she nodded more, concentrated on getting the tie perfectly knotted, her exertion gave off a slight scent. —And it was mainly his—vanilla and geranium leaves and something extra that was right between being wrong and perfect and then came so down on the good side. And how to say it? when she touched me, in that state? and brushed past my ear and smoothed my long hair back, I got an erection, not just from recalling him but believing there might, just might, be left in my life a chance with her. I know, insane. But we all of us really were just then.

Bama's plane finally lowered from nowhere, circled once while whining like some insect toy, and somehow landed. The ladder, lumbering and creaky, got maneuvered out by those two fine strong local lads. Business passengers came filing off first. On the tarmac, a great pyramid of army-green trunks and gear. Flight attendants stood at odd spots out there.

Against stark farmed winter vistas, they all faced opposite directions, till, in my disorientation, it seemed a dance piece planned by some avant-gardist of New York. All in honor of today's three strange New York arrivals.

Finally it was actual Alabama angled in the plane's door. She looked dead white, she wore a short black suit, a tiny black pillbox hat, and not-undramatic Callas-like dark glasses. She had on black gloves to hide her "peasant claws," as she called them. She already looked older. I thought how convenient black clothes are full-time since, when you're summoned from Berlin to an only half-expected Iowa funeral, you come equipped. From the start, she had always been equipped.

But now Bama seemed to pull back from garish yellow healthy sunlight.

Once again she bobbed forward before retreating. I saw, floating over her head, one corner of a sort of Jackie veil. She hung there in the metal portal, acting dubious of Cedar Rapids's even being real. She appeared disdainful, even somewhat harsh, disappointed. I knew her. I just knew that, in some griped jet-lagged part of her, she half expected to be met. And not by me. Not by his gentle, suffering folks.

"Why won't she come out?" Robert's mom asked no one who would answer.

Our Circle had always planned to travel to each other's hometowns, a personal tour, spots where we'd squandered our short-lived virginities, train tracks where a car wreck nearly took us out at nineteen.

Now the uniformed attendants meant to keep people off the runway slowly noticed her. A young lady not quite on the plane, but not coming off. She blinked, hesitating there. She did look oddly chic. She looked like someone well known if lost here. My Alabama Byrnes *was* that now.

But the one who finally ventured down those metal stairs looked more like my plain ole Angie, the kid who'd bowed to us all at the clinic, bowed like a boy forced into some family ceremony, a boy making a joke of the dark rental clothes he secretly liked.

Her free hand held a prissy black leather purse that reminded me of a carry-all for forty-five rpm records. She made it halfway down the ladder, clinging to its handrail like someone descending while on uppers. But I could tell she believed she resembled a thirties actress doing the spiral staircase while wearing chiffon to the tune of a wind machine.

"Is she . . . Bob?" Mrs. Gustafson asked. "I don't think she's well."

"She's well." I sounded overinsistent. "She's sad and she's tired but well, understand?"

Then I slid past the guards. We'd been told to stand back because of propellers and insurance restrictions, but as I jogged, I thought: What can they do to me, what's left to *do* to us now?

She, high heels having achieved asphalt, saw me. As I ran, dodging the pile of army equipment, she did too and grew bigger and, through her layers of widowhood, two white arms lifted. Angie barged so forward she ran past one of her own teetering high heels. She made a strange shrill laughing, "Hartley Airedale, son." I caught and lifted her and she, if short, still hoisted me right back, the two of us bobbing, lifting coughing, shifting weight, taking turns.

"It's true?" she shook me. She appeared far thinner; some white powder from her face was caking on the veil.

Then I saw her bend to peek under her own plane, scanning piles of luggage being carted here or there.

"What?" I asked, half stern in order to get through to her. And, beyond the dim gauze, Angie's pretty dark mouth said, "Is . . . it . . . is he *here* yet?"

I breathed. "Yeah. Signed, sealed, delivered, in your cowboy top and his historic velvet with the star pin right in place. —Now, come be nice to the parents again. I think I love the mother. I also feel I've been sitting with them at this airport all my life. She considers you a film star, so do get a grip, this is not no West Village Halloween, girlfriend."

"Honey?" she backed a foot away from me, as if afraid I would assault her. "I'm going down with it. It's everything happening at once, the show, on top of the others, on top of Robert. You actually feel it *in* you, very *Alien*. My little 'tote' is for such pills as one cute German doctor found me on short notice. Extremely in the throat. I thought it would make me feel closer to him but he is dead. I am not yet dead, one hears. I lied that day. You had so much on you already. We all did. You've guessed. I just didn't want to go *in*to it. Remember your offer? Well, since you're the last one standing, and seeing as how my mom considers sickness unladylike and won't let me cross the Georgia line, looks like you might just be stuck with me. But I warn you, even when I'm *healthy*, many intelligent people consider me the most dreadful bitch."

She stepped forward to hold me up a minute. She'd known she would probably have to. Her veil kept blowing in my mouth. I finally said to air above her shoulder, "You're not making this up. You're not playing around, are you?"

I felt her shake her head sideways just once. "Oh no."

I stumbled over then and flopped onto a trunk. I sat, as on some toilet, knees against elbows, hands loose, gaping down. I studied tar. I saw her bare stocking foot. It looked comic, pitiful. This was Iowa in winter. "It's just lucky for me," I stood, "that you're beautiful, a genius, and good. Here's what we're going to do together. You'll move to North Carolina, room with me. You'll rent a tobacco warehouse, northern exposure, then paint your absolute ass off. I can just see you and Mother, in her new white Miata convertible, you girls wearing white kerchiefs and your biggest sunglasses, youall slipping off to estate-jewelry auctions statewide. —It'll mainly be all right. Know one reason? We got his bed."

"Which helps," she blinked. "Funny how some Robbie hospitality still helps. So you *did* ask them. And they coughed it right over. —Hartley? you know? you've gotten braver."

"*I'm happy to learn that.* —So, Angie. How'd your paintings look, up?"

"Never better. Your Alabama is just three inches more immortal. Lot of fuckin' good it does *me*. But you've got the burden now. I honestly pity you. You are a hell of a nurse, though. Remember the fat RN at St. Vincent's coming in to ask you about the contact-lens fluid you used to clean his catheter? And now Cinderella finally gets the benefit of all your princely training-on-the-job. I'm afraid I'll be quite a number, patient-wise. Do my best, though. —We played so hard so well together. What *hap*pened to us?"

"Not a clue."

"Well, get one. Because, Hart?" She lifted my writing hand, then kissed, like a strand of lucky pearls, every single knuckle.

"Hart? You figure you can *make* something out of it? Our all ending up like this?"

"Yeah. Slow learner, but he learns. Yes ma'am. Believe I can."

My saying that, it worked on her like the finest of all drugs. Across a beloved face that had only been confusion—I saw something slip— something like the warmth of a whole new career.

"Say 'I do,' " I said.

" 'I do.' "

"Okay then. Because our bed is huge."

I could see the crowd near the depot watching. I felt conspicuous. What matter? She was here. So, then, propping each other up, we hobbled toward the Gustafsons. Best behavior, the little hardened-sugar couple came down off the wedding cake. I soon noticed that, behind us, a stewardess was bringing Angie's lost high heel; I saw how that pretty uniformed girl was lifting it aloft, as if it were some valuable slipper that meant something in a fairy tale. Which this was. Is. —The princess's shoe that'll fit only one gal in the kingdom and deserves, due to magic, respect. Then I spied, tucked beneath the hostess's other arm, a glossy brochure. For its cover, an Angie painting reproduced big in living color, then inscribed to the stewardess. I decided, with a mixture of betrayal and delight, "They Know Who She Is. Thanks to *HER*, They Know. And Thanks, I Guess, to *US*."

We approached Robert's tall blond mother and his short white-collared father, both of them freely waving, crying some. Maybe from watching us out there. Worried, guessing. We'd been being fully who we were, I think, at least in part for them.

Angie neared them first, gloved hand out, poise itself. "Reverend and Mrs. Gustafson—Bob, Beka, I am so sorry. He gave us everything he had, didn't he? Held nothing back, our love. —How are *you* all bearing up?"

Other passengers lingered, turning back this way. Angie's widow's weeds must've helped make plain at least her role in this. Strangers appeared a bit confused, but they surely acted interested. They seemed to understand at least a few things—somebody important had just arrived, someone who could use this whole town's epic caretaking. I still felt embarrassed, but why?

Let them learn a little.
We were worth it.
Let them go ahead and stare.

Payday

urns out, there are at least four days in the history of Manhattan: the day you first see it, the day you get to move there, that day you—far smarter, far less intact—still find the strength to leave; and the morning you go back, as New York's most loving, humbled, overqualified tourist.

Been here, done this, know which train.

My agent's office is being painted, terrible fumes. We need a place to meet midtown. I've owned my house in North Carolina for, what? Going on five years. Amazing. My original accent is seeping back to sticky authenticity; my speed has changed from nursing's gallop to recovery's full stop; now it's regained a smoother lope between. I have a few new friends; my first ones were the guys who helped me restore my house. Then acquaintance spread out through the village. Isolation was, for me, a hard state to achieve; I only got there by subtraction. Despite my resolution of solitude, it proved a toughie to maintain. You get pulled back into the world so soon. Especially if you're nosy. Nosy is another word for hopeful. —You might laugh to hear I have been asked to join the volunteer fire department, just blocks from my house. I'm still debating. But you should see the talent-level in their busy shower room.

My agent, loyal through everything, suggested that we meet here at the Museum of Modern Art. She's usually ten minutes late, for effect. That's the birthright of physically beautiful people, a right I grew used to long ago. I settle on one of those backless benches to the lobby's east, the wall nearest their bookshop.

It's December and, through revolving doors, people maneuver huge giftwrapped packages. It has just begun to snow. Must be the season's first storm, judging from how pleased-looking people appear lunging in here. Two women arrive smiling, shaking white powder from their hair, purging fat fur collars.

I sit reading the *Times*, waiting, though basically I have no talent for waiting. So I try to engage myself by studying tourists (pretending I am not one). These days, I am so out of all things art world; I subscribe to no glossy national magazines, just one local paper; instead I garden, putter, eat, birdwatch. And remember. I have learned to sit in each rocker for up to eleven minutes. Sit there, blank, safe, fatter, stiller.

I know I miss a lot up here in the city. If you lived in Manhattan for fifteen years and if you have the kind of memory I do, you still recognize certain faces from back then. Older, of course, they're looking more prosperous or seedier. But over there, I see two people, both artists, long married, our age. We all attended openings together; they wouldn't know a dropout like me but I recall them. They're older but still seem flourishing, a pair.

Sometimes when you're feeling agitated, your eyes will choose some arbitrary resting spot. Behind the dark coats of scruffy gorgeous Swedish students, beyond the usual Park Avenue matrons using art as their respectable starting place for luncheon-shopping expeditions, I come to idly focus on a new painting. It is the only picture in this lobby.

I've never before seen it. A huge oil, done in blacks and whites, and subtlest pinkish-grays. At once, of course, I know the artist. My sinuses burn. For a moment, part of me wants to bolt from here; another longs to turn toward those audibly revolving doors, expecting a two-part appointment made years ago.

Schoolgirls in gray pleated skirts and blue blazers cluster before the huge canvas. They bunch around their lady teacher, who is pointing out one portion of it—careful not to make actual contact with the valuable surface.

I fold my newspaper and, feeling a strange kind of hunter's excitement, almost a nausea of attention, rise. I approach the painting, but slow, as if stalking the rarest of game. It might move. It might leap away, achieve the street, run straight for woods.

I feel atypically tall, somewhat wobbly, older than seems possible, thicker at my palpitating center. And yet I somehow make my Airedale way across this crowded public civic space. I keep my head down, fearful that, if I confront my goal too directly, someone, something, might push me back from it.

A fear comes: I will die before I get to it.

But no, you don't even need a ticket to see this one. It's the "teaser" that they stick in front of sideshows. Surefire bait to draw you in. I slide through conversations in three languages I can identify but not speak.

Its underpainting has a snapping and splashed energy. Raw X's form the basic grid. These marks have been set down with an enviable sense of brushy freedom. Paint was trusted to do what it must at this impossible speed.

Hidden among the darks, stenciled digits, letters resting on their sides, paint scraped very thick, runes arranged—it seems—with a sort of archaic grandeur. Since the picture stretches six by nine feet, you feel that any artist who could manage so long a reach must be someone of immense physical scale.

Set overtop this whorl and slap, a frame of draperies, rendered as if around some puppet stage, valance swags around the picture's entire top. Within curtains, susceptible to blackness underneath—a faint pink over-sketch shows a cottage, grayish rose. It has shutters, an opened half door, thatched roof, hollyhocks and azaleas standing sentinel, drifts of sea foam. This home seems the witch's, as overly inviting as one in some fairy tale that is all violent twists. The kitschy sketch, though done with much ironic haste, still seems full of longing. There's something childlike in its false cheer, the pathos of promised shelter.

Up and down either six-foot end, words show through the paint. First these look like accidental squiggles, until, closer, you see they're sentences; each has been speckled with paint so as to at first seem hidden.

But I just saw two schoolgirls cock their heads, deciphering the flanking statements. One, to the right, offers the promise of fond slavery, a hope for free meals ahead; the left one threatens the artist's very hands, promises the artist will soon suffer terribly and never paint again.

Finally, in the picture's lower center, two human hands are outlined, then painted to appear dimensional. They exist side by side, small puppets downstage within too large a proscenium. A His, a Hers. Her hand wears a ring.

From its stone, a compass radiates. Elaborate directional arrows reach the picture's farthest edges. The arrows are rendered in many fine lines as from some antique engraved map. At the center of this compass, in the picture's bottom center, on the ring finger of the smaller hand, hers, a collage element.

The third finger seems dwarfed by so huge a gemstone, a big pale chunk, three-dimensional. I bend nearer to see it better:

It is a block of wood, maybe eight inches square. It has been enameled white—the outer edges outlined in sloppy double stripes of black. And, as on some child's nursery building block, in the center of each, freely hand-painted, rests the number 282.

I try ignoring the teacher's standardized lecture on this artist. Gender role questioning, "masculine" approach to paint application but a psychological . . . etc. I wait. A pretty droopy girl finally scuffs off, revealing the wall-mounted label. Not wanting to whip out my reading glasses (they date me so), instead I ease back two full feet. Back, more back, till these official modernist block letters playing before my eyes finally swim into a clarity that holds.

Artist: Alabama Byrnes
American. Female. b. 1952. d. 1990.
Oil and collage. 9 by 6 feet.
Former estate of the
artist, recent gift of
the Vincent Astor
Foundation.
Title:
Patient Number

We found it impossible to express the change that appeared in the very countenances of the people . . . . . .They would open their windows and call from one house to another, "What good news?" And when they answered that the plague was abated, and the bills (of deaths) decreased almost two thousand, they would cry out, "God be praised!" and would weep aloud for joy . . . And such was the joy of the people, that it was, as it were, life to them from the grave.

They shook one another by the hands in the streets, who would hardly go on the same side of the way before. I could also set down many extravagant things done in the excess of their joy as of their grief; but that would be to lessen the value of it . . .

Human help and human skill were at an end. The common people went along the streets, giving God thanks for their deliverance. . . . Indeed, we were no more afraid now to pass by a man with a white cap upon his head, or with a cloth wrapped round his neck, or with his leg limping—all which were frightful to the last degree but the week before.

But now these streets were full of them, and these poor recovering creatures, give them their due, appeared very sensible of their unexpected delivery . . .

I can go no further here. I should be counted censorious, and perhaps unjust, if I should enter into the unpleasing work of reflecting . . . upon the unthankfulness and return of all manner of wickedness among us, which I was an eyewitness of myself.

I shall therefore conclude the account of this calamitous year with a coarse but a sincere stanza of my own, placed at the end of my ordinary memorandums the same year they were written:

A dreadful plague in London was.
In the year sixty-five,
Which swept an hundred
thousand souls
Away, Yet I alive.

Appendix

July 3, 1984
Fiction: Approx. 50,000 wds.
Please return in SASE to:
Hartley Mims jr.
PO Box 6114, Canal Street Station
New York, New York 10011

TOWARD A MORE PRECISE IDENTIFICATION OF THE NEWER ANGELS

Having just died, having been judged unexpectedly worthy, you—new recruit—find yourself transposed up those infinite octaves separating you, the truly righteous, from the rest of those deadbeats left down there.

Glad you're aboard. You've earned it.

You are saved from the ranks of the dull and greedy. You are set apart from the recent attorneys general whose one defense ran, "I have not been indicted yet." How does it feel, being finally unlatched from pain? I am here to welcome you.

I have greeted many.

(Some complain that during these wake-up calls, I "editorialize." But, for me, you see, strong opinion is paradise.) Been here for absolute ever. My exact age, thank God, is finally irrelevant. I can't believe how much I cared. Time was such a Drag. My dears, we are well shut of it.

In Paradise, we organize by color. Later, God will put on such a show for you. You'll see hues that you cannot yet name. I will teach you what we call each one.

What do you thousands of souls have in common? A superstitious fondness for the lucky numbers 1, 3, and 7. For the color red. Among you, find more Geminis and Scorpios than any other sign—(we notice astrology but don't quite believe it here either).

As a group, you all exhibit a sense of humor often criticized as "infantile." You have a secret sweet tooth. You enjoy playing around. You show a passion for collecting anything from salt-cellars to orphans. There's real talent at empathy, a quiet yet profound interest in sex (more about that later). You've each kept a garden, if only a window-box. The amount of fund-raising you did, we angels first admired, then pitied. Your virtue runs alongside a scofflaw's hatred for paying parking tickets.

And, today there's the surprise element. First, you feel astonished at the fact of a Paradise, any paradise. Then you're shocked on being picked for it. But, see, that constitutes your righteousness, you silly willies!

Yes, there is a Hell. And it's becoming quite the crowded spot just now. But why bother your pretty little heads about

1

that? My job is to situate you here. —Even so, is it not delicious? Picturing the pain endured by certain lowlifes who divorced you, overborrowed from you, and, in forty-nine cases present, killed you!—They're finally really paying. Hell is their constant root canal. Torture will keep them screaming through eternity. (Never doubt God loves you.)

We find our entering class gets annually smaller. Even so, what still ascends to us, it deeply edifies. You constitute whatever center of the moral universe still holds. Lately, little has. Attendant rewards await you.

It is those I wish to sketch. Among your group, find no representative of the Executive or Legislative branches. A handful from Judicial did squeak through. As usual, very few of the professionally religious made our last cut. There is some fairness, after all. A shocker in itself, no?

—Odd, but Immortality is quite easy to embrace (especially one's own). What's harder to accept is justice.

(This, you're in, is the indoctrination for Westerners. We have an African and an Asian session going on concurrently. Though you can now speak every language, God considers certain rewards untranslatable except into the language that you used most recently. —Even here, nobody's everybody.)

How does it feel, opening your eyes on pure vista-possibility? It's all horizon here, and never dark, and your very feet are planted on gelatinous light. What is it you miss most? That too shall find you on high. Room service knows your every wish; it'll be up shortly.

Let's call this Freshman Orientation, shall we? You will soon learn house rules for The Conversation. It is my joy to describe certain literal facts of your sudden exquisite setup.

Magna—Blue: II

Shall we begin with your new shapes? I see a few in back starting to notice each other. No criticism implied, go on. True, you're altered. Actually "transformed" (to do the Miracle full credit).

You will each find, upon more careful examination, that you've been minted into an envelope of white light. Your brand-new semi-see-through carapace is composed of cloud salt-granules. Your body-packet contains only about as much gummy connective tissue as is found in, say, one good-sized fertile earthly salamander, or, the glue of nine, count 'em, nine, commemorative stamps.

Touch your face. It is still yours. We, the angelic, might at first appear similar. But our essential personal differences have been archivally and lovingly preserved. God has quite the filing system. This is a Soul Museum. It stars only those souls that remained transitive and evolving, not ones long since exhausted, set and stuffed. Certain traces of the old world have come along with you intact. Many other saints will seem, like you, dark horses for eternal life. There is a woman here who seduced her son unknowingly. There is a someone present who murdered another. The top crowd is never quite what you expect. The skills rewarded here are not wage-earning ones. You were mainly kind to others. You were each very good with your hands. You were all pretty good in the sack.

Paradise would not deprive you of that most beautiful achievement constructed during your earthly sentence. I mean, of course, your hard-won Character. We all struggled to stay honest, we each endured a different set of trials. We are not just another army. Soon I will lead you into touching those few outward parts of yourself left utterly intact.

First, caress your face. Fingertips will hint: You now wear a cataracted helmet shielding your former features. You are pressing your new face. It encloses and eternally preserves the old one. —I must say, the new one looks far better. Believe me. I'm out here. I can see you.

The wings are there, of course, behind. Not to fret, don't consider them a responsibility. Clear of your sight, they're useful should you ever need them, like overabundant closet space. In time, we'll be getting back to your wings.

I note your expression, 89th from the left, 140 rows back. I'm like you. On first arriving, I also found the whole concept of Wingedness a little retro. This far into time's vertical future, "wing shapes" are more a tradition than a flight requirement. Since we can now time/space travel at will, such canaryish trappings strike me as coy, vestigial, and pesky as were appendixes last go-round. —But nobody asked.

Still, I am allowed to dissent. Crabbiness has always offered me a pleasure supernatural. So, God—having somehow slipped up and made me an angel—allows this level of crossness to grumble on forever. God's really sorta good at this.

Heaven has been tailored to our former faults, not just our dull on-rolling merits. Bliss is never general.

If you envisioned something in your last life, you can fully do that here. Not "do," but "have done." For, to picture a deed in Paradise is to enact it, is to instantly recall it. That is a paradox of God—He/She has never been an entity dwelling in Present tense. God is perfect Memory, the energy to Play, plus endless Time. Anything that was ever forgotten (that is, absolutely everything) eventually finds us here, in our ecstatic Lost and Found.

But I get ahead of myself, or behind . . .

If you nursed one unacted wish below, if you loved some-one who ignored you, here that yen has already been ful-filled to the point of sorest satiation. Find it well-stowed in the gelid honeyed aspic of collective memory. This is not the zone of Desires Transacted. Heaven is the zone of Desires Recalled. Maybe you wish you had once wisely bro-ken a rule. —Done.

Example? I might say, oh, "Homemade lemon meringue pie, cooling on a Rhode Island windowsill before its browned peaks even get to harden toward stickiness. A confection made twenty minutes back by your own mom who'll be dead (drunk driver, laundry truck) before supper time—her final creation and gift, steam rising, set in the kitchen window on a tea towel, with a view beyond, of your backyard's blooming fruit trees. You wander home from school. Mom's car is gone. You see Mom's pie waiting. Her baked goods—good, as usual—smell of her standard grated lemon rind, all held by the lightest possible crust. And you, age nine, aching to sneak a wedge, eucharist. In life, you did not. The wreck happened. You could hear it from the house. Aunts converged. Casseroles arrived. The pie was first refrigerated then—as newer treats swarmed in—'tossed,' uneaten. But now, in Para-dise, wise wisher, you get to taste both it and her." There, I hear those new lips smacking.

O but I love the sound of your laughter. You cannot imag-ine the music of first laughs hatching into light here. I spent much of my earthly energy loving others. Know what they did? They all left me. Coming in through the backdoor, I dreaded seeing the note again on the kitchen table, "You were nice and always gentle and so I am not sure why, but I do know I'm gone for good." The dresser drawers half emp-tied, our bundled savings fully cleared.

But this time, for all time, for me, it's always Hello. Hello, forever. Thank you, Gracious God . . . Such plea-sure. I've been volunteering for this duty since . . . you've no idea . . .

If, sudden friends, you find you're itching under those new wing blades? that's usual. Not your fault. It comes from burning toward your present purified un-matter. It comes via simple sea salts so missing their other cruder, merely chemi-cal, reality. The early need to scratch is just one of Transformation-retooling's minor techno-glitches.

That roar you will be hearing intermittently forever is called Euphoria. You'll learn to tamp it back a bit should

4

it ever interfere with The Conversation. Nothing must ever obscure one glorious word of that, our communal enterprise:

The Conversation, our highest form of folk art. Cerebral, circular, sexual, musical, celestial—you have just arrived midsentence at the longest dormitory bull session on record. Heaven is pure communion with your own source in others, with theirs in you.

The scale of Heavenly talk is not symphonic . . . that was merely poignant human overreaching. Heaven is Chamber Music, a give-take chat and revelation, confusion finally fully harmonized, a gossip where history, picnic sensation, philosophy, mathematical verity, and especially the earthly acts of eating, eliminating, plus all deeds sexual, have been conjoined to form a single round-the-clock state, a forward beating rolling motion we call Joy.—There, I heard a giggle over there. Good. Go with that.

Some mortals do their weekly Meals-on-Wheels gig just to appease a superstitious prospect of heavenly reward. They missed The Boat. Such climbers and overachievers are not, alas, for us. Not one of them stands among you. Fact is, 39 percent of you are atheists. Were . . .

All of you got here the hard way, via the back stairs' long spiral climb. —Among us, find not a single glad-hander from the Business Community of Atlanta. We've included only two "career" Manhattanites, and no Parisians. Our ranks . . . our

Uhum, excuse me. I see you three whispering, on the two hundred and ninety-fifth queue back? Yes, you. Look, I'm sure you're keyed up. I don't doubt you have scads to chat about. But I ain't exactly your average flight attendant up here delivering the same old crash-lore, my dears.

There'll be mucho time for your little personal exchanges later, thank you . . . (—I swear, in every group, we get a few . . .) Where was I? Oh yes, Paradise, etc. Our ranks are comprised solely of seeming nonbelievers who somehow found ways to live believingly.

Having devoted yourselves to the chance of finding meaning—you each came, if-half-by-accident, to actually believe.

In something.

What is the rarest commodity left down there on your self-tainting, self-pitying planet? Belief.

And you bottled your homebrew of it. Belief is a vintage that can only be created a bathtubful at a time. Micro-breweries predominate. You fermented your own, for home use only. And now your joy is just commencing. Believe God. Believe me.

How you suffered. We saw. I know.

5

What's coming is such sweet payback, my fellow survivors. Oh, but we tried hard, didn't we? The wasteful cruelty of that rigged game.

You know my own last conscious thoughts? An awareness of my teeth!

Among you, I see former postmen, four invaluable dental assistants (all were blond and coincidentally named "Sandy"). Back there, transformed today, we have a man from Estonia who drowned and the complete stranger who saw him going under, stopped the car, plunged off a bridge to save him, and drowned trying. Yes, we've put you side by side, how lovely, look at them clinging. —Say hello. You'll know each other here.

Your life alone did not win you Paradise. Your dying did, new children. Yours showed acceptance, subtlety, patience with a bad plan that none of us created. You opened to it, let it roll through you like smoke.

—Perpetual glee is spread luminous before you. And your joy is not just cavorting on those wings (low-maintenance, two in number, semipermeable, and soon as easy to use as were your earthly eyes). No, Heaven's truest reward is the good company of your cocitizens. Even here, God is best seen refracted among the varieties of human character.

Timbre—Red: III

One of our surprising customs is a pleasure largely unpracticed on Earth for decades: I mean Uninterrupted Visiting. "Hell is other people," wrote one sad man.
—But, you see, if Hell is other people, so is Heaven. Heaven is just Other other people.

Imagine speaking steadily, commingling your wings, merging your new skin salamander-fine with, say, Plato? Leonardo, Bach, Mozart, Jane Austen, Rembrandt—who'd still rather draw and does so with a finger in the air. You're comfortable with George Eliot, Chekhov, Thelonious Sphere Monk, Virginia Woolf, Montaigne, Billie Holiday, and one of the Wright brothers (I can never remember which, but he's definitely on my side of the antiwing debate).

We've Shakespeare (a sexual athlete and absolute stitch). Shakespeare and Lincoln have become inseparable here lately, thick as thieves; Shakespeare thinks he invented Lincoln and—a very funny man, his sense of humor dark as corn syrup—Lincoln lets Shakespeare. Typical.

Einstein always mostly wanted to play his violin better and now he's cosmically fantastical at that. He'll engage in physics shoptalk solely by performing Mozart, Brahms, and a little Korngold. Buster Keaton, when things get slow, does one of his "falls"—going straight down through clouds, you'll love it. George Washington? He's always just sort of standing around, lovely man I guess, but has nothing to say. Jefferson? In Hell. Go figure. —Gandhi, surprisingly, is something of a stick. We do have Henry James, fine company, but—even by our eternal standards—God love him—he can go on.

All these and you are interchangeable, best friends. You have entered a domain of ease and genius known as Play. Competition has been forever expunged. Here, everyone's achievement becomes everyone's, circular. The glad ironies pile up.

Yes, we have a Heavenly Choir but its chapel master is not J. S. Bach. Bach feels happy to serve as second in command under one Thomas K. Pine, a former Baptist "Minister of Music" at Hot Springs, Arkansas, whose compositional gifts are, according to Bach, "one hundred thousand times my own."
Thomas K. Pine was leading a huge youth choir through his own brilliant contrapuntal setting of "Nearer My God to Thee." This happened in 1901 in a park's green metal bandshell during a July Fourth celebration when, soaked from the sudden downpour, Mr. Pine was struck and killed by lightning at the age of twenty. For Heaven, the gangly red-haired boy proved something of a shoo-in. Now Bach goes to school to Thomas K. Pine and we're all the richer for their daily playing. Trust me.

Tips on Things to Try First? You have sudden access to all languages and patois, all facts and contradictions of intergalactic history, and these are constantly at play, as Heaven is daylight steadily. Your mind can go anywhere, can become anyone in any language of any period; some of you have always known this. But here, see, you enjoy God's own fact-finding support system, all the enabling knowledge ever available—now yours.

Which fact to pull forth as your initiating example? I do love examples, don't you? Heavenly light has the yellow-white clarity of Fairy Tale, of pure Continuous Example. May I ask someone to volunteer the name of a well-known historical figure? Good, "Elizabeth the First." I should warn you that, here at the beginning, it's all going to sound like we're all constantly showing off, umkay? —But, what real-life Elizabethanism presently seems most striking? well . . .

On the day Elizabeth decided if she should execute Mary Queen of Scots, she prayed for some omen. Queen

Bess—carrot-topped and balding, pockmarked, beaky, brilliant—did, of course, feel a certain poisonous jealousy toward all usurping Papist cousins, especially prettier younger female ones.

At luncheon, Elizabeth bit into a ripe raspberry. What she did not swallow, popped forth, speckling her white neck ruff, four spots of glistening crimson. This became the Proof she sought. Cousin Mary's beheading was ordered, loud, at once. (The farmer who grew the luscious berries that inspired assassination was one Ezekiel Booth, the latent great-great-great-grandfather of a bad actor who'd shoot Lincoln.) After Elizabeth's own death, molecules retained from the portentous berry departed her remains, entered a nearby elder bush whose wood became marquetry in the captain's quarters of a fourmaster that in 1771 sailed to America, where the great ship was finally scrapped in 1804, its better interior surfaces purchased by a clock maker whose elaborate gonging mantel timepiece rode a Conestoga wagon West where, honored as an heirloom in Sacramento, it burned during a housefire, the splinters rendered into mulch taken up by the very strawberries then served to Bette Davis, on camera, as she played Elizabeth I with such psychic skill.

I could go on. It being Paradise, you can . . . Rest assured, You will.

The promised show is coming. Nine thousand new colors. You will be essential in God's promised show.

Eating here and sleeping here and the nuisance of elimination are optional. But many of our ranks still choose to exercise these functions in memory (and therefore deed). Old habits die hard. Habits seem, in fact, less willing to stop living than does any single human life!

Sneezes have lately proved popular. Sneezing is a hobby as arbitrary as taking snuff. But sneeze these silly angels do, remembering.

I find such fads endearing. They're unpredictable as our former species itself, and just as lavishly perverse. Certain rituals of the bathroom recall our lower starter-life as little else here can. "Voiding" is catching on in certain circles—you see them seated, knee to knee, salamander-smooth backsides exposed. Quaint, loggy, primitive, hopeless, soporific, yet engaging as human life itself.

Sex? You think we're superior to that on high? With all this time on our hands? Rethink, my new beauties. You'll find no virgins in Paradise—at least not for long. (O, sure, they're a few holdouts. Emily Dickinson, Winslow Homer,

Joseph Cornell, and Vincent van Gogh, actually. And I mean everybody's after them.)

But, on this plane, there is, as the hit song tried saying, "a whole lot of fuckin' going on." You need only consider trying the act with someone, need only find a pooled majority vote, and instantly—indeed almost involuntarily—you two are at it. Oftentimes midair. Others, materialized nearby, get to watch. All in the family. No need for your partner to even announce his/her name or former occupation or death date—you know that already. (You know everything, my dear ones. And instead of being phone-book boring, Omniscience—one now realizes—is such a turn-on.)

Before, you had to sneak off somewhere fugitive to "do it." But, here, anytime-anywhere, you ARE it.

And, hey, no need for messy debilitating anticlimactic contraception. Deadly diseases? No sweat. You are midair, you are your featherbed, and you are at it, in it, you're guiltless (unless, of course, guilt alone still gets your overmortal mojo going).

Joined to your latest beloved, you utterly inwardly know each other's deepest trigger spots—all your encoded prelingual animal oinks are placed before you like piano keyboards. "Higher," "There," "Unnnnh," "Wetter," "Less Teethies," etc.

Imagine the sensation of "simultaneous orgasm" stretched out to ejaculatory increments across pearly eternity entire. The screaming can be funny.

Mainly, genital-mentally, we communicate.

Arriving, you just saw the gigantic Crystal Gate. You read its simple yet profound inscription.

By heavenly standards, the Gate is new. I suppose its design must have a few proponents. The thing does glisten becomingly. But, while icy in its perfect form, though all but planetary in its scale—for me, The New Gate is no better than, say, the St. Louis Arch. A leetle bor-ing.

For Reasons all Her/His Own, God has lately set a Mr. Steuben loose "improving" our monuments. Back when I arrived, the great Bernini was still in charge. —And, as clean and World's Fairish as these immense crystal paperweight thingums do look, you can't imagine . . . before.

The choice of Mr. Steuben—and the recalled ruins of our former lives—both make clear the obvious: God's Got Everything but Taste.

Insecurities persist. From here, my dears, all our earthly struggles look puppet-dumb if labor-intensive. From way up here, it all appears Claymation.

Some of you are wondering if you "deserve" such epic

rewards. If you're "up" to Heaven. You never thought of yourself as particularly GOOD, right? Actually, you often weren't. It's the contrast to those other slugs that makes you seem a total saint.

The others said, "Who'll know?" "What difference will it make in fifty years?" "As long as you've already taken off your knickers, tramp, maybe just this once." Meanwhile you were down there, muddling through, sweating out your quarterly estimateds, still playing by the rules, sweet fool.

Alive, I myself did most everything wrong. I even did wrong wrong. I can't say more. I had a sort of life, I guess. I overtrusted. Let us all enjoy eternal After. As for my life, Before—I don't want to go into it.

—Soon you will see the promised Show. How can I place Heaven's Spectacle of Light in proper perspective? Earthlings go on and on about the Aurora Borealis. You know what the Aurora Borealis is? Leakage.

Imbue—Yellow: IV

Though nine and a half percent of you died illiterate, the largest single occupation among your group is/was teachers. Any teacher who would submit to that low a salary, to the inner-city parking situation, and who then—en route to a graffitied classroom—also daily agreed to being frisked by early-morning metal detectors, well, you caught our eye.

Among you, find a fifty-year-old daughter from Brest, France. She lived with her talented pianist mother, was her mother's best friend. She eventually killed her mother because that cheerful woman, in such pain from spinal cancer, begged begged begged her to. The obliging daughter, using Mom's own favorite pillow, succeeded, died in prison for her kindness. There, back there, step out, you two—reunited. Look, yes, there you both are again. Embrace. Hello. Forever.

I see among you a breeder of Labradors despite her severe allergy to dog hair, a shoe manufacturer, a young man who gave away his fortune saving the historic homes of North Carolina, several Kiwanians, and the destitute Monte Carlo aristocrats who are married (very unusual, both halves of a couple turning up together here . . . and not just because of the time factor). Over there, a mortician accused of having Heimlich sexual sessions with his female dead. He kept feeling that certain bodies contained angels. We've put him back there in a cluster of the talent he intuited. Among you, a young painter who gave away his only tube of his period's most costly blue, hand-delivered it via subways taken from Harlem at three a.m. Welcome. All of you have managed to transcend to this exalted rank, the most exclusive "key club" in the cosmos.

But do know, please, Homesickness is inevitable. It's lonely, waking alone at so far a new camp—lonely even waking to dewy celestial consciousness. Lonesome also is the wing-itching, aforementioned. But, not to fret on finding yourselves weaned from overtly resembling your former fleshly self. Some remnants blessedly persist. We'll touch upon those shortly. I believe you'll be not unpleased . . .

Bye the bye, nothing is required here. Certain of our denizens opted for a good nap upon arriving in 1491 and have chosen never to end that supernal siesta. So be it. Little is demanded, and maybe it's just me, but that far row on the end? Looks a teensy bit ragged, almost unattractive, thank you, there, I'm feeling better and you're kind.

You appear if not exactly alike, then as similar as any given pair of shoes coming off the conveyor belt at the Thom McAn wing-tip factory outside Sag Harbor, New York, formerly managed, and most humanely, I must say, by the 19th from the left in Sub-Row 3. Yes, excellent. The maternity leave you implemented, madam, did not go unnoticed and still helps many. Welcome.

Your new face has been rendered only about as much like your old one (which it contains) as a brand-new pair of shoes in your proper size can be called personal and deeply yours. Your face has become wonderful-looking if generic. True, here at first, it appears a tad blank. There are but two ways that you can—with precision—be visually identified post-Transformation.

Say you died; as you so recently did, actually. Now you're waking, half alarmed (I know, my dears, believe me, I have been there), waking to this mystic scumbly light. You snap to, alert. First you hear my perhaps annoying babble, sounding like the nurse's prodding chat that roused you from the outer edges of an anesthetic or—in thirty cases present—that did not.

You've re-become yourself but, in addition—wriggling beneath an overlay unsought—you're also, confusingly, an angel. Disconcerting to find all telltale traces of your fond mortal coil gone. Even within your Ziploc envelope of powder-white light, you feel nude . . . deprived of a single youlike souvenir. You're shivering, that cold.

You were just getting almost used to the earthly you. You'd set up the bank draft program that freed you from writing those depressing monthly utility checks. You'd started acknowledging certain thorny traits that, in resembling your same-sex parent, you always feared most—

qualities you'd begun to joke about and even crankily accept, love almost. —Then, whammo, that missed left turn, a new lump under your ear, and here you are, one semi-translucent flame of soul, grafted with wings, no less.

Well, be calmed. You fear that, in gaining Paradise, you've sacrificed your own true earned identity. You miss your friends. My dears, all is not lost.

The earthen stamp has been preserved. Certain features wholly yours. Back there, I see a few of you start noticing. Excellent. Go ahead.

There are echelons of virtue here as there are echelons of filth and lust and greed below. I will now tell you how the highest forms of the Once-Earth get recognized. Say you are standing here, winged, similar, if merely "designed." All our torsos are single-sex units—chests, sizable for pecs, if small for breasts. Your silver ectoplasmic wings are tucked behind.

What has stayed constant from that depressed old world to this inspirited new one? What, on you Job-patient postmen so schnauzer-gnawed, on you unpredictably bighearted Monte Carlo gamblers, on the twin brother Kiwanians who broke records selling Christmas trees for Cerebral Palsy in sub-zero weather only to catch pneumonia as your one thanks? What? That's yours? Looks exactly as before? Yes, I see more of you back there catching the drift. Good, explore, feel.

The single portrait-fixtures still serving as Autobiography for all we otherwise-samish angels?

Yes, your original genitals have stayed intact. Those, and your beginning hands.

The dear baubles—be they cleft or sceptered—plus your clever mitts—are still themselves, no? And in their every cuticle particular. Open and close your hands. Look between your legs. "Hello," right? Now, don't you feel a heap less alone?

Go ahead, check yours out. Flex those digits. Your hands are more fully yours than was your face. Our nail-biters will find those nails yet gnawed. Your wedding rings? They vaporized in transit, dear ones. But the grooves still dent and dignify. Laden with typing skills, able to tie fly-fishing lures in the dark, still so attuned to others' genital pleasures—your particular hands were more instinctually clever than your head's best try. Manual labor matters mucho to our Lord. Your hands contain your own most automatic kindness: your soul. Maybe touch your very own underparts for starters? I know I never tire of doing so. Oh, the memories!

Your surviving portions are made of slightly finer stuff than that first rude stab at getting them right. Here they're more satiny, slightly sleeker, euphemized. Plus there's a wee bonus: So much sudden time, such distance as you just

blurred through in getting here, mercifully served your
lower body as a depilatory. That helps, design-wise. It was
patchy, pubic hair, admit it. Even ours.

—So this, my dears, is how we separate our two classes of
the Angelic. You are all now Angels Republican Second-Rank
(that's honorary, just "for showing up"). But, way far
higher stand the Angels Imperial-First-Class.

Though I do belong to that crowd, I was not consulted in
the matter of celestial "haves and have nots." Paradise
should not feature such elitist structure, I'm sorry.

You, future Angels Imperial-First-Class, will be immediately subsumed as God's minions, His/Her Teacher's Pets,
Her/His Handpicked Gofers, the confidantes to Utter Know-
ingness, Complete Enfolding Compassion. And, in my experience, I swear, the best Company, like, ever. You cannot
imagine the level of God's Smartness and Steadying Quantum
Joy. God, however tasteless, is the Original Sense of Humor.
Total Recall for All Jokes. And, you alone, of your opaque
crowd, "got" it.

How will some few of you become Angels Imperial-First-
Class as, unexpectedly, yours truly did?

—Simple.

If, among the other wandering angels, those newly transformed and those already recodified/refined—if among the
millions greeting you, there should chance past you any—any
single soul who, upon doing a "high-five," feels your original palm-to-palm portrait energy, one who—on glancing at
your telltale lower regions Knows you and can name your
name, then that—even amid this level of piled-on cumulus
virtue—marks yours as a soul judged Ultimate Good.

It proves you did the maximum while still so painfully
earthlocked.

Your discoverer-namer might be your predeceased spouse or
lover. Perhaps an overadoring elder brother or sister. Some
intimate friend. Maybe your gynecologist or even some did-
dling scoutmaster with a great memory for detail, up-close
and personal. Maybe simply a regular customer whose hand you
shook every week for sixty years.

But, if just one such perusing angel can, merely from the
feel of your right palm's heat, from the characteristic
moundness, roundness, mole, depth or breadth, raggedness,
rosiness, heft or tinyness, from any twist or suppleness of
your mortal generative area—if just one angel (are they
ready to come in? fine, hold them just a wing beat more,
please) . . . should just one know your touch, should one
among the millions of formerly dead about to file past you
(quite a spectacle of breeze and beauty, the promised show),
should one suddenly point down, should just one, with glee,
call but a single of your names, say, "Verne!" . . . then

you, my dearest new angel, will soon be known as an Angel Imperial-First-Class forever. You will automatically advance to the right hand of God the Mother Father Almighty.

Am I making any sense here? They about ready? Excellent.

At surge, they now come drifting. Here it all starts, my dears. Above you, note four million fetal planets become visible at once. Fish farm for the firmament. "Ahh," you say, your heads back, loveliest of sounds.

Heaven's colors, this emotive and inventive, are renewed. Most hues will still lack names for you. Colors here are granted the volition and mischief accorded human souls. They play above—in cloud formation—their own form of tag, hopscotch, and chess.

That dramatic wine-dark hue over there is Magna. This one above us is mainly Timbre. And the other, lightest, farthest, God calls Imbue.

To shield you, dear beginners, uncoiling in your Genesis, we've tamped back the Euphoria at first. We don't want its jagged playful force to scare you.

Good, there . . . you'll feel the Dynamos of Ecstasy come purring on, in lights. Settle over the sensation. It's not unsexual, is it? Hmnnmm. —Yes, laugh, do.

Your own well-being thrums forward, like some upper-end harp string long ignored, newly plucked, and oh so glad to be found by Music's uses.

—NOW, let The Great Celestial March and Fugue commence! Feel the scented airs increase? Note how colors this intense press their nap against your palms and crotch? The washes of green light (green especially) soothe those itchy upper wings. See the range of blues go pink go oh so yellow. Magna to Timbre clear off to Imbue! Feel light burning cool across your new-old body. Recognitions will soon occur.

First thing, check out your own variouses. Having done that, freely browse among each other's, some of you will know the others despite years. Go hand to hand. A strong impression was made by you once chanting, "I'll let you see mine, if you'll let me . . ." You did see, didn't you? Seeing others' is God's will.

Here, lines devolve. Mill, ogle, scout, waggle, point, chat, giggle, gab, prod, whatever. Freely, good, keep gazing, good, freely at your classmates' last innocent ties to the old corrupted world, good. Touch. Should you come, good, upon anyone/anything you simply know, then by all means, Blurt! You were picked for your Enthusiasm plus your diehard talent at Belief. Don't get shy on us now! Far nobler to lay claim to an overwide test group than knowing too few.

14

*   *   *

There will be no more talking for one-tenth of a nanosecond millennium. Simply drift among each other now. Steer and pirouette. Skate atop the attendant crust of light always blooming beneath each foot in time to perfectly support you. This is the smallest group of angels from that awful present age down there. You winged ones escaped your century's major peril: self-pity's flypaper.

All forms of Physics are now bent upon contenting you forever. Which means amusing you (which means instructing you). Heaven is secretly a school. Its only subject, the past and future history of Love . . .

Observe, fondle, stroke, Indian wrestle, hand-hold. Try several brands of hearty handshakes to make sure. Winnow forth from among yourselves those known most fully—via love—to you other saints. Shout a beloved name. Feel each other, feel each other up, my darling sudden angels. You're allowed now, anything, always.

Pray, continue.

We have only time here, only time, our memories, and charity. You'll all soon be absolutely crazy about each other. Fascinated, and I mean forever.

Here, no one will ever again leave you.

Heaven's code name is "Hello."

You have managed, you—of all your kinds and gangs. You have broken through the leaky outer edges of parlous actual love. You persisted when the wiser ones turned back. They retreated toward mere dignity, security. They're in Hell or, worse, are nowhere. You chanced loving those that, trying, just . . . could . . . not . . . quite . . . fully . . . love . . . you . . . back.

Mother hold daughter. Man who drowned while clinging to a stranger, hold him close. You are strangers reborn brothers. "Hello" say "Hello" to "Hello."

Let true pleasure—innocent and richly deep—at last begin. How can you know you've just found Paradise?

The Celestial offers you privacy. Plus perfect, funny, erotic company eternally.

BrotherSister, here we live beyond Race and Class and Shame. You need never again fear your own body. We all now play toward working. Existence is finally precisely understood because it is so perfectly recalled. Life's become, at last, pure meaning.

There is nothing left to do beyond the one great promise.

Sound the Tympany, Master Pine, the Promise it is come.

Play the gong, the flute, and strike the lyre, First Assistant Bach.

Now that Promise shall be heard!

The Conversation contains all God's own favorite forms of bliss.

This is the single IOU ever due you.

This is the promise you saw carved clear through the overarching Gates of Paradise.

These few words encircle all there is of Happiness.

Turn to face those recent angels nearest you.

Let your saved hands join others'. Touch new/old faces, old/new genitals.

Eleven words—through Magna past Timbre toward Imbue—are burned deep within our Gate's colossal crystal. Heaven's motto lights you toward your vertical future. Finally, encircled, we conclude commencing.

The Celestial offers you perfect, funny, erotic company, eternally.

This is Paradise.

This, my dears, is all God ever promised us:

HELLO AT LAST.
YOU HAVE ONLY
JUST BEGUN TO
KNOW EACH OTHER.